RESTLESS

WILLIAM BOYD

B L O O M S B U R Y
LONDON • OXFORD • NEW YORK • NEW DELHI • SYDNEY

Bloomsbury Paperbacks
An imprint of Bloomsbury Publishing Plc

50 Bedford Square
London
WC1B 3DP
UK

1385 Broadway
New York
NY 10018
USA

www.bloomsbury.com

BLOOMSBURY and the Diana logo are trademarks of Bloomsbury Publishing Plc

First published in Great Britain 2006
This paperback edition first published in 2017

British Library Cataloguing-in-Publication Data
A catalogue record for this book is available from the British Library.

ISBN: PB: 978–1–4088–9137–7
ePub: 978–1–4088–0712–5

2 4 6 8 10 9 7 5 3 1

Printed and bound in Great Britain by CPI Group (UK) Ltd, Croydon CR0 4YY

RESTLESS

for Susan

We may, indeed, say that the hour of death is uncertain, but when we say this we think of that hour as situated in a vague and remote expanse of time; it does not occur to us that it can have any connection with the day that has already dawned and can mean that death may occur this very afternoon, so far from uncertain, this afternoon whose timetable, hour by hour, has been settled in advance. One insists on one's daily outing, so that in a month's time one will have had the necessary ration of fresh air; one has hesitated over which coat to take, which cabman to call; one is in the cab, the whole day lies before one, short because one must be back home early, as a friend is coming to see one; one hopes it will be as fine again tomorrow; and one has no suspicion that death, which has been advancing within one on another plane, has chosen precisely this particular day to make its appearance in a few minutes' time . . .

Marcel Proust, *The Guermantes Way*

I

Into the Heart of England

WHEN I WAS A child and was being fractious and contrary and generally behaving badly, my mother used to rebuke me by saying: 'One day someone will come and kill me and then you'll be sorry'; or, 'They'll appear out of the blue and whisk me away – how would you like that?'; or, 'You'll wake up one morning and I'll be gone. Disappeared. You wait and see.'

It's curious, but you don't think seriously about these remarks when you're young. But now – as I look back on the events of that interminable hot summer of 1976, that summer when England reeled, gasping for breath, pole-axed by the unending heat – now I know what my mother was talking about: I understand that bitter dark current of fear that flowed beneath the placid surface of her ordinary life – how it had never left her even after years of peaceful, unexceptionable living. I now realise she was always frightened that someone was going to come and kill her. And she had good reason.

It all started, I remember, in early June. I can't recall the exact day – a Saturday, most likely, because Jochen wasn't at his nursery school – and we both drove over to Middle Ashton as usual. We took the main road out of Oxford to Stratford and then turned off it at Chipping Norton, heading for Evesham, and then we turned off again and again, as if we were following a descending scale of road types; trunk road, road, B-road, minor road, until we found ourselves on the metalled cart track that led through the dense and venerable beech wood down to the narrow valley that contained the tiny village of Middle Ashton. It was a journey I made at least twice a week and each time I did so I felt I was being led into the lost heart of England – a green, forgotten, inverse Shangri-La where everything became older, mouldier and more decrepit.

Middle Ashton had grown up, centuries ago, around the Jacobean manor house – Ashton House – at its centre, still occupied by a distant relative of the original owner-builder-proprietor, one Trefor Parry, a seventeenth-century Welsh wool-merchant-made-good who, flaunting his great wealth, had built his grand demesne here in the middle of England itself. Now, after generation upon generation of reckless, spendthrift Parrys and their steadfast, complacent neglect, the manor house was falling down, on its last woodwormed legs, giving up its parched ghost to entropy. Sagging tarpaulins covered the roof of the east wing, rusting scaffolding spoke of previous vain gestures at restoration and the soft yellow Cotswold stone of its walls came away in your hand like wet toast. There was a small damp dark church near by, overwhelmed by massive black-green yews that seemed to drink the light of day; a cheerless pub – the Peace and Plenty, where the hair on your head brushed the greasy, nicotine varnish of the ceiling in the bar – a post office with a shop and an off-licence, and a scatter of cottages, some thatched, green with moss, and interesting old houses in big gardens. The lanes in the village were sunk six feet beneath high banks with rampant hedges growing on either side, as if the traffic of ages past, like a river, had eroded the road into its own mini-valley, deeper and deeper, a foot each decade. The oaks, the beeches, the chestnuts were towering, hoary old ancients, casting the village in a kind of permanent gloaming during the day and in the night providing an atonal symphony of creaks and groans, whispers and sighs as the night breezes shifted the massive branches and the old wood moaned and complained.

I was looking forward to Middle Ashton's generous shade as it was another blearily hot day – every day seemed hot, that summer – but we weren't yet bored to oblivion by the heat. Jochen was in the back, looking out of the car's rear window – he liked to see the road 'unwinding', he said. I was listening to music on the radio when I heard him ask me a question.

'If you speak to a window I can't hear you,' I said.

'Sorry, Mummy.'

He turned himself and rested his elbows on my shoulders and I heard his quiet voice in my ear.

'Is Granny your real mummy?'

'Of course she is, why?'

'I don't know . . . She's so strange.'

'Everybody's strange when you come to think of it,' I said. 'I'm strange . . . You're strange . . .'

'That's true,' he said, 'I know.' He set his chin on my shoulder and dug it down, working the muscle above my right collar-bone with his little pointed chin, and I felt tears smart in my eyes. He did this to me from time to time, did Jochen, my strange son – and made me want to cry for annoying reasons I couldn't really explain.

At the entrance to the village, opposite the grim pub, the Peace and Plenty, a brewer's lorry was parked, delivering beer. There was the narrowest of gaps for the car to squeeze through.

'You'll scrape Hippo's side,' Jochen warned. My car was a seventh-hand Renault 5, sky blue with a (replaced) crimson bonnet. Jochen had wanted to christen it and I had said that because it was a French car we should give it a French name and so I suggested Hippolyte (I had been reading Taine, for some forgotten scholarly reason) and so 'Hippo' it became – at least to Jochen. I personally can't stand people who give their cars names.

'No, I won't,' I said. 'I'll be careful.'

I had just about negotiated my way through, inching by, when the driver of the lorry, I supposed, appeared from the pub, strode into the gap and histrionically waved me on. He was a youngish man with a big gut straining his sweatshirt and distorting its Morrell's logo and his bright beery face boasted mutton-chop whiskers a Victorian dragoon would have been proud of.

'Come on, come on, yeah, yeah, you're all right, darling,' he wheedled tiredly at me, his voice heavy with a weary exasperation. 'It's not a bloody Sherman tank.'

As I came level with him I wound down the window and smiled.

I said: 'If you'd get your fat gut out of the way it'd be a whole lot easier, you fucking arsehole.'

I accelerated off before he could collect himself and wound up the window again, feeling my anger evaporate – deliciously, tinglingly – as quickly as it had surged up. I was not in the best of moods, true, because, as I was attempting to hang a poster in my study that morning, I had, with cartoonish inevitability and ineptitude, hit my thumbnail – which was steadying the picture hook – square on with the hammer instead of the nail of the picture hook. Charlie Chaplin would have been proud of me as I squealed and hopped and flapped my hand as if I wanted to shake it off my wrist. My thumbnail, beneath its skin-coloured plaster, was now a damson purple, and a little socket of pain located in my thumb throbbed with my pulse like some kind of organic timepiece, counting down the seconds of my mortality. But as we accelerated away I could sense the adrenalin-charged heart-thud, the head-reel of pleasure at my audacity: at moments like this I felt I knew all the latent anger buried in me – in me and in our species.

'Mummy, you used the F-word,' Jochen said, his voice softened with stern reproach.

'I'm sorry, but that man really annoyed me.'

'He was only trying to help.'

'No, he wasn't. He was trying to patronise me.'

Jochen sat and considered this new word for a while, then gave up.

'Here we are at last,' he said.

My mother's cottage sat amidst dense, thronging vegetation surrounded by an unclipped, undulating box hedge that was thick with rambling roses and clematis. Its tufty hand-shorn lawn was an indecent moist green, an affront to the implacable sun. From the air, I thought, the cottage and its garden must look like a verdant oasis, its shaggy profusion in this hot summer almost challenging the authorities to impose an immediate hosepipe ban. My mother was an enthusiastic and idiosyncratic gardener: she planted close and pruned hard. If a plant or bush flourished she let it go, not worrying if it stifled others or cast inappropriate shade. Her garden, she claimed, was designed to be a controlled wilderness – she did not own a mower; she cut her lawn with shears – and she knew it annoyed others in the village where neatness and order were the pointed and visible virtues. But none could argue or complain that her garden was abandoned or unkempt: no one in the village spent more time in her garden than Mrs Sally Gilmartin and the fact that her industry was designed to create lushness and wildness was something that could be criticised, perhaps, but not condemned.

We called it a cottage but in fact it was a small two-storey ashlar house in sandy Cotswold stone with a flint tiled roof, rebuilt in the eighteenth century. The upper floor had kept its older mullioned windows, the bedrooms were dark and low, whereas the ground floor had sash windows and a handsome carved doorway with fluted half-columns and a scrolled pediment. She had somehow managed to buy it from Huw Parry-Jones, the dipsomaniac owner of Ashton House, when he was more than particularly hard up, and its rear backed on to the modest remnants of Ashton House park – now an uncut and uncropped meadow – all that was left of the thousands of rolling acres that the Parry family had originally owned in this part of Oxfordshire. To one side was a wooden shed-cum-garage almost completely overwhelmed by ivy and Virginia creeper. I saw her car was parked there – a white Austin Allegro – so I knew she was at home.

Jochen and I opened the gate and looked around for her, Jochen calling, 'Granny, we're here,' and being answered by a loud 'Hip-hip hooray!' coming from the rear of the house. And then she appeared, wheeling herself along the brick path in a wheelchair. She stopped and held out her arms as if to scoop us into her embrace, but we both stood there, immobile, astonished.

'Why on earth are you in a wheelchair?' I said. 'What's happened?'

'Push me inside, dear,' she said. 'All shall be revealed.'

As Jochen and I wheeled her inside, I noticed there was a little wooden ramp up to the front step.

'How long have you been like this, Sal?' I asked. 'You should have called me.'

'Oh, two, three days,' she said, 'nothing to worry about.'

I wasn't feeling the concern that perhaps I should have experienced because my mother looked so patently well: her face lightly tanned, her thick grey-blond hair lustrous and recently cut. And, as if to confirm this impromptu diagnosis, once we had bumped her inside she stepped out of her wheelchair and stooped easily to give Jochen a kiss.

'I fell,' she said, gesturing at the staircase. 'The last two or three steps – tripped, fell to the ground and hurt my back. Doctor Thorne suggested I got a wheelchair to cut down on my walking. Walking makes it worse, you see.'

'Who's Doctor Thorne? What happened to Doctor Brotherton?'

'On holiday. Thorne's the locum. Was the locum.' She paused. 'Nice young man. He's gone now.'

She led us through to the kitchen. I looked for evidence of a bad back in her gait and posture but could see nothing.

'It does help, really,' she said, as if she could sense my growing bafflement, my scepticism. 'The wheelchair, you know, for pottering about. It's amazing how much time one spends on one's feet in a day.'

Jochen opened the fridge. 'What's for lunch, Granny?' he asked.

'Salad,' she said. 'Too hot to cook. Help yourself to a drink, darling.'

'I love salad,' Jochen said, reaching for a can of Coca-Cola. 'I like cold food best.'

'Good boy.' My mother drew me aside. 'I'm afraid he can't stay this afternoon. I can't manage with the wheelchair and whatnot.'

I concealed my disappointment and my selfish irritation – Saturday afternoons on my own, while Jochen spent half the day at Middle Ashton, had become precious to me. My mother walked to the window and shaded her eyes to peer out. Her kitchen/dining-room looked over her garden and her garden backed on to the meadow that was cut very haphazardly, sometimes with a gap of two or three years, and as a result was full of wild flowers and myriad types of grass and weed. And beyond the meadow was the wood, called Witch Wood for some forgotten reason – ancient woodland of oak, beech and chestnut, all the elms gone, or going, of course. There was something very odd happening here, I said to myself: something beyond my mother's usual whims and cultivated eccentricities. I went up to her and placed my hand reassuringly on her shoulder.

'Is everything all right, old thing?'

'Mmm. It was just a fall. A shock to the system, as they say. I should be fine again in a week or two.'

'There's nothing else, is there? You would tell me . . .'

She turned her handsome face on me and gave me her famous candid stare, the pale blue eyes wide – I knew it well. But I could face it out, now, these days, after everything I'd been through myself: I wasn't so cowed by it anymore.

'What else could it be, my darling? Senile dementia?'

All the same, she asked me to wheel her in her wheelchair through the village to the post office to buy a needless pint of milk and pick up a newspaper. She talked at some length about her bad back to Mrs Cumber, the postmistress, and made me stop on the return journey to converse over a drystone wall with Percy Fleet, the young local builder, and his long-term girlfriend (Melinda? Melissa?) as they waited for their barbecue to heat up – a brick edifice with a chimney set proudly on the paving in front of their new conservatory. They commiserated: a fall was the worst thing. Melinda recalled an old stroke-ridden uncle who'd been shaken up for weeks after he'd slipped in the bathroom.

'I want one of those, Percy,' my mother said, pointing at the conservatory, 'very fine.'

'Free estimates, Mrs Gilmartin.'

'How was your aunt? Did she enjoy herself?'

'My mother-in-law,' Percy corrected.

'Ah yes, of course. It was your mother-in-law.'

We said our goodbyes and I pushed her wearily on over the uneven surface of the lane, feeling a growing itch of anger at being asked to take part in this pantomime. She was always commenting on comings and goings too, as if she were checking on people, clocking them on and clocking them off like some obsessive foreman checking on his work-force – she'd done this as long as I could remember. I told myself to be calm: we would have lunch, I would take Jochen back to the flat, he could play in the garden, we could go for a walk in the University Parks . . .

'You mustn't be angry with me, Ruth,' she said, glancing back at me over her shoulder.

I stopped pushing and took out and lit a cigarette. 'I'm not angry.'

'Oh, yes you are. Just let me see how I cope. Perhaps next Saturday I'll be fine.'

When we came in Jochen said darkly, after a minute, 'You can get cancer from cigarettes, you know.' I snapped at him and we ate our lunch in a rather tense mood of long silences broken by bright banal observations about the village on my mother's part. She persuaded me to have a glass of wine and I began to relax. I helped her wash up and stood drying the dishes beside her as she rinsed the glasses in hot water. Water-daughter, daughter-water, sought her daughter in the water, I rhymed to myself, suddenly glad it was the weekend, with no teaching, no tutees and thinking it was maybe not such a bad thing to be spending some time alone with my son. Then my mother said something.

She was shading her eyes again, looking out at the wood.

'What?'

'Can you see someone? Is there someone in the wood?'

I peered. 'Not that I can spot. Why?'

'I thought I saw someone.'

'Ramblers, picnickers – it's Saturday, the sun is shining.'

'Oh, yes, that's right: the sun is shining and all is well with the world.'

She went to the dresser and picked up a pair of binoculars she kept there and turned to focus them on the wood.

I ignored her sarcasm and went to find Jochen and we prepared to leave. My mother took her seat in her wheelchair and pointedly wheeled it to the front door. Jochen told the story of the encounter with the driver of the brewer's lorry and my unashamed use of the F-word. My mother cupped his face with her hands and smiled at him, adoringly.

'Your mother can get very angry when she wants to and no doubt that man was very stupid,' she said. 'Your mother is a very angry young woman.'

'Thank you for that, Sal,' I said and bent to kiss her forehead. 'I'll call this evening.'

'Would you do me a little favour?' she said and then asked me if, when I telephoned in future, I would let the phone ring twice, then hang up and ring again. 'That way I'll know it's you,' she explained. 'I'm not so fast about the house in the chair.'

Now, for the first time I felt a real small pang of worry: this request did seem to be the sign of some initial form of derangement or delusion – but she caught the look in my eye.

'I know what you're thinking, Ruth,' she said. 'But you're quite wrong, quite wrong.' She stood up out of her chair, tall and rigid. 'Wait a second,' she said and went upstairs.

'Have you made Granny cross again?' Jochen said, in a low voice, accusingly.

'No.'

My mother came down the stairs – effortlessly, it seemed to me – carrying a thick buff folder under her arm. She held it out for me.

'I'd like you to read this,' she said.

I took it from her. There seemed to be some dozens of pages – different types, different sizes of paper. I opened it. There was a title page: *The Story of Eva Delectorskaya.*

'Eva Delectorskaya,' I said, mystified. 'Who's that?'

'Me,' she said. 'I am Eva Delectorskaya.'

The Story of Eva Delectorskaya

Paris. 1939

EVA DELECTORSKAYA FIRST SAW the man at her brother Kolia's funeral. In the cemetery he stood some way apart from the other mourners. He was wearing a hat – an old brown trilby – which struck her as odd and she seized on that detail and allowed it to nag at her: what sort of man wore a brown trilby to a funeral? What sign of respect was that? And she used it as a way of keeping her vast angry grief almost at bay: it kept her from being overwhelmed.

But back at the apartment, before the other mourners arrived, her father began to sob and Eva found she could not keep the tears back either. Her father was holding a framed photograph of Kolia in both hands, gripping it fiercely, as if it were a rectangular steering wheel. Eva put her hand on his shoulder and with her other quickly spread the tears off her cheeks. She could think of nothing to say to him. Then Irène, her stepmother, came in with a chinking tray holding a carafe of brandy and a collection of tiny glasses, no bigger than thimbles. She set it down and went back to the kitchen to fetch a plate of sugared almonds. Eva crouched in front of her father, offering him a glass.

'Papa,' she wailed at him, unable to control her voice, 'have a little sip – look, look, I'm having one.' She drank a small mouthful of the brandy and felt her lips sting.

She heard his fat tears hit the glass of the picture. He looked up at her and with one arm pulled her to him and kissed her forehead.

He whispered: 'He was only twenty-four . . . Twenty-four? . . .' It was as if Kolia's age was literally incredible, as if someone had said to him, 'Your son disappeared into thin air,' or 'your son grew wings and flew away'.

Irène came over and took the frame from him gently, gently prising his fingers away.

'*Mange, Sergei,*' she said to him, '*bois – il faut boire.*'

She propped the frame on a nearby table and started to fill the little glasses on the tray. Eva held out the plate of sugared almonds to her father and he took a few, carelessly, letting some tumble to the floor. They sipped their brandy and nibbled at the nuts and talked of banalities: how they were glad the day was overcast and windless, how sunshine would have been inappropriate, how it was good of old Monsieur Dieudonné to have come all the way from Neuilly and how meagre and tasteless the dried flowers from the Lussipovs had been. Dried flowers, really! Eva kept glancing over at the picture of Kolia, smiling in his grey suit, as if he were listening to the chatter, amused, a teasing look in his eye, until she felt the incomprehension of his loss, the affront of his absence, rear up like a tidal wave and she looked away. Luckily the doorbell rang and Irène rose to her feet to welcome the first of the guests. Eva sat on with her father, hearing the muffled tones of discreet conversation as coats and hats were removed, even a stifled burst of laughter, signalling that curious mixture of condolence and exuberant relief that rises up, impromptu, in people after a funeral.

Hearing the laughter Eva's father looked at her; he sniffed and shrugged his shoulders hopelessly, helplessly, like a man who has forgotten the answer to the simplest of questions, and she saw how old he was all of a sudden.

'Just you and me, Eva,' he said, and she knew he was thinking of his first wife, Maria – his Masha, her mother – and her death all those years ago on the other side of the world. Eva had been fourteen, Kolia ten, and the three of them had stood hand in hand in the foreigners' graveyard in Tientsin, the air full of windblown blossom, shredded petals from the giant white wisteria growing on the cemetery wall – like snowflakes, like fat soft confetti. 'Just the three of us, now,' he had said then, as they stood beside their mother's grave, squeezing their hands very hard.

'Who was the man in the brown trilby?' Eva asked, remembering and wanting to change the subject.

'What man in the brown trilby?' said her father.

Then the Lussipovs edged cautiously into the room, smiling vaguely, and with them her plump cousin Tania with her new little husband, and the perplexing question of the man in the brown trilby was momentarily forgotten.

But she saw him again, three days later on the Monday – the first day she'd gone back to work – as she left the office to go to lunch. He was standing under the awning of the *épicerie* opposite, wearing a long tweed overcoat – dark green – and his incongruous trilby. He met her glance, nodded and smiled and crossed the road to greet her, removing his hat as he approached.

He spoke in excellent, accentless French: 'Mademoiselle Delectorskaya, my sincere condolences about your brother. My apologies for not speaking to you at the funeral but it did not seem appropriate – especially as Kolia had never introduced us.'

'I hadn't realised you knew Kolia.' This fact had already thrown her: her mind was clattering, panicked slightly – this made no sense.

'Oh, yes. Not friends, exactly, but we were firm acquaintances, shall we say?' He gave a little bow of his head and continued, this time in flawless, accented English. 'Forgive me, my name is Lucas Romer.'

The accent was upper class, patrician, but Eva thought, immediately, that this Mr Lucas Romer did not look particularly English at all. He had wavy black hair, thinning at the front and swept back and was virtually – she searched for the English word – swarthy, with dense eyebrows, uncurved, like two black horizontal dashes beneath his high forehead and above his eyes – which were a muddy bluey grey (she always noticed the colour of people's eyes). His jaw, even though freshly shaved, was solidly metallic with incipient stubble.

He sensed her studying him and reflexively ran the palm of his hand across his thinning hair. 'Kolia never spoke to you about me?' he asked.

'No,' Eva said, speaking English herself now. 'No, he never mentioned a "Lucas Romer" to me.'

He smiled, for some reason, at this information, showing very white, even teeth.

'Very good,' he said, thoughtfully, nodding to show his pleasure and then added, 'it *is* my real name by the way.'

'It never crossed my mind that it wasn't,' Eva said, offering her hand. 'It was a pleasure to meet you, Mr Romer. If you'll excuse me I have only half an hour for my lunch.'

'No. You have two hours. I told Monsieur Frellon that I would be taking you to a restaurant.'

Monsieur Frellon was her boss. He was obsessive about employee punctuality.

'Why would Monsieur Frellon permit that?'

'Because he thinks I'm going to charter four steamships from him and, as I don't speak a word of French, I need to sort the details out with his translator.' He turned and pointed with his hat. 'There's a little place I know on the rue du Cherche Midi. Excellent seafood. Do you like oysters?'

'I detest oysters.'

He smiled at her, tolerantly, as if she were a sulky child, but this time not showing her his white teeth.

'Then I will show you how to make an oyster edible.'

The restaurant was called Le Tire Bouchon and Lucas Romer did indeed show her how to make an oyster edible (with red-wine vinegar, chopped shallots, black pepper and lemon juice with a roundel of cold-buttered brown bread to follow it down). In fact Eva enjoyed oysters from time to time but she had wanted to dent this curious man's immense self-assurance.

During lunch (sole bonne femme after the oysters, cheese, tarte tatin, a half bottle of Chablis and a whole bottle of Morgon) they talked about Kolia. It was clear to Eva that Romer knew all the relevant biographical facts about Kolia – his age, his education, the family's flight from Russia after the Revolution in 1917, the death of their mother in China, the whole saga of the Delectorskis' peripatetic journeying from St Petersburg to Vladivostock to Tientsin to Shanghai to Tokyo to Berlin, finally, in 1924, and then, eventually, in 1928, to Paris. He knew about the marriage of Sergei Pavlovitch Delectorski to the childless widow Irène Argenton in 1932 and the modest financial upturn in the family's fortunes that Madame Argenton's dowry had produced. He knew even more, she discovered, about her father's recent heart problems, his failing health. If he knows so much about Kolia, Eva thought, I wonder how much he knows about me?

He had ordered coffee for them both and an eau-de-vie for himself. He offered her a cigarette from a bashed, silver cigarette tin – she took one and he lit it for her.

'You speak excellent English,' he said.

'I'm half English,' she told him, as if he didn't know. 'My late mother was English.'

'So you speak English, Russian and French. Anything else?'

'I speak some German. Middling, not fluent.'

'Good . . . How is your father, by the way?' he asked, lighting his own cigarette, leaning back and exhaling dramatically, ceilingward.

Eva paused, uncertain what to tell this man: this complete stranger who acted like a familiar, like a cousin, a concerned uncle eager for family news. 'He's not well. He's crushed, in fact – as we all are. The shock – you can't imagine . . . I think Kolia's death might kill him. My stepmother's very worried.'

'Ah, yes. Kolia adored your stepmother.'

Eva knew all too well that Kolia's relationship with Irène had been strained at the best of times. Madame Argenton thought Kolia something of a wastrel – a dreamer, but an irritating one.

'The son she never had,' Romer added.

'Did Kolia tell you that?' Eva asked.

'No. I'm guessing.'

Eva stubbed out her cigarette. 'I'd better be getting back,' she said, rising to her feet. Romer was smiling at her, annoyingly. She felt that he was pleased at her sudden coldness, her abruptness – as if she had passed some kind of minor test.

'Haven't you forgotten something?' he said.

'I don't think so.'

'I'm meant to be chartering four steamers from Frellon, Gonzales et Cie. Have another coffee and we'll sketch out the details.'

Back in the office Eva was able to tell Monsieur Frellon, with complete plausibility, the tonnage, the timing and the ports of call Romer had in mind. Monsieur Frellon was very pleased at the outcome of her protracted lunch: Romer was a 'big fish', he kept saying, we want to reel him in. Eva realised that Romer had never told her – even though she had raised the matter two or three times – where, how and when he and Kolia had met.

Two days later she was on the metro going to work when she saw Romer step into her carriage at Place Clichy. He smiled and waved through the other commuters at her. Eva knew at once this was no coincidence; she didn't think coincidence played much part in Lucas Romer's life. They exited at Sèvres-Babylone and together they made their way towards the office together – Romer informing her he had an appointment with Monsieur Frellon. It was a dull day, a mackerel sky, with odd patches of brightness; a sudden breeze snatched at her skirt and the violet-blue scarf at her throat. As they reached the small café at the junction of the rue de Varenne and the boulevard Raspail, Romer suggested they pause.

'What about your appointment?'

'I said I'd pop by sometime in the morning.'

'But I'll be late,' she said.

'He won't mind – we're talking business. I'll call him.' He went to the bar to purchase the *jetons* for the public phone. Eva sat down in the window and looked at him, not resentfully but curiously, thinking: what game are you playing here, Mr Lucas Romer? Is this a sex-game with me or a business-game with Frellon, Gonzalez et Cie? If it was a sex-game he was wasting his time. She was not drawn to Lucas Romer. She attracted too many men and, in distorted compromise, was attracted herself by very few. It was a price beauty sometimes exacted: I will make you beautiful, the gods decide, but I will also make you incredibly hard to please. She did not want to think about her life's few complicated, unhappy love affairs this early in the morning and so she took down a newspaper from its hook. Somehow she didn't think this was a sex-game – something else was at stake, some other plan was brewing here. The headlines were all of the war in Spain, of the Anschluss, of Bukharin's execution in the USSR. The vocabulary was scratchy with aggression: rearmament, territory, reparations, arms, bluster, warnings, war and future wars. Yes, she thought, Lucas Romer had another objective but she would have to wait and see what it was.

'No problem at all.' He was standing above her, returning to the table with a smile on his face. 'I've ordered you a coffee.'

She asked him about M. Frellon and Romer assured her that M. Frellon couldn't be happier about this propitious encounter. Their coffees arrived and Romer sat back, at his ease, liberally sugaring his *express*, then stirring it assiduously. Eva looked at him as she re-hung her newspaper, contemplating his dark face, his slightly smirched and crumpled soft collar, his thin, banded tie. What would one have said: a university lecturer? A moderately successful writer? A senior civil servant? Not a ship broker, for sure. So why was she sitting in this café with this perplexing Englishman when it was something she had no particular desire to do? She determined to put him to the test: she decided to ask him about Kolia.

'When did you meet Kolia?' she asked, taking out a cigarette from a pack in her handbag, as casually as she could manage and not offering him one.

'About a year ago. We met at a party – someone was celebrating the publication of a book. We got talking – I thought he was charming –'

'What book?'

'I can't remember.'

She continued her cross-examination and watched Romer's pleasure grow: he was enjoying this, she saw, and his enjoyment began to anger her. This wasn't some pastime, some idle flirtation – her brother was dead and she suspected that Romer knew far more about Kolia's death than he was prepared to admit.

'Why was he at that meeting?' she asked. 'Action Française, for heaven's sake: Kolia wasn't a Fascist.'

'Of course he wasn't.'

'So why was he there?'

'I asked him to go.'

This shocked her. She wondered why Lucas Romer would

ask Kolia Delectorski to go to an Action Française meeting, and wondered further why Kolia would agree, but could find no quick or easy answers.

'Why did you ask him to go?' she asked.

'Because he was working for me.'

All day in the office, trying to do her work, Eva thought about Romer and his baffling answers to her questions. He had abruptly ended their conversation after this declaration that Kolia was working for him – leaning forward, his eyes fixed on hers – and which seemed to say: yes, Kolia was working for me, Lucas Romer, and then announced suddenly that he had to go, he had meetings, my goodness, look at the time.

In the metro on her way home after the office had closed, Eva tried to be methodical, tried to put things together, to make the various extraneous pieces of information mesh, somehow, but it wasn't working. Lucas Romer had met Kolia at a party; they had become friends – more than friends, obviously, colleagues of a sort, with Kolia working for Romer in some unnamed capacity . . . What manner of work took you to a meeting of the Action Française in Nanterre? And at this meeting, as far as the police could determine, Kolia Delectorski had been called out to answer a telephone call. People remembered him leaving in the middle of the main speech, delivered by Charles Maurras, no less, remembered one of the stewards coming down the aisle and passing him a note, remembered the small upheaval of his departure. And then the gap of time of forty-five minutes – the last forty-five minutes of Kolia's life – to which there were no witnesses. People leaving the hall (a large cinema) by the side entrances had found his twisted body in the alleyway running along the cinema's rear, a thickening lacquered pool of blood on the paving stones, a serious wound – several heavy blows – on the back of his head. What happened in the last forty-five minutes of Kolia Delectorski's life? When he was found his wallet was missing, his watch was missing and his hat was missing. But what kind of thief kills a man and then steals his hat?

Eva walked up the rue des Fleurs, thinking about Kolia, wondering what had made him 'work' for a man like Romer and why he had never told her about this so-called job. And who was Romer to offer Kolia, a music teacher, a job that would put his life in danger? A job that had cost him his life? As what and for what, she wanted to know? For his shipping line? His international businesses? She found herself smiling sardonically at the whole absurdity of the idea as she bought her usual two baguettes and tried to ignore Benoit's eager responsive smile to what he took to be her levity. She became solemn, instantly. Benoit – another man who wanted her.

'How are you, Mademoiselle Eva?' Benoit asked, taking her money.

'I'm not so well,' she said. 'My brother's death – you know.'

His face changed, went long in sympathy. 'Terrible, terrible thing,' he said. 'These times we live in.'

At least now he can't ask me out again for a while, Eva thought, as she left and turned into the apartment block's small courtyard, stepping through the small door in the large one and nodding hello to Madame Roisanssac, the concierge. She walked up the two flights of stairs, let herself in, left the bread in the kitchen and moved on through to the salon, thinking: no, I can't stay in again tonight, not with Papa and Irène – I shall go and see a film, the film playing at the Rex: *Je Suis Partout* – I need to have a change in routine, she thought, some room, some time for myself.

She walked into the salon and Romer rose to his feet with a lazy welcoming smile. Her father stepped in front of him, saying in his bad English, with false disapprobation, 'Eva, really, why are you not telling me you've met Mr Romer?'

'I didn't think it was important,' Eva said, her eyes never leaving Romer's, trying to keep her gaze absolutely neutral, absolutely unperturbed. Romer smiled and smiled – he was very calm – and more smartly dressed, she saw, in a dark blue suit, a white shirt and another of his striped English ties.

Her father was fussing, pulling a chair forward for her, making small talk – 'Mr Romer was knowing Kolia, can you believe it?' – but Eva only heard a stridency of questions and exclamations in her head: How dare you come here! What have you told Papa? What nerve! What did you think I would say? She saw the glasses and the bottle of port on the silver tray, saw the plate of sugared almonds and knew that Romer had engineered this welcome effortlessly, confident of the solace his visit would bring. How long had he been here? she wondered, looking at the level of the port in the bottle. Something about her father's mood suggested more than one glass each.

Her father practically forced her to sit; she declined the glass of port she dearly wanted. She noticed Romer sitting back, discreetly, one leg casually crossed over the other, that small calculating smile on his face. It was the smile, she realised, of a man who was convinced he knew exactly what was going to happen next.

Determined to frustrate him, she stood up. 'I have to go,' she said. 'I'll be late for the film.'

Somehow, Romer was at the door before her, his fingers on her left elbow, restraining.

'Mr Delectorski,' Romer said to her father, 'is there anywhere I can speak privately with Eva?'

They were shown into her father's study – a small bedroom at the end of the corridor – decorated with formal, wooden photographic portraits of Delectorski relatives and containing a desk, a divan and a bookshelf full of his favourite Russian authors: Lermontev, Pushkin, Turgenev, Gogol, Chekhov. The room smelt of cigars and the pomade that her father used for his hair. Moving to the window Eva could see Madame Roisanssac hanging out her family's washing. She felt suddenly very ill at ease: she thought she knew how to deal with Romer but now alone in this room with him – alone in her father's room – everything suddenly had changed.

And, as if he sensed this, Romer changed too: gone was the overweening self-confidence, now replaced by a manner more direct, more fiercely personal. He urged her to sit down and drew a chair for himself from behind the desk, setting it opposite her, as if some form of interrogation was about to begin. He offered her a cigarette from his battered case and she took one before saying, no, thank you, I won't, and handed it back. She watched him refit it in his case, clearly mildly irritated. Eva felt she'd won a tiny, trivial victory – everything counted if that vast easy confidence was to be even momentarily discomfited.

'Kolia was working for me when he was killed,' Romer said.

'You told me.'

'He was killed by Fascists, by Nazis.'

'I thought he was robbed.'

'He was doing . . . ' he paused. 'He was doing dangerous work – and he was discovered. I think he was betrayed.'

Eva wanted to speak but decided to say nothing. Now, in the silence, Romer removed his cigarette case again and went through the rigmarole of putting the cigarette in his mouth, patting his pockets for his lighter, removing the cigarette from his mouth, tapping both ends on the cigarette case, pulling the ashtray on her father's desk towards him, lighting the cigarette and inhaling and exhaling strongly. Eva watched all this, trying to stay completely impassive.

'I work for the British government,' he said. 'You understand what I mean . . .'

'Yes,' Eva said, 'I think so.'

'Kolia was working for the British government also. He was trying to infiltrate l'Action Française on my instructions. He had joined the movement and was reporting back to me on any developments he thought might be of interest to us.' He paused and, seeing she was not going to interject, leant forward and said, reasonably, 'There will be a war in Europe in six months or a year – between Nazi Germany and several European countries – that much you can be sure of. Your brother was part of that struggle against this coming war.'

'What are you trying to say?'

'That he was a very brave man. That he didn't die in vain.'

Eva checked the sardonic laugh in her throat and almost immediately felt tears begin to flood her eyes.

'Well, I wish he'd been a cowardly man,' she said, trying to keep the tremble out of her voice, 'then he wouldn't have died at all. In fact he might have been walking through this door in ten minutes.'

Romer stood up and crossed to the window, where he too studied Madame Roisanssac hanging out her washing, before turning and sitting on the edge of her father's desk, staring at her.

'I want to offer you Kolia's job,' he said. 'I want you to come and work for us.'

'I have a job.'

'You will be paid £500 a year. You will become a British citizen with a British passport.'

'No, thank you.'

'You will be trained in Britain and will work for the British government in various capacities – just as Kolia did.'

'Thank you – no. I'm very happy in my current work.' Suddenly, impossibly, she wanted Kolia to come into the room – Kolia with his wry smile and his languid charm – and tell her what to do, what to say to this man with his insistent eyes and his insistent demands of her. What do you want me to do, Kolia? She heard the question loud in her head. You tell me what I should do and I'll do it.

Romer stood up. 'I've talked to your father. I suggest you do the same.' He walked to the door, touching his forehead with two fingers as if he'd just forgotten something. 'I'll see you tomorrow – or the next day. Think seriously about what I've proposed, Eva, and what it'll mean to you and your family.' Then his mood seemed to change abruptly, as if he were affected by some kind of sudden zeal and the mask dropped for a moment. 'For god's sake, Eva,' he said. 'Your brother was murdered by these thugs, these filthy vermin – you've a chance to get your revenge. To make them pay.'

'Goodbye, Mr Romer, it was very nice meeting you.'

Eva looked out of the carriage window at the Scottish countryside as it sped by. It was summer, yet under the low white sky she thought there lingered in the landscape a memory of many winters' hardships – the small tough trees bent and shaped by a prevailing wind, the tussocky grass, the soft green hills scabbed by their dark patches of heather. It may be summer, the land seemed to be saying, but I won't let my guard down. She thought of other landscapes she had seen from trains over her life – in fact sometimes it seemed to her that her life was one composed of train journeys through whose windows she had watched a succession of alien countrysides flash by. From Moscow to Vladivostock, from Valdivostock to China . . . Luxury wagons-lits, troop trains, goods trains, provincial stoppers on branch lines, days spent stationary, trainless, waiting for another locomotive. Sometimes crowded carriages, insufferable, overcome with the stench of packed human bodies – sometimes the melancholy of empty compartments, the lonely clatter of the wheels in their ears, night after night. Sometimes travelling light with one small suitcase, sometimes burdened with all their possessions, like helpless refugees, it seemed. All these journeys: Hamburg to Berlin, Berlin to Paris and now Paris to Scotland. Still moving towards an unknown destination, she told herself, wishing vaguely that she felt more thrill, more romance.

Eva checked her watch – ten minutes to go until Edinburgh, she reckoned. In her compartment a middle-aged businessman nodded over his novel, his head lolling, his features slack and ugly in repose. Eva removed her new passport from her handbag and looked at it for maybe the hundredth time. It had been issued in 1935 and there were immigration stamps from certain European countries: Belgium, Portugal, Switzerland and, interestingly enough, the United States of America. All places she had visited, apparently. The photograph was blurry and overlit: it looked like her – a sterner, more obstinate Eva (where had they found it?) – but even she could not tell if it was wholly genuine. Her name, her new name, was Eve Dalton. Eva Delectorskaya becomes Eve Dalton. Why not Eva? She supposed 'Eve' was more English and, in any event, Romer had not given her the option of christening herself.

That evening, after Romer had left so peremptorily, she had gone through to the salon to talk to her father. A job for the British government, she told him, £500 a year, a British passport. He feigned surprise but it was obvious that Romer had briefed him to a certain extent.

'You'd be a British citizen, with a passport,' her father said, his features incredulous, almost abjectly so – as if it were unthinkable that a nonentity such as he should have a daughter who was a British citizen. 'Do you know what I would give to be a British citizen?' he said, all the while with his left hand miming a sawing motion at his right elbow.

'I don't trust him,' Eva said. 'And why should he be doing this for me?'

'Not for you: for Kolia. Kolia worked for him. Kolia died working for him.'

She poured herself a small glass of port, drank and held its sweetness in her mouth for a second or two before swallowing it.

'Working for the British government,' she said, 'you know what that means.'

He came over to her and took her hands. 'There are a thousand ways of working for the British government.'

'I'm going to say no. I'm happy here in Paris, happy in my job.'

Again her father's face registered an emotion so intense it was almost parodic: now it was a bafflement, an incomprehension so complete it made him dizzy. He sat down as if to prove the point.

'Eva,' he said, seriously, weightily, 'think about it: you have to do it. But don't do it for the money, or the passport, or to be able to go and live in England. It's simple; you have to do it for Kolia – for your brother.' And he pointed at Kolia's smiling face in the photograph. 'Kolia's dead,' he went on, dumbly, almost idiotically, as if only now facing up to the reality of his dead son. 'Murdered. How can you not do it?'

'All right, I'll give it some thought,' she said coolly, determined not to be affected by his emotion, and left the room. But she knew, whatever the rational side of her brain was telling her – weigh everything up, don't be hasty, this is your life you're dealing with – that her father had said all that mattered. In the end it was nothing to do with money, or a passport, or safety: Kolia was dead. Kolia had been killed. She had to do it for Kolia, it was as simple as that.

She saw Romer two days later across the street as she left for lunch, standing under the awning of the *épicerie* just as he had that first day. This time he waited for her to join him and, as she crossed the road, she felt a sense of profound unease afflict her, as if she were deeply superstitious and the most maleficent sign had just been made evident to her. She wondered, absurdly: is this what people feel when they agree to marry someone?

They shook hands and Romer led her to their original café. They sat, ordered a drink and Romer handed her a buff envelope. It contained a passport, £50 in cash and a train ticket from the Gare du Nord, Paris, to Waverley Station, Edinburgh.

'What if I say no?' she asked.

'Just give it back to me. Nobody wants to force you.'

'But you had the passport ready.'

Romer smiled, showing his white teeth, and for once she thought it might be a genuine smile.

'You've no idea how easy it is to have a passport made up. No, I thought . . .' he paused and frowned. 'I don't know you, Eva, in the way I knew Kolia – but I thought, because of him, and because you remind me of him, that there was a chance you might join us.'

Eva smiled ruefully at the memory of this conversation – its mix of sincerity and vast duplicity – and leant forward as they steamed into Edinburgh and craned her head up to look at the castle on the rock, almost black, as if, made of coal, it sat on a crag of coal, as they slowed beneath it, slipping into the station. Now there were shreds of blue amongst the hurrying clouds – it was brighter, the sky no longer white and neutral – perhaps that was what made the castle and its rock seem so black.

She stepped down from the train with her suitcase ('Only one suitcase,' Romer had insisted) and wandered up the platform. All he had told her was that she would be met. She looked about her at the families and couples greeting each other and embracing, politely declined the services of a porter and walked out into the main concourse of Waverley Station.

'Miss Dalton?'

She turned, thinking how quickly one becomes accustomed to a new name – she had been Miss Eve Dalton for only two days now – and saw that the man facing her was stout in a too tight grey suit and a too tight collar.

'I'm Staff Sergeant Law,' the man said. 'Please follow me.' He did not offer to carry her suitcase.

2

Ludger Kleist

'"YES, MRS AMBERSON THOUGHT, it was *my doing nothing* that made the difference."'

Hugues looked more than usually puzzled, almost panicked in fact. He was always puzzled by English grammar, anyway – frowning, muttering, talking to himself in French – but today I had painted him into a corner.

'My doing nothing – what?' he said, helplessly.

'My doing nothing – nothing. It's a gerund.' I tried to look alert and interested but decided, there and then, to cut the lesson short by ten minutes. I felt the pressure of desperate concentration in my head – I had been almost furious in my application, all to keep my mind occupied – but my attention was beginning to fray badly. 'We'll tackle the gerund and gerundive tomorrow,' I said, closing the book (*Life with the Ambersons*, vol. III) then added, apologetically, aware of the agitation I'd aroused in him, '*C'est très compliqué.*'

'Ah, bon.'

Like Hugues, I too was sick of the Amberson family and their laborious journey through the labyrinth of English grammar. And yet I was still bound to them like an indentured servant – tied to the Ambersons and their horrible lifestyle – and the new pupil was due to arrive: only another two hours in their company to go.

Hugues pulled on his sports jacket – it was olive green with a charcoal check and I thought the material was cashmere. It was meant to look, I supposed, like the sort of jacket that an Englishman – in some mythological English world – would unreflectingly don to go and see to his hounds, or meet his estate manager, or take tea with his maiden aunt, but I had to confess I had yet to encounter a fellow countryman sporting clothing quite so fine and so well cut.

Hugues Corbillard stood in my small, narrow study, pensively stroking his blond moustache, a troubled expression still on his face – thinking about the gerund and gerundive, I supposed. He was a rising young executive in P'TIT PRIX, a low-cost French supermarket chain, and had been obliged by senior management to improve his English so that P'TIT PRIX could access new markets. I liked him – actually, I liked most of my pupils – Hugues was a rare lazy one: often he spoke French to me throughout the lesson and I English to him, but today had been something of an assault course. Usually we talked about anything except English grammar, anything to avoid the Amberson family and their doings – their trips, their modest crises (plumbing failures, chicken-pox, broken limbs), visits from relatives, Christmas holidays, children's exams, etcetera – and more and more our conversation returned to the unusual heat of this English summer, how Hugues was slowly stifling in his broiling bed and breakfast, about his incomprehension at being obliged to sit down to eat a three-course, starchy evening meal at 6.00 p.m., with the sun slamming down on the scorched, dehydrated garden. When my conscience pricked me and I felt I should remonstrate and urge him to speak in English, Hugues would say that it was all conversation, *n'est ce pas?* with a shy guilty smile, conscious he was breaking the strict terms of the contract, it must be helping his comprehension, surely? I did not disagree: I was earning £7 an hour chatting to him in this way – if he was happy, I was happy.

I walked him through the flat to the back stairway. We were

on the first floor and in the garden I could see Mr Scott, my landlord and my dentist, doing his strange exercises – waving his arms, stamping his big feet – before another patient arrived in his surgery down below us.

Hugues said goodbye and I sat down in the kitchen, leaving the door open, waiting for my next pupil from Oxford English Plus. This would be her first day and I knew little about her apart from her name – Bérangère Wu – her status – beginner/intermediate – and her timetable – four weeks, two hours a day, five days a week. Good, steady money. Then I heard voices in the garden and stepped out of the kitchen on to the landing at the top of the wrought-iron staircase, looking down to see Mr Scott talking urgently to a small woman in a fur coat and pointing repeatedly at the front gate.

'Mr Scott?' I called. 'I think she's for me.'

The woman – a young woman – a young oriental woman – climbed the staircase to my kitchen. She was wearing, despite the summer heat, some kind of long, expensive-looking, tawny fur coat slung across her shoulders and, as far as I could tell from an initial glance, her other clothes – the satin blouse, the camel trousers, the heavy jewels – were expensive-looking also.

'Hello, I'm Ruth,' I said and we shook hands.

'Bérangère,' she said, looking round my kitchen as a dowager duchess might, visiting the home of one of her poorer tenants. She followed me through to the study, where I relieved her of her coat and sat her down. I hung the coat on the back of the door – it seemed near weightless.

'This coat is amazing,' I said. 'So light. What is it?'

'It's a fox from Asia. They shave it.'

'Shaved Asian fox.'

'Yes . . . I am speaking English not so well,' she said.

I reached for *Life with the Ambersons*, vol. 1. 'So, why don't we start at the beginning,' I said.

* * *

I think I liked Bérangère, I concluded, as I walked down the road to collect Jochen from school. In the two-hour tutorial (as we came to know the Amberson family – Keith and Brenda, their children, Dan and Sara, and their dog, Rasputin) we had each smoked four cigarettes (all hers) and drunk two cups of tea. Her father was Vietnamese, she said, her mother, French. She, Bérangère, worked in a furrier's in Monte Carlo – Fourrures Monte Carle – and, if she could improve her English, she would be promoted to manager. She was incredibly petite, the size of a nine-year-old girl, I thought, one of those girl-women who made me feel like a strapping milkmaid or an Eastern-bloc pentathlete. Everything about her appeared cared-for and nurtured: her hair, her nails, her eyebrows, her teeth – and I was sure this same attention to detail applied to those parts of her not visible to me: her toenails, her underwear – her pubic hair, for all I knew. Beside her I felt scruffy and not a little unclean but, for all this manicured perfection, I sensed there was another Bérangère lurking beneath. As we said goodbye she asked me where was a good place in Oxford to meet men.

I was the first of the mothers outside Grindle's, the nursery school in Rawlinson Road. My two hours of smoking with Bérangère had me craving for another cigarette but I didn't like to smoke outside the school so to distract myself I thought about my mother.

My mother, Sally Gilmartin, née Fairchild. No, my mother, Eva Delectorskaya, half Russian, half English, a refugee from the 1917 Revolution. I felt the incredulous laugh clog my throat and I was aware I was shaking my head to and fro. I stopped myself, thinking: be serious, be sensible. My mother's sudden revelatory detonation had rocked me so powerfully that I had deliberately treated it as a fiction at first, reluctantly letting the dawning truth arrive, filling me slowly, gradually. It was too much to take on board in one go: never had the word 'bombshell' seemed more apt. I felt like a house shaken by some nearby explosion: tiles had fallen, there was a thick cloud of dust, windows had blown in. The house was still standing but it was fragile now, crazy, the structure askew and less solid. I had thought, almost wanting to believe, that this was the beginning of some complex type of delusion or dementia in her – but I realised that, for my part, this was a form of perverse wishful thinking. The other side of my brain was saying: No: face it, everything you thought you knew about your mother was a cleverly constructed fantasy. I felt suddenly alone, in the dark, lost: what does one do in a situation like this?

I tracked over what I knew of my mother's history. She had been born in Bristol, so the story went, where her father was a timber merchant, a timber merchant who had gone to work in Japan in the 1920s, where she had been schooled by a governess. And then back to England, working as a secretary before her parents' deaths prior to the war. I remembered talk of a much-loved brother, Alisdair, who had been killed at Tobruk in 1942 . . . Then marriage to my father, Sean Gilmartin, during the war, in Dublin. In the late 1940s they moved back to England and they settled in Banbury, Oxfordshire, where Sean was soon established in a successful practice as a solicitor. Birth of daughter Ruth occurred in 1949. So much, so relatively ordinary and middle-class – only the Japanese years adding a touch of the otherworldly and exotic. I could even remember an old photo of Alisdair, uncle Alisdair, propped on a table in the living room for a while. And talk too from time to time of emigré cousins and relatives in South Africa and New Zealand. We never saw them; they sent the odd Xmas card. The swarming Gilmartins (my father had two brothers and two sisters – there were a dozen cousins) gave us more than enough family to cope with. Absolutely nothing to take exception to; a family history like hundreds of others, only the war and its consequences being the great schism in lives of otherwise utter normality. Sally Gilmartin was as solid as this gatepost, I thought, resting my hand on its warm sandstone, realising at the same time how little we actually, really, know of our parents' biographies, how vague and undefined they are, like saints' lives almost – all legend and anecdote – unless we take the trouble to dig deeper. And now this new story, changing everything. I felt a kind of sickness in my throat about the unknown revelations that I was sure would have to come – as if what I knew now were not destabilising and disturbing enough. Something about my mother's tone informed me that she was going to tell me everything, every little personal detail, every hidden intimacy. Perhaps because I had never known Eva Delectorskaya, Eva Delectorskaya was now determined that I should learn absolutely everything about her.

Other mothers were now gathering, I saw. I leant back against the gatepost and rubbed my shoulders against it. Eva Delectorskaya, my mother . . . What was I to believe?

'Fiver for them,' Veronica Briggstock whispered in my ear and brought me out of my reverie. I turned and kissed her, for some reason – we normally never embraced as we saw each other almost every day. Veronica – never Vron, never Nic – was a nurse at the John Radcliffe Hospital, divorced from her husband, Ian, a lab technician in the university chemistry department. She had a daughter Avril, who was Jochen's best friend.

We stood together, talking about our respective days. I told her about Bérangère and her amazing coat as we waited for our children to emerge from the school. The single mothers at Grindle's seemed unconsciously – or consciously, perhaps – to gravitate towards each other, being perfectly friendly towards the divorced mothers and the still-married mothers, of course, and the occasional sheepish dad, but somehow preferring their own company. They could share their own particular problems, without need for further explanation, and there was, I thought, no need for pretence about our single state – we all had stories we could tell.

As if to illustrate this, Veronica was moaning profanely about Ian and his new girlfriend and the new problems that were mounting as he tried to duck out of his appointed weekends with Avril. She stopped talking as the kids began to come out of the school and I felt immediately the strange illogical worry that always rose up in me as I searched for Jochen amongst the familiar faces, some atavistic motherly anxiety, I supposed: the cave-woman searching for her brood. Then I saw him – saw his stern, sharp features, his eyes searching for me, also – and the moment's angst receded as quickly as it had arrived. I wondered what we would have for supper tonight and what we would watch on TV. Everything was normal again.

We – the four of us – sauntered back up the Banbury Road towards our homes. It was late afternoon and the heat seemed to possess extra gravity at this hour, as if it were physically pressing down on you. Veronica said she hadn't been this hot since she'd been on a holiday in Tunisia. Ahead of us Avril and Jochen walked, hand in hand, talking intensely to each other.

'What've they got to talk about?' Veronica asked. 'They haven't lived enough.'

'It's as if they've just discovered language, or something,' I said. 'You know: it's like when a kid learns to skip – they skip for months.'

'Yeah, well, they can certainly talk . . .' She smiled. 'Wish I'd had a little boy. Big strong man to look after me.'

'Want to swap?' I said, for some stupid, unthinking reason, and immediately felt guilty, as if I'd betrayed Jochen in some way. He wouldn't have understood the joke. He would have given me his look – dark, hurt, cross.

We'd reached our junction. Here, Jochen and I turned left on to Moreton Road, heading for the dentist's while Veronica and Avril would continue on to Summertown, where they lived in a flat above an Italian restaurant called La Dolce Vita – she liked the daily ironic reminder, Veronica said, its persistent empty promise. As we stood there making vague plans for a punting picnic that weekend I suddenly told her about my mother, Sally/Eva. I felt I had to share this with at least one person before I talked to my mother: that the act of retelling it would make the new facts in my life more real for me – easier to confront. And easier to confront my mother too. It wouldn't be kept a secret between us because Veronica was party to it as well – I needed one extra-familial buttress to hold me steady.

'My God,' Veronica said. 'Russian?'

'Her real name is Eva Delectorskaya, she says.'

'Is she all right? Is she forgetting things? Names? Dates?'

'No, she's as sharp as a knife.'

'Does she go off on errands then comes back because she can't remember why she went out?'

'No,' I said, 'I think I have to accept it's all true,' and explained further. 'But there's something else going on, almost a kind of mania. She thinks she's being watched. Or else it's paranoia . . . She's always checking on things, other people. Oh, and she's got a wheelchair – says she's hurt her back. It's not true: she's perfectly fit. But she thinks something's going on, something sinister as far as she's concerned and so now she's decided to tell me the truth.'

'Has she seen a doctor?'

'Oh, yes. She convinced the doctor about her back – he provided the wheelchair.' I thought for a moment and then decided to tell her the rest. 'She says she was recruited by the British Secret Service in 1939.'

Veronica had to smile at that, then looked baffled. 'But otherwise she seems perfectly normal?'

'Define "normal",' I said.

We parted and Jochen and I wandered along Moreton Road to the dentist's. Mr Scott was easing himself into his new

Triumph Dolomite; he eased himself out and made some show of offering Jochen a mint – he always did this when he saw Jochen, Mr Scott being constantly well supplied with mints of various sorts and brands. As he backed out of the drive we walked down the alley at the side of the house to 'our stepway', as Jochen called it, set at the back, a wrought-iron staircase that gave us our own private access to our flat on the first floor. The disadvantage was that any visitor had to come through the kitchen but it was better than going through the dentist's below with its strange pervasive smells – all mouthwash, dentifrice and carpet shampoo.

We ate cheese on toast and baked beans for supper and watched a documentary about a small round orange submarine exploring the ocean floor. I put Jochen to bed and went through to my study and found my file where I kept my unfinished thesis: 'Revolution in Germany, 1918–1923'. I opened the last chapter – 'The Five-Front War of Gustav von Kahr' – and, trying to concentrate, scanned a few paragraphs. I hadn't written anything for months and it was as if I was reading a stranger's writing. I was fortunate that I had the laziest supervisor in Oxford – a term could go by without any communication between us – and all I did was teach English as a Foreign Language, look after my son and visit my mother, it seemed. I was caught in the EFL trap, all too familiar a pitfall to many an Oxford postgraduate. I made £7 an hour tax-free and, if I wanted, I could teach eight hours a day, fifty-two weeks of the year. Even with the constraints on my time imposed by Jochen I would still make, this year, more than £8,000, net. The last job I had applied for, and failed to get, as a history lecturer at the University of East Anglia was offering a salary (gross) of approximately half what I earned teaching for Oxford English Plus. I should have been pleased at my solvency: rent paid, newish car, school fees paid, credit card under control, some money in the bank – but instead I felt a sudden surge of self-pity and frustrated resentment: resentment at Karl-Heinz, resentment at having to return to Oxford, resentment at having to teach English to foreign students for easy money, (guilty) resentment at the constraints my little son imposed on my freedom, resentment at my mother suddenly deciding to tell me the astonishing story about her past . . . It had not been planned this way: this was not the direction my life was supposed to have taken. I was twenty-eight years old – what had happened?

I called my mother. A strange deep voice replied.

'Yes.'

'Mummy? Sal? – It's me.'

'Is everything all right?'

'Yes.'

'Call me right back.'

I did. The phone rang four times before she picked it up.

'You can come next Saturday,' she said, 'and it'll be fine to leave Jochen – he can stay the night, if you like. Sorry about last weekend.'

'What's that clicking noise?'

'That's me – I was tapping the receiver with a pencil.'

'Why on earth?'

'It's a trick. It confuses people. Sorry, I'll stop.' She paused. 'Did you read what I gave you?'

'Yes, I would have called earlier but I had to take it all in. Needed some time . . . Bit of a shock, as you can imagine.'

'Yes, of course.' She was silent for a while. 'But I wanted you to know. It was the right time to tell you.'

'Is it true?'

'Of course, every word.'

'So that means I'm half Russian.'

'I'm afraid so, darling. But only a quarter, actually. My mother, your grandmother, was English, remember?'

'We have to talk about this.'

'There's much more to come. Much more. You'll understand everything when you hear the rest.'

Then she changed the subject and asked about Jochen and how his day had been and had he said anything amusing, so I told her, all the while sensing a kind of weakening in my bowels – as if I needed to shit – provoked by a sudden and growing worry about what was lying up ahead for me and a small nagging fear that I wouldn't be able to cope. There was more to come, she had said, much more – what was that 'everything' that I would eventually understand? We talked some more, blandly, made our appointment for next Saturday and I hung up. I rolled a joint, smoked it carefully, went to bed and slept a dreamless eight hours.

When I returned from Grindle's the next morning, Hamid was sitting on the top step of our staircase. He was wearing a short new black leather jacket that didn't really suit him, I thought, it made him look too boxy and compact. Hamid Kazemi was a stocky, bearded Iranian engineer in his early thirties with a weightlifter's broad shoulders and a barrel chest: he was my longest-serving pupil.

He opened the kitchen door for me and ushered me in with his usual precise *politesse*, complimenting me on how well I looked (something he'd remarked on twenty-four hours previously). He followed me through the flat to the study.

'You haven't mentioned my jacket,' he said in his direct way. 'Do you not like it?'

'I quite like it,' I said, 'but with those sunglasses and black jeans you look like you're a special agent for SAVAK.'

He tried to cover up the fact that he didn't find this comparison amusing – and I realised that for an Iranian it could be a joke in dubious taste so I apologised. Hamid, I remembered, hated the Shah of Iran with special fervour. He removed his new jacket and hung it carefully on the back of his chair. I could smell the new leather and I thought of tack rooms and saddle polish, the redolence of my distant girlhood.

'I received the news of my posting,' he said. 'I shall go to Indonesia.'

'I *am going* to Indonesia. Is that good? Are you pleased?'

'Am going . . . I wanted Latin America, even Africa . . .' He shrugged.

'I think Indonesia sounds fascinating,' I said, reaching for *The Ambersons*.

Hamid was an engineer who worked for Dusendorf, an international oil engineering company. Half the students at Oxford English Plus were Dusendorf engineers, learning English – the language of the petroleum industry – so they could work on oil-rigs around the world. I had been teaching Hamid for three months now. He had arrived from Iran as a fully qualified petro-chemical engineer, but virtually monoglot. However, eight hours of one-on-one tuition a day shared out between four tutors had, as Oxford English Plus confidently promised in their brochure, made him swiftly and completely bilingual.

'When do you go?' I asked.

'In one month.'

'My God!' The exclamation was genuine and unintended. Hamid was so much a part of my life, Monday to Friday, that it was impossible to imagine him suddenly absent. And because I had been his first teacher, because his very first English lesson had been with me, somehow I felt I alone had taught him his fluent workmanlike English. I was almost his Professor Higgins, I thought, illogically: I had come to feel, in a funny way, that this new English-speaking Hamid was all my own work.

I stood up and took a hanger off the back of the door for his jacket.

'It's going to lose its shape on that chair,' I said, trying to disguise the small emotional turmoil I was feeling at this news of his impending departure.

As I took the jacket from him I looked out of the window and saw, down below on the gravelled forecourt, standing beside Mr

Scott's Dolomite, a man. A slim young man in jeans and a denim jacket with dark brown hair long enough to rest on his shoulders. He saw me staring down at him and raised his two thumbs – thumbs up – a big smile on his face.

'Who's that?' Hamid asked, glancing out and then glancing back at me, noting my expression of shock and astonishment.

'He's called Ludger Kleist.'

'Why are you looking at him like that?'

'Because I thought he was dead.'

The Story of Eva Delectorskaya

Scotland. 1939

EVA DELECTORSKAYA WALKED DOWN through the springy grass towards the valley floor and the dark strip of trees that marked the small river that flowed there. The sun was beginning to set at the far end of the small glen so at least she knew which direction was west. Looking east, she tried to see if she could make out Staff Sergeant Law's lorry as it wound down between the folding hillsides towards, she assumed, the Tweed valley but there was a mistiness in the evening light that blurred the pinewoods and the stone walls alike and there was no possibility of picking out Law's two-ton truck at this range.

She strode on down to the river, her rucksack bumping the small of her back. This was an 'exercise', she told herself, and it had to be undertaken in the right spirit. There was no race on, so her instructors had told her, it was more to do with seeing how people coped with sleeping rough, what sense of direction they could acquire and what initiative they showed in the time it took them to find their way home when they didn't know where they were. To this end, Law had blindfolded her and driven her for at least two hours, she calculated now, glancing at the reddening sun. On the way Law had been untypically chatty – to stop her counting, she realised – and as he dropped her off at the top of the remote glen he said, 'You could be two miles away or twenty.' He smiled his thin smile. 'But you'll no be able to tell. See you tomorrow, Miss Dalton.'

The river that ran along the valley was brown, fast and shallow. Both its banks were thick with vegetation, mainly small, densely leaved trees with pale grey, twisted trunks. Eva began to walk steadily downstream, the saffron sun dappling the grass and undergrowth around her. Clouds of midges swarmed above pools and, as the late Scottish evening drew in, the birdsong grew in confidence.

When the sun slipped below the western edge of the glen and the light in the valley turned grey and neutral, Eva decided to rest up for the night. She had covered a couple of miles she reckoned, but there was still no sign of a house or any human habitation, no barn or bothy for her to shelter in. In her rucksack she had a mackintosh, a scarf, a water bottle, a candle, a box of matches, a small packet of toilet paper and some cheese sandwiches wrapped in greaseproof paper.

She found a mossy hollow between the roots of a tree and, putting on her mackintosh, huddled down in her makeshift bed. She ate one sandwich and saved the others for the night, thinking that she was rather enjoying the progress of this adventure, thus far, and almost looking forward to her night in the open air. The hurry of the fast water rushing over the round pebbly rocks of the river bed was soothing: it made her feel less alone and she felt she had no need for her candle to keep the gathering darkness at bay – in fact she was rather relieved to be away from her colleagues and the instructors at Lyne Manor.

When she had arrived at Waverley Station that day, Staff Sergeant Law had driven her south from Edinburgh and then along the Tweed valley through a succession of small and, to her eyes, almost identical mill towns. Then they had crossed the river and headed into remoter country; here and there was a long solid farmhouse with its steading and lowing herd, the hills around them higher – dotted with sheep – the woods denser, wilder. Then, to her surprise they drove through the ornamental gates of a manor house, with neat lodges on either side, and on down a winding drive flanked by mature beech trees to what looked like two large white houses, with neatly mown lawns, positioned to look up their own narrow valley to the west.

'Where are we?' she asked Law, stepping out of the car and looking at the bare round hills on either side.

'Lyne Manor,' he said, offering no more information.

The two houses, she saw, were in fact one: what had looked like a second was a long wing, stuccoed and whitewashed like the other, but of obviously later date than the main house – which looked as thick-walled as a keep, and rose a storey higher, with small irregular windows under a dark slate roof. She could hear the sound of a river and through a screen of trees across a field made out a spangle of light from some other building. Not quite the back of beyond, she thought, but almost.

Now as she lay in the rooty embrace of her tree, soothed by the ever-changing cadences of the rushing river, she thought of her two strange months at Lyne Manor and what she had learned there. She had come to think of the place as a kind of eccentric boarding school, and it had been a peculiar education she had received there: Morse code, first, interminable Morse code to the most advanced level, and shorthand also, and how to shoot a number of handguns. She had learned to drive a car and been given a licence; she could read a map and use a compass. She could trap, skin and cook a rabbit and other wild rodents. She knew how to cover up a trail and lay a false one. On other courses she had learned how to construct simple codes and how to break others. She had been shown how to tamper with documents, and was now able to change names and dates convincingly with a variety of special inks and tiny sharp implements; she knew how to forge – with a carved eraser – a blurry official stamp. She became familiar with human anatomy, how the body worked, what its essential nutritional needs were, and its many points of weakness. She had been shown, on busy mornings in those innocuous mill towns, how to follow a suspect, whether alone or as a couple or a threesome or more. She was also followed herself and began to know the signs when someone was on her tail and the various types of avoiding action to take. She learned how to make an invisible ink and how to make it visible. All this was interesting, occasionally fascinating, but 'scouting', as these skills were called at Lyne, was not a matter to be taken lightly: the minute anyone looked like they were enjoying themselves, let alone having fun, Law and his instructor colleagues were disparaging and unamused. But certain aspects of her education and training had perplexed her. When the others 'studying' at Lyne had gone to Turnhouse aerodrome near Edinburgh to learn how to parachute she had not been included.

'Why not?' she asked.

'Mr Romer says it's not necessary.'

But Mr Romer, it seemed, deemed other skills necessary. Twice a week Eva caught the train alone to Edinburgh, where she received elocution lessons from a shy woman in Barnton, who, slowly but surely, removed the last traces of her Russian accent from her English. She began to talk, she realised, like actresses in British films, voicing a formal, clipped, hard-edged English with strange vowel sounds: a 'man' was a 'men', a 'hat' was a 'het', her consonants were sharp and precise, her 'r's slightly trilled. She learned to speak like a young, middle-class English woman who had been privately educated. No one bothered about her French or her Russian.

The same exclusion occurred again when the others went on a three-day unarmed combat course at a commando base near Perth. 'Mr Romer says it's not necessary,' Eva was told when she wondered why she hadn't received the movement order. Then a strange man came to Lyne to teach her on her own. His name was Mr Dimarco and he was small and neatly turned-out with a sharp waxed moustache and he showed her his battery of mnemonic tricks – he used to work in a fairground, he said. Eva was told to associate numbers with colours and she soon found she could memorise up to twenty sequences of five numbers with no difficulty. They played complicated versions of Kim's Game with over one hundred objects gathered on one long table – and after two days she found, to her surprise, that she was recalling over eighty of them without difficulty. She would be shown a film and then be subjected to the most detailed interrogation about it: was the third man on the left in the pub hatless or not? What was the registration number of the getaway car? Was the woman at the hotel reception wearing ear-rings? How many steps led up to the door of the villain's house? . . . She realised she was being taught to see and remember as if from scratch: how to use her eyes and her brain in ways she had never required before. She was learning how to observe and recall in entirely different ways from the mass of human beings. And with these new talents she was meant to look at and analyse the world with a precision and purpose that went far beyond anybody's simple curiosity. Everything in the world – absolutely anything – was potentially worth noting and remembering. None of the others took these courses with Mr Dimarco – only Eva. Another of Mr Romer's special requirements, she was given to understand.

When it finally grew almost completely dark by the river, as dark as a Scottish summer night could become, Eva buttoned and belted her mackintosh and folded her scarf up as a pillow. There was a half moon and the light it shed made the river and the small gnarled trees on its banks look eerily beautiful as their colours left them and the monochrome world of the night established itself.

Only two other 'guests' had been at Lyne as long as she had: a young gaunt Polish man called Jerzy and an older woman, in her forties, called Mrs Diana Terme. There were never more than eight or ten guests at any one time and the staff changed regularly, also. Sergeant Law seemed a fixture but even he was absent for a two-week period, being replaced by a taciturn Welshman called Evans. The guests were fed three meals a day in a dining room in the main house with views of the valley and river, a mess staffed with young trainee soldiers who barely said a word. The guests were housed in the newer wing: women on one floor, men on another, each with their own room. There was even a residents' lounge with a wireless, a tea urn and newspapers and a few periodicals – but Eva rarely lingered in it. Their days were full: the comings and goings and the unstated but acknowledged nature of what they were all doing at Lyne made socialising seem risky and slack, somehow. But there were other currents circulating through Lyne that made personal contact diffident and guarded.

The day after she arrived a kind-looking man in a tweed suit and a sandy moustache interviewed her in an attic room in the main house. He never gave his name, nor was there any mention made of rank: she supposed he must be the 'Laird' that Law and some of the other staff referred to. We don't encourage friendships here at Lyne, the Laird told her, think of yourselves as travellers on a short journey – there's really no point in getting to know each other because you will never see each other again. Be cordial, make chit-chat, but the less other people know about you the better – keep yourself to yourself and make the most of your training, that, after all, is what you're here for.

As she was leaving the room he called her back and said, 'I should warn you, Miss Dalton, not all our guests are who they seem. One or two may be working for us – just to make sure the rules are adhered to.'

And so the guests at Lyne Manor all distrusted each other and were very discreet, polite and uncommunicative, exactly as the Laird would have wished and planned. Mrs Terme once asked Eva if she knew Paris and Eva, immediately suspecting her, said, 'Only very vaguely'. Then Jerzy once spoke to her in Russian and then apologised immediately. As the weeks went by she became convinced that these two were the Lyne 'ghosts' – as double agents were known. Lyne students were encouraged to use Lyne's own vocabulary, different from that employed by the service at large. There was no talk of 'the firm' – rather it was 'head office'. Agents were 'crows'; 'shadows' were people who followed you – it was, as she later learned, a kind of linguistic old-school tie, or Masonic handshake. Lyne graduates gave themselves away.

Once or twice she thought she saw Law giving a knowing glance to a new arrival and her doubts reintroduced themselves: were these the actual plants and Mrs Terme and Jerzy only naturally curious? After a short while she realised that everything was going to plan – the warning itself was enough to start the guests policing themselves and being watchful: constant suspicion makes for a very effective form of internal security. She was sure she was as much a potential suspect as any of the others she thought that she might have uncovered.

For ten days there had been a young man at Lyne. His name was Dennis Trelawny and he had blond hair with a long lock that fell over his forehead and a recent burn scar on his neck. On their few encounters – in the dining room, on the Morse code course, she knew he was looking at her, in that way. He only made the most nondescript remarks to her – 'Looks like rain', 'I'm a bit deaf from the firing range' – but she could tell that he was attracted to her. Then one day in the dining room when they met at the buffet, where they were helping themselves to dessert, they began to chat and sat down beside each other at the communal table. She asked him – she had no idea why – if he was in the Air Force: he just seemed like an RAF type to her. No, he said instinctively, the Navy, actually, and a strange look of fear came into his eye. He suspected her, she realised. He never spoke to her again.

After she had been a month at Lyne she was called one evening from her room to the main house. She was shown to a door, once again under the eaves, on which she knocked and walked in. Romer sat there at a desk, a cigarette on the go and a whisky bottle and two glasses in front of him.

'Hello, Eva,' he said, not bothering to stand. 'I was curious to know how you were getting on. Drink?' He gestured for her to sit and she did so. Romer always called her Eva, even in front of people who addressed her as Eve. She assumed they thought it an affectionate nickname; but she suspected that for Romer it was a little indication of his power, a gentle reminder that, unlike everyone else she would meet, only he knew her true history.

'No, thank you,' she said to the proffered bottle.

Romer poured her a small glass none the less and pushed it across to her.

'Nonsense – I'm impressed, but I can't drink alone.' He raised his glass to her. 'I hear you're doing well.'

'How's my father?'

'A bit better. The new pills seem to be working.'

Eva thought; is this true or is this a lie? Her Lyne training was beginning to take effect. Then she thought again: no, Romer wouldn't lie to me about this because I could find out. So, she relaxed a little.

'Why wasn't I allowed to go on the parachute course?'

'I swear you'll never need to parachute while you work for me,' he said. 'The accent's really good. Much improved.'

'Unarmed combat?'

'A waste of time.' He drank and refilled his glass. 'Imagine you're fighting for your life: you have nails, you have teeth – your animal instincts will serve you better than any training.'

'Will I be fighting for my life while I work for you?'

'Very, very unlikely.'

'So, what am I to do for you, Mr Romer?'

'Please call me Lucas.'

'So what am I to do for you, Lucas?'

'What are *we* to do, Eva. All will be made clear at the end of your training.'

'And when will that be?'

'When I think you are sufficiently trained.'

He asked her some more general questions, some of them to do with the organisation at Lyne – had people been friendly, curious, had they asked her about her recruitment, had the staff treated her differently, and so on. She gave him true answers and he took them in, ruminatively, sipping at his whisky, drawing on his cigarette, almost as if he were evaluating Lyne as a prospective parent might, seeking a school for his gifted child. Then he stubbed out his cigarette and stood up, slipping the whisky bottle into his jacket pocket and moving to the door.

'Very good to see you again, Eva,' he said. 'Keep up the good work.' And then he left.

Eva slept fitfully by the river, waking every twenty minutes or so. The small wood around her was full of noises – rustlings, crepitations, the constant melancholy hoot of owls – but she felt unafraid: just another night denizen trying to rest. In the small hours before dawn, she woke, needing to relieve herself, and moved to the river bank, where she lowered her trousers and shitted into the fast water. Now she could use her toilet paper, taking care to bury it afterwards. As she walked back to her sleeping-tree she paused and stood and looked about her, surveying her moon-dappled grove with the twisted grey trunks of the trees in a rough circle around her like a loose, warped stockade, the leaves above her head shifting drily in the night breeze. She felt strangely otherworldly, as if she were in some kind of suspended dream state, alone, lost in the remote Scottish countryside. Nobody knew where she was; and she didn't know where she was. She thought suddenly of Kolia, for some reason, her funny, moody, serious younger brother, and felt her sadness come over her, fill her for a moment. She was consoled by the thought that she was doing all this for him, making some small personal gesture of defiance to show that his death had not been for nothing. And she felt, also, a reluctant, grudging gratitude towards Romer for pushing her towards this. Perhaps, she considered, as she settled down between the embracing roots of her tree, Kolia had talked to Romer about her – perhaps Kolia had seeded the idea that she be recruited one day.

She doubted she would sleep any more, her brain was too active, but as she lay back she realised that she was as alone as she had ever been in her life and she wondered if this, also, was part of the exercise – to be completely and utterly alone, in the night, in an unknown wood, beside an unknown river, and to see how you coped – nothing to do with scouting or ingenuity at all, just a way of throwing you back on yourself for a few hours. She lay there, imagining that the sky was beginning to lighten, that dawn was imminent, and she realised she had felt calm all night, had never felt fear – and thought that perhaps this was the real dividend of Sergeant Law's game.

Dawn came with surprising rapidity – she had no idea what the time was: her watch had been taken from her – but it seemed absurd not to be up and about as the world awoke around her, so she went to the river, urinated, and washed her face and hands, drank water, filled her water-bottle and ate her remaining cheese sandwich. She sat on the river bank, chewing, drinking, and again felt more like an animal – a human animal, a creature, a thing of instinct and reflex – than she had in her entire life. It was ridiculous, she knew: she had spent one night out in the open, a balmy night at that, well clothed and sufficiently fed: but for the first time in her two months at Lyne she felt grateful to the place and the curious induction she was being put through. She headed off downstream with a steady, measured, comfortable pace but in her heart she was experiencing both a kind of exhilaration and a liberation that she had never expected.

After about an hour she saw a metalled single-track road and climbed up from the river valley. Within ten minutes a farmer in a pony and trap offered her a lift to the main road to Selkirk. From there it was a two-mile walk to town and once in Selkirk she would know exactly how far away she was from Lyne.

A holidaying couple from Durham gave her a lift from Selkirk to Innerleithen and from there she took a local taxi the remaining few miles to Lyne. She ordered the taxi to stop half a mile from the gates and, paying off the driver, circled round the foot of the hill opposite the house so she could approach it from across the meadows, as if she'd just been out for a pre-prandial stroll.

As she approached the house she could see that Sergeant Law and the Laird were standing on the lawn, looking out for her as she came in. She opened the gate on the bridge over the small stream and strode up to meet them.

'Last home, Miss Dalton,' Law said. 'Well, done, all the same: you were the furthest away.'

'We didn't expect to see you come in round Cammlesmuir, though,' the Laird said, shrewdly, 'did we, Sergeant?'

'Aye, true, sir. But Miss Dalton is always full of surprises.'

She went into the dining room, where a cold lunch had been left out for her – some tinned ham and a potato salad. She poured herself a glass of water from a carafe and gulped it down, then gulped down another. She sat and ate, alone, forcing herself to eat slowly, not wolf her food, though she had a huge hunger on her. She was feeling intense pleasure – intense self-satisfaction. Kolia would have been pleased with her, she thought, and laughed to herself. She could not explain why, but she felt she had changed in some small but profound way.

Princes Street, Edinburgh, a mid-week morning in early July, a breezy cool day with big packed clouds rushing overhead, threatening rain. Shoppers, holiday-makers, Edinburgh folk going about their business, filled the pavements and bulked in shifting crowds at the crossing points and bus stops. Eva Delectorskaya walked down the sloping street from St Andrews Square and turned right on to Princes Street. She was walking quickly, purposefully, not glancing back, but her head was full of the knowledge that at least six people were following her: two ahead, she thought, doubling back, and four behind, and perhaps a seventh, a stray, picking up instructions from the others, just to confuse her.

She paused at certain shop windows, looking at the reflections, relying on her eye to spot something familiar, something already seen, searching for people covering their faces with hats and newspapers and guidebooks – but she could see nothing suspicious. Off again: she crossed the broad street to the Gardens side, darting between a tram and a brewer's dray, running between motor cars to the Scott Monument. She walked behind it, turned on her heel and, picking up speed now, strode briskly back in the opposite direction towards Calton Hill. On a whim she suddenly ducked into the North British Hotel, the doorman having no time to tip his cap to her. At reception she asked to be shown a room and was taken up to the fourth floor. She did not linger as she enquired about rates and where the bathroom was. Outside, she knew, all would be temporary consternation but one of them at least would have seen her go into the hotel. Word would be passed: within five minutes they would be watching every exit. 'Go out the door you came in' – Law always said – 'it'll be the slackest watched.' Good advice, except everyone following had heard it also.

Down in the lobby again, she took a red headscarf out of her bag and tied it on. She took her coat off and carried it over her arm. When a gaggle of people, heading for an omnibus parked outside, gathered by the revolving door, she joined them and slipped out in their group, asking a man, with as much animation as possible, where she could find the Royal Mile, then darted round the rear of their charabanc, recrossed Princes Street again and then sauntered slowly, dawdling westwards, pausing to look in shop windows, only to study reflections. There was a man in a green jacket she thought she had seen before on the other side of the street, keeping pace with her, turning his back from time to time to look up at the castle.

She ran into Jenners and up three floors. She moved through haberdashery towards the milliners' department. Green Jacket would have seen her: he would have told the others she was in the department store. She went into the ladies' lavatory and strode past the stalls down to the end. There was a staff entrance here that, in her experience, was never locked. She turned the handle – the door opened and she slipped through.

'I'm sorry, Miss, this is private.' Two shop assistants on their break sat on a bench, smoking.

'I'm looking for Jenny, Jenny Kinloch. I'm her sister: there's been a terrible accident.'

'We've no Jenny Kinloch here, Miss.'

'But I was told to go to the staff room.'

So she was led through corridors and back stairways smelling of linoleum and polish to the staff room. No Jenny Kinloch was to be had, so Eva said she had to make a telephone call, perhaps she'd got the details wrong, perhaps the shop was Binns, not Jenners, and she was directed with some impatience towards a telephone cabin. Inside she took off her headscarf and combed out her long hair. She turned her coat inside out and stepped out through the staff entrance and on to Rose Street. She knew she'd lost them. She had always lost them but this was the first time she'd beaten a six-man follow –

'Eva!' The sound of running footsteps.

She turned: it was Romer, a little out of breath, his wiry hair tousled. He slowed, composed himself, ran a hand across his head.

'Very good,' he said. 'I thought the red scarf was a master-stroke. Make yourself conspicuous – tremendous.'

Her disappointment was like a bitter taste in her throat. 'But how did you –'

'I was cheating. I was close. Always. Nobody knew.' He stood in front of her now. 'I'll show you how to do a close follow. You need more props – specs, a false moustache.' He took one out of his pocket, and out of his other a flat tweed cap. 'But you were very good, Eva. Nearly shook me off.' He was grinning his white smile. 'Didn't you like the room at the North British? Jenners was tricky – the Ladies, nice touch. A few outraged Edinburgh maidens, there, I'm afraid. But I knew there must be a back way out because you'd never have gone in.'

'I see.'

He looked at his watch. 'Let's go up here. I've booked lunch. You like oysters, don't you?'

They ate lunch in a decoratively tiled oyster bar attached to a public house. Oysters, she thought, the symbol of our relationship. Perhaps he believes they're a genuine aphrodisiac and I'll like him better? As they sat and talked Eva found herself looking at Romer with as much objectivity as she could muster, trying to imagine what she would have thought of him if they hadn't been thrown together in this curious and alarming way – if Kolia's death had never happened. There *was* something attractive about him, she supposed: something both urgent and laconically mysterious – he was a kind of spy after all – and there was his rare transforming smile – and his massive self-confidence. She concentrated: he was praising her again, saying how everyone at Lyne was impressed by her dedication, her aptitude.

'But what's it all for?' she said, blurting the question out.

'I'll explain everything once you're finished,' he said. 'You'll come down to London and meet the unit, my team.'

'You have your own unit?'

'Let's say a small subdivision of an annexe to a subsidiary element linked to the main body.'

'And what does your unit do?'

'I wanted to give you these,' he said, not answering, and reached into his breast pocket, removing an envelope that turned out to contain two passports. She opened them: there was her same shadowy-eyed photograph, blurry and stiffly formal, but the names were different: now she was Margery Allerdice and Lily Fitzroy.

'What're these for? I thought I was Eve Dalton.'

He explained. Everyone who worked for him, who was in his unit, was given three identities. It was a perk, a bonus – to be used or not used as the recipient saw fit. Think of them as a couple of extra parachutes, he said, a couple of getaway cars parked near by if you ever felt the need to use them one day. They can be very handy, he said, and it saves a lot of time if you have them already.

Eva put her two new passports in her handbag and for the first time felt a little creep of fear climb up her spine. Following-games in Edinburgh were one thing; clearly whatever Romer's unit did was potentially dangerous. She clipped her handbag shut.

'Are you allowed to tell me more about this unit of yours?'

'Oh, yes. A bit. It's called AAS,' he said. 'Almost an embarrassing acronym, I know, but it stands for Actuarial and Accountancy Services.'

'Very boring.'

'Exactly.'

And she thought, suddenly, that she did like Romer – liked his brand of cleverness, his way of second-guessing everything. He ordered a brandy for himself. Eva wanted nothing more.

'I'll give you another piece of advice,' he said. 'In fact I'll always be giving you advice – tips – from time to time. You should try to remember them.'

She suddenly disliked him again: the self-satisfaction, the *amour propre*, were sometimes just too much. I am the cleverest man in the world and all I have to deal with are you poor fools.

'Find yourself a safe house. Somewhere. Wherever you happen to be for any length of time, have a safe house, a personal one. Don't tell me, don't tell anyone. Just a place you can be sure of going to, where you can be anonymous, where you can hide, if need be.'

'Romer's rules,' she said. 'Any more?'

'Oh, there are plenty more,' he said, not picking up the irony in her voice, 'but as we're on the subject, I'll tell you the most important rule. Rule number one, never to be forgotten.'

'Which is?'

'Don't trust anyone,' he said, without any portentousness, but with a kind of mundane confidence and certainty, as if he had said 'Today is Friday'. 'Don't trust anyone, ever,' he repeated and took out a cigarette and lit it, thinking, as if he'd managed to surprise himself by his acuity. 'Maybe it's the only rule you need. Maybe all the other rules I'll tell you are just versions of this rule. "The one and only rule". Don't trust anyone – not even the one person you think you can trust most in this world. Always suspect. Always mistrust.' He smiled, not his warm smile. 'It'll stand you in excellent stead.'

'Yes, I'm learning that.'

He drank the rest of his brandy down in a one-er. He drank quite a lot, she'd noticed, in her few encounters with Romer.

'We'd better get you back to Lyne,' he said, calling for the bill.

At the door they shook hands. Eva said she could catch a bus home easily enough. She thought he was looking at her more intently than usual and she remembered that she had her hair down – he's probably never seen me with my hair down, she thought.

'Yes . . . Eva Delectorskaya,' he said, musingly, as if he had other things on his mind. 'Who would've thought?' He reached out as if to pat her shoulder and then decided against it. 'Everyone's very pleased. Very.' He looked up at the afternoon sky with its great building clouds, grey, laden, threatening. 'War next month,' he said, in the same bland tone, 'or the next. The big European war.' He looked back and smiled at her. 'We shall do our bit,' he said, 'don't worry.'

'In the Actuarial and Accountancy Services.'

'Yes . . . Ever been to Belgium?' he asked suddenly.

'Yes. I went to Brussels once. Why?'

'I think you might like it. Bye, Eva.' He gave her a half salute, half wave and sauntered away. Eva could hear him whistling. She turned and walked thoughtfully to the bus station.

Later, as she sat in the waiting-room, waiting for the bus to Galashiels, she found herself looking at the other occupants of the small room also waiting for their buses – the men and women, and the few children. She was examining them, evaluating them, assessing them, placing them. And she thought: if only you knew, if only you knew who I was and what I did. Then she caught herself, almost exclaiming with surprise. She realised suddenly that everything had indeed changed, that she was now looking at the world in a different way. It was as if the nervous circuits in her brain had altered, as if she'd been rewired, and she knew that her lunch with Romer had marked both the end of something old and the beginning of something new. She understood now, with almost distressing clarity, that for the spy the world and its people were different than they were for everybody else. With a small tremor of alarm and, she had to admit, with a small tremor of excitement, she realised in that Edinburgh waiting-room that she was looking at the world around her as a spy would. She thought about what Romer had said, about his one and only rule, and she thought: was this the spy's particular, unique fate – to live in a world without trust? She wondered if she would ever be capable of trusting anyone again.

3

No More Naked

I WOKE EARLY, DISTURBED and angry after my familiar dream – the dream where I'm dead and I'm watching Jochen cope with life without me – usually perfectly and completely happily. I started to have this dream after he began to talk and I resent my subconscious mind drawing this deep worry, this sick neurosis, to my attention every now and then. Why am I dreaming of my own death? I never dream of Jochen's death, though sometimes I think about it, rarely, for a second or two before I banish it – shocked – from my mind. I'm almost sure that everyone does this about the people they love – it's a grim corollary of truly loving someone: you find yourself compelled to imagine your world without them and have to contemplate its awfulness and dread for a second or two. A peer through the crack to the emptiness, the big silence beyond. We can't help it – I can't help it, anyway, and I tell myself guiltily that everybody must do it, that it's a very human reaction to the human condition. I hope I'm right.

I slipped out of bed and padded through to his bedroom, to check on him. He was sitting up in bed, colouring in his colouring book, a fritter of pencils and wax crayons around him.

I gave him a kiss and asked him what he was drawing.

'A sunset,' he said, and showed me the lurid page, all flaming orange and yellow, capped with bruised brooding purples and greys.

'It's a bit sad,' I said, my mood still influenced by my dream.

'No it's not, it's meant to be beautiful.'

'What would you like for breakfast?' I asked him.

'Crispy bacon, please.'

I opened the door to Hamid – he wasn't wearing his new leather jacket, I noticed, just his black jeans and a white short-sleeved shirt, very crisp, like an airline pilot. Normally I'd have teased him about this but I thought that after my *faux pas* of the day before and the fact that Ludger was in the kitchen behind me it would be best to be pleasant and kind.

'Hamid, hello! Beautiful morning!' I said, my voice full of special cheer.

'The sun is shining again,' he said in a monotone.

'So it is, so it is.'

I turned and showed him in. Ludger was sitting there at the kitchen table in T-shirt and shorts, spooning cornflakes into his mouth. I could tell what Hamid was thinking – his insincere smile, his stiffness – but there was no possibility of explaining the reality behind this situation with Ludger in the room, so I opted for a simple introduction.

'Hamid, this is Ludger, a friend of mine from Germany. Ludger – Hamid.'

I had not introduced them the day before. I had gone down to the front door, brought Ludger up to the flat, installed him in the sitting-room and continued – with some difficulty – with Hamid's lesson. After Hamid was finished and gone I went to find Ludger – he was stretched out on the sofa, asleep.

Now Ludger raised his clenched fist and said, '*Allahu Akbar.*'

'You remember Ludger,' I said, brightly. 'He came yesterday, during our lesson.'

Hamid's face registered no emotion. 'Pleased to meet you,' he said.

'Shall we go through?' I said.

'Please, yes, after you, Ruth.'

I led him through to the study. He seemed very unlike his usual self: solemn, almost agonised in some way. I noticed he had had his beard trimmed – it made him look younger.

'So,' I said, continuing with the false breeziness, sitting down at my desk, 'I wonder what the Ambersons are up to today.'

He ignored me. 'This Ludger man,' he said, 'is he the father of Jochen?'

'No! Good God, no. What made you think that? No – he's the brother of Jochen's father, the younger brother of Karl-Heinz. No, no, absolutely no.' I laughed, with nervous relief, realising I'd said 'no' six times. No denial could have been more underscored.

Hamid tried to disguise how happy he was at this news, but failed. His grin was almost stupid.

'Oh. All right. No, I thought he . . .' he paused, held up both his hands in apology. 'Forgive me, I should not induct like this.'

'Deduce.'

'Deduce. So: he is Jochen's uncle.'

This was true, but I had to admit I had never thought of Ludger Kleist in this way (he didn't seem remotely avuncular – the words 'Uncle Ludger' conjoined appeared creepily anti-thetical) and, indeed, I had also introduced Ludger to Jochen as 'a friend from Germany' – and they had had no time to become better acquainted as I had to take Jochen to a birthday party. Ludger said he would go 'to a pub' and by the time he returned that evening Jochen was in bed. The uncle-revelation would have to wait.

Ludger was dossing down on a mattress on the floor of a room in the flat we called the Dining Room – in honour of the one dinner party I had given there since we had moved in. It was, in fact, and in theory, the room where I wrote my thesis. Its oval table was stacked with books and notes and drafts of my various chapters. I allowed myself to believe, contrary to the dusty evidence, that this was the room where I worked on my thesis – its very existence, its designation and compartmentalisation seemed to make my wishes somehow real, or more real: this was where my calm, scholarly, intellectual life took place – my messy disorganised real life occupied the rest of the flat. The Dining Room was my discrete little cell of mental endeavour. I dispelled the illusion quickly: we pushed the table to the wall; we laid down Ludger's inflatable mattress on the carpet – it had become a spare room again – one Ludger professed himself to be very comfortable in.

'If you could see where I have been sleeping,' he said, pulling down the bottom eyelid of his right eye with a finger, as if to exemplify a basilisk stare. 'Jesus Christ, Ruth, this is the Ritz.' And then he gave his crazy shrill laugh that I remembered better than I wished.

Hamid and I settled down with the Ambersons. Keith Amberson couldn't get his car started and the family were about to go on holiday to Dorset. Lots of conditional-perfect verbs. I could hear Ludger moving from the kitchen through the flat.

'Is Ludger staying long?' Hamid asked. Clearly Ludger was on both our minds.

'I don't think so,' I said, realising that in fact I had still to ask.

'You said you thought he was dead. Was it in an accident?'

I decided to tell Hamid the truth. 'I was told that he had been shot by the West German police. But obviously not.'

'Shot by police? Is he a gangster, a criminal?'

'Let's say he's a radical. A kind of anarchist.'

'So why is he staying here?'

'He'll be going in a couple of days,' I lied.

'Is it because of Jochen's father?'

'So many questions, Hamid.'

'I apologise.'

'Yes – I suppose I am letting him stay here for a couple of days because he is the brother of Jochen's father . . . Look, shall we continue? Will Keith get his car fixed? What *should* Keith *have* done?'

'Are you still in love with Jochen's father?'

I looked stupidly at Hamid. His brown-eyed gaze was intense, candid. He had never asked me questions like this before.

'No,' I said. 'Of course not. I left him nearly two years ago. That's why I brought Jochen back to Oxford.'

'Good,' he said, smiling, relaxing. 'I just had to know.'

'Why?'

'Because I would like to invite you to have dinner with me. In a restaurant.'

Veronica agreed to take Jochen home for supper and I drove out to Middle Ashton to talk with my mother. When I arrived she was in the garden on her knees, cutting the lawn with shears. She repudiated lawn mowers, she said; she abominated lawn mowers; lawn mowers had signalled the death of the English garden as it had existed for centuries. Capability Brown and Gilbert White had no need of lawn mowers: grass should only be cropped by sheep or be scythed in the true English garden – and as she didn't possess or know how to wield a scythe she was perfectly happy to get down on her knees once a fortnight with her shears. The contemporary English lawn was a ghastly anachronism – striped, shaved grass was a hideous modern invention. And so on, and so on. I was very familiar with the argument and never bothered to try to refute it (she was quite happy to use her motor car to go shopping, I noticed, rather than acquire a pony and trap, as old Capability or Gilbert would have done). Her lawn was therefore shaggy and unkempt, full of daisies and other weeds: this was what a cottage garden lawn was meant to look like, she would pontificate, given half a chance.

'How's the back?' I said, looking down on her.

'Bit better today,' she said, 'though I might ask you to wheel me down to the pub later.'

We went to sit in the kitchen and she poured me a glass of wine and an apple juice for herself. She didn't drink, my mother: I'd never seen her so much as sip a sherry.

'Let's have a cigarette,' she said, so we both lit up, puffed away and made small talk for a while putting off the big conversation she knew we were going to have.

'Feeling more relaxed, now?' she asked. 'I could tell you were tense. Why don't you tell me what's going on. Is it Jochen?'

'No, it's *you*, for heaven's sake. You and "Eva Delectorskaya". I can't get a grip on all this, Sal. Think what it's like for me – out of the blue like this, with never so much of a hint. I'm worried.'

She shrugged. 'Only to be expected. It's a shock, I know. If I were you I'd be a bit shocked, true, a bit unsettled.' She looked at me in a strange way, I thought: coldly, analytically, as if I were someone she'd just met. 'You don't really believe me. Do you?' she said. 'You think I'm crackers.'

'I do believe you, of course I do – how could I not? It's just hard to take it on board: all at once. Everything being so different – everything I'd blithely taken for granted all my life gone in a second.' I paused, daring myself: 'Go on, say something in Russian.'

She spoke for two minutes in Russian, getting angrier as she did so, pointing her finger at me, jabbing it.

I was wholly surprised and taken aback – it was like some form of possession, speaking in tongues. It left me short of breath.

'My God,' I said. 'What was that all about?'

'It was about the disappointment I feel about my daughter. My daughter, who's an intelligent and stubborn young woman but who, if she'd spent just a little of her considerable brain power thinking logically about what I have told her, would have realised in about thirty seconds that I'd never play such a wicked trick on her. So there.'

I finished off my wine.

'So what happened next?' I asked. 'Did you go to Belgium?

Why are you called "Sally" Gilmartin? What happened to my grandfather, Sergei, and my step-grandmother, Irène?'

She stood up, a little triumphantly, I thought, and moved to the door.

'One thing at a time. You'll find out everything. You'll have the answers to every question you could ask. I just want you to read my story carefully – use your brain. Your powerful brain. I'll have questions for you, also. Lots of questions. There's things I'm not sure even I understand . . .' This thought seemed to upset her and she frowned, then she left the room. I poured myself another glass of wine and then thought about breath-alysers – careful. My mother came back and handed me another folder. I felt a spasm of irritation: I knew she was doing this deliberately – feeding me her story in instalments, like a serial. She wanted to keep me drawn in, to make the revelations endure so that it wouldn't be over in one great emotional earthquake. A series of small tremors was what she was after – to keep me on my toes.

'Why don't you just give me the whole bloody thing,' I said, more petulantly than I wanted.

'I'm still polishing it,' she said, unperturbed, 'making small changes all the time. I want it to be as good as possible.'

'When did you write all this?'

'Over the last year or two. You can see I keep adding, crossing out, rewriting. Trying to make it read clearly. I want it to seem consistent. You can tidy it up if you want – you're a much better writer than I am.'

She came over to me and squeezed my arm – consolingly, I thought, with some feeling: my mother was not a great one for physical contact therefore it was hard to read the subtext of her rare affective gestures.

'Don't look so perplexed,' she said. 'We all have secrets. No one knows even half the truth about anybody else, however close or intimate they are. I'm sure you've got secrets from me.

Hundreds, thousands. Look at you – you didn't even tell me about Jochen for months.' She reached out and smoothed my hair – this was very unusual. 'That's all I'm doing, Ruth, believe me. I'm just telling you my secrets. You'll understand why I had to wait until now.'

'Did Dad know?'

She paused. 'No, he didn't. He didn't know anything.'

I thought about this for a while; thought about my parents and how I had always regarded them. Wipe that slate clean, I said to myself.

'Didn't he suspect?' I said. 'Suspect anything?'

'I don't think so. We were very happy, that's all that mattered.'

'So why have you decided to tell me all this? Tell me your secrets, all of a sudden?'

She sighed, looked about her, fluttered her hands aimlessly, ran them through her hair, then drummed her fingers on the table.

'Because,' she said, finally, 'because I think someone is trying to kill me.'

I drove home, thoughtfully, slowly, carefully. I was a little wiser, I suppose, but I was beginning to worry more about my mother's paranoia than what I had to accept as the truth about her strange, duplicitous past. Sally Gilmartin was – and this I had to come to terms with – Eva Delectorskaya. But, by the same token, why would anyone want to kill a 66-year-old woman, a grandmother, living in a remote Oxfordshire village? I thought I could just about live with Eva Delectorskaya but I found the murder issue much harder to accept.

I collected Jochen from Veronica's and we walked homewards through Summertown to Moreton Road. The summer night was heavy, humid, and the leaves on the trees looked tired and limp. A whole summer's heat in three weeks and summer had just begun. Jochen said he was hot, so I slipped his T-shirt off him and we walked home, hand in hand, not talking, each of us lost in our thoughts.

At the gate, he said: 'Is Ludger still here?'

'Yes. He's staying for a few days.'

'Is Ludger my daddy?'

'No! God, no. Definitely not. I told you – your father's called Karl-Heinz. Ludger's his brother.'

'Oh.'

'Why did you think he was?'

'He's from Germany. I was born in Germany, you said.'

'So you were.'

I crouched down and looked him in the face, took his two hands.

'He isn't your father. I would never lie to you about that, darling. I'll always tell you the truth.'

He looked pleased.

'Give me a hug,' I said, and he put his arms around my neck and kissed me on the cheek. I picked him up and carried him down the alleyway towards our stairs. As I set him down on the top landing I looked through the kitchen's glass door to see Ludger emerge from the bathroom and wander towards us down the corridor, heading for the dining-room. He was naked.

'Stay there,' I said to Jochen and strode quickly through the kitchen to intercept him. Ludger was drying his hair with a towel and humming to himself as he walked towards me – his cock was swaying to and fro as he rubbed his hair.

'Ludger.'

'Oh. Hi, Ruth,' he said, taking his time to cover himself up.

'Do you mind not doing that, Ludger. Please. In my house.'

'Sorry. I thought you were out.'

'Students come to the back door at all hours. They can see in. It's a glass door.'

He gave his sleazy grin. 'A nice surprise for them. But you don't mind.'

'Yes, I do mind. Please don't walk around naked.' I turned and went back to let Jochen in.

'Forgive me, Ruth,' he called plaintively after me: he could tell how cross I was. 'It was because I was in porno. I never think. No more naked, I promise.'

The Story of Eva Delectorskaya

Belgium. 1939

EVA DELECTORSKAYA WOKE EARLY, remembered she was alone in the flat and took her time washing and dressing. She made coffee and took it to the small balcony – there was a watery sun shining – where she had a view across the railway line to the Parc Marie-Henriette, its trees largely bare now, but she saw, to her vague surprise, that there was a solitary couple out on the lake, the man heaving on the oars as if he were in a race, showing off, the woman clinging on to the sides of the rowing boat for fear of falling in.

She decided to walk to work. The sun had persisted and, even though it was November, there was something invigorating about the cold air and the sharp slanting shadows. She put on her hat and her coat and wrapped her scarf around her neck. She double-locked the flat as she left, carefully placing her small square of yellow paper under the doorjamb, so that it was just visible. When Sylvia returned she'd replace it with a blue square. Eva knew that there was a war on but, in sleepy Ostend, such precautions seemed almost absurd: who, for instance, was going to break into their flat? But Romer wanted everyone in the unit to be 'operational' – to establish good habits and procedures, to make them second nature.

She strolled down the rue Leffinge and turned left on the Chaussée de Thourout, lifting her face to the mild sun, deliberately not thinking about the day ahead, trying to pretend she was a young Belgian woman – like the other young Belgian women she saw on the street about her – a young Belgian woman going about her business in a small town in a small country in a world that made some sort of sense.

She turned right at the clock tower and crossed the small square towards the Café de Paris. She thought about stopping for a coffee but realised that Sylvia would be waiting impatiently to be relieved from the night shift and so strode briskly onwards. At the tram depot she saw on the billboards the fading posters from last summer's races – Le Grand Prix Internationale d'Ostende 1939 – strange reminders from a world that was then at peace. She turned left at the post office into the rue d'Yser and immediately saw the new sign Romer had had installed. Royal blue on lemon yellow: Agence d'Information Nadal – or, as Romer preferred to call it: 'The Rumour Factory'.

The building was a 1920s three-storey rectilinear office block, with a curved, pillared *porte-cochère* over the main entrance, in austere Streamline Moderne style, an effect which was rather undermined by the decorative pseudo-Egyptian frieze that ran under the simple cornice of the top floor. On the roof was a thirty-foot wireless transmitter tower, like a mini-Tour Eiffel, painted red and white. It was this, rather than any architectural pretensions, that made the odd passer-by offer the building a second glance.

Eva walked in, nodded to the receptionist, and climbed the stairs to the top floor. The Agence d'Information Nadal was a small news agency, a minnow compared to the giants like Reuters, Agence Havas or Associated Press but which did, essentially, the same job – namely sell news and information to various customers unprepared or unable to gather that news and information themselves. A.I. Nadal serviced some 137 local newspapers and radio stations in Belgium, Holland and northern France and made a modest but steady profit. Romer had bought it in 1938 from its founder Pierre-Henri Nadal, a spruce white-haired old gent who wore co-respondent shoes and a boater in summer and who occasionally popped in to the office to see how his child was progressing under the new foster-parents. Romer had kept the essentials and discreetly added the modifications he required. The radio tower was heightened and made more powerful. The original staff, some dozen Belgian journalists, were retained but quartered on the second floor, where they continued to sift and disseminate the local news from this small corner of northern Europe – livestock sales, village fêtes, bicycle races, high and low tides, closing prices from the Brussels bourse and so on – duly passing their copy down to the telegraphists on the ground floor, who transformed the information into Morse code and telegraphed it to the agency's 137 subscribers.

Romer's unit occupied the third floor. A small team of five who spent their days reading every European and relevant foreign newspaper they could find, and who, after due process of consultation and discussion, would insert, from time to time, a particular Romer-story into the mass of trivia beamed out from the innocuous building on the rue d'Yser.

Apart from Romer and Eva the other four members of Romer's 'team' were Morris Devereux – Romer's number two – an elegant and suave ex-Cambridge don; Angus Woolf, a former Fleet Street journalist who was severely crippled by some congenital deformation of his spine; Sylvia Rhys-Meyer – Eva's flatmate – a lively woman in her late thirties, married and divorced three times and an ex-Foreign Office linguist and translator; and Alfie Blytheswood – who had nothing to do with the material that came out of the agency but was responsible for the maintenance and smooth running of the powerful transmitters and the occasional wireless encryptions. This was AAS in its entirety, Eva came to realise, very quickly: Romer's team was small and tight-knit – apart from her everyone seemed to have been working for him for several years, Morris Devereux even longer.

Eva hung her coat and hat on her usual hook and made for her desk. Sylvia was still there, flicking through yesterday's Swedish newspapers. The ashtray in front of her was brimful of cigarette butts.

'Busy night?'

Sylvia arched her back and eased her shoulders to simulate fatigue. She looked like a stout, no-nonsense county wife, the wife of the local GP or a gentleman farmer, bosomy and broad-hipped, who wore well-cut suits and expensive accessories – except that everything else about Sylvia Rhys-Meyer contradicted that initial assessment.

'Fucking boring, fucking dull boring, boring dull fucking, dull fucking boring,' she said, standing up to allow Eva to take her seat.

'Oh, yes,' Sylvia added. 'Your dead-sailors piece has been picked up all over the place.' She opened and pointed to a page in the *Svenska Dagbladet*. 'And it's in *The Times* and in *Le Monde*. Congratulations. His nibs will be very pleased.'

Eva looked at the Swedish text, recognising certain words. It was a story she had suggested at conference a few days before: the idea of twenty Icelandic sailors washed up in a remote Norwegian fjord, alleging that their fishing boat had sailed into heavily mined waters off the port of Narvik. Eva knew at once that it was the sort of story Romer loved. It had already provoked an official denial by the British War Office (Norwegian territorial waters had not been mined by British ships) – more to the point, as Romer would say, it was loose intelligence: a fishing boat sunk by a mine – where? – and it was information useful to the enemy. Any further denials would be either disbelieved or be too late – the news was out there in the world doing its dirty work. German intelligence officials monitoring the world's media would note the alleged presence of mines off the Norwegian coast. This would be conveyed to the navy; maps would be taken out, amended, altered. It was, in essence, the ideal illustration of how Romer's unit and A.I. Nadal was meant to work. Information wasn't neutral, Romer constantly repeated: if it was believed or even half believed, then everything began subtly to change as a result – the ripple effect could have consequences no one could foresee. Eva had had previous small successes during the four months she'd been in Ostend – news of imaginary bridges being planned for, of Dutch flood defences reinforced, of trains being re-routed in northern France because of new military manoeuvres – but this was the first time the international press had picked up one of her stories. Romer's idea, like all good ideas, was very simple: false information can be just as useful, influential, as telling, transforming or as damaging as true information. In a world where A.I. Nadal fed 137 news outlets, twenty-four hours a day, 365 days a year, how could you tell what was genuine and what was the product of a clever, devious and determined mind?

Eva took her seat, still warm from Sylvia's generous buttocks, and pulled a pile of Russian and French newspapers towards her. She assumed that someone high up in the British Secret Service had seen the merit in Romer's idea and that this explained the strange autonomy he seemed to possess. It was the British taxpayer, she surmised, who had bought the Agence d'Information Nadal (and thereby ensured Pierre-Henri Nadal a very comfortable retirement) and was now funding its development as part of its Political Warfare department. Romer and his 'unit' were involved in feeding careful and clever false information out into the world – through the bona-fide medium of a small Belgian press agency – and nobody really knew what the effect might be. No one could tell if the German high command was taking note, but the unit always counted it a success if their stories were picked up (and paid for) by other newspapers and radio stations. However, Romer seemed to want the stories they sent out to conform to some kind of plan to which only he had the key. In conference, he would sometimes demand stories about rumours of potential resignations of this or that minister, or scandals undermining this or that government; or he would say, suddenly: we need something on Spanish neutrality; or else call immediately for statistics about the increase in sheet-metal production in French foundries. The lies had to be constructed with all the scrupulousness of truth. Instant plausibility was the key concern – and the team laboured to supply it. But it was all somewhat vague and all – to tell the truth as Eva saw it – something of a parlour game. They never knew the consequences of their clever little fibs: it was as if the individual members of the unit were players in an orchestra, sequestered in soundproof rooms – only Romer was able to make out the harmonies of the tune they were playing.

Sylvia came back to the desk, her coat on and a smart felt hat with a feather jammed on her head.

'Supper in tonight?' she said. 'Let's have steak and red wine.'

''Fraid not,' a man's voice said.

They both turned to see Morris Devereux standing there. He was a lean, acerbic, sharp-featured young man with prematurely grey hair which he brushed sleekly back from his brow without a parting. He took care over his clothes: today he was wearing a dark navy suit and an azure bow tie. Some days he wore brilliant scarlet shirts.

'We're off to Brussels,' he said, to Eva. 'Press conference, foreign ministry.'

'What about this lot?' Eva said, pointing to her pile of newspapers.

'You can relax,' Morris said. 'Your dead sailors have been picked up by Associated Press. Nice cheque for us and you'll be all over America tomorrow.'

Sylvia grunted, said goodbye and left. Morris fetched Eva's coat and hat.

'We have our master's motor,' he said. 'He's been summoned to London. I think a rather nice luncheon is on the cards.'

They drove to Brussels, passing swiftly through Bruges with no delay but at Ghent they were obliged to detour on to minor roads to Audenarde as their way was blocked by a convoy of military vehicles, lorries filled with soldiers and small tanks on low-loaders and, strangely, what seemed to be an entire division of cavalry, horses and riders milling about the road and its verges for all the world as if preparing to advance on a nineteenth-century battlefield.

In Brussels they parked near the Gare du Nord and, as they were late for lunch, they took a taxi direct to the restaurant Morris had already booked, the Filet de Boeuf in the rue Grétry. The press conference was at the *hôtel de ville* at 3.30. They had plenty of time, Morris thought, though perhaps they should pass on dessert.

They were shown to their table and ordered an aperitif as they scanned the menus. Eva looked about her at the other clients: the businessmen, the lawyers, the politicians, she supposed – eating, smoking, drinking, talking – and at the elderly waiters bustling importantly to and fro with the orders and she realised she was the only woman in the room. It was a Wednesday: perhaps Belgian women didn't go out to eat until the weekend, she suggested to Morris – who was summoning the sommelier.

'Who knows? But your refulgent femininity more than compensates for the preponderance of males, my dear.'

She ordered museau de porc and turbot.

'It's very strange, this war,' she said. 'I keep having to remind myself it's going on.'

'Ah, but we're in a neutral country,' Morris said. 'Don't forget.'

'What's Romer doing in London?'

'Ours not to reason why. Probably talking to Mr X.'

'Who's Mr X?'

'Mr X is Romer's . . . what? Romer's Cardinal Richelieu. A very powerful man who allows Lucas Romer to do pretty much what he wants.'

Eva looked at Morris as he cut his foie gras into neat little squares.

'Why isn't the Agence in Brussels?' she asked. 'Why are we in Ostend?'

'So it'll be easier for us to flee when the Germans invade.'

'Oh yes? And when will that be?'

'Spring of next year, according to our boss. He doesn't want to be trapped in Brussels.'

Their main courses arrived and a bottle of claret. Eva watched Morris do the whole sniffing, glass held to the light, wine rolled around the mouth performance with aplomb.

'We'd eat and drink better in Brussels,' Eva said. 'Anyway, why am I on this trip? You're the Belgian expert.'

'Romer insisted. You do have your identification with you, I hope.'

She assured him she had and they ate on, chatting about their colleagues and the deficiencies and disadvantages of life in Ostend, but Eva found herself wondering as they talked, and not for the first time, about what tiny part she was playing in an invisible grander plan that only Romer really understood. Her recruitment, her training, her posting all seemed to betoken some form of logical progression – but she could not discern where it was leading. She could not see the Eva Delectorskaya cog in the big machine – she could not even see the big machine, she realised. Ours not to reason why, Morris had said, and she ruefully conceded that he was right, as she carved off a square inch of turbot and popped it in her mouth – delicious. It was a pleasure to be in Brussels, away from her French and Russian newspapers, lunching with a cultured and amusing young man – don't rock the boat looking for answers; don't make waves.

The press conference was held by a junior minister and was designed to outline the Belgian government's position with regard to Russia's recent invasion of Finland. Eva's name and details were taken at the door and she and Morris joined about forty other journalists and listened to the junior minister's speech for a minute or two before her mind began to wander. She found herself thinking of her father, whom she had last seen in Paris in August for a few days while she was on leave and before she moved to Ostend. He had looked much frailer, thinner, the wattles under his chin more pronounced and she noticed also how both his hands trembled in repose. The most disturbing tic was his constant licking of his lips. She asked him if he was thirsty and he said, no, not at all, why? She wondered if it were a side-effect of the drugs he had been given to stimulate his heart but she could not lie to herself any more: her father had embarked on a slow form of terminal decline – doughty old age was behind him, now he was entering the final fraught struggle of his time on earth. She thought he had aged ten years in the few months she had been away.

Irène was cool and incurious about her new life in England and said, when Eva asked about her father's health, that he was doing very nicely, thank you, all the doctors were very pleased. When her father asked her about her job she said she was working in 'signals' and that she was now an expert in Morse code. 'Who would have thought it?' he exclaimed, something of his old vigour returning for a moment or two, putting his trembling hand on her arm and adding, in a low voice so Irène couldn't hear, 'You did the right thing, my dear. Good girl.'

Morris tapped on her elbow, jerking her out of her reverie, and passed her a piece of paper. It was a question in French. She looked at it incomprehensibly.

'Romer wants you to ask it,' Morris said.

'Why?'

'I think it's meant to confer respectability on us.'

Therefore, when the junior minister had finished his speech and the moderator of the press conference asked for questions, Eva allowed four or five to take place before she raised her hand. She was spotted, pointed at – '*La Mademoiselle, là*' – and stood up.

'Eve Dalton,' she said, 'Agence d'Information Nadal.' She saw the moderator write her name in a ledger in front of him and then, at his nod, she asked her question – she had no real idea of its import – something to do with a minority party in parliament, the Vlaams Nationaal Verbond, and their policy of '*La neutralité rigoureuse*'. It caused some consternation: the junior minister's reply was brusque and dismissive but she noticed another half-dozen hands being raised for follow-up questions. She sat down and Morris gave her a covert smile of congratulation. After five more minutes he signalled that they should leave and they crept out, leaving by a side entrance and crossing the Grand Place at a half-run through an angled, spitting rain towards a café. They sat indoors and smoked a cigarette and drank tea, looking out through the windows at the ornate cliff faces of the buildings round the massive square, their sense of absolute confidence and prosperity still ringing out across the centuries. The rain was growing heavier and the flower sellers were packing up their stalls when they caught a taxi to the station and then drove back steadily and without delays or diversions towards Ostend.

There were no military convoys on the road at Ghent and they made good time, reaching Ostend by seven o'clock in the evening. On the journey back they talked casually but guardedly – as did all Romer's employees, Eva now realised. There was a sense of solidarity that they shared, of being in a small élite team – that was undeniable – but it was really only a veneer: no one was ever truly open or candid; they tried to restrict their conversation to frivolous observations, bland generalities – specific times and places in their past, pre-Romer lives were never identified.

Morris said to her: 'Your French is excellent. First class.'

And Eva said: 'Yes, I lived in Paris for a while.'

In her turn she asked Morris how long he had known Romer. 'Oh, a good few years now,' he said and she knew from the tone of his voice that it would not only be wrong to ask for a more precise answer but that it would also be suspicious. Morris called her 'Eve' and the thought came to her suddenly that perhaps 'Morris Devereux' was no more his real name than 'Eve Dalton' was hers. She glanced over at him as they motored towards the coast and saw his fine features lit from below by the dashboard lights and felt, not for the first time, a dull pang of regret: how this curious job they were doing – regardless of how they were working towards the same end – consistently managed to leave them essentially divided and solitary.

Morris dropped her at her flat; she said good-night and climbed the stairs to her landing. There she saw Sylvia's blue square of card protruding just beyond the doorjamb. She slipped her key into the lock and was just about to turn it when it was opened from the inside. Romer stood there, smiling at her somewhat frostily, she thought, and at the same time she noticed Sylvia standing in the hall behind him, making vague panic gestures that Eva couldn't quite decipher.

'You've been a while,' he said. 'Didn't you take the car?'

'Yes, we did,' Eva said, moving through to their small sitting-room. 'It was raining on the way back. I thought you were meant to be in London.'

'I was. And what I learned there has brought me immediately back. Air travel, wonderful invention.' He moved to the window where he had left his bag.

'He's been here two hours,' Sylvia whispered, making a

gruesome face, as Romer crouched down and rummaged in his grip and then belted it closed. He stood up.

'Pack an overnight bag,' he said. 'You and I are going to Holland.'

Prenslo was a nondescript small village on the frontier between Holland and Germany. Eva and Romer had found the journey there surprisingly tiring and taxing. They took a train from Ostend to Brussels, where they changed and caught another train to The Hague. At the main station in The Hague a man from the British Embassy was waiting with a car. Romer then drove them east towards the German border, except that he lost his way twice when he had to leave the main road to head cross-country for Prenslo, and they spent half an hour or so doubling back before they found their way. They arrived in Prenslo at 4.00 a.m. to discover that the hotel that Romer had booked – the Hotel Willems – was locked shut and completely dark with no one prepared to respond to their bell-ringing, their shouts or peremptory knocking. So they sat in their car in the car-park until seven when a sleepy lad in a dressing gown unlocked the hotel's front door and they were finally, grumpily, admitted.

Eva had spoken little during the journey to Prenslo, deliberately, and Romer had seemed more than usually self-absorbed and taciturn. She felt there was something about Romer's attitude that irked her – as if she was being indulged, spoilt, that she should feel unusually privileged to be on this mysterious night journey with the 'boss' – and so she behaved dutifully and uncomplainingly. But the three-hour wait in the Hotel Willems's car-park and their enforced proximity had made Romer more relaxed and he had told her in more detail what they were doing in Prenslo.

On his brief trip to London Romer had learned that there was an SIS mission due to take place the next day in Prenslo. A senior German general in the Wehrmacht high command wanted to sound out the British position and response in the event of an army-led coup against Hitler. Apparently there was no question of deposing Hitler – he would maintain his role as chancellor – but he would be under the absolute control of the mutinous generals. After several preliminary encounters – to check security, to verify details – a unit of the British Secret Service based in The Hague had set up this first meeting with the general himself in a café at Prenslo. Prenslo was chosen because of the ease with which the general and his collaborators could slip to and fro across the border unremarked. The café in question was a hundred yards from the frontier.

Eva listened to all this attentively, with about three dozen questions clustering in her head. She knew she probably shouldn't air them but she didn't really care: she was both tired and mystified.

'Why do you need me for this?' she asked.

'Because my face is known to the SIS men. One of them is Head of Station in Holland – I've met him half a dozen times.' Romer stretched, his elbow bumping Eva's shoulder. 'Sorry – you'll be my eyes and ears, Eva. I need to know exactly what's going on.' He smiled tiredly, having to explain. 'It would look very odd to this fellow if he spotted me poking around.'

Another question had to be asked: 'But why are we poking around? Aren't we all "Secret Intelligence Service" people, at the end of the day?' She found the whole thing faintly ridiculous, obviously the result of some inter-departmental squabble – all of which meant she was wasting her time sitting in a car in a small town in the middle of nowhere.

Romer suggested they take a turn around the car-park, stretch their legs – they did so. Romer lit a cigarette, not offering her one, and they walked in silence a full circuit before returning to their car.

'We are not really SIS, to be precise,' he said. 'My team – AAS – is officially part of GC&GS.' He explained. 'The Government

Code and Cipher School. GC ampersand GS. We have a . . . a somewhat different role to play.'

'Though we're all on the same side.'

'Are you trying to be clever?'

They sat in silence for a while before he spoke again. 'You've seen the stories we've been putting out through the Agence about disaffection in the upper ranks of the German army.'

Eva said yes: she remembered items about the threatened resignation of this or that high-ranking officer; denials that this or that high-ranking officer was being posted to a provincial command and so on.

Romer continued: 'I think this Prenslo encounter is all as a result of our stories from the Agence. It's only right that I should see what happens. I should have been informed from the outset.' In a gesture of his irritation he flicked away his cigarette into the bushes – a bit foolhardily, Eva thought, then remembered that at this time of the year the bushes would be damp and incombustible. He was angry, Eva realised, somebody was going to steal his credit.

'Does SIS know we're here in Prenslo?'

'I very much assume and hope not.'

'I don't understand.'

'Good.'

Once the sleepy lad had shown them to their rooms Eva was called into Romer's. He was on the top floor and had a good view down Prenslo's only significant street. Romer handed her a pair of binoculars and pointed out the key details in the panorama: there was the German border crossing with its striped black and white barrier; there was the railway line; there, a hundred yards back, was the Dutch custom-house, occupied only in summer months. Opposite was the café, the Café Backus, a large two-storey modern building with two petrol pumps and a glassed-in veranda with distinctive striped awnings – chocolate brown and orange – to cast shade. A new hedge and some tethered saplings had been planted around the gravelled forecourt; behind the café was a larger unpaved car-park, with swings and a see-saw at one side, and beyond it a pinewood into which the railway line ran and disappeared. The Café Backus effectively marked the end of Prenslo before Germany began. The rest of the village stretched back from it – houses and shops, a post office, a small town hall with a large clock and, of course, the Hotel Willems.

'I want you to go to the café and order breakfast,' Romer said. 'Speak French, if you have to speak English make it very accented and broken. Ask if you can get a room for the night, or something. Get a sense of the place, dither, poke around – say you'll be back for lunch. Have a look and report back to me in an hour or so.'

Eva had felt tired as she had scanned Prenslo through Romer's binoculars – she'd had a busy twenty-four hours, after all – but now, as she walked down Prenslo's main street towards the Café Backus, she suddenly felt her body taut and alive with adrenalin. She looked casually about her, noting the people out on the street, a lorry loaded with milk churns passing by, a file of schoolchildren in forest-green uniforms. She pushed open the door of the Café Backus.

She ordered her breakfast – coffee, two boiled eggs, bread and ham – and ate it alone in the large ground-floor dining-room that gave on to the glassed-in veranda. A young girl served her, who spoke no French. Eva could hear a clatter of plates and conversation from the kitchen. Then two young men came out of a double door to one side and stepped out on to the forecourt. They were young but one was bald and the other had very cropped hair in a military style. They were wearing suits and ties. They hung around the petrol pumps for a while, staring up the road at the custom post's barrier. Then they re-entered, glancing incuriously at Eva, who was having her coffee-cup refilled by the waitress. The double doors swung closed behind them.

Eva asked to see a room but was told that the rooms were only let in the summer. She asked where the lavatory was and, deliberately mishearing the directions, pushed through the double doors. There was a large conference room behind with tables ranged in a square. The bald man was all sharp angles, elbows and knees jutting, sitting on a chair looking at something on the sole of his shoe; the other man was practising a tennis serve with an invisible racquet. They looked slowly round and she backed out. The waitress pointed Eva in the right direction and she walked quickly down the corridor she should have taken to the lavatory.

There, she unlatched, shoved and wrenched open the small frosted-glass window to reveal a view of the unpaved car-park, the swings and the see-saw and the pinewoods beyond. She closed the window, leaving it unlatched.

She went back to the Hotel Willems and told Romer about the two men and the conference room. I couldn't tell their nationality, she said, I didn't hear them speaking – perhaps German or Dutch, certainly not English. While she had been away Romer had made some telephone calls: the meeting with the general was due to take place at 2.30 that afternoon. There would also be a Dutch intelligence officer with the two British agents – his name was Lt. Joos; he was expecting Eva to make contact with him. Romer gave her a slip of paper with the double passwords written on it, then he took it back from her and tore it up.

'Why should I make contact with Lt. Joos?'

'So he knows you're on his side.'

'Will it be dangerous?'

'You'll have been in the café some hours before him. You'll be able to tell him anything suspicious you might have seen. He's coming to this rendezvous cold – they're very happy to think you'll have been there.'

'Right.'

'He might not even ask you anything. They seem very relaxed about the whole show. But just watch, watch everything very closely, and then come back and tell me every detail.' Romer yawned. 'I'm going to get some sleep now, if you don't mind.'

Eva tried to doze herself but her brain was working too energetically. She felt, also, a strange excitement in her: this was new, more to the point this was real – Dutch and British agents, a conspiracy with a German general – it was a far cry from losing shadows in Princes Street.

At one o'clock she retraced her steps up Prenslo's main road to the Café Backus, where she ordered lunch. Three other elderly couples were already installed in the veranda area, their meals well under way. Eva sat in the back, across from the double doors and ordered a full menu though she wasn't in the least hungry. There was more bustle about the café: cars were stopping for petrol and in the reflection of the window Eva could see the black and white barrier of the frontier rising and falling as cars and lorries passed to and fro. There was no sign of the two young men but when she went to the lavatory she noticed a black Mercedes-Benz now parked behind the café by the swings and the see-saw.

Then, just after she had ordered her dessert, a tall young man with receding hair in a tightly waisted dark suit came into the café and, after talking to the *maître d'*, went through the double doors into the meeting room. She wondered if this was Lt. Joos; he had not even glanced at her as he walked by.

A few moments later two other men arrived; the British agents, Eva guessed at once. One was portly, in a blazer; the other was dapper with a small moustache and wearing a tweed suit. Now Joos came out of the room and spoke with the two men: some consternation and irritation was evident and there was much looking at watches. Joos went back into the meeting room and emerged with the bald young man, a short conversation ensued and the two British accompanied him back through the double doors to the meeting room. Joos hovered outside like a major-domo or a doorman at a night-club.

By now only one couple was left on the veranda finishing their meal, the wife spooning out the coffee grounds and sugar from the base of her coffee cup, the husband smoking a small cigar with all the histrionic relish of a large one. Eva approached Joos with an unlit cigarette and said, in English as programmed, 'Do you smoke, may I trouble you for a light?' Joos replied, as programmed, 'Indeed I do smoke.' Then he duly lit her cigarette with his lighter. He was quite a handsome man, lean with a fine straight nose, his good looks spoilt by a cast in his left eye: it seemed to be looking over the top of her head. Then Eva asked him: 'Do you know where I can buy any French cigarettes?' Joos thought for a bit and then said, 'Amsterdam?' Eva smiled, shrugged and went back to her table. She paid her bill as quickly as possible and went to the ladies' lavatory. She opened the window to its full extent, climbed on the lavatory and squeezed out. Her heel caught on the latch and she dropped to the ground awkwardly. Standing up and dusting herself down, she saw two cars speed through the border crossing from the German side and heard them pull up at the front, with much spraying gravel, outside the café. She moved round to catch sight of them and was in time to see half a dozen men run inside.

Eva walked quickly across the car-park, past the swings and the see-saw, and into the fringe of the pinewoods. After a minute, or less, a rear door of the café opened and she saw the two British agents, flanked by a man on each side, being marched over to the parked Mercedes. Then, suddenly, from around the front of the café, Joos came running. There was a series of flat abrupt cracks, like branches splitting, and she realised that Joos was shooting as he ran – he had a revolver in his hand. The British and their guards went down, taking cover behind the car. One of Joos's bullets hit the windscreen and there was a small bright scatter of glass.

Joos was running towards the wood, not directly at Eva, but to one side, to her right. By now the guards were standing up, their own pistols drawn and were firing back at Joos. Two more men came out of the café and started running after him, also firing. Eva noticed that Joos ran well, agilely, even in his tight-cut suit, like a boy, and he almost made the cover of the pine trees when he seemed to stumble, then stagger a bit, then the two men running after him fired again at closer range – 'Pan! Pan! Pan!' it sounded like – and he fell quickly and limply to the ground, not moving anymore. The men each grabbed him under his arms and dragged him back towards the car. The two British were pushed inside and Joos's body was lugged in after them. Then the car was started and driven out of the car-park and round the Café Backus at speed. The other men trotted after it, pushing their revolvers under their jackets.

Eva saw the black and white barrier at the frontier rise up and watched first one, then the two other cars cross safely over the border to Germany.

Eva sat still behind her tree for a while, emptying her mind as she had been trained: there was no need to move, better to pause rather than do anything sudden or rash, storing away the details of what she had seen, going back over the sequence of events, making sure she had them correct, reminding herself exactly of the words she and Lt. Joos had said to each other.

She found a path through the wood and walked slowly along it until she came to a forester's dirt track which led her in time to a metalled road. She was two kilometres from Prenslo, the first signpost she came to informed her. She walked slowly down the road towards the village, her mind full of noisy and competing interpretations of everything she had witnessed. When she reached the Hotel Willems she was told that the other gentleman had already left.

4

The Shotgun

BÉRANGÈRE CALLED IN THE morning to say she had a bad cold and could she cancel her tutorial. I acceded immediately, sympathetically and with some secret pleasure (as I knew I'd still be paid) and decided to take the opportunity of two free hours and caught the bus into the town centre. On Turl Street I stepped through the small door into my college and spent two minutes reading the notices and posters pinned to the big board under the vaulted gatehouse before going into the porters' lodge to see if there was anything interesting in my pigeon-hole. There were the usual flyers, Middle Common Room sherry-party invitations, a bill for wine I had bought four months previously and an expensive white envelope with my name – Ms Ruth Gilmartin MA – written in sepia ink by a very thick-nibbed pen. I knew instantly who was the author: my supervisor, Robert York, whom I regularly traduced by referring to him as the laziest don in Oxford.

And, as though to punish me for my casual disrespect, I saw that this letter was a subtle reprimand – as if Bobbie York were saying to me: I don't mind your taking me for granted but I do ever-so-slightly mind your telling everyone that you do take me for granted. It read:

My dear Ruth,

It has been some time since last we caught sight of each other. Dare I ask if there is a new chapter for me to read? I really think it would be a good idea if we met soon – before the end of term if possible. Sorry to be a bore.

Tanti saluti, Bobbie

I called him immediately from the phone box in the lodge. He took a long time to answer and then I heard the familiar patrician basso profundo.

'Robert York.'

'Hello. It's me, Ruth.'

Silence. 'Ruth de Villiers?'

'No. Ruth Gilmartin.'

'Ah, my *favourite* Ruth. The prodigal Ruth. Thank the Lord – you gave me quite a nasty turn there. How are you?'

We arranged to meet the following evening at his rooms in college. I hung up and stepped out into the Turl and paused for a moment, feeling oddly confused and guilty all of a sudden. Guilty, because I had done no work on my thesis for months; confused, because I was now thinking: what are you doing here in this smug provincial town? Why do you want to write a D.Phil. thesis? Why do you want to be an academic? . . .

No quick or ready answers came to these questions as I plodded slowly up Turl Street towards the High – contemplating going to a pub for a drink instead of returning home for a frugal, solitary lunch – when, as I passed the entrance to the covered market, I glanced over and saw an attractive older woman emerge who looked remarkably like my mother. It *was* my mother. She was wearing a pearl-grey trouser suit and her hair seemed blonder – recently dyed.

'What're you staring at?' she said, a little crossly.

'You. You look wonderful.'

'I'm in remission. You look terrible. Miserable.'

'I think I've reached a crossroads in my life. I was going to have a drink or two. Care to join me?'

She thought this was a fine idea so we turned about and made our way to the Turf Tavern. It was dark and cool inside the pub – a gratifying respite from the brazen June sun – the old flagstones had been recently washed and were mottled with moisture and there were very few customers. We found a corner table and I went to the bar and ordered a pint of lager for myself and a tonic water with ice and lemon for my mother. I thought about the latest episode in Eva Delectorskaya's story as I set the glasses down, tried to imagine my mother – then virtually the same age as me – watching Lt Joos shot to death before her eyes. I sat down opposite her: she had said that the more I read the more I would understand – but I felt a long way from comprehension. I raised my pint glass to her and said cheers. 'Chin-chin,' she said, in return. Then she looked at me as I drank my beer, puzzled, as if I were slightly deranged.

'How can you drink that stuff?'

'I got a taste for it in Germany.'

I told her that Karl-Heinz's brother, Ludger, was staying with us for a few days. She said she didn't think I owed the Kleist family any more favours, but she appeared unconcerned, even uninterested. I asked her what she was doing in Oxford – usually she preferred to do her shopping in Banbury or Chipping Norton.

'I was getting a permit.'

'A permit? What for? Invalid parking?'

'For a shotgun.' She saw my face move into a rictus of incredulity. 'It's for the rabbits – they're ravaging the garden. And also, darling – I must be honest with you – I don't feel safe in the house anymore. I'm not sleeping well – every noise I hear I jerk awake – but really awake. I can't get back to sleep. I'll feel safer with a gun.'

'You've lived in that house since Dad died,' I reminded her. 'Six years. You never had any problems before.'

'The village has changed,' she said, darkly. 'Cars drive through all the time. Strangers. Nobody knows who they are. And I think something's wrong with my phone. It rings once then cuts out. I hear noises on the line.'

I decided to act as unconcernedly as she had. 'Well, it's up to you. Just don't shoot yourself by accident.'

'Oh, I know how to use a gun,' she said, with a small self-satisfied chuckle. I decided to say nothing.

She rummaged in her bag and produced a large brown envelope.

'Next instalment,' she said. 'I was going to drop it off on the way home.'

I took it from her. 'Can't wait,' I said, and it wasn't, for once, a flippant remark.

Then she covered my hand with hers.

'Ruth, darling, I need your help.'

'I know you do,' I said. 'I'm going to take you to a proper doctor.'

For a moment I thought she might hit me.

'Be careful. Don't patronise me.'

'Of course I'll help you, Sal,' I said. 'Calm down: you know I'll do anything for you. What is it?'

She turned her glass around a few times on the table-top before she answered.

'I want you to try to find Romer for me.'

The Story of Eva Delectorskaya

Ostend, Belgium. 1939

EVA SAT IN THE agency's conference room. A heavy squally shower was passing, the smatter of rain making the sound of fine gravel thrown against the window panes. It was darkening outside and she could see the buildings opposite all had their lights on. But no lights were lit in the conference room – she was sitting in a curious premature winter afternoon's dusk. She picked up a pencil from the table in front of her and bounced its rubber end on her left thumb. She was trying to keep the image of Lt. Joos's boyish run across the car-park at Prenslo out of her mind – his fluid easy sprint and then his fatal stagger and stumble.

'He said "Amsterdam",' Eva repeated in a low voice. 'He should have said "Paris".'

Romer shrugged. 'A simple mistake. A silly mistake.'

Eva kept her voice calm and level. 'I only did what I have been instructed to do. You say it yourself all the time. A Romer rule. That's why we always use double passwords.'

Romer stood up and crossed the room to look out of the window at the lights across the street.

'It's not the only reason,' he said. 'It also keeps everyone on their toes.'

'Well, it didn't work for Lt. Joos.'

Eva thought back to that afternoon – yesterday afternoon. When she reached the Hotel Willems and learned that Romer had left she called the *Agence* immediately. Morris Devereux told her that Romer was already on his way back to Ostend and that he had telephoned ahead to say that Eva was either dead, wounded or a prisoner in Germany. 'He'll be pleased to know he was wrong,' Morris said drily. 'What have you two been up to?'

Eva herself made it back to Ostend by early the next morning (two buses from Prenslo to The Hague, where she had a long wait for a night train to Brussels) and went straight to the office. Neither Angus Woolf nor Blytheswood said anything to her about what had taken place; only Sylvia grabbed her arm when no one was looking and whispered, 'You all right, sweetheart?' putting her finger to her lips. Eva smiled and nodded.

In the afternoon, Morris said she was wanted in the conference room and she went through to find Romer sitting there, smart in a dark charcoal suit and a gleaming white shirt with a regimental tie – he looked like he was off to make a speech somewhere. He gestured to her to sit and said, 'Tell me everything, every slightest thing.'

And so she did, with impressive recall, she thought, and he sat and listened carefully, nodding from time to time, asking her to repeat a detail. He took no notes. Now she watched him standing by the window where, with the palp of his forefinger, he followed a rain droplet wiggling its way down the pane.

'So,' he said, not turning round, 'one man is dead and two British secret agents are prisoners of the Germans.'

'That's not my fault. I was there only to be your eyes and ears, you said.'

'They're amateurs,' he said, the scorn in his voice making it harsh. 'Fools and amateurs who're still reading Sapper and Buchan and Erskine Childers. The "Great Game" – it makes me want to vomit.' He turned back to her. 'What a coup for the Sicherheitsdienst – they must be amazed how it was so easy to hoodwink and capture two senior British agents and whisk them across the border. We must seem like complete idiots. We *are* complete idiots – well, not all of us . . .' He paused, thinking again. 'Joos was definitely killed, you say.'

'I would say so – definitely. They must have shot him four or five times. But I've never seen a man shot dead before.'

'But they took his body away, anyway. Interesting.' Now he turned and pointed a finger at her. 'Why didn't you warn the two British agents when Joos failed the second password? For all you knew, Joos could have been part of the German plan. He could have been working with them.'

Eva kept her anger banked down. 'You know what we're meant to do. The rule is abort – instantly. If you think something is wrong you don't hang around to see if you're right – and then try to patch things up. You just get out, fast. Which is exactly what I did. If I'd gone into that room to warn them . . .' She managed a laugh. 'There were the other two Germans with them anyway. I don't think I'd be sitting here talking to you.'

Romer paced around, then stopped, facing her.

'No, you're right. You're absolutely right. What you did – operationally – was absolutely correct. Everyone else around you was making mistakes, acting like complacent fools.' He gave her his wide white smile. 'Well done, Eva. Good work. Let them clean up their own filthy mess.'

She stood up. 'Can I go now?'

'Do you fancy a stroll? Let's have a drink to celebrate your baptism by fire.'

They caught a tram and it took them to the Digue, Ostend's lengthy and imposing sea-wall-cum-esplanade, with its grand hotels and boarding-houses, dominated at one end by the vast oriental bulk of the Kursaal, with its domes and tall arched windows giving on to its gaming rooms, its ballroom and concert-hall, at the other extreme of the gentle curve of the promenade, sat the solid bulky presence of the Royal Palace Hotel. The cafés on the Kursaal terraces were all closed so they went to the bar of the Continental Hotel, where Romer ordered a whisky and Eva chose a dry martini. The rain had let up and the evening slowly cleared enough for them to watch, out at sea, the twinkling lights of a ferry cruising slowly by. Eva felt the alcohol ease and calm her as she listened to Romer repeatedly running over the events of the 'Prenslo Incident', as he now termed it, warning Eva that he might require her to add to or corroborate the report he intended to submit to London.

'Schoolboys would have made a better fist of it than those fools,' he said, still seeming to be brooding on British incompetence, as if the fiasco was a personal slight, somehow. 'Why did they agree to meet so close to the border?' He shook his head in genuine disgust. 'We're at war with Germany, for God's sake.' He called for another drink. 'They still see it as a kind of game where a certain kind of English attitude will always prevail – all fair play, pluck and derring-do.' He paused and stared at the table-top. 'You've no idea how difficult it's been for me,' he said, suddenly looking weary, older. It was the first time, Eva realised, that she had ever heard him admit to or exhibit a trace of vulnerability. 'The people at the top – in our business – have to be seen to be believed . . .' he said, then, as if he was aware of the slip, he sat up smartly, smiling again.

Eva shrugged. 'What can we do?'

'Nothing. Or rather – the best we can under the circumstances. At least you were all right,' he said. 'You can imagine what I was thinking when I saw those cars race across the border and stop outside. Then I saw all the running about, heard the shooting.'

'I was in the woods by then,' Eva said, thinking back, seeing once again Joos in his tight suit sprint out of the café, firing his revolver. 'Everyone had just had lunch – still doesn't seem real, somehow.'

They left the Continental and walked back out on to the Digue and looked out across the Channel in the direction of England. The tide was out and the beach gleamed silver and orange in the esplanade lights.

'Black out in England,' Romer said. 'I suppose we shouldn't complain.'

They strolled down towards the Chalet Royal then turned down the Avenue de la Reine – it would lead them back to Eva's apartment. They were like a couple of tourists, she thought, or honeymooners – she checked herself.

'You know, I always feel uneasy in Belgium,' Romer said, continuing in this unusual personal vein. 'Always keen to leave.'

'Why's that?'

'Because I was almost killed here,' he said. 'In the war. In 1918. I feel I've used up all my Belgian luck.'

Romer in the war, she thought: he must have been very young in 1918 – barely twenty, in his teens perhaps. She considered her vast ignorance about this man she was walking beside and thought about what she had done and risked in Prenslo at his behest. Perhaps this is what happens in wartime, she thought: perhaps this is entirely normal. They had reached her street.

'I'm just down here,' she said.

'I'll walk you to the door,' he said. 'I've got to go back to the agency.' Then after a brief pause he added: 'That was very nice. Thank you: I enjoyed myself. All work and no play – etcetera.'

Eva stopped at the door and took out her keys. 'Yes, it was very nice,' she said, carefully matching his banalities. Their eyes met and they both smiled.

For a split second Eva thought that Romer was going to reach for her and kiss her and she felt a fierce giddy panic rise in her chest.

'Night,' was all he said, however. 'See you tomorrow.' He sauntered off, with one of his half-wave, half-salutes, pulling on his raincoat as the drizzle began again.

Eva stood at her door, more disturbed than she could have thought possible. It was not so much the idea of Lucas Romer kissing her that had shaken her – it was the fact that she realised, now the moment had passed and gone for ever, that she had actually rather wanted it to happen.

5

Red Army Faction

BOBBIE YORK POURED ME a small whisky, 'a tiny one,' he said, adding a splash of water, then he poured himself an extremely large whisky and filled water up to the glass's brim. He 'deplored' sherry, Bobbie would frequently say – filth, the worst drink in the world. He reminded me of my mother in the histrionic violence of his over-reaction – but only in this.

Robert York MA (Oxon) was, I had calculated, in his late fifties or early sixties. He was a tall portly man with a head of thin grey hair, the strands of which were swept back and kept under control by some pomade or unguent that smelt powerfully of violets. His room, winter or summer, was redolent of violets. He wore handmade tweed suits and heavy orange brogues and he furnished his large study in college like a country house: deep sofas, Persian rugs, some interesting paintings (a small Peploe, a Ben Nicholson drawing, a large, sombre Alan Reynolds apple tree) and, hidden in some glassed cabinets, were a few books and some fine Staffordshire figures. You would not think you were in the study of an Oxford don.

He approached me from the drinks table with my whisky, and his, set my drink down on a side-table and eased himself carefully into an armchair opposite. Every time I saw Bobbie I realised anew that he was really quite fat, but his height, a certain swiftness and balletic precision of movement and his excellent tailoring had the effect of delaying that judgement a good five minutes or so.

'That's a very attractive dress,' he said suavely. 'Suits you to a tee – shame about the bandage but one almost doesn't notice it, I assure you.'

The night before I had scalded my shoulder and neck badly in the bath and had been obliged today to wear one of my skimpier summer dresses, with slim spaghetti straps, so that no material rubbed on my burn – now covered with a gauze and Elastoplast dressing (applied by Veronica), the size of a large folded napkin, situated on the junction of my neck and my left shoulder. I wondered if I should be drinking whisky, given all the powerful painkillers Veronica had plied me with, but they seemed to be working well: I felt no pain – but I moved very carefully.

'Most attractive,' Bobbie repeated, trying not to look at my breasts, 'and, I dare say, in this infernal heat most comfortable. Anyway, *slangevar*,' he concluded, raising his glass and taking three great gulps of his whisky, like a man dying of thirst. I drank too, more circumspectly, yet felt the whisky burn my throat and stomach.

'Could I have a drop more water?' I asked. 'No, let me get it.' Bobby had surged and struggled in his chair at my request but had not managed to leave it, so I crossed a couple of densely patterned rugs, heading for the drinks table with its small Manhattan of clustered bottles. He seemed to have every drink in Europe I thought – I saw pastis, ouzo, grappa, slivovitz – as I filled my glass with cold water from the carafe.

'I'm afraid I've got nothing to show you,' I said over my scalded shoulder with its dressing. 'I'm rather stuck in 1923 – the Beer Hall Putsch. Can't quite fit everything in with the Freikorps and the BVP, all the intrigues in the Knilling government: the Schweyer-Wutzlhofer argument, Krausneck's resignation – all that.' I was busking, but I thought it would impress Bobbie.

'Yeeesss . . . tricky,' he said, suddenly looking a little panicked. 'It *is* very complicated. Mmm, I can see that . . . Still, the main thing is that we've finally met, you see. I have to write a short report on all my graduates – boring but obligatory. The Beer Hall Putsch, you say. I'll look out some books and send you a reading list. A short one, don't worry.'

He chuckled as I sat down again.

'Lovely to see you, Ruth,' he said. 'You're looking very nubile and summery, I must say. How's little Johannes?'

We talked about Jochen for a while. Bobbie was married to a woman he called 'the Lady Ursula' and they had two married daughters – 'Grandchildren imminent, so I'm told. That's when I commit suicide' – and he and the Lady Ursula lived in a vast Victorian brick villa on the Woodstock Road, not that far from Mr Scott, our dentist. Bobbie had published one book in 1948 called *Germany: Yesterday, Today and Tomorrow* that I had ordered up from the Bodleian stacks once out of interest. It was 140 pages long, printed on poor paper and had no index, and as far as I could determine it was his sole contribution to historical scholarship. As a boy he had holidayed in Germany and had spent a year at university in Vienna before the Anschluss intervened and necessitated his repatriation. During the war he had been a staff officer attached to the War Office and at its end had gone back to Oxford as a young don in 1945, married the Lady Ursula, published his slim book and had been a member of the History Faculty and a Fellow of his college ever since, pursuing, as he candidly put it, the 'way of least resistance'. He had a wide and sophisticated circle of friends in London and a large and decrepit house (thanks to the Lady Ursula) in County Cork, where he spent his summers.

'Did you have any luck with this Lucas Romer person?' I asked him, casually. I had phoned him that morning, thinking if anyone could help me, Bobbie York could.

'Romer, Romer . . .' he had said. 'Is he one of the Darlington Romers?'

'No, I don't think so. All I can tell you is that he was some kind of spy in the war and has some kind of a title. I think.'

He had said he would see what he could dig up.

Now he heaved himself out of his armchair, tugged his waistcoat down over his gut and went to his desk and searched among the papers there.

'He's not in *Who's Who* or *Debrett's*,' said Bobbie.

'I know: I did check,' I said.

'Doesn't mean a thing, of course. I assume he's still alive and kicking.'

'I assume so.'

He took some half-moon spectacles out of a pocket and put them on. 'Here it is,' he said, and looked over the rims at me. 'I called one of my brighter undergraduates who's become a clerk at the House of Commons. He did a little digging around and came up with someone called Baron Mansfield of Hampton Cleeve – family name Romer.' He shrugged. 'Could that be your man?' He read off the sheet of paper.

'Mansfield, Baron, created 1958 (Life Peer), of Hampton Cleeve. L.M. Romer, chairman Romer, Radclyffe Ltd – ah, the publishers, that's the bell that rang – 1946 to the present day. That's all I've got, I'm afraid. He does seem to live very discreetly.'

'Could be,' I said. 'I'll check him out, anyway. Many thanks.'

He looked at me shrewdly. 'Now, why would you be so interested in Baron Mansfield of Hampton Cleeve?'

'Oh, just someone my mother was mentioning.'

My mother had said two things in the Turf Tavern: one, that she was sure Romer was alive and, two, that he had been ennobled in some way – 'A knight, a lord, or something, I'm sure I read about it,' she had said. 'Mind you, that was ages ago.' We left the pub and strolled towards Keble College, where she had parked her car.

'Why do you want to find Romer?' I asked.

'I think the time has come' was all she said and from her tone of voice I knew further questioning would be fruitless.

She ran me to the end of Moreton Road: Hamid was due in five minutes and, sure enough, there he was, sitting on the top of the steps.

We spent two hours with the Ambersons, enjoying their delayed holiday near Corfe Castle, Dorset. There were a great many remonstrations about what Keith Amberson 'should have done' and many complaints from affronted wife and children about his oversights. Keith was abashed and apologetic. Hamid seemed to have caught Keith's mood as he seemed a little subdued throughout and over-studious in an untypical way, stopping me frequently to make long and laborious notes in his jotter. I wound things up earlier than usual and asked him if there was anything on his mind.

'You have still not responded to my dinner invitation,' he said.

'Oh, yes, any time,' I said, having forgotten all about it, of course. 'Just give me a couple of days' notice so I can get a baby-sitter.'

'What about this Saturday night?'

'Fine, fine. Jochen can stay with his grandmother. Saturday would be lovely.'

'There is a new restaurant on the Woodstock Road – Browns.'

'So there is, yes – Browns, that's it – I haven't been, that would be lovely.'

Hamid visibly brightened. 'Good – so, Saturday at Browns. I'll call here and collect you.'

We made the arrangements and I walked him through to the back door. Ludger was in the kitchen, eating a sandwich. He paused, licked his fingers and shook Hamid's hand.

'Hey, brother. *Inshallah*. Where are you going?'

'Summertown.'

'I'll come with you. See you later, Ruth.' He took his sandwich with him and followed Hamid down the stairs – I could hear the dull metallic boom of their steps as they clattered down.

I looked at my watch: ten to four – ten to five in Germany. I went to the phone in the hall, lit a cigarette and called Karl-Heinz on his private line at his office. I heard the phone ringing. I could picture his room, picture the corridor it was on, the building it was in, the nondescript suburb of Hamburg where it was to be found.

'Karl-Heinz Kleist.' I heard his voice for the first time in over a year and I felt it, for a second, sap all my strength. But only for a second.

'It's me,' I said.

'Ruth . . .' The pause was minimal, the surprise wholly disguised. 'Very good to hear your sweet English voice. I have your photo here on my desk in front of me.'

The lie was as fluent and as unfalsifiable as ever.

'Ludger's here,' I said.

'Where?'

'Here in Oxford. My flat.'

'Is he behaving himself?'

'So far.' I told him how Ludger had showed up, unannounced.

'I haven't spoken to Ludger for . . . oh, ten months,' Karl-Heinz said. 'We had a disagreement. I won't see him again.'

'What do you mean?' I heard him find and light a cigarette.

'I told him: You are no longer my brother.'

'Why? What had he done?'

'He's a bit crazy, Ludger. A bit dangerous, even. He was mixing with a crazy crowd. RAF I think.'

'RAF?'

'Red Army Faction. Baader-Meinhof, you know.'

I did. There was an interminable trial going on in Germany of Baader-Meinhof members. Ulrike Meinhof had committed suicide in May. It was all a bit vague – I seemed never to find the time to read newspapers these days. 'Is Ludger mixed up with these people?'

'Who knows? He talked about them as if he knew them. I told you I don't speak to him any more. He stole a lot of money from me. I kicked him out of my life.' Karl-Heinz's voice was very matter-of-fact – it was as if he was telling me he had just sold his car.

'Is that why Ludger came to England?'

'I don't know – I don't care. You have to ask him. I think he always liked you, Ruth. You were kind to him.'

'No I wasn't – not particularly.'

'Well, you were never unkind.' There was a pause. 'I can't say this for sure but I think he may be wanted by the police. I think he did some stupid crazy things. Bad things. You should be careful. I think maybe he is on the runaway.'

'On the run.'

'Exact.'

I paused this time. 'So there's nothing you can do.'

'No. I'm sorry – I told you: we had this fight. I will never see him again.'

'OK, great, thanks a lot. Bye.'

'How's Jochen?'

'He's very well.'

'Give him a kiss from his father.'

'No.'

'Don't be bitter, Ruth. You knew everything before this started between us. Everything was open. We had no secrets. I made no promises.'

'I'm not bitter. I just know what's best for both of us. Bye.'

I hung up. Time to pick up Jochen from school but I knew I shouldn't have called Karl-Heinz. I was already regretting it: it set everything stirring in me once more – everything that I had managed to tidy, order and label and store away in a locked cupboard was scattered all over the floor of my life again. I walked down the Banbury Road to Grindle's chanting to myself: it's over – calm down. It's finished – calm down. He's history – calm down.

That night, after Jochen had gone to bed, Ludger and I sat up later than usual in the sitting-room, watching the news on television. For once I was paying attention and, as malign coincidence would have it, there was a report from Germany about the Baader-Meinhof trial that had now lasted more than a hundred days. Ludger stirred in his seat when the picture of a man's face came up on the screen: handsome in a sleazy kind of way – a kind of sneering handsomeness that you see in certain men.

'Hey, Andreas,' Ludger said, pointing at the screen. 'You know, I knew him.'

'Really? How?'

'We were in porno together.'

I went over to the TV and switched it off.

'Do you want a cup of tea?' I said. We went through to the kitchen together and I switched the kettle on.

'What do you mean "in porno"?' I asked, idly.

'I was an actor in porno films for a while. So was Andreas. We used to hang out together.'

'You acted in porn films?'

'Well only one film. You can still buy it, you know, in Amsterdam, Sweden.' He seemed quite proud of this fact.

'What's it called?'

'*Volcano of Cum.*'

'Good title. Was Andreas Baader in this film?'

'No. Then he got crazy: you know – Ulrike Meinhof, RAF, the end of capitalism.'

'I spoke to Karl-Heinz today.'

He went very still. 'Did I tell you I cut him out of my life for ever?'

'No, you didn't, actually.'

'*Ein vollkommenes Arschloch.*'

He said this with unusual passion, not his usual lazy mid-Atlantic drawl. A complete fucking bastard, was the closest demotic equivalent I could come up with. I looked at Ludger sitting there thinking about Karl-Heinz and joined him in his silent rant of hate against his older brother. He twiddled a lock of his long hair between his fingers and looked for a moment as if he might suddenly cry bitter tears. I decided he could stay on a day or two more. I warmed the pot, put in the tea-leaves and added the boiling water.

'Did you do porno for long?' I asked, recalling his unselfconscious nude stroll through the flat.

'No. I quit. I began to have very serious problems.'

'What? With the idea of pornography? Ideologically, you mean?'

'No, no. Porno was great. I loved it – I love porno. No, I began to have serious problems with *mein Schwanz*.' He pointed at his groin.

'Oh . . . Right.'

He grinned his old sly grin. 'He wouldn't do what I was telling him to do, you know? . . .' He frowned. 'Do you say "tail" in English?'

'No. Not normally. We say "prick" or "cock". Or "dick".'

'Oh, right. But nobody is saying "tail"? Like a slang?'

'No. We don't say it.'

'*Schwanz* – "tail": I think to say "my tail" is better than to say "my dick".'

I wasn't keen to pursue this conversation – talking dirty with Ludger – any further. The tea was brewed so I poured him a cup. 'But hey, Ludger,' I said cheerfully, 'keep saying "tail" and maybe it'll catch on. I'm going to have a bath. See you in the morning.'

I took my pot of tea, my milk bottle and my mug into the bathroom, set them all carefully on the edge of the bath and turned on the taps. To lie in a hot bath drinking hot tea is the only sure way of calming myself when my brain is on the rampage.

I locked the door, took my clothes off and lay in my warm bath and sipped my tea, banishing all thoughts and images of Karl-Heinz and our years together from my mind. I thought about my mother, instead, and the Prenslo Incident, and what she had seen and done that afternoon on the Dutch-German frontier in 1939. It seemed impossible somehow – I still couldn't fit my mother into Eva Delectorskaya, nor the other way round . . . Life was very strange, I told myself, you can never be sure of anything. You think everything is normal and straightforward, set and fixed – and then suddenly it's all flung upside-down. I turned to refill my mug and knocked the teapot over, badly scalding my neck and left shoulder. My scream woke up Jochen and had Ludger beating on the door.

The Story of Eva Delectorskaya

London. 1940

IT WASN'T UNTIL AUGUST that Eva Delectorskaya was summoned, finally, to give her account of the Prenslo Incident. She travelled into work as usual, leaving her lodgings in Bayswater and catching a bus that took her into Fleet Street. She sat on the top deck, smoked her first cigarette of the day and looked out at the sunny expanse of Hyde Park, thinking how pretty the silvery barrage balloons looked, plumply flying in the pale blue sky, and wondering idly if the barrage balloons should be left there when this war ended, if it ever did. Better than any obelisk or martial statue, she thought, imagining a child in 1948 or 1965 asking their parent, 'Mummy, what were those big balloons for? . . .' Romer said this war would last at least ten years unless the Americans joined in. Though, she had to admit, he had made this pronouncement in a mood of some bitterness and shock in Ostend in May as they had watched the German blitzkrieg race through Holland, Belgium and France. Ten years . . . Ten years – 1950. In 1950, she thought, Kolia will have been dead for eleven years. The blunt truth distressed her: she thought about him all the time, not every day, now, but still many times a week. Would she still be thinking of him as much in 1950, she wondered? Yes, she told herself with some defiance, yes I will.

She opened her newspaper as the bus approached Marble Arch. Twenty-two enemy aircraft downed yesterday; Winston Churchill visits munition workers; new bombers can reach Berlin and beyond. She wondered if this last item was one of AAS's plants – it bore all the hallmarks and she was becoming something of an expert at recognising them. The story had a sound and plausible factual base but was also gifted with a teasing vagueness and a covert unprovability. 'An air ministry spokesman refused to deny that such a capability would soon be available to the RAF . . .' All the signs were there.

She stepped off her bus as it paused at traffic lights in Fleet Street and turned up Fetter Lane, making for the unremarkable building that housed Accountancy and Actuarial Services Ltd. She pressed the buzzer on the fourth-floor landing and was admitted into a shabby ante-room.

'Morning, darling,' Deirdre said, one hand holding out a pile of newspaper clippings while with the other she rummaged in a drawer of her desk.

'Morning,' Eva said, taking the clippings from her. Deirdre was a chain-smoking gaunt woman in her sixties who was effectively the administration of AAS – source of all equipment and material, provider of tickets and passes, medicaments and key information: who was available, who wasn't, who was sick and who was 'away travelling', and, most importantly, the provider and denier of access to Romer himself. Morris Devereux joked that Deirdre was in fact Romer's mother. She had a harsh monotone voice that rather undercut the effect of the constant, warm endearments she employed when she addressed people. She pressed the buzzer that allowed Eva to go through the interior door to the dim passageway off which the team's offices were situated.

Sylvia was in, she saw; Blytheswood and Morris Devereux were in, too. Angus Woolf was working at Reuters and Romer himself had a new executive position with the *Daily Express* but maintained a seldom-occupied office a floor above – reached by a cramped twisting stairway – that had a distant view of Holborn Viaduct. From their various rooms they tried to run the Agence in Ostend in absentia through encrypted telegrams sent to a stay-behind Belgian agent known as 'Guy'. Also certain words placed in AAS stories in foreign newspapers were meant to alert him and be circulated to their customers in occupied Belgium, such as they had. It was not at all clear that the system was working; indeed, Eva thought, they maintained a pretence of effort and confident news-gathering and dispatch that was impressive, but she knew everyone thought, individually, that what they were doing was at best insignificant, at worst, useless. Morale was becoming lower, daily, and nowhere better exemplified than in their boss's mood: Romer was visibly tense, snappy, often taciturn and brooding. It was only a matter of time, they whispered to each other, before AAS Ltd was shut down and they were all re-assigned.

Eva hung her hat and her gasmask on the back of the door, sat at her desk and looked out through the grimy window at the nondescript roofscape in front of her. Buddleia sprouted from a gutter-head across the central courtyard and three miserable-looking pigeons groomed themselves on a row of chimney pots. She spread her cuttings on her desk. Something from an Italian newspaper (her story about rumours of Marshal Pétain's failing health); a reference to low morale amongst Luftwaffe pilots in a Canadian magazine (Romer had scrawled 'More' on this), and teleprints from two American news agencies about a German spy ring being broken in South Africa.

Blytheswood knocked on her door and asked her if she'd like a cup of tea. He was a tall, fair and burly man in his thirties, with two red patches on each cheek as if permanent incipient blushes resided there, ready to flush his entire face. He was a shy man and Eva liked him: he had always been kind to her. He ran AAS's transmitters: a kind of genius, Romer claimed: he could do anything with radios and wirelesses, transmit messages across continents with nothing more than a car battery and a knitting needle.

While she was waiting for her tea, Eva began to type out a story she was working on about 'ghost ships' in the Mediterranean but she was interrupted by Deirdre.

'Hello, sweetness, his lordship wants you upstairs. Don't worry, I'll drink your tea.'

Eva climbed the stairs to Romer's office, trying to analyse the complex smell in the stairwell – a cross between mushrooms and soot, ancient stour and mildew, she decided. Romer's door was open and she went straight in without knocking or coughing politely. He had his back to her and was standing staring out of the window at Holborn Viaduct as if its wrought-iron arches held some encoded meaning for him.

'Morning,' Eva said. They had been back in England for four months now, since leaving Ostend, and she supposed, calculating swiftly, she must have seen Romer for about an hour and a half in all that time. The easy familiarity that had seemed to be building in Belgium had disappeared with the collapse of the Agence and the invariable, daily, bad news about the war. Romer, in England, was formal and closed with her (as he was with everyone, the other staff reminded her when she commented on his *froideur*). The rumours were growing that all the 'irregulars' were to be closed down by the new head of SIS. Romer's day was all but done, so Morris Devereux claimed.

He turned from the window.

'C wants to meet you,' he said. 'He wants to talk about Prenslo.'

She knew who C was and felt a little flutter of alarm.

'Why me?' she said. 'You know as much as I do.'

Romer explained about the continuing ramifications of the Prenslo 'disaster', as he termed it. Of the two British agents captured one was the station-head of SIS in Holland and the other ran the Dutch 'Z' network, a covert parallel intelligence-gathering system. Between the two of them they knew pretty much everything about Britain's spy networks in western Europe – and now they were in German hands, under stringent and unforgiving interrogation, no doubt.

'Everything's gone, or else exposed or insecure and unusable,' Romer said. 'We have to assume that – and what've we got left? Lisbon, Berne . . . Madrid's a wash-out.' He looked at her. 'I don't know why they want to see you, to be honest. Maybe they think you saw something, that you'll be able to inadvertently tell them why everything went so spectacularly, magnificently wrong.' His tone of voice made it clear he thought the whole exercise was a waste of time. He looked at his watch. 'We can walk,' he said. 'We're going to the Savoy Hotel.'

Eva and Romer strolled down the Strand towards the Savoy. Apart from the sandbags piled up around certain doorways, and the number of uniforms amongst the pedestrians, the scene looked like any other late-summer morning in London, Eva thought, realising as she formed the observation in her mind that she had never spent a peacetime late-summer morning in London before and therefore there was no valid comparison to be made. Perhaps London before the war was entirely otherwise, for all she knew. She wondered what it would be like to be in Paris. Now that *would* be different. Romer was untalkative, he seemed ill at ease.

'Just tell them everything – as you told me. Be completely honest.'

'Right, I will. The whole truth, etcetera.'

He looked sharply at her. Then he smiled, weakly, and allowed his shoulders to hang for a second.

'There's a lot at stake,' he said. 'A new operation for AAS. I have a feeling that how you come across this morning may have some bearing on all this.'

'Will it just be C?'

'Oh no, I think they'll all be there. You're the only witness.'

Eva said nothing as she took this in and tried to look unconcerned as they turned into Savoy Court and strolled towards the *porte-cochère*. The uniformed doorman spun the revolving door to admit them but Eva paused and asked Romer for a cigarette. He gave her one and lit it for her. She inhaled deeply, looking at the men and women going in and out of the Savoy. Women in hats and summer dresses, glossy motor cars with chauffeurs, a boy delivering a vast bouquet of flowers. For some people, she realised, a war hardly changed anything.

'Why are we meeting in a hotel?' she asked.

'They love meeting in hotels. Ninety per cent of intelligence meetings take place in hotels. Let's go.'

She stood on her half-smoked cigarette and they went inside.

They were met at reception by a young man and led up two floors and along a corridor of many corners to a suite of rooms. She and Romer were asked to wait in a kind of hallway with a sofa and offered tea. Then a man came in who knew Romer and they stood together in a corner, talking in low voices. This man wore a grey pin-striped suit, had a small trimmed moustache and sleek gingery hair. When he left Romer rejoined her on the sofa.

'Who was that?' she said.

'A complete arse,' he replied, putting his mouth close to her ear. She felt his warm breath on her cheek and her arm and side erupted in goose pimples.

'Miss Dalton?' The first young man stepped through the door and gestured for her to enter.

The room she entered was large and shadowy and she felt the softness and the richness of its carpet beneath her feet. She sensed Romer entering behind her. Armchairs and sofas had been pushed to the walls and the curtains had been half drawn against the August sun. Three tables had been positioned end to end in the middle of the room and four men sat behind them facing a solitary wooden chair set in the middle of the room. Eva was shown towards it, asked to sit down. She saw two other men standing at the rear, leaning against the wall.

A spry elderly man with a silver moustache spoke. No one was introduced.

'This may look like a tribunal, Miss Dalton, but I want you to think of it as just an informal chat.'

The absurdity of this statement made the other three men relax and chuckle. One was wearing a naval uniform, with many gold bands on his wrists. The other two looked like bankers or lawyers, she thought. One had a stiff collar. She noticed one of the men standing in the rear was wearing a polka-dotted bow tie. She glanced quickly behind her to see that Romer was standing by the door with the 'complete arse'.

Papers were shuffled, glances were exchanged.

'Now, Miss Dalton,' Silver Moustache said. 'Tell us in your own words exactly what happened at Prenslo.'

So she told them, taking them through the day, hour by hour. When she finished they began to ask her questions and more and more, she realised they began to centre on Lieutenant Joos and the failure of the double password.

'Who gave you the details of the double password?' a tall jowly man asked her; his voice was deep with a ragged, heavy quality to it; he spoke very slowly and deliberately. He was standing at the rear beside Polka-Dot Bow Tie.

'Mr Romer.'

'You're certain you had it correctly. You didn't make a mistake.'

'No. We routinely use double passwords.'

'We?' Silver Moustache interrupted.

'In the team – those of us who work with Mr Romer. It's completely normal for us.'

There were glances over at Romer. The naval officer whispered something to the man in a stiff collar. He put on a pair of round tortoiseshell spectacles and stared more closely at Eva.

Silver Moustache leant forward. 'How would you describe Lt. Joos's response to your second question; "Where can I buy French cigarettes?"?'

'I don't understand,' Eva said.

The jowly man spoke again from the back of the room. 'Did Lt. Joos's answer seem to you like the response to a password, or was it a casual, natural remark?'

Eva paused, thinking back to that moment in the Café Backus. She saw Joos's face in her mind's eye, his slight smile, he knew exactly who she was. He had said 'Amsterdam' instantly, confidently, sure that this was the answer she expected.

'I would say, absolutely, that he thought he was giving me the answer to the second password.'

For the briefest instant she sensed all the men in the room relax, infinitesimally. She couldn't tell how or why or what indicated this, but something she had said, the answer she had given, had clearly resolved a complex issue, had put their minds at rest on a contentious matter.

The jowly man stepped forward, putting his hands in his pockets. She wondered if this was C.

'What would you have done,' he asked, 'if Lt. Joos had given the correct password?'

'I would have told him that I was suspicious of the two Germans who were in the rear room.'

'You *were* suspicious of them?'

'Yes. Remember I had been there all day in the café, breakfast and lunch, in and out. They had no reason to suspect that I was anything to do with the meeting. I thought they were edgy, ill at ease. Now, with hindsight, I realise why.'

The man with the round spectacles raised a finger.

'I'm not quite clear about this, Miss Dalton, but how was it you came to be in the Café Backus during that day?'

'It was Mr Romer's idea. He told me to go there in the morning and observe what happened, as discreetly as possible.'

'It was Mr Romer's idea.'

'Yes.'

'Thank you very much.'

They asked her a few more questions, for form's sake, about the behaviour of the two British agents, but it was obvious that they had the information they needed. Then she was asked to wait outside.

She sat down in the ante-room and accepted the offer of a cup of tea. It was brought and when she took it from the young man she was pleased to note her hands were hardly shaking at all. She drank it and then, after about twenty minutes, Romer appeared. He was happy, she saw at once – everything about his bearing, his knowing look, his absolute refusal to smile, confirmed his deep and enormous good mood.

They walked out of the Savoy together and stood on the Strand, the traffic buzzing by them.

'Take the rest of the day off,' he said. 'You deserve it.'

'Do I? What've I done?'

'I know – what about supper this evening? There's a place in Soho – Don Luigi's – Frith Street. I'll see you there at eight.'

'I'm busy this evening, I'm afraid.'

'Nonsense. We're celebrating. See you at eight. Taxi!'

He ran off to claim his hailed taxi. Eva thought: Don Luigi's, Frith Street, eight o'clock. What was going on here?

'Hello Miss Fitzroy. Long time no see.'

Mrs Dangerfield stepped back from the front door to let Eva in. She was a plump blonde woman who wore thick and farinaceous make-up, almost as if she were about to go on stage.

'Just passing through, Mrs Dangerfield. Come to pick up some things.'

'I've got some post for you here.' She took a small bundle of letters from the hall table. 'Everything's nice and ready. Do you want me to make up the bed?'

'No, no, just here for a couple of hours. Then back up north.'

'Better off out of London, dear, I tell you.' Mrs Dangerfield listed London's wartime disadvantages as she led Eva up to her attic bedroom in number 312 Winchester Street, Battersea.

Eva closed the door behind her and turned the key in the lock. She looked round her room, reacquainting herself with it – she hadn't been here for five weeks or so. She checked her snares: sure enough Mrs Dangerfield had had a good poke around the desk and the wardrobe and the chest of drawers. She sat down on the single bed and laid out her half-dozen letters on the quilt, opening them one at a time. She threw three into the wastepaper basket and filed the rest in her desk drawer. All of them had been sent by herself. She propped the postcard on the mantelpiece above the gas fire; it was from King's Lynn – she had travelled there the previous weekend precisely to send this card. She turned it over and read it again:

> Dearest Lily,
>
> Hope all's well in rainy old Perthshire. We popped up to the coast for a couple of days. Young Tom Dawlish got married last Wednesday. Back to Norwich Monday evening.
>
> Love from Mum and Dad

She placed the card back on the mantelpiece, thinking suddenly of her own father and his flight from Paris. The latest news she had was that he was in Bordeaux – somehow Irène had managed to post a letter to her in London. 'In reasonable health in these unreasonable times,' she had written.

As she sat there thinking, she realised she was smiling to herself – a baffled smile – contemplating the bizarre reality of her situation, sitting in her safe house in Battersea, passing herself off as Lily Fitzroy. What would her father think of this work she was doing for the 'British government'? What would Kolia have thought? . . .

Mrs Dangerfield knew only that Lily Fitzroy was 'in signals', worked for the War Office and had to travel a lot, spending more and more time in Scotland and northern England. She was paid three months in advance and was perfectly happy with the arrangement. In her four months in London Eva had slept only six times at Winchester Road.

She pulled back the corner of the carpet on the floor and, taking a small screwdriver from her bag, prised up the loose nails on a short section of floorboard. Beneath the floor, wrapped in oilcloth, was a small bundle containing her Lily Fitzroy passport, a quarter bottle of whisky and three five-pound notes. She added another five-pound note and closed everything up again. Then she lay on her bed and snoozed for an hour, dreaming that Kolia came into the room and laid his hand on her shoulder. It made her wake with a jolt and she saw that a wand of afternoon sun had squeezed through the curtains and warmed her neck. She looked in the wardrobe, picked out a couple of dresses and folded them into a paper carrier bag she had brought with her.

At the door she paused, wondering about the wisdom or even the necessity of this 'safe' house. This was her training; this was how she had been taught to set up and maintain a safe house without raising suspicion. The secret safe house – one of Romer's rules. She gave a wry smile and unlocked the door: Romer's rules – more and more her life was being governed by these particular regulations. She switched out the light and stepped on to the landing – perhaps she'd learn a few more this evening.

'Bye, Mrs Dangerfield,' she called out gaily. 'That's me leaving now: see you in a week or two.'

That evening Eva dressed with more diligence and thought than usual. She washed her hair and curled its ends, deciding to surprise Romer by leaving it down. She teased a lock over her eye, Veronica Lake-style, but decided that was going too far: she wasn't trying to seduce the man, after all. No, she just wanted him to notice her more, be more aware of her in a different way. He may be thinking that all he was doing was taking an employee out for a treat but she wanted him to realise that not many of his employees looked like her. It was a matter of self-esteem in the pure sense – nothing to do with Romer at all.

She put on her lipstick – a new one, called Tahiti Nights – powdered her face and dabbed rose-water on her wrists and behind her ears. She was wearing a light woollen navy dress, with gathered maize-yellow panels on the front, with a sash belt that accentuated her slim waist. Her eyebrows were plucked into perfect arches and were perfectly black. She put her cigarettes, her lighter and her purse in a cane handbag studded with seashells, had a final check in the mirror, and decided, definitely, finally, against ear-rings.

As she walked down the stairs of the hostel, a few of the girls were queuing for the telephone in the lobby. She bowed as they wolf-whistled and mockingly marvelled.

'Who's the lucky man, Eve?'

She laughed. Romer was the lucky man: he had no idea how lucky he was.

The lucky man showed up, late, at 8.35. Eva had arrived and had been shown to Don Luigi's best table, set in a bow window looking out over Frith Street. Eva drank two gin-and-tonics while she waited and passed much of the time listening in to a French couple two tables away having an indiscreet, not so *sotto voce* argument mainly to do with the man's bitch of a mother. Romer duly arrived, made no apology, made no comment on how she was looking and immediately ordered a bottle of Chianti – 'The best Chianti in London. I only come here for the Chianti.' He was still animated and excited, his mood post-

Savoy having grown more intense, if anything, and as they ordered and ate their starters he spoke fluently and contemptuously about 'head office'. She half listened, preferring instead to look at him as he drank and smoked and ate. She heard him say that head office was stuffed with the stupidest élite in London, that the people he had to deal with were either idle Pall Mall clubmen or superannuated officials from the Indian Colonial Service. The first lot looked down on the second as petit-bourgeois careerists while the second regarded the first as washed-up remittance-men who only had a job because they had gone to Eton with the boss.

He pointed his fork at her – he was eating what purported to be Veal Milanese; she had ordered salted cod with tomatoes.

'How are we meant to run a successful company if the board of directors are so third rate?'

'Is Mr X third rate?'

He paused and she could sense him thinking: how does she know about Mr X? And then figuring out how she did know, and that it was all right, he replied slowly.

'No. Mr X is different. Mr X sees the value in AAS Ltd.'

'Was Mr X there, today?'

'Yes.'

'Which one was he?'

He didn't answer. He reached for the bottle and refilled both their glasses. This was their second bottle of Chianti.

'Here's to you, Eva,' he said with something approaching sincerity. 'You did very well today. I don't like to say that you saved our bacon – but I think you saved our bacon.'

They clinked glasses and he gave her one of his rare white smiles and for the first time that evening she was suddenly aware of him looking at her – as a man will look at a woman – noting aspects of her: her fair hair, long and curled under, her red lips, her arched black brows, her long neck, the swell of her breasts beneath her navy-blue dress.

'Yes, well . . .' he said awkwardly. 'You look very . . . smart.'

'How did I save your bacon?'

He looked around. No one was sitting close to them.

'They're convinced that the problem arose in the Dutch branch. Not the British. We were let down by the Dutch – a rotten apple in The Hague.'

'What does the Dutch branch say?'

'They're very angry. They blame us. Their executive was forcibly retired, after all.'

Eva knew that Romer enjoyed this plain-code, as it was termed. It was another of his rules: use plain-code whenever possible, not ciphers or codes – they were either too complex or too easy to crack. Plain-code made sense or it didn't. If it didn't make sense it was never incriminating.

Eva said: 'Well, I'm glad I was of some use.'

He said nothing in reply, this time. He was sitting back in his seat, looking at her as if he was seeing her for the first time.

'You look very beautiful tonight, Eva. Has anyone ever told you that before?'

But his dry and cynical tone of voice told her he was joking.

'Yes,' she said, equally drily, 'now and then.'

In Frith Street, in the dark of the black-out, they stood for a while waiting for a taxi.

'Where do you live?' he asked. 'Hampstead, isn't it?'

'Bayswater.' She felt a little drunk, what with the gins and all that Chianti they'd consumed. She stood in a shop doorway and watched Romer chase a taxi up the street vainly. When he came back towards her, his hair a bit awry, smiling ruefully, shrugging, she felt a sudden, almost physical urge to be in bed with him, naked. She was a bit shaken by her own carnality but she realised it had been more than two years since she'd been with a man – thinking of her last lover, Jean-Didier, Kolia's friend, the melancholy musician, as she privately called him – two years since Jean-Didier and now she suddenly felt the powerful desire, wanted to hold a man in her arms again – a naked man held against her naked body. It was not so much about any sex act, it was something about being close to, being able to embrace that bigger solider bulk – the strange musculature of a man, something about the different smells, the different strength. She missed it in her life and, she added, this isn't about Romer, watching him come towards her – this is about a man – about men. Romer, however, was the only man currently available.

'Maybe we should go by tube,' he said.

'A taxi'll come,' she said. 'I'm in no hurry.'

She remembered something a woman in Paris had told her once. A woman in her forties, much married, elegant, a little world-weary. There is nothing easier in this world, this woman had claimed, than getting a man to kiss you. Oh really? Eva had said, so how do you do that? Just stand close to a man, the woman had said, very close, as close as you can without touching – he will kiss you in one minute or two. It's inevitable. For them it's like an instinct – they can't resist. Infallible.

So Eva stood close to Romer in the doorway of the shop on Frith Street as he shouted and waved at the passing cars moving down the dark street, hoping one of them might be a taxi.

'We're out of luck,' he said, turning, to find Eva standing very close to him, her face lifted.

'I'm in no hurry,' she said.

He reached for her and kissed her.

Eva stood naked in the small bathroom of Romer's rented flat in South Kensington. She hadn't switched on the light and was aware of the reflection of her body in the mirror, its pale elongated shape printed with the dark roundels of her nipples. They had come back here, having found a taxi almost immediately after their kiss, and had made love without much ado or conversation. She had left the bed almost immediately afterwards to come here and try to gain a moment of understanding, of perspective, on what had happened. She flushed the lavatory and closed her eyes. There was nothing to be gained by thinking now, she told herself, there would be plenty of time to think later.

She slid back into bed beside him.

'I've broken all my rules, you realise,' Romer said.

'Only one, surely?' she said snuggling up to him. 'It's not the end of the world.'

'Sorry I was so quick,' he said. 'I'm a bit out of practice. You're too damn pretty and sexy.'

'I'm not complaining. Put your arms round me.'

He did so and she pressed herself up against him, feeling the muscles in his shoulders, the deep furrow in his back that was his spine. He seemed so big beside her, almost as if he were another race. This is what I had wanted, she said to herself: this is what I've been missing. She pressed her face into the angle of his shoulder and neck and breathed in.

'You're not a virgin,' he said.

'No. Are you?'

'I'm a middle-aged man, for God's sake.'

'There are middle-aged virgins.'

He laughed at her and she ran her hand over his flanks to grip him. He had a band of wiry hair across his chest and a small belly on him. She felt his penis begin to thicken in the loose cradle of her fingers. He hadn't shaved since the morning and his beard was rough on her lips and on her chin. She kissed his neck and kissed his nipples and she felt the weight of his thigh as he moved to cross it over hers. This is what she had wanted: weight – weight, bulk, muscle, strength. Something bigger than me. He rolled her easily on to her back and she felt the heft of his body flatten her against the sheets.

'Eva Delectorskaya,' he said. 'Who would've thought?'

He kissed her gently and she spread her thighs to accommodate him.

'Lucas Romer,' she said. 'My, my, my . . .'

He raised himself on his arms above her.

'Promise you won't tell anyone, but . . .' he said, teasingly leaving the sentence unfinished.

'I promise,' she said, thinking: Who would I tell? Deirdre, Sylvia, Blytheswood? What a fool!

'But . . .,' he continued, 'thanks to you, Eva Delectorskaya,' he dipped his head to kiss her lips briefly, 'we're all going to go to the United States of America.'

6

A Girl from Germany

ON SATURDAY MORNING JOCHEN and I went down to the Westgate shopping centre in Oxford – a shopping mall, of sorts, concrete, ugly but useful as most malls tend to be – to buy some new pyjamas for Jochen (as he was going to be spending a night with his grandmother) and to pay the penultimate hire-purchase instalment on the new cooker I'd bought in December. We parked the car in Broad Street and walked up Cornmarket, where the shops were just opening and, even though it promised to be yet another fine, hot sunny day, there seemed to be a brief sensation of freshness in the morning air – a tacit conspiracy or wishful illusion that such hot sunny days were not yet so commonplace as to have become tiresome and boring. The streets had been swept, the rubbish bins emptied and the sticky bus-and-tourist-clogged hell that was a Saturday Cornmarket in reality was still an hour or two away.

Jochen dragged me back to look at a toyshop window.

'Look at that, Mummy. It's amazing.'

He was pointing to some plastic space gun, encrusted with gimmicks and gizmos.

'Can I have that for my birthday?' he asked plaintively. 'For my birthday and next Christmas?'

'No. I've got you a lovely new encyclopaedia.'

'You're joking with me again,' he said, sternly. 'Don't joke like that.'

'You have to joke a little in life, darling,' I said, leading him on and turning down Queen Street. 'Otherwise what's the point?'

'It depends on the joke,' he said. 'Some jokes aren't funny.'

'All right, you can have your gun. I'll send the encyclopaedia to a little boy in Africa.'

'What little boy?'

'I'll find one. There'll be masses who'd love an encyclopaedia.'

'Look – there's Hamid.'

At the foot of Queen Street was a small square with an obelisk. Clearly designed to be a modest public space in the Edwardian part of the city, now, with the modern redevelopment, it served only as a kind of forecourt or ramp to the maw of the Westgate centre. Now glue-sniffing punks gathered at the steps around the monument (to some forgotten soldier killed in a colonial skirmish) and it was a favourite spot for marches and demonstrations to begin or end. The punks liked it, buskers liked it, beggars liked it, Hare Krishna groups tinkled their cymbals and chanted in it, Salvation Army bands played carols in it at Christmas. I had to admit that, nondescript though it was, it was possibly the liveliest and most eclectic public space in Oxford.

Today there was a small demonstration of Iranians – students and exiles, I supposed – a group of thirty or so assembled under banners that read 'Down with the Shah', 'Long Live the Iranian Revolution'. Two bearded men were trying to encourage passers-by to sign a petition and a girl in a headscarf was listing, in a shrill singsong voice, the Pahlavi family's iniquities through a megaphone. I followed the direction of Jochen's pointed finger and saw Hamid standing some way off behind a parked car, taking photographs of the demonstrators.

We wandered over to him.

'Hamid!' Jochen shouted and he turned, visibly surprised at first, then pleased to see who it was greeting him. He crouched in front of Jochen and offered him his hand to shake, which Jochen did with some vigour.

'Mr Jochen,' he said. '*Salaam alaikum.*'

'*Alaikum salaam,*' Jochen said: it was a routine he knew well.

He smiled at him, and then, rising, turned to me. 'Ruth. How are you?'

'What are you doing?' I said, abruptly, suddenly suspicious.

'Taking photographs.' He held up the camera. 'They are all friends of mine, there.'

'Oh. I would have thought they wouldn't want their photos taken.'

'Why? It's a peaceful demonstration against the Shah. His sister is coming here to Oxford to open a library they have paid for. Wait for that – there will be a big demonstration. You must come.'

'Can I come?' Jochen said.

'Of course.' Then Hamid turned, hearing his name shouted from the demo.

'I must go,' he said. 'I'll see you tonight, Ruth. Shall I bring a taxi?'

'No, no,' I said. 'We can walk.'

He ran over to join the others and for a moment I felt guilty and a fool, suspecting him in that way. We went into the Westgate to look for pyjamas but I found myself still brooding on the matter, wondering why anti-Shah demonstrators would be happy to have their photographs taken.

I was standing over Jochen as he packed his toys into his bag, urging him to be more ruthless in his selection, when I heard Ludger come up the iron stairs and enter through the kitchen door.

'Ah, Ruth,' he said, seeing me in Jochen's room. 'I have a favour. Hey, Jochen, how are you, man?'

Jochen looked round. 'I'm fine, thank you,' he said.

'I got a friend,' Ludger continued to me. 'A girl from Germany. Not a girlfriend,' he added quickly. 'She's saying she wants to visit Oxford and I'm wondering if she could stay here – two, three days.'

'There's no spare room.'

'She can sleep with me. I mean – in my room. Sleeping bag on the floor – no sweat.'

'I'll have to ask Mr Scott,' I improvised. 'There's a clause in my lease, you see. I'm really not allowed to have more than one person to stay here.'

'What?' he was incredulous. 'But it's your home?'

'My *rented* home. I'll just pop down and ask him.'

Mr Scott worked some Saturday mornings and I had seen his car was parked outside. I went down the stairs to the dentist's rooms and found him sitting on the reception desk, swinging his legs, talking to Krissi, his New Zealand dental nurse.

'Hello, hello, hello!' Mr Scott boomed, seeing me arrive, his eyes huge behind the thick lenses of his gold-rimmed spectacles. 'How's young Jochen?'

'Very well, thank you. I was just wondering, Mr Scott, would you object if I put some garden furniture out at the bottom of the garden? Table, chairs, an umbrella?'

'Why would I object?'

'I don't know – it might spoil the view from your surgery, or something.'

'How could it spoil the view?'

'That's great, then. Thanks very much.'

Mr Scott, as a young army dentist, had sailed into Singapore Harbour in February 1942. Four days after he arrived the British forces surrendered and he spent the next three and a half years as a prisoner of the Japanese. After that experience, he had told me – in all candour, without bitterness – he had made the decision that nothing in life was ever going to bother him again.

Ludger was waiting at the top of the stairs. 'Well?'

'Sorry,' I said. 'Mr Scott says no. Only one guest allowed.'

Ludger looked at me sceptically. I held his gaze.

'Oh, yeah?' he said.

'Yeah. In fact you're lucky he's let you stay for so long,' I lied, quite enjoying the process. 'My lease is at stake here, you know.'

'What kind of shit country is this?' he asked, rhetorically. 'Where a landlord can tell you who can stay in your home.'

'If you don't like it you can always bugger off,' I said, cheerfully. 'Come on, Jochen, let's go to granny's.'

My mother and I sat on the rear terrace of the cottage, looking out over the blond meadow at the dark green mass of Witch Wood, drinking home-made lemonade and keeping an eye on Jochen, who was galloping around the garden with a butterfly net, failing to catch butterflies.

'You were right,' I said, 'it turns out Romer is a lord. And a rich man, as far as I can tell.' Two visits to the Bodleian Library had furnished me with a little more information than the few facts provided by Bobbie York. I watched my mother's face intently as I documented Romer's life, reading from the notes I had made. He was born 7 March 1899. Son of Gerald Arthur Romer (deceased 1918). An elder brother, Sholto, had been killed at the Battle of the Somme in 1916. Romer had been educated at a minor public school called Framingham Hall, where his father had taught classics. During the First World War he had become a captain in the King's Own Yorkshire Light Infantry, and had won the Military Cross in 1918. Back to Oxford, post-war, to St John's College, where he obtained a first-class degree in history in 1923. Then there were two years at the Sorbonne, 1924–5. Then he joined the Foreign Office from 1926–35. I paused. 'Then it all goes blank, except that he was awarded the Croix de Guerre – the Belgian Croix de Guerre in 1945.'

'Good old Belgium,' she said, flatly.

I told her that the publishing enterprise had begun in 1946 – concentrating on learned journals, initially, with material from mainly German sources. The German university presses being moribund, barely under way or severely handicapped, German academics and scientists found Romer's journals very welcoming. On the back of this success, he moved increasingly into reference books, drily academic in character, expensive, and sold largely to academic libraries around the world. Romer's business – Romer, Radclyffe Ltd – soon had an impressive though specialised market presence, one that led to the firm's buyout in 1963 by a Dutch publishing group, netting Romer a personal fortune of some £3 million. I mentioned the marriage in 1949 to one Miriam Hilton (who died in 1972) and the two children – a son and a daughter – and she didn't flinch. There was a house in London – 'in Knightsbridge' was all I could discover, and a villa near Antibes. The Romer, Radclyffe imprint continued after its take-over (Romer sat on the board of the Dutch conglomerate) and he became a consultant to and director of various companies in the publishing and newspaper industries. He had been made a peer by Churchill's government in 1953, 'for services to the publishing industry'.

Here my mother chuckled sardonically: 'For services to the espionage industry, you mean. They always wait a bit.'

'That's all I can dig up,' I said. 'There's not much at all. He calls himself Lord Mansfield now. That's why it took some tracking down.'

'His middle name is Mansfield,' my mother said. 'Lucas Mansfield Romer – I'd forgotten that. Any photographs? I bet you there aren't.'

But I had found a fairly recent one in *Tatler*, of Romer standing beside his son, Sebastian, at his twenty-first birthday party. As if aware of the photographer, Romer had managed to cover his mouth and chin with one hand. It could have been anyone: a lean face, a dinner-jacket and bow tie, a head now quite significantly bald. I had had a photocopy made and I handed it over to my mother.

She looked at it expressionlessly.

'I suppose I might just have recognised him. My, he's lost his hair.'

'Oh yes. And apparently there's a portrait of him by David Bomberg in the National Portrait Gallery.'

'What date?'

'Nineteen thirty-six.'

'Now that would be worth seeing,' she said. 'You might get some idea of what he was like when I met him.' She flicked the photocopy with a nail. 'Not this old chap.'

'Why do you want to find him, Sal? After all these years?' I asked as innocuously as I could manage.

'I just feel the time has come.'

I left it at that as Jochen wandered over with a grasshopper in his net.

'Well done,' I said. 'At least it's an insect.'

'Actually, I think grasshoppers are more interesting than butterflies,' he said.

'Run and catch another one,' my mother said. 'Then we'll have supper.'

'My God, look at the time,' I said. 'I've got a date.' I told her about Hamid and his invitation but she wasn't listening. I could see she was in Romer-land.

'Do you think you could find out where his house is in London?'

'Romer's? . . . Well, I suppose I could try. Shouldn't be impossible. But what then?'

'Then I want you to arrange to meet him.'

I put my hand on her arm. 'Sal, are you sure this is wise?'

'Not so much wise as absolutely vital. Crucial.'

'How am I meant to arrange to meet him? Why would Lord Mansfield of Hampton Cleeve want to meet me?'

She leant over and gave me a kiss on the forehead.

'You're a very intelligent young woman – you'll think of something.'

'And what am I meant to do at this meeting?'

'I'll tell you exactly what to do when the time comes.' She turned to the garden again. 'Jochen! Mummy's leaving. Come and say goodbye.'

I made a bit of an effort for Hamid, though my heart wasn't really in it. I rather relished these rare evenings alone but I washed my hair and put on some dark grey eyeshadow. I was going to wear my platform boots but didn't want to tower over him so I settled for some clogs, jeans and an embroidered cheesecloth smock. My burn-dressing was less conspicuous now – under the cheesecloth of the smock it formed a neat lump the size of a small sandwich. While I waited for him I set a kitchen chair outside on the landing at the top of the stairs and drank a beer. The light was soft and hazy and dozens of swifts jinked and dived above the treetops, the air filled with their squeakings like a kind of semi-audible, shrill static. Thinking about my mother, as I sipped my beer, I concluded that the only good outcome of this Romer-search was that it seemed to have cut down on the paranoia and the invalid play-acting – there was no more talk of her bad back, the wheelchair stood unused in the hall – but then I realised I had forgotten to ask her about the shotgun.

Hamid arrived, wearing a dark suit and a tie. He said I looked 'very nice' though I could tell he was a little disappointed at the informality of my outfit. We walked down the Woodstock Road in the golden, hazy evening light. The lawns of the big brick houses were parched and ochreous and the leaves on the trees – usually so vividly, so densely green – looked dusty and tired.

'Aren't you hot?' I asked Hamid. 'You can take your jacket off.'

'No, I'm fine. Maybe the restaurant has air-conditioning?'

'I doubt it – this is England, remember.'

As it turned out, I was right, but in compensation numerous roof fans whirred above our heads. I had never been in Browns before but I liked its long dark bar and its big mirrors, the palms and greenery everywhere. Globe lights on the walls shone like small albescent moons. Some kind of jazzy rock music was playing.

Hamid didn't drink but he insisted on my having an aperitif – vodka and tonic, thanks – and then he ordered a bottle of red wine.

'I can't drink all that,' I said. 'I'll fall over.'

'I will catch you,' he said, with awkward suggestive gallantry. Then he acknowledged his awkwardness with a shy confessional smile.

'You can always leave some.'

'I'll take it home with me,' I said, wanting to end this conversation about my drinking. 'Waste not, want not.'

We ate our food, chatting about Oxford English Plus, Hamid telling me about his other tutors, how another thirty oil engineers from Dusendorf were arriving, and that he thought Hugues and Bérangère were having an affair.

'How do you know?' I asked – I'd seen no sign of any increased intimacy.

'He's telling me everything, Hugues.'

'Oh, well . . . I hope they're very happy.'

He poured some more wine into my glass. Something about the way he did this and the set of his mouth and jaw forewarned me of some serious conversation coming up. I felt a faint lowering of my spirits: life was complicated enough – I didn't want Hamid complicating it further. I drank half the glass of wine in preparation for the cross-examination and felt the alcohol kick in almost immediately. I was drinking too much – but who could blame me?

'Ruth, may I ask you some questions?'

'Of course.'

'I want to ask you about Jochen's father.'

'Oh, God, right. Fire away.'

'Were you ever married to him?'

'No. He was already married with three children when I met him.'

'So: how come you had this child with this man?'

I drank more wine. The waitress cleared our plates away.

'You really want to know?'

'Yes. I feel I don't understand this. Don't understand this in your life. And yet I know you, Ruth.'

'No you don't.'

'Well, I have seen you almost every day for three months. I feel you are a friend.'

'True. OK.'

'So: how did this happen?'

I decided to tell him, or to tell him as much as he needed to know. Perhaps the act of relating such a history would help me also, set it in some kind of a context of my life; maybe make it not less significant (because it had produced Jochen, after all) but provide its significance with some perspective and thereby transform it into a normal slice of autobiography and not some gaping, bleeding, psychological wound. I lit a cigarette and took another long sip of wine. Hamid, I saw, had leant forward on the table, his arms folded, his brown eyes fixed on mine. I am a good listener, his pose was telling me – no distractions, full focus.

'It all began in 1970,' I said. 'I had just graduated, I had a first-class degree in French and German from Oxford University – my life lay ahead of me, full of bright promise, all sorts of interesting potential options and avenues to explore, etcetera, etcetera . . . And then my father dropped down dead in the garden from a heart attack.'

'I'm sorry,' Hamid said.

'Not as sorry as I was,' I said, and I could feel my throat thicken with remembered emotion. 'I loved my dad – more than my mother, I think. Don't forget I was an only child . . . So I was twenty-one years old and I went a little crazy. In fact, I think I might have had some kind of a nervous breakdown – who knows?

'But I wasn't helped at this difficult time by my mother who, a week after the funeral – almost as if she'd been given orders by someone – put the family home on the market (a lovely old house, just outside Banbury), sold it within a month and, with the money she made, bought a cottage in the remotest village she could find in Oxfordshire.'

'Maybe for her it made sense,' Hamid ventured.

'Maybe for her it did. It didn't to me. Suddenly, I didn't have a home. The cottage was hers, her place. There was a guest room that I could use if I ever wanted to stay. But the message was plain: our family life was over – your father is dead – you're a graduated student, twenty-one years old, we will go our separate ways. And so I decided to go to Germany. I decided to write a thesis on the German revolution after the First World War. "Revolution in Germany" it was called – it *is* called – "1918–1923".'

'Why?'

'I don't know – I told you, I think I was a bit mad. And, anyway, revolution was in the air. I felt like revolutionising my life. This was something suggested to me and I grabbed it with both hands. I wanted to get away – from Banbury, from Oxford, from my mother, from memories of my father. So I went to university in Hamburg to write a thesis.'

'Hamburg.' Hamid repeated the name of the city as if logging it in his memory bank. 'And this is where you met Jochen's father.'

'Yes. Jochen's father was my professor at Hamburg. A history professor. Professor Karl-Heinz Kleist. He was supervising my thesis – amongst other things like presenting arts programmes on TV, organising demonstrations, publishing radical pamphlets, writing articles for *Die Zeit* on the German Crisis . . .' I paused. 'He was a man of many facets. A very busy man.'

I put out cigarette number one and lit cigarette number two.

'You've got to understand,' I continued, 'it was in a very strange state, Germany, in 1970 – it's still in a strange state in 1976. Some sort of upheaval was happening in society – some sort of defining process. For example, when I went to meet Karl-Heinz for the first time – in the university building where he had his office – there was a huge hand-painted sign across the façade – put up by the students – saying: *Institut für Soziale Angelegenheiten* – "The Institute for Social Conscience" . . . Not "The History Faculty", or whatever. For these students in 1970, history was about studying their social conscience –'

'What does this mean?'

'It meant how – you know – the events of the past, particularly the recent past, had shaped their ideas of themselves. It really had little to do with documented facts, of forming a consensus around a narrative about the past . . .'

I saw I was losing Hamid but I found myself remembering that first meeting with Karl-Heinz. His dark, shadowy room was filled with towers of books, leaning against the wall – there were no bookshelves. There were cushions scattered on the floor – no seats – and there were three joss sticks burning on his low desk, a Thai bed in actuality – otherwise empty. He was a tall man with fine blond hair which fell to his shoulders. He was wearing several beaded necklaces, an embroidered pale blue silk chemise and crushed-velvet mulberry flared trousers. He had big emphatic features: a long nose, full lips, heavy brows – not so much handsome as unignorable. After three years in Oxford he came as something of a shock to me – and this was a professor. At his behest I lowered myself down on to a cushion and he dragged another over to sit opposite me. He repeated my thesis title several times as if testing it for residual humour, as if it contained some hidden joke I was playing on him.

'What was he like?' Hamid asked. 'This Karl-Heinz.'

'At first he was like nobody I had ever met. Then, as I got to know him over the next year or so, he slowly but surely became ordinary again. He became just like everybody else.'

'I don't understand.'

'Selfish, vain, lazy, careless, dishonourable . . .' I tried to think of more adjectives. 'Complacent, sly, mendacious, weak –'

'But this is Jochen's father.'

'Yes. Maybe all fathers are like that, deep down.'

'You're very cynical, Ruth.'

'No, I'm not. I'm not in the least cynical.'

Hamid clearly decided not to pursue this particular line of our conversation.

'So what happened?'

'What do you think?' I said, refilling my glass. 'I fell crazily in love with him. Totally, fanatically, abjectly, in love.'

'But this man had a wife and three children.'

'This was 1970, Hamid. In Germany. In a German university. His wife didn't care. I used to see her quite a lot for a while. I liked her. She was called Irmgard.'

I thought of Irmgard Kleist – tall as Karl-Heinz – with her long, breast-sweeping, hennaed hair and her carefully cultivated air of extreme, terminal languor. Look at me, she seemed to be saying, I'm so relaxed I'm almost comatose – yet I have a famous, philandering husband, three children and I edit political books in a fashionable left-wing publishing house and still I can barely be bothered to string three words together. Irmgard's attitude was contagious – for a while even I affected some of her mannerisms. For a while nothing could stir me from my self-regarding torpor. Nothing but Karl-Heinz.

'She didn't care what Karl-Heinz did,' I said. 'She knew, with absolute confidence, that he would never leave her – so she allowed him his little adventures. I wasn't the first and I wasn't the last.'

'And then comes Jochen.'

'I got pregnant. I don't know – maybe I was too stoned one night and I forgot to take my pill. Karl-Heinz said immediately he could arrange an abortion through a doctor friend of his. But I thought: my dad is dead, my mother is a gardening hermit who I never see – I want this baby.'

'You were very young.'

'So everybody said. But I didn't feel young – I felt very grown-up, very in control. It seemed like the right thing to do and an interesting thing to do. It was all the justification that I needed. Jochen was born. Now I know that it was the best thing that could ever have happened to me.' I said this instantly, wanting to pre-empt him asking me if I had any regrets – which I felt he was about to do. I didn't want him to ask me that question. I didn't want to consider if I had any regrets.

'So Jochen was born.'

'Jochen was born. Karl-Heinz was very pleased – he told everybody. Told his own children they had a new baby brother. I had a small apartment where we lived. Karl-Heinz helped me with the rent. He would stay a few nights a week with me. We went on holidays together – to Vienna, to Copenhagen, to Berlin. Then he got bored and started having an affair with one of the producers of his television show. As soon as I found out, I knew it was over so I left Hamburg with Jochen and came back to Oxford to finish my thesis.' I spread my hands. 'And here we are.'

'How long were you in Germany?'

'Nearly four years. I came back in January '75.'

'Did you try to see this Karl-Heinz again?'

'No. I'll probably never see him again. I don't want to see him. I don't need to see him. It's over. Finished.'

'Maybe Jochen will want to see him.'

'That's fine with me.'

Hamid was frowning, thinking hard, I could see, trying to fit the Ruth he knew into this other Ruth that had just been revealed to him. I actually felt quite pleased that I had told him my story in this way: I saw its shapeliness. I saw that it had ended.

He paid the bill and we left the restaurant and ambled back up the Woodstock Road in the warm muggy night. Hamid finally removed his jacket and tie.

'And Ludger?'

'Ludger was there, around and about. He spent a lot of time in Berlin. He was crazy – taking drugs, stealing motor bikes. He was always in trouble. Karl-Heinz would kick him out and he'd go back to Berlin.'

'It's a sad story,' Hamid said. 'He was a bad man that you fell in love with.'

'Well, it wasn't all bad. He taught me a lot. I changed. You wouldn't have believed what I was like when I went to Hamburg. Timid, nervous, unsure of myself.'

He laughed. 'No – this I don't believe.'

'It's true. When I left I was a different person. Karl-Heinz taught me one important thing: he taught me to be fearless, to be unafraid. I'm not fucking frightened of anyone, thanks to him – policemen, judges, skinheads, Oxford dons, poets, parking wardens, intellectuals, yobbos, bores, bitches, headmasters, lawyers, journalists, drunks, politicians, preachers . . .' I ran out of people I wasn't fucking afraid of. 'It was a valuable lesson.'

'I suppose so.'

'He used to say that everything you did should contribute in some way to the destruction of the great myth – the myth of the all-powerful system.'

'I don't understand.'

'That your life, in every small way, should be a kind of propaganda action to expose this myth as a lie and an illusion.'

'So you become a criminal.'

'No – you don't have to. Some people did – a very few. But it makes sense – think about it. Nobody needs to be afraid of anyone or anything. The myth of the all-powerful system is a sham, empty.'

'Maybe you should go to Iran. Tell this to the Shah.'

I laughed. We had reached our driveway in Moreton Road.

'Fair point,' I said. 'Maybe it's easy to be fearless in cosy old Oxford.' I turned to him, and I thought: I'm pissed, I drank too much, I'm talking too much. 'Thanks, Hamid. That was great,' I said. 'I really enjoyed myself. I hope it wasn't boring for you.'

'No, it was wonderful, fascinating.'

He leant forward quickly and kissed me on the lips. I felt his soft beard on my face before I pushed him off.

'Hey. Hamid, no –'

'I ask you all these questions because I have something to tell you.'

'No, Hamid, no – please. We're friends: you said so yourself.'

'I'm in love with you, Ruth.'

'No you're not. Go to bed. I'll see you on Monday.'

'I am, Ruth, I am. I'm sorry.'

I said nothing more, turning away and leaving him standing on the gravel as I strode down the side of the house towards our back stairs. The wine had gone so far to my head that I felt myself swaying and had to pause to touch the brickwork on my left to keep myself steady, and at the same time I was trying to ignore the mounting confusion in my head caused by Hamid's declaration. A little unbalanced, and miscalculating the position of the bottom step, I banged my shin heavily on a supporting bar of the handrail and felt tears of pain sting my eyes. I limped up the iron stairs, cursing to myself, and once in the kitchen pulled up my jeans to see that the blow had broken the skin – there were little bubbles of blood pushing through the smashed skin – and that a dark bruise was already forming – I was bleeding under my skin. My shin throbbed like some kind of malignant tuning fork – the bone must be bruised. I swore vilely to myself – funny how a torrent of fucks and bastards and cunts acts as a kind of instant analgesic. At least the pain had driven Hamid from my mind.

'Oh, hi, Ruth. It's you.'

I looked groggily round to see Ludger standing there, in jeans, but with no shirt on. Behind him stood a grubby-looking girl wearing a T-shirt and panties. Her hair was greasy and she had a wide, slack mouth, pretty in a sulky kind of way.

'This is Ilse. She had nowhere to stay. What could I do?'

The Story of Eva Delectorskaya

New York. 1941

ROMER WAS A ROBUST and uncomplicated lover – except in one particular. At some juncture, while he and Eva were making love, he would withdraw and rock back on his haunches, taking whatever blankets and sheets and bed covers there were with him, and look at Eva lying naked, spread-eagled before him on the bed and then consider his own glossy tumescence and then, after a second or two, taking hold of himself, he would position his erect penis and carefully, slowly re-enter her. Eva began to wonder if it were the act of penetration that excited him more than the eventual orgasm. Once, when he had done this a second time to her, she had said: 'Be careful, I won't wait around for ever'. So he confined himself, by and large, to one of these contemplative withdrawals a session. Eva had to admit that the manoeuvre itself was, all things considered, rather pleasurable also, on her side of the sexual fence.

They had made love that morning, fairly swiftly, satisfyingly and with no interruptions. They were in Meadowville, a town outside Albany, New York State, staying at the Windermere Hotel and Coffee Shop on Market Street. Eva was dressing and Romer lay grandly in bed, naked, a knee up, the sheets bunched at his groin, his fingers laced behind his head. Eva clipped on her stockings and stepped into her skirt, hauling it up.

'How long will you be?' Romer asked.

'Half an hour.'

'You don't speak?'

'Not since the first meeting. He thinks I'm from Boston and work for NBC.'

She buttoned her jacket and checked her hair.

'Can't lie here all day,' Romer said, slipping out of bed and padding towards the bathroom.

'I'll see you at the station,' she said, picking up her handbag and her *Herald Tribune* and blowing him a kiss. But when he shut the door behind him she set her bag and newspaper down and quickly checked the pockets of his jacket hanging behind the door. His wallet was plump with dollars but there was nothing else of any significance. She checked his briefcase: five different newspapers (three American, one Spanish, one Canadian), an apple, a copy of *Tess of the d'Urbervilles* and a rolled-up tie. She wasn't sure why she did this – she was convinced Romer would never leave anything interesting or confidential to be found and he never seemed to take notes – but she felt he would almost expect it of her, think she was remiss not to take advantage of the opportunity (she was sure he did it to her) and so, whenever she had a minute or two, she looked, checked and poked around.

She went downstairs to the coffee shop. It was panelled in dark brown wood and there were small booths along two walls, with red leather banquettes. She looked at the display of muffins, cakes, bagels and cookies and marvelled yet again at the profligacy and generosity of America when it came to the business of eating and drinking. She thought of the breakfast that awaited her here in the Windermere Hotel Coffee Shop and compared it with the last breakfast she had had in England, in Liverpool, before she sailed for Canada: a cup of tea, two slices of thin toast and margarine spread with watered-down raspberry jam.

She was hungry – all this sex, she thought – and ordered eggs over-easy, bacon and potatoes as the proprietor's wife filled her mug with steaming coffee.

'All the coffee you can drink, miss,' she reminded her needlessly – signs everywhere proclaimed the same largess.

'Thank you,' Eva said, more humbly and more gratefully than she meant.

She ate her breakfast hungrily, quickly and sat on in the booth, drinking another two mugs of free coffee before Wilbur Johnson appeared at the door. He was the owner-manager of Meadowville's radio station, WNLR, one of two stations that she 'ran'. She spotted him step in, hat in hand, saw his gaze sweep round to take her in, sitting in her booth, saw his gaze judder a moment, and then he wandered into the coffee shop, just another customer, all innocence, looking for somewhere to sit. Eva stood up and quit her booth, leaving her *Tribune* on the banquette, and went to the cash desk to pay her bill. Johnson took her seat in the booth a moment later. Eva paid, stepped outside into the October sunshine and sauntered down Market Street towards the railway station.

In the *Tribune* was a cyclostyled news release from a news agency called Transoceanic Press, the news agency that Eva worked for. It carried reports from German, French and Spanish newspapers of the return to La Rochelle after a successful mission of the submarine U-549, the very submarine that had, the week before, torpedoed the destroyer USS *Kearny*, killing eleven American sailors. The *Kearny*, badly damaged, had limped into Reykjavik in Iceland. Visible on the conning tower of the U-549, Eva's news flash reported, as it moored in La Rochelle, were eleven freshly painted Stars and Stripes. The listeners of WNLR would be the first to know. Wilbur Johnson, a staunch New Dealer and supporter of Roosevelt and admirer of Churchill, just happened to be married to an Englishwoman.

On the train back to New York Eva and Romer sat opposite

each other. Romer was staring at her, dreamily, his head propped on a fist.

'A penny for your disgusting thoughts,' Eva said.

'When's your next trip?'

She considered: her other radio station was far upstate, in a town called Franklin Forks near Burlington, not far from the border with Canada. The manager was a taciturn Pole called Paul Witoldski who had lost several members of his family in Warsaw in 1939, hence his keen anti-Fascism – she was due another visit: she hadn't seen him for a month.

'A week or so, I suppose.'

'Make it two nights and book a double room.'

'Yes, sir.'

They rarely spent a night together in New York, there were too many people who might see or hear of it, therefore Romer preferred to accompany her on these trips out of town, to benefit from their provincial anonymity.

'What're you doing today?' she asked.

'Big meeting at head office. Interesting developments in South America, it seems . . . What about you?'

'I'm lunching with Angus Woolf.'

'Good old Angus. Say hello from me.'

In Manhattan the taxi dropped Romer at the Rockefeller Center – where the British Security Coordination, as it was blandly called, now occupied two full floors. Eva had been there once and had been amazed to see the number of personnel: rows of offices off corridors, secretaries, staff running around, type-writers, telephones, teleprinters – hundreds and hundreds of people, like a real business, she thought, a true espionage corporation with its headquarters in New York. She often wondered how the British government would feel if there were hundreds of American intelligence staff occupying several floors of a building in Oxford Street, say – somehow she thought the level of tolerance might be different, but the Americans had not seemed to mind, had raised no objection, and the British Security Coordination accordingly grew and grew and grew. However, Romer, ever the irregular, tried to keep his team dispersed or at arm's length from the Center. Sylvia worked there but Blytheswood was at the radio station WLUR, Angus Woolf (ex-Reuters) was now at the Overseas News Agency, and Eva and Morris Devereux ran the team of translators at Transoceanic Press, the small American news agency – a near replica of the Agence Nadal – that specialised in Hispanic and South American news releases, an agency that BSC (through American intermediaries) had quietly acquired for Romer at the end of 1940. Romer had travelled to New York in August of that year to set everything up, Eva and the team following a month later – first to Toronto in Canada before establishing themselves in New York.

Unable to pull out because of a passing bus, her taxi stalled. As the driver restarted his engine Eva turned to look through the rear window, watching Romer stride along the concourse into the main entrance of the Center. She felt a warmth for him flood her suddenly, watching his brisk progress as he dodged the shoppers and the sightseers. This is what Romer is like to the rest of the world, she thought, a little absurdly – a busy, urgent man, suited, carrying a briefcase, going into a skyscraper. She sensed her privileged intimacy, her private knowledge of her strange lover and she briefly revelled in it. Lucas Romer, who would have thought?

Angus Woolf had arranged to meet her in a restaurant on Lexington Avenue and 63rd Street. She was early and ordered a dry Martini. There was the usual small commotion at the door as Angus arrived: chairs were moved, waiters hovered, as Angus negotiated the doorway with his twisted body and splayed sticks and made determinedly for the table where Eva was waiting. He swung himself into his seat with much grunting and puffing – refusing all offers of help from the staff – and carefully hung his sticks on the back of an adjacent chair.

'Eve, my dear, you look radiant.'

Eva coloured, ridiculously, as if she were giving something away and muttered excuses about a cold coming on.

'Nonsense,' Angus said. 'You look positively splendid.'

Angus had a big handsome face on his tiny warped torso and specialised in a line of extravagant polished compliments, all uttered with a slight breathy lisp as if the effort it took to inflate and deflate his lungs were another consequence of his disability. He lit a cigarette and ordered a drink.

'Celebrating,' he said.

'Oh, yes? Are we doing well, all of a sudden?'

'I wouldn't go as far as that,' he said, 'but we managed to get an America First meeting closed in Philadelphia. Two thousand photographs of Herr Hitler found in the organisers' office. Irate denials, accusations of a set-up – but, still, a little victory. All going out on the ONA wire today if you people want to pick it up.'

Eva said they probably would. Angus asked her how life was at Transoceanic and they chatted unguardedly about work, Eva admitting to a real disappointment about the response to the *Kearny* attack: everyone at Transoceanic had seen it as a godsend, thought it would provoke more shock. She told Angus about her follow-up stories, all designed to stir up a little more outrage. 'But,' she said, 'no one seems that concerned, at all. German U-boat kills eleven neutral American sailors. So what?'

'They just don't want to be in our nasty European war, dear. Face it.'

They ordered T-bone steaks and fries – still two ravenous Britons – and talked circumspectly about interventionists and isolationists, of Father Coughlin and the America First Committee, pressures from London, Roosevelt's maddening inertia, and so on.

'What about our esteemed leader? Have you seen him?' Angus asked.

'This morning,' Eva said, unthinkingly. 'Going into head office.'

'I thought he was out of town.'

'He had some big meeting to go to,' she said, ignoring Angus's implication.

'I get the impression they're not very happy with him,' he said.

'They're never very happy with him,' she said, unreflectingly. 'That's how he likes it. They don't see that his being a wild card is his strength.'

'You're very loyal – I'm impressed,' Angus said, a little too knowingly.

Eva had regretted the words the minute she had uttered them – she became flustered suddenly and spoke on, instead of shutting up.

'I mean, only that he likes being challenged, you know, likes being awkward. It puts everybody on their mettle he says. He functions better that way.'

'Point taken, Eve. Steady on: no need to defend yourself. I agree.'

But she wondered if Angus suspected something and worried that her uncharacteristic volubility might have given more away. In London it had been easy to be discreet, hidden, but here in New York it had been harder to meet regularly and securely. Here they – the British – were more conspicuous and, moreover, objects of curiosity too, fighting their war against the Nazis – with, since May of this year, their new allies the Russians – while America looked on concernedly but otherwise got on with her life.

'How're things generally?' she said, wanting to change the subject. She sawed away at her steak, suddenly not quite so ravenous. Angus chewed, thinking, looking first frowningly thoughtful, then slightly troubled, as if he were a reluctant bringer of bad news. 'Things,' he said, dabbing at his mouth prissily with his napkin, 'things are pretty much as they've always been. I don't think anything will happen, to tell the truth.' He talked about Roosevelt and how he didn't dare risk putting entry to the war to the vote in Congress – he was absolutely sure that he'd lose. So everything had to remain confidential, done on the sly, backhandedly. The isolationist lobby was incredibly powerful, incredibly, Angus said. 'Keep our boys out of that European quagmire,' he said, trying and failing for a convincing American accent. 'They'll give us arms and as much help as they can – for as long as we can hold out. But you know . . .' He tackled his meat again.

She felt a sudden impotence, almost a demoralisation, hearing all this and wondered to herself, if this was indeed the case, what was the point of all this stuff they did: all the radio stations, the newspapers, the press agencies – all that opinion and influence out there, the stories, the column inches, the pundits, the famous broadcasters, all designed to bring America into the war, to cajole and nudge, persuade and convince – if it were not going to make Roosevelt act.

'Got to do our best, Eve,' Angus said brightly, as if he were conscious of the effect of his cynicism on her and trying to counterbalance it. 'But, short of Adolf declaring war unilaterally I can't see the Yanks joining in.' He smiled, looking pleased, as if he'd just heard he'd been given a huge raise. 'We have to face it,' he lowered his voice, glancing left and right. 'We're not exactly the most popular people in town. So many of them hate us, detest us. They hate and detest FDR too – he has to be very careful, very.'

'He just got re-elected for the third time, for God's sake.'

'Yes. On an "I'll keep us out" ticket.'

She sighed: she didn't want to feel depressed today, it had started so well. 'Romer says there are interesting developments in South America.'

'Does he, now?' Angus affected indifference but Eva could sense his interest quicken. 'Did he give you any more details?'

'No. Nothing.' Eva wondered if she had blundered again. What was happening to her today? She seemed to have lost her poise, her balance. They were all crows after all, all interested in carrion.

'Let's have another cocktail,' Angus said. 'Eat, drink and be merry – and all that.'

But Eva did feel strangely depressed after her lunch with Angus and she also continued to worry that she had given away information, subtext, hints about her and Romer – nuances that someone with Angus's agile brain would be able to turn into a plausible picture. As she walked back to the Transoceanic office, across town, crossing the great avenues – Park, Madison, Fifth – looking down the wide, unique vistas, seeing everywhere around her the hurry, chatter, noise and confidence of the city, the people, the country, she thought that maybe she too, if she had been a young American woman, a Manhattanite, happy in her work, cherishing her security, her opportunities, with all her life ahead of her – perhaps she too, however much she might sympathise and empathise with Britain and her struggle for survival, would think: why should I sacrifice all this, risk the lives of our young men, to become involved in some sordid and deadly war taking place 3,000 miles away?

Back at Transoceanic she found Morris busy with the Czech and Spanish translators. He waved at her and she went to her office, thinking that there seemed to be every kind of community in the United States – Irish, Hispanic, German, Polish, Czech, Lithuanian, and so on – but no British community. Where were the British-Americans? Who was going to put their case to counter the arguments of the Irish-Americans, the German-Americans, the Swedish-Americans and all the others?

To cheer herself up and to deflect her mind from these defeatist thoughts, she spent the afternoon compiling a small dossier on one of her stories. Three weeks previously, in a feigned-tipsy conversation with the *Tass* New York correspondent (her Russian suddenly very useful), she had let slip that the Royal Navy was completing trials on a new form of depth charge – the deeper it went the more powerful it became: there would be no hiding place for submarines. The *Tass* correspondent was very sceptical. Two days later, Angus – through the offices of ONA – covertly placed the story with the *New York Post*. The *Tass* correspondent phoned to apologise and said he was cabling the story back to Moscow. When it appeared in Russian newspapers, British newspapers and news agencies picked it up and the news agencies cabled the story back to the USA. Full circle: she ranged the clippings on her desk – the *Daily News*, the *Herald Tribune*, the *Boston Globe*. 'New deadlier depth charge to obliterate U-boat menace'. The Germans would read it now, now that it was an American story. Maybe U-boats would be instructed to be more cautious as they approached convoys. Maybe German submariners would be demoralised. Maybe the Americans would root for the plucky Britons a little bit more. Maybe, maybe . . . According to Angus it was all a waste of time.

A few days later Morris Devereux came into her office at Transoceanic and handed her a cutting from the *Washington Post*. It was headlined: 'Russian professor commits suicide in DC hotel'. She skimmed through it quickly: the Russian's name was Aleksandr Nekich. He had emigrated to the USA in 1938 with his wife and two daughters and had been an associate professor of international politics at Johns Hopkins University. Police were mystified as to why he should have killed himself in a clearly low-rent hotel.

'Means nothing to me,' Eva said.

'Ever heard of him?'

'No.'

'Did your friends at *Tass* ever talk about him?'

'No. But I could ask them.' There was something about the tone of Morris's questioning that was untypical. Something hard had replaced the debonair manner.

'Why's it important?' she asked.

Morris sat down and seemed to relax a little. Nekich, he explained, was a senior NKVD officer who had defected to the States after Stalin's purges in 1937.

'They made him a professor for form's sake – he never taught at all. Apparently he's a mine of information – was a mine of information – about Soviet penetration here in the US . . .' he paused. 'And in Britain. Which is why we were rather interested in him.'

'I thought we were all on the same side now,' Eva said, knowing how naïve she sounded.

'Well, we are. But look at us; what're we doing here?'

'Once a crow always a crow.'

'Exactly. You're always interested in what your friends are up to.'

A thought struck her. 'Why are you concerned about this dead Russian? Not your beat, is it?'

Morris took back the clipping. 'I was meant to meet him next week. He was going to tell us about what had happened in England. The Americans had got everything they wanted out of him – apparently he had some very interesting news for us.'

'Too late?'

'Yes . . . very inconvenient.'

'What do you mean?'

'I would say it looked like somebody didn't want him to talk to us.'

'So he committed suicide.'

He gave a little chuckle. 'They're bloody good, these Russians,' he said. 'Nekich shot himself in the head in a locked hotel room, gun in his hand, the key still in the lock, the windows bolted. But when it looks like a hard-and-fast, grade-A, genuine suicide it usually ain't.'

Eva was thinking: why is he telling me all this?

'They'd been after him since 1938,' Morris went on. 'And they got him. Shame they hadn't waited an extra week . . .' He gave a mock-rueful smile. 'I was quite looking forward to my encounter with Mr Nekich.'

Eva said nothing. This was all new to her: she wondered if Romer was involved with these meetings. As far as she was concerned Morris and she were only meant to be preoccupied with Transoceanic. But then, she thought – what do I know?

'The *Tass* people haven't mentioned any new faces in town?'

'Not to me.'

'Do me a favour, Eve – make a few calls to your Russian friends – see what the word is on Nekich's death.'

'All right. But they're just journalists.'

'Nobody's "just" anything.'

'Romer's rule.'

He snapped his fingers and stood up. 'Your "German naval manoeuvres off Buenos Aires" story is doing well. All of South America very angry, protests all over.'

'Good,' she said flatly. 'Every little helps, I suppose.'

'Cheer up, Eve. By the way – the lord above wants to see you. Eldorado diner in fifteen minutes.'

Eva waited in the diner for an hour before Romer turned up. She found these professional encounters very strange: she wanted to kiss him, touch his face, hold his hands, but they had to observe the most formal of courtesies.

'Sorry I'm late,' he said, sitting down opposite. 'You know – it's the first time in New York, but I think I had a shadow. Maybe two. I had to go into the park to be sure I'd lost them.'

'Who would put shadows on you?' She stretched her leg out under the table and rubbed his calf with the toe of her shoe.

'FBI.' Romer smiled at her. 'I think Hoover's getting worried about how large we've grown. You've seen BSC. Frankenstein's monster. You'd better stop that, by the way, you'll get me excited.'

He ordered a coffee; Eva had another Pepsi-Cola.

'I've got a job for you,' he said.

She covered her mouth with her fingers and said softly, 'Lucas . . . I want to see you.'

Romer looked fixedly at her; she sat up straight. 'I want you to go to Washington,' he said. 'I want you to get to know a man there called Mason Harding. He works in Harry Hopkins's press office.'

She knew who Harry Hopkins was – Roosevelt's right-hand man. Secretary of Commerce, notionally, but, in reality, FDR's adviser, envoy, fixer, eyes and ears. Quite probably the second most important man in America – as far as the British were concerned.

'So I have to get to know this Mason Harding. Why?'

'Approach the press office – say you want to interview Hopkins for Transoceanic. They'll probably say no – but, who knows? You might meet Hopkins. But the key thing is to get to know Harding.'

'What then?'

'I'll tell you.'

She felt that little flutter of pleasurable anticipation; it was the same as when Romer had sent her into Prenslo. The strange thought came to her: maybe I was always destined to be a spy?

'When do I go?'

'Tomorrow. Make your appointments today.' He passed her a scrap of paper with a Washington telephone number on it. 'That's Harding's personal line. Find a nice hotel. Maybe I'll pop down and visit. Washington's an interesting town.'

Mention of the name reminded her of Morris's questions.

'Do you know anything about this Nekich killing?'

There was the briefest pause. 'Who told you about that?'

'It was written up in the *Washington Post*. Morris was asking me about it – if my *Tass* friends had anything to say.'

'What's it got to do with Morris?'

'I don't know.'

She could practically hear his brain working. His mind had spotted some link, some connection, some congruence that seemed odd to him. His face changed: his lips pouted then made a kind of grimace.

'Why should Morris Devereux be interested in an NKVD assassination?'

'So it *was* an assassination – not a suicide.' She shrugged. 'He said he was due to meet this man – Nekich.'

'Are you sure?' She could see that Romer found this unusual. 'I was meant to meet him.'

'Maybe you both were. That's what he told me.'

'I'll give him a call. Look, I'd better go.' He leant forward. 'Call me once you've made contact with Harding.' He raised his coffee-cup to his lips and spoke over the rim and mouthed something at her, an endearment, she hoped but she couldn't make it out. Always cover your mouth when you have something important to convey – another Romer rule – against lip-readers. 'We'll call it Operation Eldorado,' he said. 'Harding is "Gold".' He put his cup down and went to pay the bill.

7

Super-Jolie Nana

I WAS RATHER HOPING that Hamid would cancel his tutorial – perhaps even put in a request for a change of tutor – but there was no call from OEP so I worked my way, somewhat distractedly, through Hugues's lessons, trying to keep my mind off the advancing hour when Hamid and I would meet again. Hugues seemed to notice nothing of my vague agitation and spent a large part of his tutorial telling me, in French, about some vast abattoir in Normandy he had visited once and how it was staffed almost exclusively by fat women.

I walked him to the landing outside the kitchen door and we stood in the sun, looking down on the garden below. My new furniture – white plastic table, four plastic chairs and an unopened cerise and pistachio umbrella – was set out at the end under the big sycamore. Mr Scott was doing his jumping exercises around the flowerbeds, like a Rumplestilt-skin in a white coat trying to stamp through the surface of the earth to the seething magma beneath. He flapped his arms and leapt up and down, moved sideways and repeated the exercise.

'Who is that madman?' Hugues asked.

'My landlord and my dentist.'

'You let that lunatic fix your teeth?'

'He's the sanest man I've ever met.'

Hugues said goodbye and clanged down the stairs. I rested my rump against the balustrade, watching Mr Scott move into his deep-breathing routine (touch the knees, throw back arms and inflate lungs), and heard Hugues bump into Hamid in the alleyway that ran along the side of the house. Some trick of the acoustics – the tone of their voices and the proximity of the brickwork – carried their words up to me on the landing.

'*Bonjour*, Hamid. *Ça va?*'

'*Ça va.*'

'She's in a strange mood today.'

'Ruth?'

'Yeah. She's sort of not connecting.'

'Oh.'

Pause. I heard Hugues light a cigarette.

'You like her?' Hugues asked.

'Sure.'

'I think she's sexy. In an English way – you know.'

'I like her very much.'

'Good figure, man. *Super-jolie nana.*'

'Figure?' Hamid was not concentrating.

'You know.' At this point Hugues must have gestured. I assumed he would be delineating the size of my breasts.

Hamid laughed nervously. 'I never really notice.'

They parted and I waited for Hamid to climb the stairs. Head down, he might have been mounting a scaffold.

'Hamid,' I said. 'Morning.'

He looked up.

'Ruth, I come to apologise and then I am going to OEP to request a new tutor.'

I calmed him down, took him into the study and reassured him that I wasn't offended, that these complications happened between mature students and teachers, especially in one-on-one tutorials, also given the long relationships that the OEP teaching programme necessitated. One of those things, no hard feelings, let's carry on as if nothing has happened. He listened to me patiently and then said,

'No, Ruth, please. I am sincere. I am in love with you.'

'What's the point? You're going to Indonesia in two weeks. We'll never see each other again. Let's forget it – we're friends. We'll always be friends.'

'No, I have to be honest with you, Ruth. This is my feeling. This is what I feel in my heart. I know you don't feel the same for me but I am obliged to tell you what my feelings was.'

'Were.'

'Were.'

We sat in silence for a while, Hamid never taking his eyes off me.

'What're you going to do?' I said, finally. 'Do you want to carry on with the lessons?'

'If you don't mind.'

'Let's see how we get on, anyway. Do you want a cup of tea? I could murder a cup of tea.'

On uncanny cue, there was a knock on the door.

Ilse pushed it open and said, 'Sorry, Ruth. Where is tea? I am looking but Ludger is sleeping still.'

We went into the kitchen and I made a pot of tea for Hamid, Ilse, myself and, in due course, a sleepy Ludger.

Bobbie York feigned huge astonishment – hand on forehead, staggering backward a few feet – when I called round to see him, unannounced.

'What have I done to deserve this?' he said as he poured me one of his 'tiny' whiskies. 'Twice in one week. I feel I should – I don't know – dance a jig, run naked through the quad, slaughter a cow, or something.'

'I need to ask your advice,' I said, as flatteringly as possible.

'Where to publish your thesis?'

'Fraid not. How to arrange a meeting with Lord Mansfield of Hampton Cleeve.'

'Ah, the plot thickens. Just write a letter and ask for an appointment.'

'Life doesn't work like that, Bobbie. There's got to be a reason. He's retired, he's in his seventies, by all accounts something of a recluse. Why would he want to meet me, a complete stranger?'

'Fair point.' Bobbie handed me my drink and slowly sat down. 'How's that burn of yours, by the way?'

'Much better, thank you.'

'Well, why don't you say you're writing an essay – about something he was involved in. Publishing, journalism.'

'Or what he did in the war.'

'Or what he did in the war – even more intriguing.' Bobbie was no fool. 'I suspect that's where your interest lies. You're a historian, after all – tell him you're writing a book and that you want to interview him.'

I thought about this. 'Or a newspaper article.'

'Yes – much better. Appeal to his vanity. Say it's for the *Telegraph* or *The Times*. That might flush him out.'

On my way home I stopped at a newsagent and bought copies of all the broadsheets just to refresh my memory. I thought to myself: can one just say one is writing an article for *The Times* or the *Telegraph*? Yes, I told myself, it's not a lie – anyone can write an article for these newspapers but there's no guarantee they'll accept it; it would only be a lie if you said you'd been commissioned when you hadn't. I picked up the *Telegraph*, thinking this was more likely to appeal to a noble lord, but then bought the others – it had been a long time since I had read my way through a bundle of British newspapers. As I gathered the broadsheets together I saw a copy of the *Frankfurter Allgemeine*. On the front page was a picture of the same man who I had seen on television – Baader, the one Ludger claimed to have known in his porno days. The headline was about the trial of the Baader-Meinhof gang in Stammheim. July 4th – the trial was in its 120th day. I added it to my pile. First Ludger staying, now the mysterious Ilse – I felt I needed to reacquaint myself with the world of German urban terrorism. I drove home with my reading matter and that night, after I had put Jochen to bed (Ludger and Ilse had gone out to the pub), I wrote a letter to Lucas Romer, Baron Mansfield of Hampton Cleeve, care of the House of Lords, requesting an interview for an article I was writing for the *Daily Telegraph* about the British Secret Service in World War Two. I felt strange writing 'Dear Lord Mansfield', writing to this man who had been my mother's lover. I was very brief and to the point – it would be interesting to see what reply he made, if at all.

The Story of Eva Delectorskaya

Washington DC. 1941

EVA DELECTORSKAYA CALLED ROMER in New York.

'I've struck gold,' she said and hung up.

Arranging an appointment with Mason Harding had been very straightforward. Eva took the train from New York to Washington and booked into the London Hall Apartment Hotel on 11th and M streets. She realised she was subconsciously drawn to hotels that carried some echo of England. Then she thought that if it was becoming a habit then it was one she should change – another Romer rule – but she liked her one-room apartment with its tiny galley kitchen and ice-box and the gleaming clean shower. She reserved it for two weeks and, once she had unpacked, she called the number Romer had given her.

'Mason Harding.'

She introduced herself, saying that she worked for Trans-oceanic Press in New York and she would like to request an interview with Mr Hopkins.

'I'm afraid Mr Hopkins is unwell,' Harding said, then added, 'Are you English?'

'Sort of. Half Russian.'

'Sounds a dangerous mixture.'

'Can I call by your office? There may be other stories we can run – Transoceanic has a huge readership in South and Latin America.'

Harding was very amenable – he suggested the end of the afternoon the following day.

Mason Harding was a young man in his early thirties, Eva guessed, whose thick brown hair was cut and severely parted like a schoolboy's. He was putting on weight and his even, handsome features were softened by a layer of fat on his cheeks and his jaw-bone. He wore a pale fawn seersucker suit and on his desk a sign said 'Mason Harding III'.

'So,' he said, offering her a seat and looking her up and down. 'Transoceanic Press – can't say I've heard of you.'

She gave him a rough outline of Transoceanic's reach and readership; he nodded, seemingly taking it in. She said she'd been sent down to Washington to interview key officials in the new administration.

'Sure. Where are you staying?'

She told him. He asked her a few questions about London, the war and had she been there in the Blitz? Then he looked at his watch.

'You want to get a drink? I think we close at five or thereabouts, these days.'

They left the Department of Commerce, a vast classical monster of a building – with a façade more like a museum than a department of state – and they walked a few blocks north on 15th Street to a dark bar that Mason – 'Please call me Mason' – knew and where, once settled inside, they both ordered Whisky Macs, Mason's suggestion. It was a chilly day: they could do with some warming up.

Eva asked some dutiful questions about Hopkins and Mason told her a few bland facts, except for the information that Hopkins had had 'half his stomach removed' in an operation some years ago for stomach cancer. Mason was careful to mention his department's and the Roosevelt administration's admiration of British resolve and pluck.

'You got to understand, Eve,' he said, savouring his second Whisky Mac, 'it's incredibly hard for Hopkins and FDR to do anything more. If it was up to us we'd be in there beside you, shoulder to shoulder, fighting those damn Nazis. Want another? Waiter! Sir?' He signalled for another drink. 'But the vote in Congress has to be won before we go to war. Roosevelt knows he'll never win it. Not now. Something has to happen to change people's attitudes. You ever been to an America First rally?'

Eva said she had. She remembered it well: an Irish-American priest hectoring the crowd about British iniquity and duplicity. Eighty per cent of Americans were against entering the war. America had intervened in the last war and had gained nothing except the Depression. The United States was safe from attack – there was no need to help England again. England was broke, finished: don't waste American money and American lives trying to save her skin. And so on – to massive cheers and applause.

'Well, you see the problem writ large,' Mason said, with a resigned apologetic tone, like a doctor diagnosing an incurable illness. 'I don't want a Nazi Europe, God no – we'll be next on the list, for sure. Trouble is hardly anybody else reads it that way.'

They talked on and in the course of their conversation it emerged that Mason was married and had two children – boys: Mason junior and Farley – and that he lived in Alexandria. After his third Whisky Mac he asked her what she was doing, Saturday. She said she had no plans and so he volunteered to show her around the city – he had to come into the office, anyway, to tidy up a few things.

So, on Saturday, Mason picked her up in the morning outside the London Hall Hotel in his smart green sedan and toured her around the city's key sights. She saw the White House, the Washington Monument, the Lincoln Memorial, the Capitol and finally the National Gallery. They lunched at a restaurant called Du Barry on Connecticut Avenue.

'Look, I mustn't keep you any longer,' Eva said as Mason paid the bill. 'Don't you have to get to your office?'

'Oh, heck, it can wait till Monday. Anyway, I want to take you out to Arlington.'

He dropped her back at her hotel before six. He told her to come by the office on Monday afternoon when he would have some news on Hopkins's state of health and if and when he were likely to be available for interview. They shook hands, Eva thanking him warmly for her 'great day', then she went to her hotel room and made the call to Romer.

Mason Harding tried to kiss her on Monday evening. After their meeting – 'Still no Harry, I'm afraid' – they had gone back to his bar and he had drunk too much. Coming out, it had been raining and they waited under a shop awning until the brisk shower passed over. As the rain abated, they dashed for his car. She thought it was a little strange that he combed his hair before starting the engine and driving her back to the London Hall. It was while they were making their farewells that he lunged at her and, averting her face just in time, she felt his lips on her cheek, her jaw, her neck.

'Mason! For God's sake.' She pushed him away.

He recoiled and sat glowering, staring at the steering wheel. 'I'm very attracted to you, Eve,' he said, in a strangely sulky voice, not looking at her, as if this were all the explanation she required.

'I'm sure your wife is very attracted to you, also.'

He sighed and his body sagged in mock fatigue as if this was a tired and over-familiar rebuke.

'We both know what this is about,' he said, turning finally. 'Let's not act like a couple of innocents. You're a beautiful woman. My personal situation has nothing to do with it.'

'I'll call you on Monday,' Eva said and opened the car door.

He grabbed her hand before she could step out and kissed it. She tugged but he wouldn't let it go.

'I've got to go out of town tomorrow,' he said. 'I've got to go to Baltimore for two days. Meet me there – at the Allegany Hotel, 6.00 p.m.'

She said nothing, shook her hand free and slipped out of the car.

'The Allegany Hotel,' he repeated. 'I can get you that Hopkins interview.'

'The gold is very bright and shiny,' Eva said. 'It almost seems to have heat coming off it.'

'Good,' Romer said. She could hear through the receiver the sound of people talking around him.

'Is everything all right?' she asked.

'I'm in the office.'

'They want me to make a sale at the Allegany Hotel, Baltimore, tomorrow, Tuesday, at 6.00 p.m.'

'Don't do or say anything. I'll come down and see you in the morning.'

Romer was in Washington by ten. She went down to the lobby when the front desk called up to her room to tell her he was there and she felt such a leaping and thudding in her heart as she looked around for him that she paused, surprised at herself, surprised that she was reacting this way.

He was sitting in a corner vestibule but, annoyingly, there was another man with him, whom he introduced simply as Bradley. Bradley was a small slim fellow, dark, with a grin that flickered on and off like a faulty light bulb.

When Romer saw her he stood and came to greet her. They shook hands and he led her over to another part of the lobby. When they sat down she reached surreptitiously for his hand.

'Lucas, darling –'

'Don't touch me.'

'Sorry. Who's Bradley?'

'Bradley's a photographer that works for us. Are you ready? I think we should go.'

They caught a train from Union Station. It was a terse almost wordless journey what with Bradley sitting opposite them. Every time Eva looked at him he flashed his short-lived grin at her, like a nervous tic. She preferred to look out of the window at the autumn leaves. She was grateful that the journey was a short one.

At Baltimore Station she told Romer pointedly that she felt like a coffee and a sandwich, so Romer asked Bradley to go ahead to the Allegany and wait for them. Finally, they were alone.

'What's happening?' she said when they sat down in a corner of the station cafeteria, half knowing what the answer would be. There was condensation on the window and with the heel of her hand she wiped a porthole of clarity to see a near-empty street, a few passers-by, a black man selling brilliant posies.

'We need a photograph of you and Harding entering the hotel and leaving the hotel the next morning.'

'I see . . .' She felt sick, suddenly nauseous, but decided to press on. 'Why?'

Romer sighed and looked round before taking hold of her hand under the table.

'People only betray their country for three reasons,' he said, quietly, seriously, cueing her next question.

'And what are they?'

'Money, blackmail and revenge.'

She thought about this, wondering if it were another Romer rule.

'Money, revenge – and blackmail.'

'You know what's going on, Eva. You know what it'll take to make Mr Harding suddenly become very helpful to us.'

She did, thinking of Mrs Harding with all the money and little Mason jun. and Farley.

'Did you plan all this?'

'No.'

She looked at him: liar, her eyes said.

'It's part of the job, Eva. You have no idea how this would change everything. We'd have someone in Hopkins's office, someone close to him.' He paused. 'Close to Hopkins means close to Roosevelt.'

She put a cigarette in her mouth – to confuse any passing lip-readers – and said, 'So I have to sleep with Mason Harding so that SIS can know what Roosevelt and Hopkins are up to.'

'You don't have to sleep with him. As long as we have the photographs – that's all the evidence we require. You can finesse it any way you like.'

She managed a dry little laugh, but it didn't convince her. ' "Finesse" – nice word,' she said. 'I know: I could tell him I was having my period.'

He wasn't amused. 'You're being stupid, now. You're letting yourself down. This actually isn't about your feelings – this is why you joined us.' He sat back. 'But if you want to abort – just tell me.'

She said nothing. She was thinking about what lay ahead of her. She wondered if she were capable of doing what Romer required of her. She wondered also what he was feeling – he seemed so cold and matter-of-fact.

'How would you feel?' she asked him. 'If I did it.'

He said, immediately, flatly: 'We've got a job to do.'

She tried not to show the hurt that was growing in her. There were so many other things you could have said, she thought, that would have made it a little easier.

'You have to think of it as a job, Eva,' he continued, in a softer voice, as if he could read her mind. 'Keep your feelings out of it. You may have even more unpleasant things to do before this war is over.' He covered his mouth with his hand. 'I shouldn't be telling you this, but the pressures from London are huge, immense.' He went on. BSC had one solitary vital task: to persuade America it was in her interest to join the war in Europe. That was all, pure and simple – get America in. He reminded her that it was over three months since the first meeting between Churchill and Roosevelt. 'We've got our wonderful, much-heralded Atlantic Charter,' he said, 'and what's happened? Nothing. You've seen the press back at home. "Where are the Yanks?", "What's keeping the Yanks?" We have to get closer. We have to get inside the White House. You can help – simple as that.'

'But how do *you* feel about it?' It was the wrong question to ask again, she knew, and she saw his face change, but she wanted to be brutal, wanted him to confront the reality of what she was being asked to do. 'How do *you* feel about me and Mason Harding in bed together.'

'I just want us to win this war,' he said. 'My feelings are irrelevant.'

'All right,' she said, feeling ashamed and then feeling angry for feeling ashamed. 'I'll do what I can.'

She was waiting in the lobby at six when Mason arrived. He kissed her on the cheek and they registered at reception as Mr and Mrs Avery. She could sense his tension as they stood at the front desk – she felt that adultery was not run-of-the-mill in Mason Harding's life. As he signed the register she looked around; somewhere she knew Bradley was taking pictures; later someone would pay the clerk for a copy of the booking. They went up to their room and, once the bellhop had left, Mason kissed her with more passion, touched her breasts, thanked her, told her she was the most beautiful woman he had ever met.

They dined in the hotel restaurant, early, and Mason spent most of the meal quietly but forcefully denigrating his wife and her family and their financial hold over him. This mood of petulance helped her, she found; it was boring, small-minded and selfish and it allowed her to step back from any vision of what was about to ensue. It made her colder. People betray their country for only three reasons, Romer had said. Mason Harding was about to take the first step along that narrow, winding road.

They both drank too much, from different motives, she supposed, but as they went up to their room she felt her head whirl with the alcohol. Mason kissed her in the elevator, using his tongue. In the room, he called room service and ordered up a pint of whisky, and once it was delivered, began almost immediately to undress her. Eva switched on a smile, drank some more and thought, at least he isn't ugly or nasty – he was just a kind foolish man who wanted to betray his wife. To her surprise she found she was able to switch her feelings off. It's a job, she said to herself, one only I can do.

In bed, he tried but was unable to control himself and was ashamed at how quickly he came, blaming it on the condoms – 'Damn Trojans!' Eva soothed him, said it was more important just being together. He drank more whisky and tried again later but with no success.

She consoled him again, letting him hold her and caress her, huddling in his arms, feeling the room tilt and sway from all the booze she had drunk.

'It's always crap the first time,' he said. 'Don't you find that?'

'Always,' she said, not hating him – indeed feeling a little sorry for him and wondering what he would think in a day or so when someone – not Romer – approached him and said, Hello, Mr Harding, we have some photographs that I think your wife and father-in-law would be most interested in viewing.

He fell asleep quickly and she eased herself across the bed from him. She managed to sleep, herself, but woke early and ran a deep bath, soaked in it, and then ordered up a room-service breakfast before Mason awoke to pre-empt any early-morning amorousness, but he was crapulous and out of sorts – guilty, perhaps – and had turned moody and monosyllabic. She let him kiss her again in the room before they went down to the lobby.

He paid the bill and she stood close to him, picking some lint off his jacket as he paid the clerk in cash. Click. She could practically hear Bradley's camera. Outside at the taxi rank he seemed self-conscious and stiff all of a sudden.

'I've got meetings,' he said. 'What about you?'

'I'll get back to town,' she said. 'I'll call you. It'll be better next time, don't worry.'

This promise seemed to revive him and he smiled warmly.

'Thanks, Eve,' he said. 'You were great. You're beautiful. Call me next week. I got to take the kids . . .' he stopped. 'Call me next week. Wednesday.'

He kissed her on the cheek and in her head she heard another Bradley 'click' go off.

When she returned to London Hall there was a message – a note shoved under her door.

'ELDORADO is over,' it read.

'Oh, you're back,' Sylvia said when she came home from work and found Eva in the apartment, sitting in the kitchen. 'How was Washington?'

'Boring.'

'I thought you'd be gone for a couple of weeks.'

'There was nothing doing. Endless round of insignificant press conferences.'

'Meet any nice men?' Sylvia said, putting on a grotesque leer.

'I wish. Just a fat under-secretary of state at Agriculture, or something, who tried to feel me up.'

'I might just settle for that,' Sylvia said, heading for her bedroom, taking off her coat.

Sometimes it amazed Eva how fluently and spontaneously she

could lie. Think that everybody is lying to you all the time, Romer said, it's probably the safest way to proceed.

Sylvia came back in and opened the ice-box and took out a small pitcher of Martini.

'We're celebrating,' she said, then made an apologetic face. 'Sorry. Wrong word. The Germans have sunk another Yank destroyer – the *Reuben Jones*. One hundred and fifteen dead. Hardly a cause for rejoicing, I know. But . . .'

'My God . . . One hundred and fifteen –'

'Exactly. This has got to change everything. They can't stand on the sidelines now.'

So much for Mason Harding, Eva thought. She had a sudden image of Mason, slipping out of his underwear, his thickening cock jutting beneath the eave of his young man's belly, coming to sit on the bed, fumbling with the foil on the condom. She found she could think about it with dispassion, coldly, objectively. Romer would have been pleased with her.

As she poured their Martinis, Sylvia told her that Roosevelt had made a fine, stirringly belligerent speech – his most belligerent since 1939, talking of how the 'shooting war' had begun.

'Oh yes,' she said, sipping her drink. 'And he has this wonderful map – some map of South America. How the Germans plan to divide it up into five huge new countries.'

Eva was half listening but Sylvia's enthusiasm provoked in her a small surge of confidence – a strange feeling of temporary elation. Similar spasms had come and gone in the two years since she'd joined Romer's team. Although she tried to tell herself to treat such instinctive reactions with suspicion she couldn't prevent them from blossoming in herself – as if wishful thinking were an innate attribute of being human: the thought that things were bound to improve being stitched into our human consciousness. She sipped her cold drink – maybe that's just the definition of an optimist, she thought. Maybe that's all I am: an optimist.

'So maybe we're getting there,' she said, drinking her chilled Martini, yielding to her optimism, thinking that if the Americans join us we must win. America, Britain and the Empire, and Russia – then it could only be a matter of time.

'Let's eat out tomorrow,' she said to Sylvia as they went to their bedrooms. 'We owe ourselves a little party.'

'Don't forget we're saying goodbye to Alfie.'

Eva remembered that Blytheswood was leaving the radio station and was going back to London, to Electra House, the GC&CS's radio interception station in the basement of Cable & Wireless's Embankment office.

'Then we can go dancing afterwards,' she said. She felt like dancing, she thought as she undressed and tried to empty her mind of Mason Harding and his hands on her body.

The next day in the office Morris Devereux showed her a transcript of the Roosevelt speech. She took it from him and flicked through the pages until she came to the relevant passage:

'I have in my possession a secret map,' she read, 'made in Germany by Hitler's government. It is a map of South America as Hitler proposes to reorganise it. The geographical experts of Berlin have divided South America into five vassal states . . . They have also arranged that one of these new puppet states includes the Republic of Panama and our great lifeline, the Panama Canal . . . This map makes clear the Nazi design not only against South America but against the United States as well.'

'Well,' she said to Devereux, 'pretty strong stuff, don't you think? If I were an American I'd be beginning to feel just a little uneasy. A tiny bit worried, no?'

'Let's hope they share your sentiments – and what with the *Reuben Jones*'s sinking . . . I don't know: you'd think they wouldn't sleep quite so securely.' He smiled at her. 'How was Washington?'

'Fine. I think I've made a good contact in Hopkins's office,' she said offhandedly. 'A press attaché. I think we can feed him our stuff.'

'Interesting. Did he drop any hints?'

'No, not really,' she said carefully. 'He was actually very discouraging, if anything. Congress ranged against war. FDR's hands tied, and so forth. But I'm going to give him translations of all our Spanish stories.'

'Good idea,' he said vaguely and drifted away.

Eva started thinking: Morris seemed more and more interested in her movements and her work. But why hadn't he asked her the name of the press attaché she had lassoed? That *was* odd . . . Did he know who it was already?

She went to her office and checked her in-tray. A newspaper in Buenos Aires, *Critica*, had picked up her story about German naval manoeuvres off the South American Atlantic coast. She had her opening, now: she re-transcribed the story but gave it a Buenos Aires date-line and put it out to all of Transoceanic's subscribers. She called Blytheswood at WRUL and, using their verbal priority code – 'Mr Blytheswood, this is Miss Dalton here' – said she had an intriguing story out of Argentina. Blytheswood said they might indeed be interested but it would have to have an American date-line before it could be broadcast around the world. So she sent a cablegram to Johnson in Meadowville, and Witoldski in Franklin Forks, signed simply Transoceanic, plus a transcript of the key lines from Roosevelt's speech. She suspected they would guess it was from her. If either Johnson or Witoldski broadcast the *Critica* report she could reconfigure it once more as a story from an independent US radio station. And so the fiction would move on steadily through the news media, accumulating weight and significance – more date-lines, more sources somehow confirming its emerging status as a fact and nowhere revealing its origins in the mind of Eva Delectorskaya. Eventually one of the big American newspapers would pick it up (perhaps with a little help from Angus Woolf) and the German

Embassy would cable it back home to Berlin. Then denials would be issued, ambassadors would be called in to deliver explanations and rebuttals and this would provide yet another story, or a series of stories, for Transoceanic to distribute over its wire services. Eva felt a small sense of power and pride as she contemplated the future life of her falsehood – thinking of herself as a tiny spider at the centre of her spreading, complex web of innuendo, half-truth and invention. But then she felt a hot flush of embarrassed remembrance, recalling suddenly her night with Mason Harding, and its fumbling inadequacies. It was always going to be a dirty war, Romer repeatedly said, nothing should be discounted in the waging of it.

She was walking homewards along Central Park South, looking out at the trees in the park, already yellow and orange with the advancing fall, when she became aware of a set of footsteps maintaining the exact same cadence as hers. This was one of the tricks she had learned at Lyne – it was almost as effective as someone tapping you on the shoulder. She stopped to adjust the strap on her shoe and, looking casually round, saw Romer three or four paces behind her, staring intently into the window of a jeweller's shop. He turned on his heel and, after a brief pause, she followed him back along Sixth Avenue, where she saw him go into a large delicatessen. She joined the queue at the counter further down from him and watched him order a sandwich and a beer and go to sit in a busy corner. She bought a coffee and walked over to him.

'Hello,' she said. 'May I join you?'

She sat down.

'All very clandestine,' she said.

'We all have to take more precautions,' he said. 'Double-check, triple-check. To tell the truth, we're a little worried that some of our American friends have become too intrigued by what we're up to. I think we've grown too large – impossible to ignore the scale of the thing, anymore. So: extra effort, more snares, watch for shadows, friendly crows, strange noises on the telephone. Just a hunch – but we've all been getting a bit complacent.'

'Right,' she said, watching him bite into his vast sandwich. Nothing that size had ever been seen in the British Isles, she thought. He chewed and swallowed for a while before speaking.

'I wanted to tell you that everyone's very pleased about Washington. I've been taking all the compliments but I wanted to say that you did well, Eva. Very well. Don't think that I take it for granted. Don't think that we take it for granted.'

'Thank you.' She didn't exactly feel a warm glow of self-satisfaction.

' "Gold" is going to be our golden boy.'

'Good,' she said, then thought. 'Is he already –'

'He was activated yesterday.'

'Oh.' Eva thought about Mason: she had an image of somebody spreading photos on a table before his appalled face. She could see him weeping, even. I wonder what he thinks about me now? she thought, uncomfortably. 'What if he calls me?' she asked.

'He won't call you.' Romer paused. 'We've never been so close to the chief before. Thanks to you.'

'Maybe we won't need him for long,' she suggested vaguely, as if to assuage her mounting guilt, to keep the tarnish to a minimum for a while.

'Why do you say that?'

'The *Reuben Jones* going down.'

'It doesn't seem to have made any material difference to public opinion,' Romer said, with some sarcasm. 'People seem more interested in the result of the Army–Notre Dame match.'

She couldn't understand this. 'Why? There's a hundred dead young sailors, for God's sake.'

'U-boats sinking US ships got them into the last war,' he said, putting two-thirds of his sandwich down, admitting defeat. 'They've got long memories.' He smiled at her unpleasantly. His mood was odd that evening, she thought, almost angry in some way. 'They don't want to be in this war, Eva, whatever their president or Harry Hopkins or Gale Winant thinks.' He gestured at the crowded deli: the men and women, the working day over, the children, laughing, chatting, buying their enormous sandwiches and their fizzy drinks. 'Life's good here. They're happy. Why mess it up going to war 3,000 miles away? Would you?'

She had no ready, convincing answer.

'Yes, but what about this map?' she said, sensing herself losing the argument. 'Doesn't that change things?' She thought further, as if she were trying to persuade herself. 'And Roosevelt's speech. They can't deny it's getting closer. Panama – it's their back yard.'

Romer, she saw, allowed himself a slight smile at her earnest ardour.

'Yes, well, I have to admit we're quite pleased with that,' he said. 'We never expected it to work so efficiently or so quickly.'

She waited a second before asking her question, trying to seem as unconcerned as possible.

'It's ours, you mean? The map is ours – is that what you're saying?'

Romer looked at her with mild rebuke in his eyes, as if she were being too slow, lagging behind the class. 'Of course. Here's the story: German courier crashed his car in Rio de Janiero. Careless fellow. He was taken to hospital. In his briefcase was this fascinating map. Rather too convenient, don't you think? I was very reluctant to go down that road but our friends seem to have bought it wholesale.' He paused. 'By the way, I want you to get all this out on Transoceanic tomorrow. Everywhere – date-line US government, Washington DC. Have you pen and paper?'

Eva rummaged in her handbag for notebook and pencil and took down in shorthand everything that Romer listed: five new countries in the South American continent as displayed on Roosevelt's secret map. 'Argentina' now included Uruguay and Paraguay and half of Bolivia; 'Chile' took in the other half of Bolivia and the whole of Peru. 'New Spain' was composed of Colombia, Venezuela and Ecuador and, crucially, the Panama Canal. Only 'Brazil' remained substantially as it was.

'I must say it was a rather beautiful document: "*Argentinien, Brasilien, Neu Spanien*" – all criss-crossed by proposed Lufthansa routes.' He chuckled to himself.

Eva put her notebook away and used the excuse to sit quiet for a while, taking this in and realising that her gullibility, her susceptibility was still an issue – was she too easy to deceive, perhaps? Never believe anything, Romer said, never, never. Always look for the other explanations, the other options, the other side.

When she raised her eyes she found he was looking at her differently. Fondly, she would have said, with an undercurrent of carnal interest.

'I miss you, Eva.'

'I miss you, too, Lucas. But what can we do about it?'

'I'm going to send you on a course to Canada. You know, care of documents, filing, that sort of thing.'

She knew this meant Station M – a BSC forging laboratory run under cover of the Canadian Broadcasting Company. Station M produced all their fake documentation – she assumed the map had come from them, also.

'For how long?'

'A few days – but you can have a bit of leave before you go, as reward for all your good work. I suggest Long Island.'

'Long Island? Oh, yes?'

'Yes. I can recommend the Narragansett Inn in St James. A Mr and Mrs Washington have a room booked there this weekend.'

She felt an instinctive sexual quickening within her. A slackening, then a tightening of her bowels.

'Sounds nice,' she said, her eyes steady on his. 'Lucky Mr and Mrs Washington.' She stood up. 'I'd better go. Sylvia and I are going out on the town.'

'Well, be careful, be watchful,' he said, seriously, suddenly like an anxious parent. 'Triple-check.'

At that moment Eva wondered if she was in love with Lucas Romer. She wanted to kiss him, more than anything, wanted to touch his face.

'Right,' she said. 'Will do.'

He stood up, and left some coins on the table as a tip. 'Have you got your safe place?'

'Yes,' she said. Her safe house in New York was a one-room cold-water apartment in Brooklyn. 'I've got somewhere out of town.' It was almost true.

'Good.' He smiled. 'Enjoy your leave.'

On Friday evening Eva caught a train to Long Island. At Farmingdale she stepped off and caught another immediately back to Brooklyn. She left the station and wandered around for ten minutes before catching another train on the branch line that ended at Port Jefferson. There, she took a taxi to the bus station at St James. As they motored away from Port Jefferson she watched the cars that were behind them. There was one that seemed to be keeping its distance but when she asked the taxi driver to slow down it swiftly overtook. From the bus station she walked to the Narragansett Inn – she had no shadow as far as she could tell – she was rigorously obeying Romer's instructions. She was pleased to see that the inn was a large, comfortable, cream clapboard house set in a well-kept garden on the outskirts of town, with a distant view of the dunes. She felt a cold wind blowing off the Sound and was glad of her coat. Romer was waiting for her in the residents' sitting-room, where there was a snapping driftwood fire burning in the grate. Mr and Mrs Washington went straight upstairs to their room and didn't emerge until the next morning.

8

Brydges'

I READ THE LETTER out loud to my mother:

> Dear Ms Gilmartin,
>
> Lord Mansfield thanks you for your communication but regrets that, owing to pressure of work, he is unable to comply with your request for an interview.
>
> Yours sincerely,
> Anna Orloggi
> (Assistant to Lord Mansfield)

'It's on House of Lords notepaper,' I added. My mother crossed the room and took the sheet from me, scrutinising it with unusual concentration, her lips moving as she reread the terse message of refusal. I wasn't sure if she was excited or not. She seemed calm enough.

'Anna Orloggi . . . I love it,' she said. 'I bet she doesn't exist.' Then she paused. 'Look,' she said. 'There's the telephone number.' She began to pace up and down my sitting-room. She'd come for an appointment with Mr Scott – a crown had loosened – and she had popped up, unannounced, to see me. The letter had arrived that morning.

'Do you want a glass of something?' I asked. 'Squash? Coca-Cola?' It was my lunch break: Bérangère had just left and

Hamid was due at two. Ludger and Ilse had gone to London to 'see a friend'.

'I'll have a Coke,' she said.

'When did you stop drinking?' I said, going through to the kitchen. 'You certainly drank a lot in the war.'

'I think you know why,' she said drily, following me through. She took the glass from me and had a sip but I could see her mind was working. 'Actually, call that number now,' she said, her face suddenly animated. 'That's the thing: and say you want to talk to him about AAS Ltd, that should work.'

'Are you sure about this?' I asked. 'You could be opening some hideous can of worms.'

'Yes, that's exactly the idea,' she said.

I dialled the London number with some reluctance and then listened to it ring and ring. I was about to hang up when a woman's voice answered.

'Lord Mansfield's office.'

I explained who I was and that I'd just received a letter from Lord Mansfield.

'Ah, yes. I'm very sorry but Lord Mansfield is abroad and in any event does not grant interviews.'

So he doesn't 'grant' interviews, I thought. The woman's voice was clipped and patrician – I wondered if this was Anna Orloggi.

'Would you be so kind as to tell him,' I said, deciding to emphasise the patrician qualities in my own voice, 'that I want to ask him some questions about AAS Ltd.'

'It won't make any difference, I'm afraid.'

'I'm afraid it will if you *don't* tell him, especially to your continued employment. I know absolutely that he'll want to speak to me. AAS Ltd – it's very important. You have my phone number on my original letter. I'd be most grateful. Thank you so much.'

'I can't promise anything.'

'AAS Ltd. Please be sure to tell him. Thank you. Goodbye.' I hung up.

'Good girl,' my mother said. 'I'd rather hate to have you on the end of a phone.'

We wandered back through to the kitchen. I pointed out my new garden furniture and my mother duly admired it, but she wasn't concentrating.

'I know he'll see you now,' she said, thoughtfully. 'He won't be able to resist.' Then she turned and smiled. 'How was your date?'

I told her about Hamid and his declaration of love.

'How marvellous,' she said. 'Do you like him?'

'Yes,' I said. 'Very much. But I don't love him back.'

'Shame. But is he kind?'

'Yes. But he's a Muslim, Sal, and he's going to work in Indonesia. I can see where this conversation is going. No – he is not going to become Jochen's stepfather.'

She wouldn't stay for lunch but she told me to call her the minute I heard from Romer. Hamid arrived for his lesson and he seemed fine, more composed. We spent our time on a new chapter with the Ambersons – now returned from their unsatisfactory holiday at Corfe Castle only to have Rasputin run away – and explored the mysteries of the present perfect progressive. 'Rasputin has been acting a little strangely lately.' 'The neighbours have been complaining about his barking.' The fear of poisoning entered the cloistered world of Darlington Crescent. As he left Hamid asked me again to have dinner with him at Browns on Friday night but I said instantly that I was busy. He took me at my word: he seemed to have lost the agitation of our previous conversations but I noted the new invitation – it clearly wasn't over yet.

Veronica and I – the single-mother sluts – stood smoking outside Grindle's, waiting for our children.

'How's Sally?' Veronica asked. 'Any better?'

'I think so,' I said. 'But there are still worrying signs. She's bought a shotgun.'

'Christ . . .'

'To kill rabbits, she says. And the story about what she did in the war gets ever more . . . extraordinary.'

'Do you believe her?'

'Yes, I do,' I said bluntly, as if confessing to some crime. I had thought about this matter regularly and repeatedly but the story of Eva Delectorskaya was too textured, detailed and precise to be the product of a mind convulsed with fantastical re-invention, let alone on the verge of senile dementia. I had found the experience of reading the regular supply of pages disturbing because the Eva/Sally figures still refused to converge in my mind. When I read that Eva had slept with Mason Harding so that he could be blackmailed I couldn't connect that historical fact, that act of personal sacrifice, that deliberate surrender of a personal moral code, with the rangy, handsome woman who had been pacing about my sitting-room a few hours ago. What did it take to have sex with a stranger for your country? Maybe it was straightforward – a rational decision. Was it any different from a soldier killing his enemy for his country? Or, more to the point, lying to your closest allies for your country? Perhaps I was too young – perhaps I needed to have been living during World War Two? I had a feeling I'd never truly understand.

Jochen and Avril came bounding out of the school and the four of us wandered back up the Banbury Road.

'We're having a heatwave,' Jochen said.

'A tropical heatwave. That's what it is.'

'Is it like a wave in the sea? A wave of heat washing over us?' he asked, making a swooping wave gesture with his hand.

'Or,' I said, 'is the sun waving at us, making the heat blow down on earth.'

'That's just silly, Mummy,' he said, unamused.

I apologised and we wandered homeward, chatting. Veronica and I made plans to have supper together on Saturday night.

In the flat I was setting about making Jochen his tea when the phone rang.

'Ms Gilmartin?'

'Speaking.'

'This is Anna Orloggi.' It was the same woman – she pronounced her surname without a hint of an Italian accent, as if she were from one of the oldest families in England.

'Yes,' I said, aimlessly. 'Hello.'

'Lord Mansfield will see you in his club on Friday evening at 6.00 p.m. Have you a pen and paper?'

I took down the details: Brydges' was his club – not Brydges Club, just Brydges' – and an address off St James's.

'Six p.m. this Friday,' Anna Orloggi repeated.

'I'll be there.'

I hung up and felt an immediate elation that our ruse had worked and also a disturbing nervousness, knowing that I was finally going to be the one to meet Lucas Romer. Everything had become real, all of a sudden, and I felt the elation give way to a small squirm of nausea and my mouth seemed suddenly dry of all saliva as I thought about this encounter. I knew I was experiencing an emotion that I claimed to be immune to – I was feeling just a little bit frightened.

'Are you all right, Mummy?' Jochen asked.

'Yes. Fine, darling. Twinge of toothache.'

I called my mother to tell her the news.

'It worked,' I reported, 'just like you said.'

'Good,' she said, her voice quite calm. 'I knew it would. I'll tell you exactly what to say and do.'

As I hung up a knock came on the door that led down from the flat to the surgery below. I opened the door to find Mr Scott standing there, beaming, as if – through the floor – he'd heard me say 'twinge of toothache' and had bounded upstairs to minister to me. But behind him was a hot, short-haired young man in a cheap dark suit.

'Hello, hello, Ruth Gilmartin,' Mr Scott said. 'Great excitement. This young man's a policeman – a detective, no less – wants to have a word with you. See you later – maybe . . .'

I showed the detective into the sitting-room. He took a seat, asked if he might remove his jacket – steaming hot outside – and said his name was Detective Constable Frobisher, a name I found reassuring, for some perverse reason, I thought, as DC Frobisher hung his jacket carefully over the arm of a chair and sat down again.

'Just a few questions,' he said taking out and flicking through his notebook. 'We've had a request from the Metropolitan Police. They're interested in the whereabouts of a young woman named . . . Ilse Bunzl.' He pronounced it with care. 'Apparently she's called this number from London. Is that right?'

I kept my face impassive. If they knew Ilse had called here, then, I reasoned, somebody's phone must be tapped.

'No,' I said. 'I never got a call. What was her name again?'

'Ilse Bunzl.' He spelt her surname.

'I teach foreign students, you see. So many of them come and go.'

Detective Frobisher made a note – 'teaches foreign students' no doubt – asked a few questions (Was there anyone I was teaching who might know this girl? Were there many Germans signed up to OEP?) and apologised for taking up my time. I showed him out the back door, not wanting to increase Mr Scott's glee. I hadn't lied – everything I had said to the policeman was true.

I walked back through the hall, wondering where Jochen was, then I heard his voice – low, nearly inaudible – coming from the sitting-room: he must have slipped in behind us as we left, I thought. I paused at the door and peered through the crack by the hinge and I saw him sitting on the sofa, a book open in his lap. But he wasn't reading, he was talking to himself and making little placing gestures with his hands as if he were sorting out invisible piles of beans or playing some invisible board game.

I felt, of course, a spontaneous, engulfing, near-intolerable surge of love for him, all the more acute because it was voyeuristic and he had no idea I was watching – his unselfconsciousness was as pure as it could be. He set his book aside and went to the window, still muttering to himself but now pointing things out, in the room and out of the window. What was he doing? What on earth was going on in his head? Who was that writer who said that 'people lead their real, most interesting lives under cover of secrecy'? I knew Jochen better than any being on the planet, yet in some sense, in some degree, the guileless child was already beginning to develop the opacities of the growing boy, the youth, the adult, where the veils of ignorance and unknowing existed even between the people you were closest to. Look at my mother, I thought, wryly – not so much a veil as a thick woollen blanket. And no doubt the same could be said from her side, I reflected, and coughed loudly before I stepped into the sitting-room.

'Who was that man?' Jochen asked.

'A detective.'

'A detective! What did he want?'

'He said he was looking for a dangerous bank robber called Jochen Gilmartin and did I know anyone of that name.'

'Mummy!' He laughed, jabbing his finger repeatedly at me – something he did when he was either particularly amused or extremely angry. He was pleased; I was worried.

I went back to the hall, picked up the phone and called Bobbie York.

The Story of Eva Delectorskaya

New York. 1941

IT WAS TOWARDS THE middle of November that Eva Delectorskaya took the call from Lucas Romer. She was in the Transoceanic offices one morning, working on the spiralling ramifications of her naval-manoeuvres story – every newspaper in South America had picked it up in one way or another – when Romer telephoned himself and suggested meeting on the steps of the Metropolitan Museum. She took the subway to 86th Street and walked down Fifth, crossing the road from the grand apartment buildings to be closer to Central Park. It was a cold breezy day and she tugged her hat down over her ears and knotted her scarf higher round her throat. There was a scatter of autumn leaves on the pavements – or fall leaves on the sidewalks, as she should learn to call them – and the chestnut sellers were out on the street corners, the salty, sweet smoke from their braziers wafting by her from time to time as she sauntered down towards the great edifice of the museum.

She saw Romer standing waiting for her on the steps, hatless and wearing a long dark grey overcoat she hadn't seen before. She smiled instinctively, happily, thinking again of their two days in Long Island. To be in New York in November in 1941, going to meet her lover on the steps of the Metropolitan Museum seemed the most normal and natural of activities in the world – as if her whole life had somehow been steering her in the direction of this particular moment. But the realities massing elsewhere behind this encounter – the war news she'd read in the newspapers this morning, the Germans advancing on Moscow – made her realise that what she and Romer were experiencing was, in actual fact, utterly absurd and surreal. We may be lovers, she reminded herself, but we are also spies: therefore everything is entirely different from what it seems.

He came down the steps to meet her. She saw his frowning, serious face and wanted to kiss him, wanted to go immediately to that hotel across the road and make love all afternoon – but they didn't even touch; they didn't even shake hands. He circled round her and pointed to the park.

'Let's go for a stroll,' he said.

'Nice to see you. I've missed you.'

He looked at her in a manner as if to say: we simply can't talk to each other like this.

'Sorry,' she said, 'Chilly, isn't it?' and walked briskly ahead of him into the park.

He increased his speed and caught up with her. They walked along the pathway in silence for a while and then he said, 'Fancy a bit of winter sunshine?'

They found a bench with a view of a small valley and some craggy rocks. A boy was throwing a stick for a dog that refused to chase it. So the boy would fetch the stick, walk back to the dog and throw it again.

'Winter sunshine?'

'It's a simple BSC courier job,' he said. 'To New Mexico.'

'If it's so simple why don't they do it?'

'Since the Brazil map they want to seem extremely kosher. They're a bit worried that the FBI might be watching them. So they asked me if someone from Transoceanic could do it. I thought of you. You don't have to if you don't want to. I'll ask Morris if you don't fancy it.'

But she did fancy it, as she knew he knew she would.

She shrugged. 'I suppose I could do it.'

'I'm not doing you a favour,' he said. 'I know you'd do a good job. A good secure job. That's what they want. You pick up a package and you give it to someone else and you come home.'

'Who'll run me? Not BSC.'

'Transoceanic will run you.'

'All right.'

He gave her a piece of paper and told her to read it until she'd memorised the details. She studied the words that were written down, remembering Mr Dimarco at Lyne, all his tricks, match colours to words, match memories to numbers. She handed the piece of paper back to Romer.

'Usual telephone code to base?' she asked.

'Yes. All the variations.'

'Where do I go after Albuquerque?'

'The contact there will tell you. It'll be in New Mexico. Possibly Texas.'

'And then what?'

'Come back here and carry on as normal. It should take you three or four days. You'll get some sun, see an interesting part of the country – it's big.'

He moved his hand along the bench and interlinked his little finger with hers.

'When can I see you again?' she said, softly, looking away. 'I loved the Narragansett Inn. Can we go back?'

'Probably not. It's difficult. Things are heating up. London is getting frantic. Everything is rather . . .' He paused, as if to say the words was distasteful. 'Rather out of control.'

'How's "Gold"?'

' "Gold" is our only ray of sunshine. Very helpful, indeed. Which reminds me: this operation you're on is "Cinnamon". You're "Sage".'

' "Sage".'

'You know how they love procedure. They'll have opened a file and written "Cinnamon" on it. "Top Secret".' He reached in his pocket and took out and gave her a bulky, buff envelope.

'What's this?'

'Five thousand dollars. For the man at the end of the line, wherever that is. I would leave tomorrow if I were you.'

'Right.'

'Do you want a gun?'

'Will I need a gun?'

'No. But I always ask.'

'Anyway, I have my nails and my teeth,' she said, making claws with her hands and baring her fangs.

Romer laughed, giving her his wide white smile and she suddenly flashed to Paris and that day when they first met. She had a sudden vision of him crossing the street towards her. She felt weak.

'Bye, Lucas,' she said, then looked at him meaningfully. 'We have to sort something out when I come back.' She paused. 'I don't know if I can carry on like this – it's getting to be a strain. You know what I mean – I think –'

He interrupted her. 'We'll sort something out, don't worry.' He squeezed her hand.

She was going to say it, she didn't care. 'I think I'm in love with you, Lucas, that's why.'

He didn't say anything, just took this in with a slight pursing of the lips. He squeezed her hand again and then let go.

'*Bon voyage*,' he said. 'Be careful.'

'I'm always careful. You know that.'

He stood up, turned and walked away, striding down the path. Eva watched him go, saying to herself: I command you to turn, I insist you turn and look at me again. And sure enough he did – he turned and walked backwards for a few paces and smiled and gave her his familiar half-wave, half-salute.

The next morning Eva went to Penn Station and bought a ticket to Albuquerque, New Mexico.

9

Don Carlos

'PEOPLE WILL THINK WE'RE having an affair,' Bobbie York said. 'All these impromptu visits. I'm not complaining. I'll be very discreet.'

'Thank you, Bobbie,' I said, refusing to participate in his banter. 'You are my supervisor, after all. I'm supposed to come to you for advice.'

'Yes, yes, yes. Of course you are. But how can I advise someone as capable as you?'

I had postponed Bérangère's tutorial so I could see Bobbie in the morning. I didn't want to sit in his rooms as he plied me with whisky again.

'I need to talk to somebody who can tell me about the British Security Services in World War Two. MI5, MI6 – that sort of thing. SIS, SOE, BSC – you know.'

'Yeeesss,' Bobbie said. 'Not my strong point. I sense Lord Mansfield has bitten.'

Bobbie was no fool, however hard he strove to seem like an amiable one.

'He has,' I said. 'I'm to meet him on Friday – at his club. I just feel I need to be a bit more clued-up.'

'My, what drama. You've got to tell me all about this one day, Ruth, I insist. It seems splendidly cloak-and-dagger.'

'I will,' I said. 'I promise. I'm a bit in the dark myself, to tell the truth. As soon as I know I'll fill you in.'

Bobbie went to his desk and searched through some papers.

'One of the very few advantages of living in Oxford,' he said, 'is that there is an expert on just about every subject in the world, sitting on your doorstep. From medieval astrolabes to particle accelerators – we can usually serve one up. Ah, here's the man. Fellow of All Souls called Timothy Thoms.'

'Timothy Thoms?'

'Yes. Thoms spelt with an "h". I know he sounds like a character in a children's book or some harassed clerk in Dickens but he's actually a hundred times cleverer than I am. Mind you – so are you. So you and Timothy Thoms should get along like the proverbial conflagrating house. There: Dr T.C.L. Thoms. I've met him a couple of times. Agreeable fellow. I shall procure you a meeting.' He reached for his telephone.

Bobbie arranged for me to see Dr Thoms two days later at the end of the afternoon. I deposited Jochen with Veronica and Avril and I went into All Souls and was directed to Dr Thoms's staircase. The afternoon was sultry, oppressive and threatening, the sun seemed sulphurously hazed, producing an odd yellow light in the air that amplified the yellow in the stones of the college walls and I wondered for a moment – prayed for a moment – that it would storm. The grass in the quadrangle was the colour of desert sand.

I knocked on Dr Thoms's door and it was opened by a burly young man in jeans and a T-shirt – in his late twenties, I would have said – who had a shock of curly brown hair tumbling to his shoulders and an almost painfully neatly trimmed beard, all angles and hard edges.

'Ruth Gilmartin,' I said. 'I've come to meet Dr Thoms.'

'You've found him. Come in.' He had a strong Yorkshire or Lancashire accent – I couldn't tell them apart – 'Coom in' he had said.

We sat down in his study and I refused his offer of tea or coffee. I noticed he had a computer with a screen like a television on his desk. Bobbie had told me that Thoms had written his doctorate on Admiral Canaris and MI5 penetration of the Abwehr in World War Two. He was now writing a 'vast book' for 'vast sums of money' on the history of the British Secret Service from 1909 to the present day. 'I think he's your man,' Bobbie had said, rather pleased with his efficiency.

Thoms asked me how he could help me and so I started to tell him, in the most circumspect and vague terms I could manage, given my limited knowledge of the subject. I said I was going to interview a man who had been fairly high up in the Secret Intelligence Service during the war. I just needed some background information, particularly about what was going on in America in 1940–1, before Pearl Harbor.

Thoms made no effort to conceal his quickening interest.

'Really,' he said. 'So he was high up in the British Security Coordination.'

'Yes,' I said. 'But I get the impression he was something of a freelance – had his own small operation.'

Thoms looked more intrigued. 'There were a few of them – irregulars – but they were all reeled in as the war went on.'

'I have a source who worked for this man.'

'Reliable?'

'Yes. This source worked for him in Belgium and then in America.'

'I see,' Thoms said, impressed, looking at me with some fascination. 'This source of yours could be sitting on a goldmine.'

'What do you mean?'

'He could make a fortune if he told his story.'

He. Interesting, I thought – let's keep him a he. And I had never thought of money, either.

'Do you know about the Prenslo Incident?' I asked.

'Yes. It was a disaster, blew everything wide open.'

'This source was there.'

Thoms said nothing – only nodded several times. His excitement was palpable.

'Have you heard of an organisation called AAS Ltd?' I asked.

'No.'

'Does the name "Mr X" help you identify anyone?'

'No.'

'Transoceanic Press?'

'No.'

'Do you know who "C" was in 1941?'

'Yes, of course,' he said. 'These names are beginning to come out now – now the whole Enigma/Bletchley Park secret is exposed. Old agents are talking – or talking so you can read between the lines. But,' he leant forward, 'this is what is fascinating – and it makes me sweat a little, to be completely honest – as to what SIS was really doing in the United States in the early days – what the BSC was doing in their name – is the greyest of grey areas. *Nobody* wants to talk about that. Your source is the first one I've ever heard of – from an agent in the field.'

'It's a stroke of luck,' I said carefully.

'Can I meet your source?'

'No, I'm afraid not.'

'Because I have about a million questions, as you can imagine.' There was a strange light in his eye – the light of the scholar-hunter who has smelt fresh spoor, who knows there is an unblazed trail out there.

'What I might do,' I offered, cautiously, 'is write some of it down, in broad outline, see if it made any sense to you.'

'Great. Happy to oblige,' he said, and leant back in his seat as if, for the first time, he were just taking in the fact that I was, for example, a member of the female sex, and not simply a new mine of exclusive information.

'Fancy going to the pub for a drink?' he said.

We crossed the High and went to a small pub in a lane near

Oriel and he gave me a potted synopsis of SIS and BSC and the pre-Pearl Harbor operations as far as he understood them and I began to understand something of the context for my mother's particular adventure. Thoms spoke fluently and with some passion about this covert world with its interconnecting lines of duplicity – effectively a whole British security and intelligence apparatus right in the middle of Manhattan, hundreds of agents all striving to persuade America to join the war in Europe despite the express and steadfast objections of the majority of the population of the United States.

'Astonishing, really, when you come to think of it. Unparalleled . . .' He stopped suddenly. 'Why are you looking at me like that?' he asked, a bit discomfited.

'Do you want an honest answer?'

'Yes, please.'

'I can't decide whether the hair doesn't go with the beard or the beard doesn't go with the hair.'

He laughed: he seemed almost pleased by my bluntness.

'I don't usually have a beard, actually. But I've grown it for a role.'

'A role?'

'In *Don Carlos*. I'm playing a Spanish nobleman called Rodrigo. It's an opera.'

'Yeah. That Verdi bloke, innit? You can obviously sing, then.'

'It's an amateur company,' he explained. 'We're doing three performances at the Playhouse. Want to come and see it?'

'As long as I can get a baby-sitter,' I said. That usually scared them off. Not Thoms, though, and I began to sense Thoms's interest in me might extend further than any secrets I possessed about the British Security Coordination.

'I take it you're not married,' he said.

'That's right.'

'How old's the kid?'

'Five.'

'Bring him along. You're never too young to start going to the opera.'

'Maybe I will,' I said.

We chatted a bit more and I said I'd call him when I had my summary complete – I was still waiting for more information. I left him in the pub and wandered down the High Street to where I'd parked my car. Some students, wearing gowns and carrying champagne bottles, burst out of University College, singing a song with a nonsensical refrain. They capered off down the street, whooping and laughing. Exams over, I thought, term nearly finished and a hot summer of freedom ahead. Suddenly I felt ridiculously old, remembering my own post-exam euphoria and celebrations – an aeon ago, it seemed – and the thought depressed me for the usual reasons. When I took my final exams and celebrated their conclusion my father had been alive; he died three days before I had my results – and so he never learned that his daughter had got a first. As I made for my car, I found myself thinking about him in that last month of his life, that summer – six years ago, already. He had looked well, my unchanging Dad, he wasn't unwell, he wasn't old, but in those final weeks of his life he had started behaving oddly. One afternoon he dug up a whole row of new potatoes, five yards' worth, tens and tens of pounds. Why did you do that, Sean? I remember my mother asking. I just wanted to see if they were ready, he said. Then he cut down and burned on a bonfire a ten-foot lime sapling he'd planted the year before. Why, Dad? I just couldn't bear the thought of it growing, was his simple, baffling reply. Most strange, though, was a compulsion he developed in what was to be his last week on earth, for switching out electric lights in the house. He would patrol the rooms, upstairs and down, looking for a burning light bulb and extinguish it. I'd leave the library to make a cup of tea and come back to find it in darkness. I caught him waiting to slip into rooms we were about to vacate, poised to make sure the lights went off within seconds of their being no longer required. It began to drive me and my mother mad. I remember shouting at him once: what the hell's going on? And he replied with unusual meekness – it just seems a terrible waste, Ruth, an awful waste of precious electricity.

I now think he knew that he was soon going to die but the message had somehow become scrambled or unintelligible to him. We are animals, after all, and I believe our old animal instincts lurk deep inside us. Animals seem to be able to read the signals – perhaps our big, super-intelligent brains can't bear to decipher them. I'm sure now my father's body was somehow subtly alerting him to the impending shutdown, the final systems malfunction, but he was confused. Two days after I had shouted at him about the lights he collapsed and died in the garden after lunch. He was deadheading roses – nothing strenuous – and died immediately, we were informed, a fact that consoled me, but I still hated to dwell on his few, bewildered, frightened weeks of *timor mortis*.

I unlocked my car and sat down behind the wheel, feeling blue, missing him badly all of a sudden, wondering what he would have made of my mother's, his wife's, astounding revelations. Of course, it would have all been different if he'd been alive – a pointless hypothesis, then – and so, to move my mind away from this depressing subject I tried to imagine Timothy Thoms without his hidalgo's beard. 'Rodrigo' Thoms. I liked that better. Perhaps I would call him Rodrigo.

The Story of Eva Delectorskaya

New Mexico. 1941

EVA DELECTORSKAYA STEPPED QUICKLY off the train at Albuquerque's Santa Fe station. It was eight o'clock in the evening and she was arriving a day later than she had planned – but better to be sure and safe. She watched the passengers disembark – a dozen or so – and then waited until the train pulled out, heading for El Paso. There was no sign of the two crows she had lost in Denver. All the same, she walked a couple of blocks around the station, checking, and, being shadow-free, went into the first hotel she found – The Commercial – and paid six dollars in advance for a single room, three nights. Her room was small, could have been cleaner, had a fine view of an air shaft, but it would do. She left her suitcase there, walked back to the station and told a taxi driver to take her to the Hotel de Vargas, her original destination and where she was due to meet her first contact. The de Vargas proved to be ten minutes away in the business district but after the scare in Denver she needed a bolt-hole. One town: two hotels – standard Lyne training.

The de Vargas lived up to its pretentious name. It was over-decorated, had a hundred rooms and a cocktail lounge. She put a wedding ring on her finger before she checked in and explained to the receptionist that her luggage was lost in Chicago and the railway would be sending it on. No problem, Mrs Dalton, the receptionist said, we'll be sure to let you know the moment it arrives. Her room looked out over a small faux-Pueblo courtyard with a pattering fountain. She freshened up and went down to the cocktail lounge, dark and virtually empty, and ordered a Tom Collins from a plump waitress in a short orange dress. Eva wasn't happy, her brain was working too hard. She nibbled peanuts and drank her liquor and wondered what was the best thing to do.

She had left New York and travelled to Chicago, where she spent a night, deliberately not making her connecting train to Kansas City. She saw the trajectory of her journey across America as a thrown stone, heading westwards, slowly falling on New Mexico. The next day she travelled to Kansas City, missed another connection to Denver and waited three hours in the station for the next. She bought a newspaper and found some items on the war on page nine. The Germans were closing in on Moscow but winter was impeding their advance – as for what might be going on in England she could find nothing. On the next section of her journey, as the train was approaching Denver, she did a routine walk through the coaches. She spotted the crows in the observation platform. They were sitting together, a silly, slack mistake: if they'd been apart she might not have noticed them but she had seen those two charcoal-grey suits in Chicago as well as the two ties, one burnt-amber, one maroon. The maroon tie had a diamond-patterned weave to it that reminded her of a tie she had once given to Kolia as a Christmas present – he wore it with a pale blue shirt, she remembered. She had made him promise that it would be his 'favourite' tie and he had solemnly promised – the tie of ties, he had said, how can I ever thank you? trying to keep his face serious. That's how she had remembered the crows. There was a young man with an undershot lantern-jaw and an older man with greying hair and a moustache. She walked by them and sat down looking out at the prairies rolling by. In the window's reflection she saw them separate immediately: Lantern-Jaw went downstairs, Moustache pretended to read his newspaper.

From Denver she had planned to go straight on to Santa Fe and Albuquerque but clearly now she had shadows she had to lose them. Not for the first time she was grateful for what she had learned in Lyne: broken journeys always make it easier to spot the shadow. Nobody would ever travel as she had done – so coincidence was ruled out. It wouldn't be difficult to get rid of them, she thought – they were either inept or complacent, or both.

At Denver Station she bought a locker, left her suitcase in it, and then walked out into the city and went into the first multi-storey department store she encountered. She looked around, browsing, moving up through the floors until she found what she wanted: an elevator close to a stairway on the third floor. She made her way slowly back to the first floor, buying a lipstick and compact on the way. At the elevator she dithered, letting others go by her as she scrutinised the store directory, then slipped in at the last minute. Moustache had been hovering but was too far away. 'Five, please,' she said to the operator but stepped out on three. She waited behind a rack of dresses by the doorway. Seconds later Moustache and Lantern-Jaw thundered up the stairs, quickly scanned the floor, and, not seeing her, and spotting that the lift was still going up, bolted out again. Eva was down the stairs and out on the street a minute later. She doubled back and jinked around but they were gone. She collected her suitcase and took a bus to Colorado Springs, four stops down the line to Santa Fe and spent a night there in a hotel opposite the station.

That evening she called in from a pay phone in the lobby. She let it ring three times, hung up, called again, hung up after the first ring and called once more. She suddenly wanted to hear Romer's voice.

'Transoceanic. How can I help you?' It was Morris Devereux. She checked her disappointment, angry with herself at being disappointed it wasn't Romer.

'You know the party I went to?'

'Yes.'

'There were two uninvited guests.'

'Unusual. Any idea who they were?'

'Local crows, I would say.'

'Even more unusual. Are you sure?'

'I'm sure. I've lost them anyway. Can I speak to the boss?'

'I'm afraid not. The boss has gone home.'

'Home?' This meant England. 'A bit sudden.'

'Yes.'

'I was wondering what I should do.'

'If you're happy, I would proceed as normal.'

'All right. Bye.'

She hung up. It was illogical but for some reason she felt more insecure knowing that Romer had been called away. Proceed as normal as long as you're happy. There was no reason not to, she supposed. Standard operating procedure. She wondered who the two men were – FBI? Romer had said the FBI were growing worried at the size and scale of the British presence. Perhaps this was the first sign of penetration . . . All the same, she changed trains twice more on the way to Albuquerque, making slow progress.

She sighed and ordered another cocktail from the waitress. A man came up to her and asked if he could join her but he didn't use the passwords, just wanting to pick her up. She said she was on her honeymoon, waiting for her husband and he wandered away looking for more promising material. She finished her drink and went to bed where, try as she might to calm herself, she slept badly.

The next day she wandered around the old town, went into a church on the plaza and took a stroll through Rio Grande Park under the tall cottonwood trees and looked out at the broad turbid river and the hazy mauve mountains to the west and, as she frequently did, marvelled that she should find herself here, at this stage of her life, in this town, at this time. She lunched at the de Vargas and, as she passed through the lobby afterwards, the desk clerk suggested she might appreciate a tour of the university, telling her that the library was 'magnificent'. She said she'd save it for another day. Instead she took a taxi to her other hotel and lay on her hard bed, reading a novel – *The Hollow Mountain* by Sam M. Goodforth – with dogged concentration throughout the rest of the afternoon.

She was back in a booth in the cocktail lounge at six, enjoying a dry Martini, when a man slipped into the seat opposite.

'Hi, glad to see you looking so well.' He had a plump, pasty face and his tie had grease stains on it. He had a local newspaper in his hand and was wearing a frayed straw trilby that he didn't remove.

'I just had a two-week vacation,' she said.

'Go to the mountains?'

'I prefer the seaside.'

So far so good, she thought. Then said, 'Have you anything for me?'

He pointedly placed the newspaper on the seat beside him. Very BSC, she thought, we love newspaper drops – anyone can carry a newspaper. Keep it simple.

'Go to Las Cruces. A man called Raul will contact you. The Alamogordo Inn.'

'How long am I meant to stay there?'

'Until Raul shows up. Nice talking to you.' He slipped out of the booth and was gone. She reached over and picked up the newspaper. Inside was a brown envelope sealed with sticky tape. She went up to her room and sat and looked at it for ten minutes then she tore it open to find a map of Mexico with the printed title: LUFTVERKEHRSNETZ VON MEXIKO. HAUPTLINEN.

She called Transoceanic.

'Sage, hello.' It was Angus Woolf – she was surprised to hear his voice.

'Hello. Moonlighting?'

'Sort of,' he said. 'How's the party going?'

'Interesting. I've made contact but my gift is particularly intriguing. Inferior material, I would say.'

'I'd better call the manager.'

Devereux came on the line. 'Inferior?'

'Not that you'd spot it immediately but it wouldn't take you long.'

The map looked professional and official and was printed in black and white and two colours, blue and red. Mexico was divided up into four districts – Gau 1, Gau 2, Gau 3 and Gau 4 – and blue lines between red cities indicated air routes; Mexico City to Monterrey and Torreón; Guadalauara to Chihuahua and so on. Most unusual were lines extending beyond Mexico's boundaries: one south 'für Panama', and two north 'für San Antonio, Texas' and another, 'für Miami, Florida'. The implication, Eva thought at once, was too clear – where was the subtlety? But more worrying too were the errors; HAUPTLINEN should have been HAUPTLINIEN, and 'für' in the sense of 'to' was not correct either – it should have been 'nach' – 'nach Miami, Florida'. To her eyes the positive first impression was quickly undermined and subverted by these factors. The spelling mistakes might just be explained by a compositor who didn't speak German (perhaps the map had been printed in Mexico) but the mistakes plus the territorial ambitions enshrined in the air routes seemed too much to her – trying too hard to get the message across.

'Are you sure this is our product?' she asked Devereux.

'Yes, as far as I know.'

'Will you tell the boss what I think and I'll call back later.'

'Are you going to proceed?' he asked.

'With due caution.'

'Where are you going?'

'A place called Las Cruces,' she said instantly, then thinking: why am I being so honest? Too late now.

She hung up, went to the front desk and asked where she could hire a car.

The road to Las Cruces was due south on Highway 85, some 220 miles or so on the old Camino Real that followed the Rio Grande valley all the way to Mexico. It was two-lane tarmacadam most of the way, with some sections in concrete on which she made good, steady going, driving a tan-coloured Cadillac touring car with a retractable roof that she did not bother to retract. She barely looked at the scenery as she drove south but was aware, all the same, of the rugged mountain ranges to the east and west, the *ranchitos* with their melon and corn patches clustered around the river and, here and there, she saw from the road the rocky stretches of desert and the lava beds of the fabled *jornada del muerte* – beyond the river valley the land was hard and arid.

She arrived in Las Cruces in the late afternoon and drove down the main street, looking for the Alamogordo Inn. These small towns already seemed familiar to her having driven through some half-dozen or so identical ones on her journey south: Los Lunas, Socorro, Hatch – they all blended into a homogenous image of New Mexican provinciality. After the adobe ranch houses came the gas stations and the auto shops, then the neat suburbs on the outskirts, then the freight yards, the grain silos and the flour mills. Each town had its wide main street with its garish shop-fronts and neon advertisements, its awnings and shaded walkways, dusty cars parked at an angle on both verges of the road. Las Cruces looked no different: there was the Woolworths, a jeweller with a winking plastic gem the size of a football, signs for Florsheim Shoes, Coca-Cola, Liberty Furniture, the drugstore, the bank and, at the end of the street, opposite a small park with a stand of shady cottonwoods, the plain concrete façade of the Alamogordo Inn.

She parked in the lot at the back and went into the lobby. A couple of roof fans stirred the air, there was a cracked-leather, three-seater sofa and worn Indian rugs on the wooden floor. A cobwebbed cactus stood in a pot of sand studded with cigarette butts, below a sign that said: 'Positively no loitering. Electric light in every room'. The desk clerk, a young man with a weak chin and a shirt collar three sizes too big for his neck looked at her curiously as she asked for a room.

'You sure you want this hotel?' he asked, meekly. 'There are much nicer ones just out of town.'

'I'm quite happy, thank you,' she said. 'Where can I get a bite to eat?'

Turn right out the front door for a restaurant, turn left for a diner, he said. She chose the diner and ordered a hamburger. The place was empty: two grey-haired ladies manned the soda fountain and an Indian with a sternly handsome, melancholic face swept the floor. Eva ate her burger and and drank her Coca-Cola. She experienced a strange form of inertia, an almost palpable heaviness, as if the world had stopped turning and only the swish of the Indian's broom on the cement floor was marking the passage of time. Somewhere in a back room jazz was playing on the radio and Eva thought: what am I doing here? What particular destiny am I playing out? She felt she could sit on here in this diner in Las Cruces for all eternity – the Indian man would be sweeping the floor, her hamburger would remain half eaten, the thin jazz would continue to play. She allowed the mood to linger, steeping herself in it, finding it oddly calming, this late-afternoon stasis, knowing that whatever she did next would set a new chain of events in motion that would be out of her control. Better to savour these few moments of stillness where apathy ruled unchallenged.

She went to the diner pay phone, in a small booth by some shelves stacked with tins, and called Transoceanic. Devereux answered.

'Can I speak to the boss?' she asked.

'Alas, no. But I spoke to him yesterday evening.'

'And what did he say?' For some reason Eva felt sure that Romer was in the room with Devereux – then she dismissed the idea as absurd.

'He says it's all up to you. It's your party. If you want to leave – leave. If you want to change the music – do so. Trust your instincts, he said.'

'You told him what I thought about my gift.'

'Yes, he's checked. It's our product, so they must want it out there.'

She hung up, thinking hard. So: everything was up to her. She walked slowly back to the Alamogordo, keeping to the shady side of the street. A large truck went by loaded with massive tree trunks followed by a rather smart red coupé with a man and a woman in the front seat. She stopped and looked behind her: some kids stood chatting to a girl on a bicycle. But she had the strangest feeling that she was being shadowed – which was crazy, she knew. She went and sat in the small park for a few minutes and read her guidebook to drive these demons from her mind. Las Cruces – 'The Crosses' – so called after the massacre by local Apaches of a freight party in the eighteenth century *en route* to Chihuahua and the tall crosses that were erected over their subsequent graves. She hoped it wasn't a bad omen.

The small red coupé passed by again: no man – the woman at the wheel.

No: she was being jumpy, naïve, unprofessional. If she was

worried there were procedures she could follow. It was her party. Use your instincts, Romer had said. All right – she would.

She went back to the Alamogordo and drove her car out on the Mesa Road towards the state college and found the new motel her guidebook had promised – the Mesilla Motor Lodge. She rented a cabin at the end of a wooden walkway and hid the map in the back of the wardrobe, behind a panel that she eased away with her nail file. The hotel was only a year old, the bellhop told her as he led her to her cabin. It smelt new: the odour of creosote, putty and woodshavings seemed to linger in her room. The cabin was clean and modern, its furniture pale and undecorated. A semi-abstract painting of a Pueblo village hung above the desk, which was fitted out with a bowl of cellophane-wrapped fruit, a tiny yucca in a terracotta pot and a folding blotter and writing kit of paper, envelopes, postcards and half a dozen monogrammed pencils. Everything is complimentary, the bellhop told her, with our compliments. She professed herself very pleased with the arrangement. When she was alone again she took 2,000 dollars out of the envelope and stashed the rest with the map.

She drove back to Las Cruces, parked behind the Alamogordo and went into the lobby. A man was sitting on the sofa, wearing a pale blue cotton suit. He had white blond hair and an unusually pink face – an almost albino she thought – with his pale blue suit he looked like a big baby.

'Hi,' he said, standing up. 'Good to see you looking so well.'

'I just had a two-week vacation.'

'Go to the mountains?'

'I prefer the seaside.'

He offered his hand and she shook it. He had a pleasant, husky voice.

'I'm Raul.' He turned to the desk clerk. 'Hey, sonny, can we get a drink here?'

'No.'

They walked outside and looked vainly for a bar for five minutes.

'I got to get some beer,' he said. He went into a liquor store and came out with a can of beer in a brown paper bag. They walked back to the park and sat on a bench under the cotton-wood trees while Raul opened his beer with a can opener that he had in his pocket and drank it in great draughts, not removing the can from the bag. I will always remember this small park in Las Cruces, Eva thought.

'Sorry,' he said, letting air escape from his belly with a whispery wheeze. 'I was dying of thirst.' Eva noticed his voice was markedly less husky. 'Water doesn't work for me,' he added by way of explanation.

'There's been a problem,' Eva said. 'A delay.'

'Oh yeah?' He looked suddenly shifty, displeased. 'Nobody told me nothing.' He stood up, walked to the trashcan and dumped his beer-bag. He stood with his hands on his hips and looked around as if he were being set up in some way.

'I've got to come back next week,' she said. 'They told me to give you this in the meantime.'

She opened her handbag and let him see the money. He came over quickly and sat beside her. She slipped him the wad of notes.

'Two thousand. The rest next week.'

'Yeah?' He couldn't keep the surprise and delight off his face. He wasn't expecting money, she thought: what's happening here?

Raul stuffed the money in his jacket pocket.

'When next week?' he said.

'You'll be contacted.'

'Okay,' he said, standing up again. 'See ya.' He sauntered away. Eva waited five minutes, still checking for shadows. She walked up the main street and went into Woolworths, where she bought a pack of tissues. She turned down a narrow lane between the bank and a realtor's and immediately retraced her steps back up it at speed. Nothing. She did a few other manoeuvres, finally convincing herself that no one had or could have been tailing her, before going back to the Alamogordo and checking out – no refunds, sorry.

She drove back to the Mesilla Motor Lodge. It was dusk now and the setting sun was striking the peaks of the mountains to the east, turning them a dark-fissured, dramatic orange. Tomorrow she would return to Albuquerque and catch a plane to Dallas and make her way home from there – the sooner the better.

She ate in the hotel restaurant ordering a steak – tough – and creamed spinach – cold – washed down with a bottle of beer ('We don't serve wine, Mam'). There were a few other people in the dining-room, an elderly couple with guides and maps, a plump man who propped his newspaper in front of him and never looked up, and a well-dressed family of Mexicans with two silent, beautifully behaved little girls.

She walked along the walkway towards her cabin, thinking back over her day and wondering if Romer would approve of what her instincts had led her to do. She looked up at the stars and felt the desert air chill on her skin. Somewhere a dog barked. She checked the other cabins routinely before she unlocked her door: no new cars, all accounted for. She turned the key and pushed the door open.

The man was sitting on her bed, his thighs spread wide, his revolver pointing at her face.

'Shut the door,' he said. 'Move over there.' His accent was heavy, Mexican. He rose to his feet, a big burly man with a hanging gut on him. He had a dense wide moustache and his suit was dull green.

She moved across the room as he wagged his gun at her, obeying him, her mind frantic with questions, receiving no answers.

'Where's the map?' he said.

'What? Who?' She thought he had said 'Where's the man?'.

'The map.' He made the 'p' plosive. Spittle flew.

How could he know she had a map?

She noticed that her room and her suitcase had been searched, as her glance flicked about its four corners. Like some super-calculating machine her brain was running through the permutations and the implications of this encounter. It became clear to her almost instantly that she should give the map to this person.

'It's in the cupboard,' she said, walking over to it and hearing him cock his gun.

'I'm unarmed,' she said, gesturing for his permission to go further and then, when he nodded his head, reaching behind the loose partition and removing the map and the remaining 3,000 dollars. She handed them to the Mexican. Something about the way he took them from her, checked them and kept her covered made her think he was a policeman, not a crow. He was used to doing this, he did this all the time; he was very calm. He put the map and the money on the desk.

'Take your clothes off,' he said.

As she undressed she felt sick. No, not this, she thought, please no. She felt a horrible foreboding now: his bulk, his easy professionalism – he wasn't like Raul or the man in Albuquerque – it made her think that she was going to die very soon.

'Okay, stop.' She was down to her brassière and panties. 'Get dressed.' There was no leering, no prurience.

He went to the window and pulled back the curtain. She heard a car start up some way off and approach the cabin and stop outside. A door slammed and the engine stayed running. There were others, then. She dressed faster than she had ever dressed in her life. She was thinking: don't panic, remember your training, maybe he just wants the map.

'Put the map and your money in the handbag,' he said.

She felt her throat swell and her chest tighten. She was trying not to think what might happen, to stay in the absolute here and now, but she realised the awful implication of what he had just said. It wasn't the map or the money he was after – he was after her: she was the prize.

She walked to the desk.

Why had she refused Romer's offer of a gun? Not that it would have made any difference now. A simple courier's job, he had said. Romer didn't believe in guns or unarmed combat: you have your teeth and your nails, he had said, your animal instincts. She needed more than that to fight this big confident man: she needed a weapon.

She put the map and the 3,000 dollars in her handbag while the Mexican went to the door. He kept her covered, opened the door and glanced outside. She shifted her body. She had one second and she used it.

'Come,' he said, as she was adjusting the combs that held her hair up in a loose chignon. 'Don't bother with that.' He linked arms with her, the snout of his revolver pressed into her side and they walked out to his car. Over at another cabin she could see the little Mexican girls playing on the porch – they paid her and her companion no attention.

He pushed her in and followed her, making her slide over behind the wheel. The headlights were on. There was no sign of the person who had delivered the car.

'Drive,' he said, looping his arm along the back of the front seat, the muzzle of his revolver now pressing into her ribs. She put the car in gear – the shift was on the steering column – and they pulled away slowly from the Mesilla Motor Lodge.

As they left the compound and turned on to the road to Las Cruces she thought he gave a sign – a wave, a thumbs-up – to someone standing in the shadows on the verge under a poplar. She glanced over and she thought she saw two men there, waiting by a parked car with its lights off. It looked like a coupé but it was too dark to tell what colour it was. And then they were past them and he told her to drive through Las Cruces and take Highway 80 heading for the Texas line.

They drove on Highway 80 for about half an hour. Just when she saw the city limits for Berino he told her to turn right on a gravel road sign-posted to Leopold. The road was in bad repair and the car bucked and juddered as she hit the ruts and the ridges, the Mexican's gun banging into her side painfully.

'Slow down,' he said. She cut the speed to about ten miles per hour and after a few minutes he told her to stop.

They were at a sharp bend in the road and the headlights lit up a section of scrub and stony ground crossed by what looked like a deep-shadowed arroyo.

Eva sat there, conscious of the adrenalin surge running through her body. She felt remarkably clear-headed. By any reasonable calculation she would be dead in a minute or two, she realised. Trust your animal instincts. She knew exactly what she had to do.

'Get out of the car,' the Mexican said. 'We're going to meet some people.'

This was a lie, she thought. He just doesn't want me to think this is the end of the road.

She reached for the door latch with her left hand and with her right looped a stray lock of hair that had fallen, back behind her ear. A natural gesture, a womanly reflex.

'Switch the lights off,' he said.

She needed light.

'Listen,' she said, 'I have more money.'

The fingers of her right hand that were in her hair touched the rubber eraser on the Mesilla Motor Lodge pencil that she had slipped in amongst her bunched and gathered folds of hair – one of the half-dozen new, sharpened, complimentary pencils that had been laid out on the blotter beside the notepaper and the postcards. New and newly sharpened with the name Mesilla Motor Lodge, Las Cruces, stamped in gold along their sides. This was the pencil she had picked up and slid into her hair as the Mexican peered briefly out of the door, checking on his car.

'I can get you another ten thousand,' she said. 'Easy. In one hour.'

He chuckled. 'Get out.'

She grabbed the sharp pencil in her hair and stabbed him in the left eye.

The pencil went in smoothly and instantly without resistance, almost to its full six-inch length. The man gave a kind of gasp-inhalation and dropped his gun with a clatter. He tried to raise his trembling hands to his eye as if to draw the pencil out then fell back against the door. The end of the pencil with the rubber eraser stuck out an inch above the punctured jelly of his left eyeball. There was no blood. She knew immediately from his absolute stillness that he was dead.

She switched out the lights and stepped out of the car. She was shivering, but not excessively, telling herself that she had probably been a minute or two from her own death – the moment of life-or-death exchange – she felt no shock, no horror, at what she had done to this man. She forced herself away from that topic and tried to be rational: what now? What next? Run away? Perhaps there was something to be salvaged from this disaster: one step at a time, use your brain, she said to herself – think. Think.

She climbed back into the car and drove it a few yards off the road behind a clump of greasewood bushes and killed the lights. Sitting there in the dark beside the dead Mexican she methodically considered her options. She switched on the interior light above the rear-view mirror and picked up the gun, using her handkerchief to keep her prints off it. She opened his jacket and replaced it in his shoulder holster. There was still no blood from his wound, not even a trickle – just the end of a pencil sticking out of his unblinking eye.

She went through his pockets and found his wallet and his identification: Deputy Inspector Luis de Baca. She also found some money, a letter and a bill of sale from a hardware store in

Ciudad Juárez. She put everything back. A Mexican policeman would have been her killer: it made no sense at all. She switched off the light again and carried on thinking: she was safe for a short while, she knew – she could flee back to her friends one way or another now – but tracks had to be covered.

She stepped out of the car again and paced about thinking, planning. There was a sickle moon casting no light and it was getting colder. She hugged her arms to her chest, crouching down at one stage when a truck bumped along the road to Leopold but the sweep of its headlights didn't come close. A plan began to form slowly and she teased it out in her mind, second-guessing, raising objections, considering advantages and disadvantages. She opened the boot of the car and found a can of oil, a rope and a spade. In the dashboard glove compartment was a flashlight, some cigarettes and chewing gum. It seemed to be his own car.

She walked a few paces along the road to Leopold where the corner was and saw, with the flashlight, that the arroyo at the bend was little more than a gulley about twenty feet deep. She started the car, switching on the headlights and drove to the edge, gunning the engine as she left the road, making the wheels spin, scattering gravel. She let the car roll to the very edge of the gulley and put on the handbrake. She made a final check, picked up her bag and stepped out, releasing the handbrake as she did so. The car began to move forward slowly and she ran round the back and pushed. The car toppled over the gulley rim and she listened to the heavy thump and tear of metal as it nosedived to the gulley floor. She heard the windscreen pop out and the shatter of glass.

With the flashlight she picked her way down to the wreck. One headlight was still on and the hood had buckled and sprung open. There was a smell of petrol leaking and the car had canted over forty-five degrees on the passenger side. She was able to wrench open the driver's door and put the gear lever into fourth.

Luis de Baca had fallen forward in the descent and smashed his forehead on the dashboard. A small trickle of blood was now running from his eye to his moustache. The moustache filled and began to drip blood on to his shirt. She hauled him over to the driver's side noticing that one of his legs looked broken, skewed at an odd angle. Good, she thought.

She took the map out of her bag and carefully tore a large corner off it, leaving 'LUFTVERK' and the lines for San Antonio and Miami. She put the rest of the map in her bag, then, taking out a pen and spreading the torn corner on the bonnet, wrote notes on it in German: '*Wo befinden sich die Ölreserven für den transatlantischen Verkehr?*' and '*Der dritte Gau scheint zu gross zu sein.*' In the margin she wrote a small sum adding up some figures: 150,000 plus 35,000 = 185,000 then some meaningless letters and numbers – LBF/3, XPD 77. She smeared the torn corner against de Baca's bloodstained shirt and crumpled it up, then she slipped it under the shoe of his unbroken leg. She put the 3,000 dollars in the glove compartment in the dashboard under a road map and an instruction manual. Then with her handkerchief she wiped down the surfaces and the steering wheel, taking particular care with the gear lever. Finally she heaved de Baca up and propped him against the steering wheel so she could see his face. She knew that what she had to do next would be the hardest but she was so involved in the construction of the accident that she was operating almost automatically, with conscious efficiency. She scattered some windscreen glass over him and snapped off a bent windscreen wiper, tearing away the rubber blade.

She reached for the pencil in his eye and drew it out. It came easily, as if oiled, and with it blood welled up and flowed over the lids. She jammed the end of the windscreen wiper into the wound and stepped backwards. She left the door open and made a final check with the flashlight. Then she picked up her bag, scrambled up the gulley side and walked back along the road towards Highway 80. After about half a mile she left the road and buried the remains of the map, the flashlight and the pencil under a rock. She could see the lights of cars on the highway and the glow of lights from Berdino's main street. She headed off again. She knew what she had to do next: call the police and anonymously report a crashed car in a gulley between the highway and Leopold. A taxi would take her back to the Mesilla Motor Lodge. She would pay her bill and drive through the night to Albuquerque. She had done everything she could but she could not stop thinking as she walked into a Texaco gas station on the outskirts of Berdino – the truth had to be faced: someone, somehow, had betrayed her.

10

Meeting Lucas Romer

I STOOD IN FRONT of David Bomberg's portrait of Lucas Romer for a good twenty minutes, searching for clues, I suppose, and also trying to identify the man my mother had met in 1939 in order to distinguish him from the man I was about to meet in 1976.

The portrait was virtually life-size – a head and shoulders on a canvas of about 12 inches by 18. The simple broad black wooden frame made the small painting look more imposing but it was still, none the less, stuck away in a corridor on an upper floor of the National Portrait Gallery. The artist in this case was more important than the sitter: the notes on the wall were all about David Bomberg – the sitter was identified simply as 'Lucas Romer, a friend' – and its date was given as '1936(?)' – three years before Romer had met Eva Delectorskaya.

The picture was clearly a sketch, notable for its fluent impasto surface – perhaps a study that might have been worked up later to something more polished had there been more sittings. It seemed to me a good painting – a good portrait – the sitter's character emerged from it powerfully, though I had no idea if it were a good likeness. Lucas Romer stared out of the canvas at the viewer – making emphatic eye contact – his eyes a pale grey-blue, and his mouth was set, not relaxed, almost slightly pushed to one side, betokening reluctance, impatience at the posing procedure, the time spent being still. His hair was thinning at the front, as my mother had described, and he was wearing a white shirt, a blue jacket almost the same colour as his eyes and what looked like a nondescript greenish-beige tie. Only the knot of the tie was in the frame.

Bomberg had outlined the head with a thick band of black that had the effect of concentrating your eye on the painted surface within that boundary. The style was bold: blue, verdigris, chartreuse, raw pinks, browns and charcoal combined to render the flesh tones and the incipient heavy beard. The brush strokes were broad, impetuous, confident, loaded with pigment. I had an instant sense of a personality – a strong one, perhaps an arrogant one – and I didn't think I was bringing any privileged knowledge to that assessment. Big hooded eyes, a conspicuous nose – perhaps the only sign of weakness was in the mouth: full, rather slack lips, pursed in their temporary tolerance. A bully? An over-confident intellectual? A complex neurotic artist? Perhaps you needed all these qualities to be a spymaster and run your own team of spies.

I wandered down to the gallery lobby and decided to walk to Brydges'. But first I went to the ladies' lavatory and considered myself in the mirror. What did *this* portrait say of the sitter? My hair was down, thick and long and freshly washed, I was wearing a pale pink lipstick and my usual dark eyeshadow. I had on a newish black trouser suit with ostentatious white stitching on the seams and the patch pockets – and I had my platforms on under the trousers. I was tall – I wanted to be tall today – and I thought I looked pretty damn good. The worn leather briefcase I was carrying added a nice incongruous touch to the picture, I felt.

I walked across Trafalgar Square towards Pall Mall and then cut up through St James's Square to the network of small streets between the square and Jermyn Street, where I would find Brydges'. The door was discreet, glossy black – no nameplate, just a number – with a fanlight with elaborate tracery, all curlicues and ogees. I rang the brass doorbell and was admitted suspiciously by a porter in a navy-blue frock coat with red lapels. I said I had an appointment with Lord Mansfield and he retreated into a kind of glass phone box to consult a ledger.

'Ruth Gilmartin,' I said. 'Six o'clock.'

'This way, Miss.'

I followed the man up a wide swerving staircase, already aware that the modest entrance concealed a building of capacious and elegant Georgian proportions. On the first floor we passed a reading-room – deep sofas, dark portraits, a few old men reading periodicals and newspapers – then a bar – a few old men drinking – then a dining-room being set up for dinner by young girls in black skirts and crisp white blouses. I sensed it was very unusual ever to have a female in this building who wasn't a servant of some kind. We then turned another corner to go down a corridor past a cloakroom and a gentleman's toilet (a smell of disinfectant mingled with hair oil, the sound of urinals discreetly flushing) from which an old man with a walking-stick emerged and, on seeing me, gave a start of almost cartoon-like incredulity.

'Evening,' I said to him, becoming at once both calmer and angrier. Angry because I knew what was obviously, crassly, going on here; calmer because I knew that Romer could have no idea that it would not only not work, but that it would be counter-productive as well. We turned another corner and arrived at a door that had written on it: 'Ladies' Drawing Room'.

'Lord Mansfield will see you here,' the porter said, opening the door.

'How can you be sure I'm a lady?' I said.

'Beg pardon, Miss?'

'Oh, forget it.'

I pushed past him and went into the Ladies' Drawing Room. It was poky and cheaply furnished and smelt of carpet shampoo and polish – everything about its décor signalled disuse. There were chintz curtains and puce shades with saffron fringes on the wall sconces; a selection of unread 'ladies' magazines' – *House & Garden*, *Woman's Journal*, the *Lady* itself – was fanned out on the coffee table; a spider plant was dying of thirst on the mantelpiece above the unlaid fire.

The porter left and I moved the largest armchair over a few feet so that the solitary window was behind it; I wanted to be backlit, my face in shadow, so that the summer evening light would fall on Romer. I opened my briefcase and took out my clipboard and pen.

I waited fifteen minutes, twenty, twenty-five. Again I knew this was deliberate but I was glad of the wait because it made me confront the fact that, unusually for me, I was actually rather nervous about meeting this man – this man who had made love to my mother, who had recruited her, who had 'run' her, as the parlance went, and to whom she had declared her love, one chilly day in Manhattan in 1941. Eva Delectorskaya, I felt for perhaps the first time, was becoming real. But the longer Lucas Romer kept me waiting, the more he tried to intimidate me in this bastion of aged establishment masculinity, the more pissed off I became – and therefore the less insecure.

Eventually the porter opened the door: a figure loomed behind him.

'Miss Gilmartin, your lordship,' the porter said and melted away.

Romer slipped in, a smile on his lean, seamed face.

'So sorry to have kept you waiting,' he said, his voice gravelly and slightly hoarse as if his larynx were choked with polyps. 'Tiresome phone calls. Lucas Romer.' He extended his hand.

'Ruth Gilmartin,' I said, standing up, tall as he was, and gave him one of my firmest handshakes, trying not to stare, trying not to gawp, though I would have loved a good few minutes' scrutiny of him through a one-way mirror.

He was wearing a perfectly cut, single-breasted midnight-blue suit with a cream shirt and a dark maroon knitted tie. His smile was as white and immaculate as my mother had described, though there was now, in the recesses of his mouth, the gold gleam of expensive bridgework. He was bald, his longish oiled hair above his ears combed into two grey sleek wings. Though he was slim he was a little stooped but the handsome man he had been lingered in this 77-year-old like a ghostly memory: in certain lights it would have been hard to guess his age – he was, I suppose, still a good-looking older man. I sat down in my positioned armchair before he could claim it or wave me into any other seat. He chose to sit as far away from me as possible and asked if I wanted tea.

'I wouldn't mind an alcoholic drink,' I said, 'if such things are served in a Ladies' Drawing Room.'

'Oh, indeed,' he said. 'We're very broad-minded in Brydges'.' He reached for and pressed a wired bell push that sat on the edge of the coffee table and almost immediately a white-jacketed waiter was in the room with a silver tray under his arm.

'What will you have, Miss Martin?'

'Gilmartin.'

'Forgive me – an old man's imbecility – Miss Gilmartin. What is your pleasure?'

'A large whisky and soda please.'

'All whiskies are served large, here.' He turned to the waiter. 'A tomato juice for me, Boris. A touch of celery salt, no Worcestershire.' He turned back to me. 'We only have J&B or Bell's as blends.'

'A Bell's, in that case.' I had no idea what a J&B was.

'Yes, your lordship,' the waiter said and left.

'I must say I've been looking forward to this meeting,' Romer said with patent insincerity. 'At my age one feels wholly forgotten. Then all of a sudden a newspaper rings up wanting to interview one. A surprise, but gratifying, I suppose. The *Observer*, wasn't it?'

'The *Telegraph*.'

'Splendid. Who's your editor, by the way? Do you know Toby Litton-Fry?'

'No. I'm working with Robert York,' I said, quickly and calmly.

'Robert York . . . I'll ring Toby about him.' He smiled. 'I'd like to know who'll be correcting your copy.'

Our drinks arrived. Boris served them on paper coasters with a supplementary saucer of salted peanuts.

'You can take those away, Boris,' Romer said. 'Whisky and peanuts – no, no, no.' He chuckled. 'Will they ever learn?'

When Boris left the mood changed suddenly. I couldn't analyse precisely how, but Romer's false charm and suavity seemed to have quit the room with Boris and the peanuts. The smile was still there but the pretence was absent: the gaze was direct, curious, faintly hostile.

'I want to ask you a question, if you don't mind, Miss Gilmartin, before we begin our fascinating interview.'

'Fire away.'

'You mentioned something to my secretary about AAS Ltd.'

'Yes.'

'Where did you come across that name?'

'From an archive source.'

'I don't believe you.'

'I'm sorry you should think that,' I said, suddenly on my guard. His eyes were on me, very cold, fixed. I held his gaze and continued. 'You can have no idea what's become available to scholars and historians in the last few years since the whole Ultra secret came out. Enigma, Bletchley Park – the lid has been well and truly lifted: everybody wants to tell their story now. And a lot of the material is – what shall I say? – informal, personal.'

He thought about this.

'A printed source, you say?'

'Yes.'

'Have you seen it?'

'No, not personally.' I was playing for time now, suddenly a little more worried. Even though my mother had warned me that there would be particular curiosity about AAS Ltd. 'I was given the information by an Oxford don who is writing a history of the British Secret Service,' I said quickly.

'Is he really?' Romer sighed and his sigh said: what a complete and utter waste of time. 'What's this don's name?'

'Timothy Thoms.'

Romer slipped a small, leather-encased notepad from his jacket pocket and then a fountain pen and wrote the name down. I had to admire the bluff, the bravado.

'Dr T.C.L. Thoms. T,h,o,m,s. He's at All Souls,' I added.

'Good . . .' He wrote all this down and looked up. 'What exactly is this article about, that you're writing?'

'It's about the British Security Coordination. And what they were doing in America before Pearl Harbor.' This was what my mother had told me to say: a large catch-all subject.

'Why on earth would anyone be interested in all that? Why are you so intrigued by BSC?'

'I thought I was meant to be interviewing you, Lord Mansfield.'

'I just want to clarify a few things before we begin.'

The waiter knocked on the door and came in.

'Telephone, Lord Mansfield,' he said. 'Line one.'

Romer raised himself to his feet and walked a little stiffly to the telephone on the small writing-desk in the corner. He picked up the receiver.

'Yes?'

He listened to whatever was being said and I picked up my whisky, took a large sip, and took my chance to study him a little more closely. He stood in profile to me, the receiver in his left hand and I could see the glint of the signet ring on his little finger against the black bakelite. With the heel of his right hand he smoothed the wing of hair above his ear.

'No, I'm not concerned,' he said. 'Not remotely.' He hung up and stood for a moment looking at the telephone, thinking. The two wings of his hair met at the back of his head in a small turbulence of curls. It didn't look well groomed but of course it was. His shoes were brilliantly polished as if by an army batman. He turned back to me, his eyes widening for a moment, as if suddenly remembering I was in the room.

'So, Miss Gilmartin, you were telling me about your interest in BSC,' he said, sitting down again.

'My uncle was involved in BSC.'

'Really, what was his name?'

My mother had told me to watch him very closely at this juncture.

'Morris Devereux,' I said.

Romer reflected, repeated the name a couple of times. 'Don't think I know him. No.'

'So you do admit you were part of BSC.'

'I admit nothing, Miss Gilmartin,' he said, smiling at me. He was smiling at me a lot, was Romer, but none of his smiles were genuine or friendly. 'Do you know,' he said, 'I'm sorry to be a bore, but I've decided not to grant this interview.' He stood up again, moved to the door and opened it.

'May I ask why?'

'Because I don't believe a word you've told me.'

'I'm sorry,' I said. 'What can I say? I've been completely honest with you.'

'Then let's say I've changed my mind.'

'Your privilege.' I took my time: I had another sip of whisky and then put my clipboard and my pen away in my briefcase, stood up and walked through the door ahead of him. My mother had warned me that it would probably end like this. He would have had to see me, of course, after the AAS Ltd revelation, and he would try to determine what my agenda was and the moment he sensed it was unthreatening – simple journalistic curiosity, in other words – he would have nothing more to do with me.

'I can find my own way out,' I said.

'Alas, you're not allowed to.'

We moved past the dining-room, now with a few male diners, past the bar – fuller than when I arrived, with a low susurrus of conversation within – past the reading-room, where there was one old man sleeping, and then down the grand curving staircase to the simple black door with its elaborate fanlight.

The porter opened the door for us. Romer didn't offer his hand.

'I hope I haven't wasted too much of your time,' he said, signalling beyond me to a sleek, heavy car – a Bentley, I thought – that started up and pulled over to the Brydges' side of the road.

'I'll still be writing my article,' I said.

'Of course you will, Miss Gilmartin, but be very careful you don't write anything libellous. I have an excellent lawyer – he happens to be a member here.'

'Is that a threat?'

'It's a fact.'

I looked at him squarely in the eye, hoping that my gaze was saying: I don't like you and I don't like your disgusting club and I'm not remotely frightened of you.

'Goodbye,' I said, and I turned and walked away, past the Bentley, from which a uniformed chauffeur had appeared and was opening the passenger's door.

As I walked away from Brydges' I felt an odd mixture of emotions uncoiling inside me: I felt pleased – pleased that I'd met this man who had played such a key role in my mother's life and that I hadn't been cowed by him. And I also felt a little angry with myself – suspecting and worried that I hadn't handled the encounter well enough, hadn't extracted enough from it, had allowed Romer to dictate its course and tenor. I had been reacting too much to him, rather than the other way round – for some reason I had wanted to rattle him more. But my mother had been very insistent: don't go too far, don't reveal anything that you know – only mention AAS Ltd, Devereux and BSC – that'll be enough to set him thinking, enough to spoil his beauty sleep, she'd said with some glee. I hoped I'd done enough for her.

I was home in Oxford by nine o'clock and picked up Jochen from Veronica's.

'Why did you go to London?' he said, as we climbed the back stairs towards the kitchen door.

'I went to see an old friend of Granny's.'

'Granny says she hasn't got any friends.'

'This is someone she knew a long time ago,' I said, moving to the phone in the hall. 'Go and put your pyjamas on.' I dialled my mother's number. There was no reply so I hung up and dialled again, using her stupid code and she still didn't pick up. I put the phone down.

'Shall we go on a little adventure?' I said, trying to keep my voice light-hearted. 'Let's drive out to Granny's and give her a surprise.'

'She won't be pleased,' Jochen said. 'She hates surprises.'

When we reached Middle Ashton I saw at once that the cottage was dark and there was no sign of her car. I went to the third flower pot on the left of the front door, suddenly very worried for some reason, found the key and let myself in.

'What's happening, Mummy?' Jochen said. 'Is this some kind of a game?'

'Sort of.'

Everything in the cottage seemed in order: the kitchen was tidy, the dishes were washed, clothes hung drying on the clothes-horse in the boiler room. I climbed the stairs to her bedroom, Jochen following, and looked around. The bed was made and on her desk was a brown envelope with 'Ruth' written on it. I was about to pick it up when Jochen said, 'Look, there's a car coming.'

It was my mother in her old white Allegro. I felt both stupid and relieved. I ran downstairs, opened the front door and called to her as she stepped out of the car.

'Sal! It's us. We came out to see you.'

'What a lovely surprise,' she said, her voice heavy with irony, bending down to kiss Jochen. 'I didn't remember leaving the lights on. Somebody's up very late.'

'You told me to call you the minute, the second, I got back,' I said, more accusingly and more annoyed than I intended. 'When you didn't reply what was I meant to think?'

'I must have forgotten I'd asked you,' she said, breezily, moving past me into the house. 'Anyone like a cup of tea?'

'I saw Romer,' I said, following her. 'I spoke to him. I thought you'd be interested. But it didn't go well. In fact, I would say he was thoroughly unpleasant.'

'I'm sure you were more than a match for him,' she said. 'I thought you both looked a bit frosty when you said goodbye.'

I stopped. 'What do you mean?' I said.

'I was outside: I saw you both leave the club,' she said, her face utterly open, guileless, as if this were the most natural thing in the world. 'Then I followed him home and now I know where he lives: 29 Walton Crescent, Knightsbridge. Great big white stucco place. It'll be much easier getting to him the next time.'

The Story of Eva Delectorskaya

New York. 1941

EVA CALLED TRANSOCEANIC FROM a pay phone on the street outside her safe house in Brooklyn. Five days had gone by since the events in Las Cruces, during which she had made her way slowly back to New York, taking advantage of all the means of transport available – plane, train, bus and automobile. The first day in New York she had staked out her own safe house. When she was sure no one was watching she moved in and laid low. Finally, when she assumed they'd be growing increasingly worried by her silence, she telephoned.

'Eve!' Morris Devereux almost shouted, forgetting procedure. 'Thank God. Where are you?'

'Somewhere on the eastern seaboard,' she said. 'Morris: I'm not coming in.'

'You have to come in,' he said. 'We have to see you. Circumstances have changed.'

'You don't know what happened down there,' she said with some venom. 'I'm lucky to be alive. I want to speak to Romer. Is he back?'

'Yes.'

'Tell him I'll call on Sylvia's number at BSC. Tomorrow afternoon at four.'

She hung up.

She went down the street to a grocery store and bought some tinned soup, a loaf of bread, three apples and two packs of Lucky Strike before going back to her room on the third floor of the brownstone building on Pineapple Street. Nobody bothered her, none of her anonymous neighbours seemed to register that Miss Margery Allerdice was in residence. If she opened the bathroom window, and leant out as far as she could, the top of one of the towers of Brooklyn Bridge was just visible – on a clear day. She had a pull-down bed, two armchairs, a radio, a galley kitchen with two electric rings, a soapstone sink with one cold tap and a lavatory screened by a plastic curtain with tropical fish all swimming in the same direction. When she arrived back she made some soup – mushroom – ate it with some bread and butter and then smoked three cigarettes while wondering what to do. Perhaps, she thought, the best thing would be to fly now . . . She had her identification, she could be Margery Allerdice and be gone before anyone really noticed. But where to? Mexico? From there she could catch a ship to Spain or Portugal. Or Canada, perhaps? Or was Canada too close? And BSC had a substantial organisation there also. She ran through the pros and cons, thinking she could manage better in Canada, that it would be easier to be inconspicuous; in Mexico she'd stand out – a young English woman – though from there she could go to Brazil, or even better, Argentina. There was a sizeable English community in Argentina; she could find a job, translating, invent a past for herself, become invisible, bury herself underground. That was what she wanted to do – to disappear. But as she thought on she realised that all this planning and speculation, however worthwhile, wasn't going to be put into effect until she'd seen and spoken to Romer: she had to tell him what happened – perhaps he could sort out and solve the crowding mysteries. After that she could make up her mind, but not before.

As the evening drew in she listened to some music on the radio and in her mind went back over the events in Las Cruces. 'The Events in Las Cruces' – the euphemism was rather comforting: as if her hotel room had been double-booked or her car had broken down on Highway 80. She felt no guilt, no compunction about what she had done to de Baca. If she hadn't killed him she knew he would have killed her in the next minute or two. Her plan had been only to stab him in the eye and run. She only had a sharpened pencil, after all – one of his eyes was the only possible target if he was to be immobilised. But thinking back over those few seconds in the car, remembering de Baca's reactions, his total, shocking incapacity followed by his immediate death, she realised that the force of her blow must have driven the pencil point through the eyeball and the eye-hole in his skull, deep into his brain puncturing, in the process, the carotid artery – or perhaps hit the brain-stem, causing instant cardiac arrest. There could be no other explanation for his almost instant death. Even if she had missed the artery and the pencil had penetrated his brain de Baca might not have died. But she would have been able to make her escape, though. However, her luck – her luck – her aim and the sharpness of the pencil point had killed him as swiftly and as surely as if he had taken prussic acid or had been strapped to an electric chair. She went to bed early and dreamt that Raul was trying to sell her a small speedy red coupé.

She called Sylvia's number at BSC exactly at 4.01 p.m. She was standing at a pay phone outside the entrance of the Rockefeller Center on Fifth Avenue with a good view of the main doors. Sylvia's phone rang three times and then was picked up.

'Hello, Eva,' Romer said, his voice level, unsurprised. 'We want you to come in.'

'Listen carefully,' she said. 'Leave the building now and walk south down Fifth. I'll give you two minutes, otherwise there won't be any meeting.'

She hung up and waited. After about three and a half minutes, Romer emerged – fast enough, she thought: he would have had no time to set up any team. He turned right down Fifth Avenue. She shadowed him from across the street and behind, watching his back, watching his manner, letting him walk some six blocks before she was sure there was no one on his tail. She was wearing a headscarf and spectacles, flat shoes and a camel coat she'd bought in a thrift shop that morning. She crossed the street at an intersection and began to follow him closely for another block or two. He was wearing a trench coat, an old one with a few repaired tears, and a navy-blue scarf. He was bareheaded. He seemed very at ease, strolling southwards, not looking around, waiting for contact to be made. They had reached 39th Street before she walked up beside him and said, 'Follow me.'

She turned east and on Park Avenue turned north again, heading towards 42nd Street and Grand Central Station, going in by the Vanderbilt Avenue entrance and walking up the ramp to the main concourse. Thousands of commuters criss-crossed the vast space, swarming, jostling, hurrying: it was rush hour – probably as secure a place to meet as any in the city, Eva reasoned: hard to jump her, easy to cause confusion and escape. She didn't look behind her but made for the central information booth. When she reached it only then did she turn, taking off her spectacles.

He was right behind her, face expressionless.

'Relax,' he said. 'I'm alone. I'm not that stupid.' He paused, moving closer to her, lowering his voice. 'How are you, Eva?'

To her intense irritation the genuine concern in his voice made her suddenly want to cry. She had only to think of Luis de Baca to go hard and resilient again. She took off her headscarf, shook her hair loose.

'I was sold,' she said. 'Somebody sold me.'

'Not any one of us. I don't know what went wrong but Transoceanic is tight.'

'I think you're wrong.'

'Of course you think that. I would think that. But I would know, Eva. I'd figure it out. We're tight.'

'What about BSC?'

'BSC would give you a medal if they could,' he said. 'You did a brilliant job.'

This threw her and she looked around at the hundreds of people hurrying by and then, as if for inspiration, up at the immense vaulted ceiling with its constellations winking out of the blue. She felt weak: the pressure of the last days overcoming her now, all of a sudden. She wanted nothing more than for Romer to put his arms around her.

'Let's go downstairs,' he said. 'We can't talk properly here. I've got a lot to tell you.'

They went down a ramp to the lower concourse and found a place at the counter of a milk bar. She ordered a cherry milkshake with a scoop of vanilla ice-cream, suddenly craving sweetness. She checked the room as the order was prepared.

'There's no need to look around,' Romer said. 'I'm on my own. You've got to come in, Eva – not now, not today, or tomorrow. Take your time. You deserve it.' He reached over and took her hand. 'What you managed to do was astonishing,' he said. 'Tell me what happened. Start from when you left New York.' He let her hand go.

So she told him: she talked him through every hour of the entire trip from New York to Las Cruces and Romer listened, still, without saying a word, only asking her when she had finished to repeat the period of time from her saying farewell to Raul to the encounter with de Baca.

'What's happened in the days you've been out is this,' he told her when she had finished. 'The sheriff of Dona Ana County was called to the crash after you reported it. They found the corner of the map and the money and called in the local FBI agent from Santa Fe. The map went to Hoover in Washington and Hoover himself put it on the President's desk.' He paused. 'Nobody can quite figure it out – so they called us in, naturally enough, as it seemed to have a connection with the Brazilian map. How do you explain it? The death of a Mexican detective in a road crash near the border. There's a sizeable amount of cash and what appears to be a portion of a map, in German, detailing potential air routes within Mexico and the United States. Foul play? Or an unlucky accident? Did he buy the map? Was he selling it and the sale went wrong? Did someone try to steal it from him and was spooked and ran?' He spread his hands. 'Who knows? The investigation continues. The key thing from our point of view – BSC's – is that it confirms the validity of the Brazilian map. Unequivocally.' He chuckled. 'You could never have foreseen this, Eva, but the sheer exceptional beauty of this episode is that the map reached Roosevelt and Hopkins without a trace, without a hint of a smell, of BSC on it. From county sheriff to FBI operative to Hoover to the White House. What's going on south of the border? What are these Nazis planning with their airlines and their Gaus? Couldn't have worked out better.'

Eva thought. 'But the material was inferior.'

'They thought it was good enough. Raul was simply going to plant it, send it to a local newspaper. That was the plan. Until your plan superseded.'

'But I didn't have a plan.'

'All right. Your . . . improvisation. Necessity is the mother of invention and all that.' He paused, looked at her, almost checking her out, she felt, to see if she had changed, somehow. 'The key thing,' he continued, 'the amazing thing, is that it's all worked out about a hundred times better than anyone could have hoped. They can't point a finger at the British and BSC and say: look, another of your dirty tricks to hoodwink us into your European war. They turned this up themselves in a forgotten corner of their own backyard. What can the Bund say? Or America First? It's as clear as day: the Nazis are planning flights from Mexico City to San Antonio and Miami. They're already on your doorstep, USA, it's not something happening across the Atlantic Ocean – wake up.' He didn't need to say anything more: Eva could see how it fitted only one interpretation.

'London's very happy,' he said. 'I can tell you that – very. It might have made the crucial difference.'

She felt the tiredness gather on her again as if she were carrying a heavy rucksack. Maybe it was relief, she thought: she didn't have to fly, didn't have to run, everything had turned out all right – somehow, mystifyingly.

'All right. I'll come in,' she said. 'I'll be back in the office on Monday.'

'Good. There's lots to do. Transoceanic has to follow this up in various ways.'

She climbed down from her stool as Romer paid for her milkshake.

'It was a very close-run thing, you know,' she said, a little residual silt of bitterness in her voice. 'Very.'

'I know. Life's a close-run thing.'

'See you on Monday,' she said. 'Bye.' She turned away, craving her bed.

'Eva,' Romer said and caught her elbow. 'Mr and Mrs Sage. Room 340. The Algonquin Hotel.'

'Tell me exactly what happened,' Morris Devereux said, 'from the minute you left New York.'

They were sitting in his office at Transoceanic on a Friday morning. Outside it was a cold late-November day, snow-flurries were threatened. Eva had spent Saturday and Sunday at the Algonquin with Romer. She had slept all day Saturday, Romer being sweet and considerate. On Sunday they went for a walk in Central Park and had a brunch at the Plaza, then they went back to the hotel and made love. She had gone home to her apartment in the evening. Sylvia had been waiting, forewarned – don't tell me anything, she said, take your time, I'm here if you want me. She had felt restored again and, for a while, all the nagging questions in her head had receded until Morris Devereux's request brought them charging back. She told him everything that she had told Romer, leaving nothing out. Devereux listened intently and made brief notes on a pad in front of him – dates, times.

When she finished he shook his head in some amazement. 'And it's all turned out so well. Fantastically well. Bigger than the Belmonte Letter, bigger than the Brazil Map.'

'You make it sound like some Machiavellian superscheme,' she said. 'But there was no plan. Everything was spontaneous, on the spur of the moment. I was only trying to cover tracks – to muddy water, to give me some time. Confuse people. I had no plan,' she reiterated.

'Maybe all great schemes are like that,' he said. 'Happenstance intersecting with received wisdom produces something entirely new and significant.'

'Perhaps. But I was *sold*, Morris,' she said, with some harshness, some provocativeness. 'Wouldn't you say so?'

He made an uncomfortable face. 'I would have to say it looks like it.'

'I keep thinking of *their* plan,' she said. 'And that's what bothers me, not the fact that I somehow, by luck and accident, foiled it and turned it into our so-called triumph. I'm not interested in that. I was meant to be found dead in the desert with a dodgy map of Mexico on me and 5,000 dollars. That was the real plan. Why? What's it all about?'

He looked baffled, as he thought through the logic of what she had said. 'Let's go over it again,' he said. 'When did you first spot the two crows at Denver?'

They ran through the sequence of events again. She could see that now there was something further troubling Morris, something that he wasn't prepared to tell her – yet.

'Who was running me, Morris?'

'I was. I was running you.'

'And Angus and Sylvia.'

'But under my instructions. It was my party.'

She looked shrewdly at him. 'So, I should probably be very suspicious of you.'

'Yes,' he said, thoughtfully, 'so it would seem.' He sat back and locked his fingers behind his head. 'I would be suspicious of me, too. You lost the crows in Denver. Hundred per cent sure?'

'Hundred per cent.'

'But they were waiting for you in Las Cruces.'

'I didn't even know I was going to Las Cruces until the man in Albuquerque told me. I could have been going anywhere.'

'So he must have set you up.'

'He was an envoy. A fetch-and-carry man.'

'The crows in Denver were local.'

'I'm pretty sure. Standard FBI.'

'Which suggests to me,' Morris said, sitting up, 'that the crows in Las Cruces weren't.'

'What do you mean?' Now she was interested.

'They were bloody good. Too bloody good for you.'

This was something she hadn't thought of. Neither had Romer. Denver and Las Cruces had always seemed like two ends of the same operation. Devereux's suggestion implied that there were two parties running – simultaneously, unconnected.

'Two sets of crows? Makes no sense – one inept, one good.'

Devereux held up his hand. 'Let's proceed with the assumption and ignore the solution. Didn't they teach you that at Lyne?'

'They needn't have been waiting for me,' she said, thinking fast. 'They could have been with me all the way from New York if they were that good.'

'Possibly. Exactly.'

'So who were the second lot if they weren't FBI?' Eva said:

her mind was beginning that old mad clamour again – questions, questions, questions and no answers. 'The Bund? America First? Private hire?'

'You're looking for a solution. Let's play it through first. They wanted you dead with the map on you. You would be identified as a British crow because the FBI were following you out of New York even though you lost them.'

'But what's the point? One dead British agent.'

She noticed Morris now had a worried expression on his face. 'You're right: it doesn't add up. There's something we're missing . . .' he looked like a man faced with half a dozen urgent options, all of them unsavoury.

'Who knew I was in Las Cruces?' Eva prompted, trying to get the momentum going again.

'Me, Angus, Sylvia.'

'Romer?'

'No. He was in England. He only knew about Albuquerque.'

'Raul knew,' Eva said. 'And the fellow in Albuquerque. So other people knew apart from you three . . .' Something struck her. 'How come de Baca knew I was in the Motor Lodge? Nobody knew I was going to the Motor Lodge except me – you didn't know, Angus and Sylvia didn't know. I jinked, I weaved, I backtracked. I had no shadows, I swear.'

'You must have,' he said, insistently. 'Think about it: that's why the Las Cruces lot had nothing to do with the Denver crows. They had a big team on you, or waiting for you. A brigade – four, six. And they were good.'

'There was a woman in the red coupé,' Eva said, remembering. 'Maybe I wasn't looking for a woman. Or women.'

'What about the desk clerk at the Alamogordo Inn. He knew you were checking out.'

She thought: that little twerp on the desk? And remembered the Lyne mnemonic – the best often seem the worst. Maybe

Raul, also. Albino Raul, the desk clerk, the couple in the coupé – a brigade, Morris said – two others she hadn't spotted. And who were the men de Baca had made the sign to as they left the Motor Lodge? It suddenly seemed more possible. She looked at Morris as he sat in thought, tugging at his bottom lip with finger and thumb. Isn't he rather leading me, she wondered? Is this Morris's smart intuition or is he steering me? She decided to stop: circles were rotating within rotating circles.

'I'll keep thinking,' she said. 'I'll call you if I have a brainwave.'

As she walked back to her office she remembered what the desk clerk had said to her when she'd checked into the Alamogordo Inn. You sure you want to stay here? There are nicer places out of town. Had he deliberately seeded an idea in her head? No, she thought, this is becoming absurd – it was driving her insane.

That night Sylvia fried her a steak and they opened a bottle of wine.

'Everything's buzzing at the office,' she said, hinting heavily. 'They say you're the star of the show.'

'I will tell you, I promise,' Eva said. 'Only I still haven't worked half of it out yet.'

Just before she went to bed, Morris Devereux telephoned. His voice sounded tense, on edge – he had abandoned his usual languid drawl.

'Can you speak?' he asked. Eva looked round and saw that Sylvia was clearing the dishes from the table.

'Yes, absolutely fine.'

'Sorry to call you so late, but something's bothering me and only you can provide the answer.'

'What is it?'

'Why didn't you just give the map to Raul?'

'Sorry?'

'I mean: those were your instructions, weren't they? You were simply meant to give a "package" to Raul along with the money.'

'Yes.'

'So why didn't you?'

She looked round, she could hear the clatter of dishes from the kitchen.

'Because I checked it and I thought it was botched. Inferior material – something rotten.'

'Did anyone tell you to check the merchandise?'

'No.'

'So why did you?'

'Because . . . Because I thought I should . . .' She asked herself why: it had been a matter of complete instinct. 'I just thought it was good procedure.'

He went quiet. Eva listened for a second and then said: 'Hello? Are you there?'

'Yes,' Morris said. 'The thing is, Eve, that if you'd just given the merchandise to Raul as instructed, then none of this would have happened. Don't you see? It all happened precisely because you *didn't* do what you were supposed to.'

Eva thought about this for a moment: she couldn't see what he was driving at.

'I don't follow,' she said. 'Are you saying that this is somehow all my fault?'

'Jesus Christ!' he said softly, abruptly.

'Morris? Are you all right?'

'I see it now . . .' he said, almost to himself. 'My God, yes . . .'

'See what?'

'I have to do some checks tomorrow. Let's meet tomorrow. Tomorrow afternoon.' He gave her instructions to go to a cartoon-news theatre on Broadway, just north of Times Square – a small cinema that showed cartoons and newsreels on a 24-hour loop.

'It's always empty around four,' Morris said. 'Sit in the back row. I'll find you.'

'What's going on, Morris,' she said. 'You can't leave me dangling like this.'

'I have to make some very discreet enquiries. Don't mention this to anyone. I'm worried that it may be very serious.'

'I thought everyone was thrilled to bits.'

'I think the crows in Las Cruces may have been our friends in grey.'

Our friends in grey were the German-American Bund.

'Locals?'

'Further afield.'

'Jesus.'

'Don't speak. See you tomorrow. Good-night.'

She hung up. Morris was talking about the Abwehr or the SD – the Sicherheitsdienst. No wonder he was worried – if he was right then the Germans must have someone in BSC – a ghost at the heart of the operation.

'Who was that?' Sylvia asked coming out of the kitchen. 'Coffee?'

'Yes, please. It was Morris. Some accounting problem at Transoceanic.'

'Oh, yes?' They all knew when they were lying to each other but nobody took offence. Sylvia would just log this fact away: it was too unusual – it showed how worried Morris must be to have drawn attention to himself in this way. They drank their coffee, listened to some music on the radio and went to bed. As she drifted off to sleep Eva thought she heard Sylvia making a short phone call. She wondered if she should have told Sylvia of Morris's suspicions but decided, on balance, that it was better to have them confirmed or denied before she shared them. As she lay in her bed she reran their conversation: Morris had seen something in the events at Las Cruces that she hadn't or couldn't. She wondered further if she should tell someone about this meeting with him tomorrow – as insurance. But she decided not to – she should just let Morris explain how he saw things. For some reason she trusted him and to trust someone, she knew all too well, was the first and biggest mistake you could make.

But there was no sign of Morris at the office the next morning – even by lunchtime he still hadn't put in an appearance. Eva was working on a follow-up story to the Mexican map, all about a new generation of four-engined German passenger planes – based on the Condor Fw 200 submarine hunter – that had a non-stop range of 2,000 miles, more than enough to cross the Atlantic to South America from West Africa. She thought that if she could place the story with a Spanish newspaper – *El Diario* or *Independiente* – that an Argentine airline had ordered six, then it might have some legs.

She drafted it out and took it through to Angus, who seemed to be more and more a presence at Transoceanic, these days, and less and less at OBA.

He read it quickly.

'What do you think?' she said.

Angus seemed distracted – not particularly friendly – and she noticed the ashtray in front of him was dense with buckled cigarette butts.

'Why Spain?'

'Better to start it there so Argentina can deny it. We get more mileage if it starts in Spain and then is picked up in South America. Then maybe we can try it here in the US.'

'Do these planes exist?'

'Condors exist.'

'Right. Seems fine. Good luck.' He reached for his cigarette case again – he clearly couldn't care less.

'Have you seen Morris, by any chance?' she asked.

'He said he had to spend the day at Rockefeller – following something up.'

'Is something wrong, Angus? Is something going on?'

'No, no,' he said, just about managing a convincing smile. 'Rather too many Martinis last night.'

She left him, feeling slightly disturbed: so Morris was at BSC – interesting that Angus knew that. Had Morris told Angus anything? Could this explain Angus's untypical brusqueness? She pondered these issues as she typed up her Condor story and took it to one of the Spanish translators.

She had a late lunch at an automat on Seventh Avenue, where she bought a tuna sandwich, a slice of cheesecake and a glass of milk. She wondered what Morris could possibly glean at Rockefeller. The Las Cruces job had originated at BSC, of course . . . She ate her sandwich and for about the hundredth time ran through the events that had led to her encounter with de Baca, looking for something she might have missed. What had Morris seen that she hadn't? So: de Baca shoots her and makes sure that her body is quickly found. The map is discovered and some $5,000. What does this say to anybody? A young female British agent is discovered murdered in New Mexico with a suspect map. All eyes – all FBI eyes – would turn to BSC and wonder what they had been planning here. It would be highly, damagingly embarrassing – a nice Abwehr counter-plot, she could see. A British agent exposed distributing anti-Nazi propaganda. But we did nothing else, she said to herself, given the chance, and everybody at the FBI must be aware of this state of affairs – what would be so sensational about that?

But various rogue details tugged at her sleeve. Nobody had ever suggested that the Abwehr could run such an operation in the United States. A whole shadowing brigade from New York to Las Cruces – moreover, one with such resources and such refinements that she couldn't spot it and its members somewhere along the way. She had been highly suspicious – which is how she had snared the local crows. How big would the team have had to be? Six, eight? Changing over all the time, maybe with one or two women? She would have spotted them, she kept saying to herself, or would she: the whole time in Las Cruces she had been suspicious. It's very hard to follow a suspicious target, but she had to say she had never thought about women. But then again, she thought: why was I suspicious? Was I semi-consciously aware of the rings being run around me. She stopped thinking and decided to go early to the cartoon theatre. A laugh or two might be just what she needed.

She waited two hours for Morris at the theatre, sitting in the back row of the near-empty cinema, watching a succession of Mickey Mouse, Daffy Duck, and Tom and Jerry cartoons interspersed with newsreels that occasionally contained news of the war in Europe. 'Germany's war machine falters at the gates of Moscow,' the announcer intoned with massive, hectoring insistence, 'General Winter takes command of the battlefield.' She saw horses floundering up to their withers in mud as fluid and gluey as melted chocolate; she saw exhausted, gaunt German soldiers with sheets tied around them as camouflage, numbly running from house to house; frozen bodies in the snow taking on the properties of shattered trees or outcrops of rock: iron-hard, wind-lashed, unmovable; burning villages lighting the thousands of Russian soldiers scurrying forward across the icy fields in counter-attack. She tried to imagine what was happening there in the countryside around Moscow – Moscow, where she had been born, and which she couldn't remember at all – and found that her brain refused to supply her with any answers. Donald Duck took over, to her relief. People began to laugh.

When it was apparent Morris was not going to show up, and the theatre began slowly but surely to fill up as offices closed, she made her way back to the apartment. She was not that bothered – three out of four of these prearranged meetings never took place – it was too complex and too risky to try to alert people of a postponement or a delay, but worries still nagged at her. Or were they genuine worries? Perhaps her own curiosity about what Morris would have had to say made her more edgy and concerned. He would call in the fullness of time, she told herself; they would meet again; she would discover what he had discovered. Back in the apartment she checked the snares in her room – Sylvia had not been poking around, she was glad, almost stupidly happy, to note. Sometimes she grew tired of this endless, vigilant suspicion – how can you live like that, she thought? Always watching, always checking, always fearful that you were being betrayed and undone. She made herself a cup of coffee, smoked a cigarette and waited for Morris to call.

Sylvia came home and Eva asked her – very by the way – had she seen Morris at the Center today? Sylvia said no, reminding her of just how many hundreds of people worked there now, how huge BSC had grown – like a giant business enterprise, two entire floors of the skyscraper filled, crammed, overflow offices on other floors – Morris could have been there for a week and she'd have still not seen him.

At about eight o'clock a slight but poisonous unease began to afflict Eva. She telephoned Transoceanic and was told by a duty clerk that Mr Devereux had not been in all day. She telephoned Angus Woolf at his apartment but his phone just rang and rang.

At nine Sylvia went out to see a movie – *The Maltese Falcon* – with a friend, leaving Eva alone in the apartment. She sat and watched the phone – a stupid thing to do, she knew, but she felt better for doing it, all the same. She tried to recall her last conversation with Morris. She could hear in her mind his quiet 'Jesus Christ' as something profound had struck him, some missing piece in the puzzle had fitted into place. It had been more shock in his voice, she decided, than alarm, as if this potential solution was so . . . so unexpected, so drastic, that it had drawn this exclamation from him spontaneously. He had fully intended to tell her, otherwise he wouldn't have set up the cartoon-theatre meeting and, more importantly, he had wanted to tell her face to face. Face to face, she thought: why couldn't he have told me in plain-code? I would have got the message. Too shocking for plain-code, perhaps. Too earth-shattering.

She decided to ignore procedure and call his apartment.

'Yes,' a man's voice answered. American accent.

'Could I speak with Elizabeth Wesley, please?' she said, instantly Americanising her own voice.

'I think you have the wrong number.'

'So sorry.'

She hung up and ran to fetch her coat. In the street she found a taxi quickly and told it to go to Murray Hill. Morris lived there in a tall block of anonymous service apartments, as they all did. She made the taxi stop a couple of streets away and walked the rest of the distance. Two police patrol cars were parked outside the lobby entrance. She walked past and saw the doorman sitting behind his lectern, reading a newspaper. She hovered for five minutes, waiting for someone to go in and eventually a couple appeared who had their own key and she followed them quickly through the door, chatting – 'Hi. Excuse me, you don't happen to know if Linda and Mary Weiss are on the sixteenth or the seventeenth floor? I just left them and left my purse there. Five A – sixteen or seventeen. Just running out to a club. Can you believe it?' – the man waved at the doorman, who looked up from his newspaper at the animated trio and looked down again. The couple didn't happen to know the Weiss sisters but Eva rode up to the tenth floor with her new friends – where they exited – and then went on up to thirteen and came down the fire stairs to twelve, where Morris lived.

She saw two policemen and Angus Woolf standing outside the door to Morris's apartment. Angus Woolf? What's he doing here, she thought? And a nausea hit her stomach as she realised, almost immediately, that Morris must be dead.

'Angus,' she called quietly, walking down the corridor towards him, 'what's happened?'

Angus signalled to the cops that she was admissible and swung quickly toward her on his sticks.

'You'd better get out, Eve,' he said, his face pale, 'this is System Blue, here.'

System Blue was as bad as it could get.

'Where's Morris?' she asked, trying to keep her head, trying to seem calm and normal, knowing the answer.

'Morris is dead,' Angus said. 'He killed himself.' He was shocked and upset, she could tell: she remembered they had been colleagues, friends, for a long time, long before she'd arrived at AAS.

Eva felt her mouth go dry as if some small vacuum inside her was siphoning off all her saliva. 'Oh my God,' she said.

'You'd better go, Eve,' Angus repeated. 'All kinds of shit are hitting the fan.'

And then Romer came out of Morris's apartment to have a word with the policemen, turned, glanced down the passageway, and saw her. He strode towards her.

'What're you doing here?'

'I'd arranged to meet Morris for a drink,' she said. 'He was late so I came over.'

Romer's face was immobile, almost vacant, as if he were still taking in and computing the fact of Eva's presence.

'What happened?' Eva said.

'Pills and whisky. Doors locked, windows locked. A note that makes no sense. Something about some boy.'

'Why?' Eva said, unthinkingly, spontaneously.

'Who knows? How well do we know anyone?' Romer turned to Angus. 'Call head office again. We need a big-wig on this one.' Angus limped off and Romer turned back to her. Somehow she felt his whole attention was on her now.

'How did you get in here?' he asked her, his voice unfriendly. 'Why didn't the doorman ring up?'

Eva realised she had made a mistake: she should have gone to the doorman, not used her little subterfuge. That would have been normal: the normal, innocent thing a friend would do if another friend was late for a drink.

'He was busy. I just came up.'

'Or maybe you were looking for Elizabeth Wesley.'

'Who?'

Romer chuckled. Eva realised he was too clever – and he knew her too well, anyway.

Romer looked at her, his eyes were cold: 'Never underestimate the scrupulous resourcefulness of our Miss Dalton, eh?'

And she knew.

She felt a shrilling in her ears, a keening note of hysterical alarm. She put her hand on his arm.

'Lucas,' she said softly. 'I want to see you tonight. I want to be with you.'

It was all she could do – it was pure instinct. She needed to buy a few seconds of time before he realised everything.

He looked over his shoulder at the policemen.

'It's impossible,' he said. 'Not tonight.'

In those seconds she was thinking: he knows Morris and I have talked. He knows Morris told me something, which is why I came covertly into the building. He thinks I have the crucial information and he's trying to calculate how dangerous I am. She saw his expression change as he turned back to her again. She could almost hear their two brains – supercharged – churning. Two turbines going in their separate directions.

'Please,' she said, 'I miss you.' It might just throw him, she was thinking, this lover's plea. Just over twenty-four hours ago we were making love – it might just throw him for five minutes.

'Look – maybe,' he said. He reached for her hand and squeezed it then let it go. 'Stephenson wants to meet you. It seems Roosevelt's going to mention your map in a speech next week – on the tenth. Stephenson wants to congratulate you himself.'

This is so far-fetched it might almost be true, she thought.

'Stephenson wants to meet me?' she repeated, dumbly. It seemed inconceivable. William Stephenson was BSC: it was his party, every nut and bolt – every cracker, cookie and slice of cake.

'You're our shining star,' he said insincerely and looked at his watch. 'Let me sort out this mess. I'll pick you up outside your apartment at ten.' He smiled. 'And don't tell Sylvia. All right?'

'See you at ten,' she said. 'And then, afterwards, maybe we can . . .'

'I'll think of something. Listen, you'd better go before one of these cops takes your name.'

He turned and walked away towards the policemen.

As Eva rode down to the street in the elevator she began to calculate. She checked her watch: 8.45. Romer would be waiting for her outside her apartment at ten. When she didn't show after five minutes he would know she was flying. She had just over an hour to disappear.

She decided she had no time to go back to the apartment – everything had to be left behind in the interests of immediate safety and flight. As she waited for a subway she checked what she had in her handbag: her Eve Dalton passport, some thirty dollars, a packet of cigarettes, lipstick, a compact. Was this enough, she wondered, smiling ruefully to herself, to start a new life?

On the train to Brooklyn she began to go back over that last encounter with Romer and slowly, methodically, examine all its implications. Why was she so suddenly, immediately convinced that Romer was somehow behind the events in Las Cruces and Morris Devereux's death? Maybe she was wrong? . . . Maybe it was Angus Woolf. Maybe it had been Morris playing an elaborate game of entrapment with her, acting the innocent party? But she knew Morris hadn't committed suicide: you don't make a vitally important appointment and then decide to cancel it by ending your life. Romer had given nothing away, though, she had to admit – so why this unshakeable certainty? Why did she feel she had to fly now, at once, as though her life depended on it? The commonplace phrase disturbed her, made her come out in goose bumps – her life did depend on it, she realised. For Morris it was the fact that she hadn't given the map to Raul that was the key indication, the essential clue. Why hadn't she given the map to Raul? Because she had inspected it and found it wanting. Who told her to check the merchandise? No one.

She heard Romer's voice, her lover's voice, as if he were standing beside her: 'Never underestimate the scrupulous resourcefulness of our Miss Dalton, eh?'

That was what had clinched it for her. That was what had made her understand what Morris had seen. She couldn't see the whole picture, how the game was meant to end, but she had realised, standing talking to Romer outside poor dead Morris's flat, that Romer had sent her on the Las Cruces mission, knowing one thing for sure: he knew – absolutely, confidently – that she would never hand over merchandise without examining it. He *knew* her, he knew completely what she would do in that situation. She felt a blush of shame glow on her face as she came to terms with the fact that she could be so easily read, so perfectly programmed and positioned. But why feel shame, she said to herself, with a little flare of anger? Romer knew she would never be an automatic, press-all-the-buttons, courier – that was why he had volunteered her for the job. It had been the same at Prenslo – she used her initiative, took spontaneous decisions, made hard judgements. And the same with Mason Harding. Her head began to reel: it was as if he had been testing her, evaluating how she behaved in these circumstances. She suddenly thought: had Romer put the FBI crows on to her as well, knowing, confident, that she would lose them – and thereby rouse suspicions? She began to feel outmanoeuvred, as if she were playing chess with a grandmaster who was always working ten, twenty, thirty moves ahead. But why would Lucas Romer want her dead?

In the Brooklyn apartment she went straight to the bathroom and took down the medicine cabinet from the wall. She pulled away the loose brick behind it and removed her Margery Allerdice passport and a small wad of dollar bills: she had nearly 300 dollars saved. As she rehung the cabinet she paused.

'No, Eva,' she said out loud.

She had to remember this – she could never forget this – she was dealing with Lucas Romer, a man who knew her all too well, as well as anybody had ever known her in her life, it seemed. She sat down, almost giddy with the thought that had just come to her: Romer *wanted* her to fly, he was expecting her to fly – it would be much easier to deal with her if she was on the run, far from home. So think, she urged herself – double-think, triple-think. Put yourself in Romer's mind – assess his knowledge and opinion of you, Eva Delectorskaya – and then surprise him.

She reasoned to herself: Romer would not have fallen for her heartfelt invitation to spend the night together, not for one second. He would know that she suspected him; he would know that she didn't believe Morris had killed himself. He probably knew, also, that it was over the second she appeared in the corridor outside Morris's apartment and therefore his suggestion to meet at ten was almost an invitation for her to fly. She was suddenly aware that she didn't have a head start: not an hour, not half an hour – she had no time at all.

She left the apartment immediately, wondering if Romer would be aware of its address. She thought not, and as she walked down the street she confirmed that no one was following her. She slipped her Eve Dalton passport through a grating in the gutter and heard it splash gently in some water below. She was now Margery Allerdice – someone Romer knew, of course; he would know all the aliases he provided for his agents – Margery Allerdice would only take her so far.

But take her where? she thought, as she hurried on to the subway station. She had two clear simple choices: south to Mexico or north to Canada. As she deliberated she found herself wondering what Romer would expect her to do. She had just come from the Mexican border – would he assume she would head back, or go north – the other way? She saw a cab cruising by and hailed it. Take me to Penn Station, she said – south, then, to Mexico, the best decision, it made sense – she knew how and where to cross the border.

On the cab journey she continued to ponder the ramifications of this plan. Train – was that the right thing to do? He wouldn't expect her to take a train: too obvious, too easy to check, easier to be trapped on a train – no, Romer would think bus or car, so taking a train might actually buy her some time. She kept thinking about Romer and the way his mind worked as she crossed the East River, heading for the lucent towers of Manhattan, aware that only this would ensure her survival. Eva Delectorskaya versus Lucas Romer. It wouldn't be easy – more to the point, he had trained her, everything she knew came from Romer, handed down in one way or another. So the thing to do was turn his own methods, his own little tricks and specialities, against him . . . But she just needed a little time, she realised, weakly, just a day or two's start on him, time enough to cover her tracks, make it harder for him . . . She huddled down in the back of the cab: it was a chilly November night – some Mexican sun would be nice, she thought, some Brazilian sun. Then she realised she had to go north. She reached over and tapped the taxi driver on the shoulder.

At Grand Central she bought a ticket for Buffalo – twenty-three dollars – and handed over two twenties. The clerk counted out her change and gave her the ticket. She said thank you and walked away, waiting until he had served two other customers, before she came back to the booth, interrupting the next transaction and said, 'This is change for forty. I gave you a fifty.'

The row was impressive. The ticket clerk – a middle-aged man with a middle parting so severe that it looked like it was shaved in place – refused to budge or apologise. An under-manager was called; Eva demanded to see a supervisor. The crowd waiting in line became restive – 'Hurry it up there, lady!' somebody shouted – and Eva rounded on them, crying that she had been cheated out of ten dollars. When she began to weep the under-manager led her away to an office where, almost instantly, she calmed down and said she would be in touch with her lawyers. She made a point of writing down the under-manager's name – Enright – and the ticket clerk's – Stefanelli – and warned him that he and Stefanelli had not heard the last of this, no sirree: when the Delaware & Hudson Railway started robbing its innocent customers somebody had to stand up and fight.

She walked back across the huge concourse, feeling quite pleased with herself – she was surprised at just how easily she had managed to produce genuine tears. She went to a more distant booth and bought another ticket, this time for Burlington. The last train was leaving in three minutes – she ran down the ramp to the platform and boarded it with thirty seconds to spare.

She sat in her seat, watching the lit suburbs flit by and tried to put herself once more in Romer's position. What would he think about the kerfuffle at Grand Central? He would know it was staged – it was an old training ploy to deliberately draw attention to yourself: you make a fuss while buying a ticket to the Canadian border because that's precisely where you're *not* heading. But Romer wouldn't buy that – too easy – he wouldn't be looking south at all, now. No, Eva, he would say to himself, you're not going to El Paso or Laredo – that's what you want me to think. In fact you're going to Canada. Romer would intuit the double bluff immediately, but then – because one must never underestimate the scrupulous resourcefulness of Eva Delectorskaya – doubts would creep in: he would start thinking, no, no . . . maybe it's a triple bluff. That's precisely what Eva wants me to think, to conclude that she was going to Canada when in actual fact she was going south to Mexico. She hoped she was right: Romer's mind was devious enough – would her quadruple bluff be sufficient to fool him? She thought it would. He would read the play thoroughly and should think: yes, in winter birds fly south.

At the station in Burlington she made a phone call to Paul Witoldski in Franklin Forks. It was after midnight.

'Who is it?' Witoldski's voice was harsh and irritated.

'Is this the Witoldski bakery?'

'No. It's the Witoldski Chinese Laundry.'

'Can I speak to Julius?'

'There's no Julius here.'

'It's Eve,' she said.

There was a silence. Then Witoldski said, 'Did I miss a meeting?'

'No. I need your help, Mr Witoldski. It's urgent. I'm at Burlington Station.'

Silence again. 'I'll be there in thirty minutes.'

While Eva waited for Witoldski to arrive she thought to herself: we are urged, implored, instructed, ordered, beseeched never to trust anyone – which is all very well, she reflected, but sometimes in desperate situations trust is all you can rely on. She had to trust Witoldski to help her; Johnson in Meadowville would have been the obvious choice – and she thought she could trust Johnson too – but Romer had been in Meadowville with her. At some stage he would call Johnson; he knew about Witoldski also but he would check on Johnson first. Witoldski might buy her another hour or two.

She saw a muddy station wagon pull into the car-park with 'WXBQ Franklin Forks' printed along its side. Witoldski was unshaven and wearing a plaid jacket and what looked like waxed fishing trousers.

'Are you in trouble?' he asked, looking around for her suitcase.

'I'm in a spot of trouble,' she admitted, 'and I have to be in Canada tonight.'

He thought for a while and rubbed his chin so she could hear the rasp of his bristles.

'Don't tell me any more,' he said and opened the car door for her.

They drove north, barely saying a word to each other; he smelt of beer and other staleness – old sheets, perhaps, a body not recently washed – but she was not complaining. They stopped to fill up at a gas station in Champlain and he asked her if she was hungry. She said she was and he came back to the car with a packet of fig rolls – Gouverneur Fig Rolls, it said on the wrapping. She ate three, one after the other, as they turned west and headed for a town sign-posted Chateaugay, but just before they reached it he turned on to a gravel road and they began to climb up through pine forests, the road narrowing to a single track, the tips of the pine trees brushing the car as they moved slowly along, a thin metallic whisper in her ears. Hunters' trails, Witoldski explained. She nodded off for a while and dreamt of figs and fig trees in the sun until the lurch as the car came to a halt woke her up.

Dawn was close, there was a tarnished silveriness in the sky above her that made the pines seem blacker still. Witoldski pointed to a junction, lit by his headlights.

'A mile down that road you come to Sainte-Justine.'

They stepped out of the car and Eva felt the cold hit her. She saw Witoldski was looking at her thin city shoes. He went round to the back of the station wagon, opened the tail-gate and came back with a scarf and an old greasy cardigan that she put on under her coat.

'You're in Canada,' he said. 'Quebec. They speak French here. You speak French?'

'Yes.'

'Dumb question.'

'I'd like to give you some money for the gas – and your time,' she said.

'Give it to charity, buy a war bond.'

'If anybody comes,' she said. 'If anybody asks you about me, tell them the truth. There's no need to cover up.'

'I never saw you,' he said. 'Who are you? I been out fishing.'

'Thank you,' Eva said, thinking she should perhaps embrace this man. But he held out his hand and they shook hands briefly.

'Good luck, Miss Dalton,' he said, climbed back in his car, turned it at the junction and drove away, leaving Eva in a darkness so absolute Eva did not trust herself to take even one step. But slowly her eyes accustomed themselves to the gloom and she began to make out the jagged tips of the trees against the slowly greying sky and she could see the pale path of the road where it forked. She wrapped Witoldski's scarf tighter around her throat and set off down the track to Sainte-Justine. She was truly flying now, she thought, she had flown to another country and for the first time she began to feel a little safer. It was a Sunday morning, she realised, listening to the noise of her feet crunch on the gravel of the roadway, and the first birds beginning to sing – Sunday, 7 December 1941.

11

Begging with Threats

I LOCKED THE KITCHEN door – Ilse and Ludger were out, but somewhere in Oxford, and I didn't want any surprises. It was lunchtime and I had an hour before Hamid arrived. I felt strange pushing open the door to Ludger and Ilse's room – *my* dining room, I reminded myself – and I reminded myself again that I hadn't set foot in there since Ludger had arrived.

The place looked as if refugees had been holed up there for a month or so. It smelt of old clothes, cigarettes and joss sticks. There were two inflatable mattresses on the floor with unzipped sleeping-bags on them – ancient, khaki, army issue, creased, almost like something once living, a cast-off skin, a decomposing giant limb – that served as beds. There were small stashes of food and drink here and there – tins of tuna and sardines, cans of beer and cider, chocolate bars and biscuits – as if the occupants were expecting to undergo a short siege of some kind. The table and chairs had been pushed against the wall and served as a form of open wardrobe – jeans, shirts, smocks, underwear were hung or laid flat on every edge, chair back or level surface. In another corner I saw the grip that Ludger had arrived with and a bulky rucksack – ex-army – that I supposed was Ilse's.

I very carefully noticed its position against the wall and just before I opened the main flap the thought came to me that she might have placed some snares. 'Snares,' I said out loud, and forced an ironic chuckle: I was spending too much time in my mother's past, I thought to myself – and yet had to admit that here I was indulging in a clandestine search of my lodgers' room. I undid the buckle and rummaged inside – I found a few dog-eared paperbacks (in German – two Stefan Zweigs), an Instamatic camera, a tattered teddy-bear mascot with the name 'Uli' stitched on to it, several packs of condoms and something the size of a half-brick wrapped in kitchen foil. I knew what this was and smelt it: dope, marijuana. I unpeeled a corner of the foil and saw a dense dark-chocolate mass. I took a tiny pinch of it between forefinger and thumb and tasted it – I don't know why: was I some kind of drug connoisseur who could identify its provenance? No, not at all, even though I enjoyed a joint from time to time, but it seemed the sort of thing to do when one was secretly investigating other people's belongings. I folded the foil shut again and put everything away. I searched the other pockets of the rucksack and found nothing interesting. I wasn't sure exactly what I was looking for: a weapon? A gun? A hand-grenade? I closed the door behind me and went to make myself a sandwich.

When Hamid arrived for his lesson, he handed me an envelope and a flyer. The flyer was to announce a demonstration outside Wadham College to protest at the official visit of the Shah of Iran's sister, Ashraf. In the envelope was a xeroxed invitation to a party in the upstairs room at the Captain Bligh pub on the Cowley Road on Friday night.

'Who's having the party?' I asked.

'I am,' Hamid said. 'To say goodbye. I go to Indonesia the next day.'

That evening when Jochen was in bed and Ludger and Ilse had gone to the pub – they always asked me; I always said no – I rang Detective Constable Frobisher.

'I've had a phone call from this Ilse girl,' I said. 'She must have been given my number by mistake – she was asking for someone I didn't know – some "James". I think it was from London.'

'No, she's now definitely in Oxford, Miss Gilmartin.'

'Oh.' This threw me. 'What's she meant to have done?'

There was a pause. 'I shouldn't really tell you this but she was living in a squat in Tooting Bec. We think she might have been selling drugs but the complaints made about her were to do with aggressive begging. Begging with threats, if you know what I mean.'

'Oh right. So she's not some kind of anarchist terrorist, then.'

'What makes you say that?' There was new interest in his voice.

'No reason. Just all this stuff in the papers, you know.'

'Right, yeah . . . Well, the Met just want us to pick her up. We don't want her type in Oxford,' he added a bit priggishly and foolishly, I thought: Oxford was full of all sorts of types – as odd and deranged and as unpleasant as they came: one Ilse more or less wouldn't make any difference.

'I'll be sure to call if she makes contact again,' I said, dutifully.

'Much obliged, Miss Gilmartin.'

I hung up and thought of thin, moody, grubby Ilse and wondered how aggressively she could beg. I began to wonder if I had made a mistake calling Frobisher – he was very keen – and what had made me mention terrorism? That was a blunder, really stupid. Here I was thinking I might be inadvertently harbouring the second generation of the Baader-Meinhof gang but had discovered that they were just the usual sad sacks and losers.

The demonstration outside Wadham College was billed for 6.00 p.m., when the Shah's sister was due to arrive for a reception to declare open the new library that the Shah's money had paid for. I picked up Jochen from Grindle's and we caught a bus into town. We had time for a pizza and a coke in the St Michael's street pizzeria before we wandered hand in hand along the Broad towards Wadham.

'What's a demonstration, Mummy?' he asked.

'We're protesting. Protesting that the University of Oxford should take money from a tyrant and a dictator, a man called the Shah of Iran.'

'The Shah of Iran,' he repeated, liking the sounds of the words. 'Will Hamid be there?'

'Definitely, I would say.'

'He comes from Iran as well, doesn't he?'

'Indeed he does, my clever lad . . .'

I stopped, astonished – there seemed to be about 500 people gathered in two groups on either side of the main entrance to the college. I had been expecting the usual small quorum of earnest lefties and some punks looking for fun but here were dozens of police, arms linked, keeping the entrance to the college as wide and as clear as possible. Others stood in the street on their walkie-talkies, impatiently waving cars on. There were banners – saying DICTATOR, TRAITOR, MURDERER and OXFORD'S SHAME and (more wittily) THE SHAM OF IRAN – and orchestrated chanting in Farsi led by a masked man with a megaphone. Yet the mood was strangely festive – perhaps because it was a beautiful warm summer evening, perhaps because it was a decorous Oxford demonstration, or perhaps because it seemed hard to be really outraged and revolutionary about the opening of a new library. There were a lot of grins, laughter, banter – still, I was impressed: it was the largest political demonstration I had seen in Oxford. It reminded me of my Hamburg days and, thinking of Hamburg, I was reminded of Karl-Heinz and all the fervent, angry marches and demonstrations we had been on together. My mood collapsed somewhat.

I spotted Hamid with a group of other Iranians, chanting along with the megaphone man, and pointing their fingers in emphatic unison. The larking English students, in their combat jackets and *keffiyehs*, looked like amateurs; for them this protest was a kind of extra-curricular luxury, nothing was really at stake – a bit of fun on a sunny evening.

I looked around at the crowd and at the sweating, harassed policemen holding back the protestors' half-hearted surges. I saw another two dozen coppers coming down the road from vans parked outside Keble – the Shah's sister must be due. Then I spotted Frobisher – he was standing on a low wall with other journalists and press photographers – snapping away with a camera at the crowd of demonstrators. I turned my back on him quickly and almost bumped into Ludger and Ilse.

'Hey, Ruth,' Ludger said with a wide smile, seemingly pleased to see me. 'And Jochen too. Great! Have an egg.'

He and Ilse each had two boxes of a dozen eggs that they were handing out to the crowd.

Jochen took one carefully. 'What do I do with this?' he said, uneasily – he had never really warmed to Ludger, despite Ludger's ceaseless, amiable jocularity, but he liked Ilse. I reached out and took an egg as well, to encourage him.

'When you see the rich lady getting out of the limousine you throw it at her,' Ludger said.

'Why?' Jochen asked – reasonably enough, I thought – but before anyone could give him a cogent answer Hamid had picked him up and set him on his shoulders.

'Now you can have a good view,' he said.

I wondered if I should be playing the responsible mother but decided not to – it was never too early in your life to try to destroy the myth of the all-powerful system. What the hell, I thought: the counter-culture dies hard, and in any event it might be good for Jochen Gilmartin to throw an egg at a Persian princess, I reckoned. As Jochen surveyed the scene from Hamid's shoulders I turned to Ilse.

'You see that photographer in the denim jacket – on the wall with the others, the journalists?' I said.

'Yes. And so?'

'He's a policeman. He's looking for you.'

She turned away at once and fished in the pockets of her jacket for a hat – a pale blue bush hat with a floppy brim – that she pulled on low on her head, and added a pair of sunglasses. She whispered something to Ludger and they slipped away into the crowd.

Suddenly the police started to call and gesture to each other. All traffic was stopped and a motorcade of cars led by two outriders with flashing lights came at some speed down Broad Street. The noise of the jeering and the shouting became shrill as the cars stopped and the bodyguards stepped out, shielding a small figure in a silk turquoise dress and short jacket. I saw dark, lacquered bouffant hair, big sunglasses and, as she was ushered quickly towards the porters' lodge and the nervous dons in the welcome committee, the eggs began to fly. I thought that the sound of their cracking open as they hit was like distant gunshots.

'Throw, Jochen!' I shouted spontaneously – and saw him hurl his egg. Hamid let him stay up a second longer and then slid him down his front to the ground.

'I hit a man on the shoulder,' Jochen said, 'one of the men in sunglasses.'

'Good boy,' I said. 'Now let's go home. That's enough excitement for the day.'

We said our goodbyes and walked away from the demonstration up Broad Street and on to the Banbury Road. After a minute or two we were joined, surprisingly, by Ludger and Ilse. Jochen began at once to explain to them that he had deliberately not aimed at the lady because her dress looked pretty – and expensive.

'Hey, Ruth,' Ludger said stepping in beside me, 'thanks for the warning about the pig.'

I saw Ilse had taken Jochen's hand; she was talking to him in German.

'I thought she was in more serious trouble,' I said. 'I think they just want to warn her.'

'No, no,' Ludger said, with a nervous laugh. He lowered his voice. 'Her head is a bit fucked-up. A bit crazy. Nothing heavy, you know.'

'Fine,' I said. 'Just like the rest of us, then.'

Jochen reached for Ludger's hand. 'Give me a swing, Ludger.'

So Ludger and Ilse between them began to swing Jochen off his feet as we walked homewards, Jochen laughing with uncontrolled pleasure, calling at every swing to be launched higher, higher.

I dropped back a little, bent down to adjust the strap on my shoe, and didn't spot the police car until it had pulled up alongside me. Through the open window Detective Constable Frobisher smiled at me.

'Miss Gilmartin – I thought it was you. Could I have a quick word?' He stepped out of the car, the driver remaining inside. I sensed Ludger, Ilse and Jochen continuing on their way regardless and managed not to look at them.

'I just wanted you to know,' Frobisher said. 'The German girl – seems she's back in London again.'

'Oh, right.'

'Did you see the demo?'

'Yes, I was in Broad Street. Some of my students were participating. Iranians, you know.'

'Yeah, that was what I was wanting to talk to you about,' he said, stepping away from the car. 'You move, I take it, among the foreign-student community.'

'I wouldn't say "move", exactly – but I do teach foreign students all year round, pretty much.' I flicked my hair back out of my eyes and used the gesture to glance up the road. Ludger, Ilse and Jochen were about a hundred yards off, standing still now, looking back at me, Ilse holding Jochen's hand.

'Let me put it this way, Miss Gilmartin,' Frobisher said,

making his voice confidential, semi-urgent. 'We'd be very interested if you saw and heard anything unusual – political, like: anarchists, radicals. The Italians, the Germans, the Arabs . . . Anything that strikes you – just give us a call, let us know.' He smiled, genuinely, not politely, and I suddenly saw the real Frobisher for an instant, saw his serious zeal. Under the formulaic pleasantries and the air of earnest dullness, was someone shrewder, cleverer, more ambitious. 'You can get closer to these people than we can, you hear things we'd never hear,' he said, letting his guard drop again, 'and if you gave us a call from time to time – doesn't matter if it's just a hunch – we'd really appreciate it.'

Is this how it begins? I thought. Is this how your life as a spy begins?

'Sure,' I said. 'If I ever heard anything. But they're fairly innocuous and ordinary – all trying to learn English.'

'I know. Ninety-nine point nine per cent. But you've seen the graffiti,' he said. 'We're talking Italian far right, German far left. They must be here if they're writing that stuff on the walls.' It was true: Oxford was more and more spattered with meaningless Euro-agitprop slogans – *Ordine Nuevo, das Volk wird dich rachen, Caca-pipi-talisme* – meaningless to the English, that is.

'I understand,' I said. 'If I hear anything I'll give you a call. No problem: I've got your number.'

He thanked me again, said he'd be in touch, told me to 'take care', shook my hand and climbed back into his car, which did a swift U-turn and headed back down the road towards the city centre.

I rejoined the waiting trio.

'Why did that policeman want you, Mummy?'

'He said he was looking for a boy who threw an egg.' The adults all laughed but Jochen wasn't amused.

'You've used that joke before. It's still not funny.'

As we headed off, I drew Ilse back a pace or two.

'They think you're back in London, for some reason. So I suppose you're safe here.'

'Thank you for this, Ruth. I'm very grateful.'

'Why are you begging? They said you were begging aggressively – with threats.'

She sighed. 'Only at the beginning I was begging. Yeah. But not any more.' She shrugged. 'On the streets there is much indifference, you know. It was making me angry.'

'What were you doing in London, anyway?'

'I left my home – in Düsseldorf. My best friend from school started to fuck my father. It was impossible, I had to leave.'

'Yes,' I said, 'yes, I can see how you might have had to . . . What're you going to do now?'

Ilse thought for a while, made a vague gesture with her hand. 'I think Ludger and I will find a flat in Oxford. We can squat, maybe. I like Oxford. Ludger says maybe we can do some porno.'

'In Oxford?'

'No, in Amsterdam. Ludger says he knows a guy who's making videos.'

I glanced at the skinny blonde girl walking along beside me as she rummaged in her bag for a cigarette – almost pretty, just something blunt and rounded about her features keeping her ordinary. An ordinary girl.

'I wouldn't do porno, Ilse,' I said. 'It's just to help sad men wank.'

'Yeah . . .' She thought a bit. 'You're right. I rather selling drugs.'

We caught up with Ludger and Jochen and wandered homewards, chatting about the demo and Jochen's bull's-eye with the egg, first throw. But I found I was thinking of Frobisher's offer, for some reason: anything you hear, even a hunch – we'd really appreciate it.

The Story of Eva Delectorskaya

Ottawa. Canada. 1941

EVA DELECTORSKAYA LOOKED OUT of the bus window at the coloured lights and the Christmas decorations in the windows of Ottawa's department stores. She was on her way to work and had managed to find a seat close to the front, as usual, not far from the driver, so she could more easily monitor who stepped aboard and who stepped off. She opened her novel and pretended to read. She was headed for Somerset Street in downtown Ottawa but she tended to get off either a few stops before her destination or a few stops after and, wherever she chose to disembark, she would take a different, roundabout route before she arrived at the Ministry of Supply. Such precautions added about twenty minutes to her journey to work but she felt calmer and more at ease during the day, knowing she had carried them out.

She was sure, almost 100 per cent sure, as sure as anyone could be, that no one had ever followed her during these few days she'd been living and working in Ottawa, but the constant routine checks were a part of her life now: it was almost two weeks since she had flown from New York – two weeks tomorrow, she realised – but she could still take nothing for granted.

She had walked into Sainte-Justine as the village was beginning to wake and stir and had ordered a coffee and doughnut with the first customers at the drugstore before catching the early bus to Montreal. There, she had had her long hair cut short and dyed a chestnut brown and spent that night in a small hotel near the station. She had taken to her bed at eight and slept through twelve hours. It wasn't until the next morning, the Monday, that she bought a newspaper and read about Sunday's attack on Pearl Harbor. She skimmed the story quickly, incredulously, and then reread it more slowly: eight battleships sunk, hundreds dead and missing, a date which will live in infamy, war declared on Japan. And she thought, buoyantly, simply: we've won. This is what we had wanted and now we will win – not next week, not next year, but we will win. She became almost tearful because she knew how important it was, trying to imagine how the news was being received at BSC, and had a sudden crazy urge – immediately rejected – to telephone Sylvia. What would Lucas Romer be feeling, she wondered? Was she more secure now? Would they call off the search?

Somehow she doubted it, she said to herself, as she walked up the steps to the new annexe of the Ministry of Supply and took the elevator to the typing pool on the third floor. She was early, the first of the four women who acted as shorthand typists for the half-dozen civil servants who occupied this floor of this division of the ministry. She began to relax, somewhat: she always felt safer at work because of the anonymity provided by the number of people in the building and because she could cover herself journeying there and homeward. It was during her time off that the caution and the constant suspicion re-established itself – as if she became an individual once she left the office, an individual who might attract attention. Here on the third floor she was just a member of a typing pool amongst innumerable typing pools.

She took the cover off her typewriter and leafed through the documents in her in-tray. She was quite happy with her work: it made no demands on her and it was going to provide her with a ticket home, or so she hoped.

Eva knew there were only two ways for a single woman to obtain passage to England from Canada: either in uniform – the Red Cross, nursing, or signals – or in government. She considered government the swiftest route and so had travelled to Ottawa from Montreal on Monday 8 December and had registered with a secretarial agency specialising in providing secretaries for government departments and Parliament. Her shorthand, her fluent French and her typing speed were more than adequate qualifications and within twenty-four hours she had been sent for interview at the new annexe of the Ministry of Supply on Somerset Street, a solid unadorned office block of grey stone, the colour of old snow.

On her first night in Montreal, in her hotel, she had spent an hour with a powerful magnifying glass, a needle and some black Indian ink diluted with a little milk, painstakingly altering her passport name from 'Allerdice' to 'Atterdine'. There was nothing she could do about 'Margery' but decided to call herself 'Mary' as if it were a preferred diminutive. The passport would not survive inspection by an expert with a microscope but it would certainly pass muster beneath the hurried glance of an immigration official. Eva Delectorskaya became Eve Dalton became Margery Allerdice became Mary Atterdine – her tracks, she hoped, were slowly being erased.

After a few days at her job she began asking around the women and girls in the ministry's canteen what the chances were of being posted to the London embassy. She discovered there was a fairly regular traffic of staff to and fro: every month or two some went out, some came back. She had to go to personnel and fill in a form; the fact that she was British might make the whole process easier. The story she grudgingly, shyly, told to any who asked was that she had come to Canada to be married and had been grievously let down by her Canadian fiancé. She had moved to Vancouver to be with him but as the marriage plans remained suspiciously vague she realised she had been cruelly misled and misused. Alone and adrift in Vancouver, she had travelled east to seek passage home, one way or another. Anyone who asked her more precise questions – Who was the man? Where had she lived? – prompted sniffles or genuine tears: she was still raw and humiliated, it was all too upsetting to talk about. Sympathetic questioners understood and tended not to probe further.

She had found a boarding-house on a quiet street – Bradley Street – in the bourgeois suburb of Westboro, run by Mr and Mrs Maddox Richmond, all of whose clients were young ladies. Bed and breakfast was offered at ten dollars a week; half board at fifteen, rates by the week or the month. 'Open fires on chilly days' it said on the small sign attached to the gatepost. Most of their 'paying guests' were immigrants: two Czech sisters, a Swedish woman, a country girl from Alberta, and Eva. Family prayers were held in the downstairs parlour at 6.00 p.m. for those who wished to attend and from time to time Eva duly and with unostentatious piety did. She ate out, choosing diners and restaurants near the ministry, anonymous places, busy, where the turnover of hungry clients was swift. She found a public library that opened late where some nights she could read undisturbed until 9.00 p.m. and, on her first weekend off, travelled to Quebec City, simply to be away. She really only used the Richmond Guest House to sleep in and she never came to know the other paying guests better than as nodding acquaintances.

This quiet life, this regular routine suited her and she found she came to enjoy living in Ottawa almost without effort: its wide boulevards, its well-kept parks, its solid, Gothically grandiose public buildings, its tranquil streets and civic cleanliness were exactly what she needed, she realised, as she pondered her next move.

But all the while she was there she covered herself. In a notebook she logged the registration of every car parked in the street and learned to which household they belonged. She noted down the names of the owners of the twenty-three houses on Bradley Street, opposite and on either side of the Richmonds, and kept track of the comings and goings in casual chats with Mrs Richmond: Valerie Kominski had a new boyfriend, Mr and Mrs Doubleday were on vacation, Fielding Bauer had just been 'let go' from the building firm he worked for. She wrote everything down, adding new facts, crossing out redundant or outdated ones, looking all the time for the anomaly that would alert her. With her first weekly salary check she had purchased some sensible items of clothing and dipped into her dollar supply to buy a bulky beaver coat against the cold that was growing as Christmas approached.

She tried to analyse and second-guess what might be going on at BSC. Despite the euphoria of Pearl Harbor and the arrival of the USA as the long-awaited ally, she imagined that they would still be investigating, digging deep, following up leads. Morris Devereux dies and Eve Dalton disappears that very night – not events that can be casually ignored. She was sure that everything that Morris had suspected of Romer would now be laid at his door: if there were Abwehr ghosts in BSC did anyone need to look any further than Devereux and Dalton? But she also knew – and this gave her satisfaction, made her more determined – that her continued disappearance, her invisibility, would be a persistent, annoying worry and goad to Romer. If anyone would be urging that the search be maintained at its highest level it would be he. She would never be complacent or relax, she told herself: Margery – 'call me Mary' – Atterdine would continue to lead her life as unobtrusively and as cautiously as she could.

'Miss Atterdine?'

She looked up from her typewriter. It was Mr Comeau, one of the under-secretaries in the ministry, a neat middle-aged man with a trimmed moustache and a nervous manner that was at once shy and punctilious. He asked her to come into his office.

He sat at his desk and searched through his papers.

'Please sit.'

She did so. He was a proper man, Mr Comeau, never acting in a superior or dismissive manner – as some of the other under-secretaries did as they thrust their documents at the typists and issued their instructions as if they were talking to automata – but there was something melancholy about him, too, about his neatness, his propriety, as if it were his guard against a hostile world.

'We have your application for the London posting here. It's been approved.'

'Oh, good.' She felt a heart-thud of pleasure: something would happen now, she sensed her life taking a new direction again, but she kept her face expressionless.

Comeau told her there was a new draft of five 'young women' from the Ottawa ministries leaving St John on 18 January for Gourock in Scotland.

'I'm very pleased,' she said, thinking she must make some comment. 'It's very important to me –'

'Unless . . .' he interrupted, trying for a playful smile and failed.

'Unless what?' Her voice was more sharp and abrupt than she meant it to be.

'Unless we can persuade you to stay. You've fitted in very well here. We're very pleased with your diligence and ability. We're talking about promotion, Miss Atterdine.'

She was flattered, she said, indeed she was surprised and overwhelmed, but nothing could persuade her otherwise. She alluded, discreetly, to the unhappy experiences in British Columbia, how all that was behind her and she wished simply to go back home now, home to her widowed father, she added, throwing in this new biographical information spontaneously.

Mr Comeau listened, nodded sympathetically, said he understood, and told her that he too was a widow, that Mrs Comeau had died two years ago and that he also knew that loneliness her father must be experiencing. She realised now where his air of melancholia originated.

'But think again, Miss Atterdine,' he said. 'These Atlantic crossings are dangerous, there's risk involved. They're still bombing London. Wouldn't you rather be here in Ottawa?'

'I think my father wants me back,' Eva said. 'But thank you for your concern.'

Comeau raised himself from his chair and went to look out of the window. A small rain was spitting on the glass and he traced the squirming fall of a raindrop on the pane with his forefinger. And Eva was instantly back in Ostend, in Romer's office, the day after Prenslo, and she felt a giddiness overcome her. How many times a day did she think of Lucas Romer? She thought of him deliberately, wilfully all the time, thought of him organising the search for her, thought of him thinking about her, wondering where she was and how to find her, but these inadvertent moments when memories pounced on her took her unawares and were overwhelming.

Comeau was saying something.

'I'm sorry?'

'I was wondering if you had plans for the Christmas holiday,' he said, a little shyly.

'Yes, I'm staying with friends,' she said, instantly.

'I go to my brother's, you see,' he continued as if he hadn't heard her. 'He has a house near North Bay, on the lake.'

'Sounds wonderful, unfortunately –'

Comeau was determined to make this invitation, overriding all interruptions. 'He has three sons, one of them married, a very nice family, eager, friendly young people. I wondered if you'd like to join us for a night or two, as my guest. It's very relaxed and informal – log fires, fishing on the lake, home cooking.'

'You're very kind, Mr Comeau,' she said, 'but I've already made all the arrangements with my friends. It wouldn't be fair on them to cancel at such short notice.' She put on a frustrated smile to console him a little, sorry to let him down.

The sadness crossed his face again – he had had his hopes high, she realised. The lonely young English woman who worked in the typing pool – so attractive, leading such a drab, quiet life. The London transfer would have galvanised him, she knew, made him act.

'Yes, well, of course,' Comeau said. 'Perhaps I should've asked you earlier.' He spread his hands abjectly and Eva felt sorry for him. 'But I had no idea you would be leaving us so soon.'

It was three days later when Eva saw the car for the second time, a moss-green '38 Ford parked outside the Pepperdines' house. Before that it had been outside Miss Knox's and Eva knew the car belonged to neither Miss Knox (an elderly spinster with three terriers) nor the Pepperdines. She walked quickly past it, glancing inside. There was a newspaper and a map on the passenger seat and what looked like a thermos flask in the door pocket on the driver's side. A thermos flask, she thought: someone spends a lot of time in that car.

Two hours later she went out 'for a stroll' and it was gone.

She thought long and hard that night, telling herself initially that if she saw the car a third time she would move out. But she knew that was wrong, remembering her Lyne training: when the anomaly appears react to it immediately was the rule – a Romer rule. If she saw it for a third time it would almost definitely be sinister and by then perhaps too late, as far as she was concerned. That night she packed her small grip and looked out of her dormer window at the houses opposite and wondered if there was a BSC team already installed there waiting for her. She put her grip by the door, thinking how light it weighs, how few possessions I have. She did not sleep that night.

In the morning she told Mr and Mrs Richmond that she had to leave urgently – a family matter – and was going back to Vancouver. They were sorry to see her go, they said, but she had to understand that at such short notice they couldn't possibly reimburse the residue of her month's rent paid in advance. Eva said she understood, completely, and apologised for any inconvenience.

'By the way,' she asked, pausing at the door, 'has anyone left any messages for me?'

The Richmonds looked at each other, consulting silently, before Mrs Richmond said, 'No, I don't think so. No, dear.'

'No one's called round to see me?'

Mr Richmond chuckled. 'We had a young man drop by yesterday asking to rent a room. We told him it was ladies only – he seemed very surprised.'

Eva thought: it's probably nothing, a coincidence, but she suddenly wanted to be away from Bradley Street.

'If anyone does call say I've gone back to Vancouver.'

'Of course, dear. Take care now, it's been lovely knowing you.'

Eva left the house, turned left instead of her usual right, and briskly walked a meandering, convoluted mile to a different bus stop.

She moved into the Franklin Hotel on Bank Street, one of Ottawa's largest, a functional, modest establishment with over 300 rooms 'completely fireproof and all with shower and phone' but no restaurant or coffee shop. However, even with her single room at three dollars a night, she realised she was going to run out of money. There were no doubt cheaper hotels and more frugal lodgings to be had in Ottawa but she required the security and anonymity of a large central hotel. She had a little over three weeks to go until her voyage back to Britain: she just needed to bury herself away.

Her room was small, plain and on the seventh floor and

through a gap in the buildings opposite she could see the green expanse of the Exhibition Grounds and a swerve of the Rideau River. She unpacked and hung her few clothes in the wardrobe. The one advantage of the move was that she could at least walk to work and save on bus fares.

But she kept wondering if she had done the right thing, if she had been too jumpy, and that the very suddenness of her move from the Richmonds might have signalled something itself . . . A strange car in a suburban street – what could be so alarming about that? But she reminded herself that she had chosen Bradley Street and the Richmond Guest House precisely because its location made it easy to spot anything unusual occurring. Everybody knew everyone and knew everyone's business on Bradley Street – it was that kind of neighbourhood. And who was the young man who had failed to read the 'Ladies Only' rubric on the guest-house sign? A careless traveller? Not a policeman, she thought, for a policeman would have simply identified himself and asked to see the register. Someone from BSC, then, instructed to check out the hotels and guest-houses in Ottawa. Why Ottawa, she reasoned further, why not Toronto? How could anyone guess or deduce she had gone to Ottawa? And so the questions continued, badgering her, sapping her energy. She went to work as usual, typed letters and documents in the typing pool and came home to her room. She barely inhabited the city. She bought sandwiches on her way home from work, stayed in her room with its view of the Exhibition Grounds and the Rideau River and listened to the radio, waiting for Christmas and 1942 to arrive.

The Ministry of Supply offices closed on Christmas Eve and opened again on 27 December. She chose not to go to the ministry's staff Christmas party. On Christmas Day she slipped out of the hotel early and bought some turkey roll, a loaf of bread, butter and two bottles of beer. She sat on her bed, eating her sandwich, drinking her beer and listening to music on the radio and managed not to cry for an hour or so. Then she allowed herself to weep for ten minutes, thinking she had never been so alone in her life, disturbed by the thought that not one person in the entire world knew where she was. She found herself thinking of her father, an old sick man, living in Bordeaux, and she remembered his encouragement and his zeal when Romer came to recruit her. Who would have thought it would end like this? she said to herself, alone in a hotel room in Ottowa . . . But no, she thought: no self-pity, she angrily reminded herself, wiping her eyes and steeling herself anew. She cursed Lucas Romer for his cruelty and his betrayal. Then she slept for an hour or so and woke more determined, more composed and calculating, stronger. Now she had an ambition, a purpose: to defeat the worst intentions of Lucas Romer became her mission and she began to wonder, in her solitude, if he had been manipulating her from the very beginning of her recruitment; if he had been observing and honing her habits, her cast of mind and her particular diligence – trying her out in Prenslo and in Washington, waiting for the day when she would become suddenly very useful indeed . . . It was futile stuff, she knew, and to think like that would drive her to madness. The simple fact that he could not find her was her hold over him – her little portion of power. While Eva Delectorskaya was at large in the world, Lucas Romer could never truly relax.

And then she wondered if this was what her life would always be like, from now on: covert, fearful, always watchful, always restless, always watching, suspecting. It was something she didn't particularly want to contemplate or consider. Forget that, she ordered herself: one step at a time. Get home, first, then see what happens.

She went back to work on the 27th only to be faced with another holiday looming at the New Year. But having survived Christmas she felt she could cope with welcoming in 1942. German forces were retreating from Moscow but the Japanese had taken Hong Kong: this was the way it would go, she thought, for a long time to come. She bought a pint of whisky and woke to discover that she had managed to construct a presentable hangover for herself on the morning of 1 January. The year began with a persistent day-long headache – but there was another headache approaching that she knew could not be avoided.

On her second day back at work, just before the office closed for the evening, she asked if she could see Mr Comeau. He was free and she knocked on his door and was admitted. Comeau was visibly pleased to see her – he had been keeping his distance since she had turned down his holiday invitation, but now he was up and around from his side of the desk, drawing out a chair for her and sitting himself rakishly on the edge of his desk, a leg dangling, an unfortunate inch of hirsute shin exposed below his trouser cuff. He offered her a cigarette and the small ceremony of lighting took place, Eva being careful not to touch his hand as he held his lighter tremblingly in place.

'Second thoughts, Miss Atterdine?' he asked. 'Or is that too much to hope for?'

'I have to ask you an enormous favour,' she said.

'Oh, I see.' The dying fall of the words expressed his huge disappointment eloquently. 'What can I do for you? A reference? A letter of introduction?'

'I need to borrow a hundred dollars,' she said. Unforeseen expenses, she explained; she couldn't wait until her salary started in England.

'Go to your bank,' he said, a little stiffly, offended. 'I'm sure they'll listen to you.'

'I don't have a bank account,' she said. 'I'll pay you back from England. It's just that I need the money now, here, before I go.'

'Are you in some kind of trouble, as they say?' His cynicism didn't suit him, and she could see he knew it.

'No. I just need the money. Urgently.'

'It's a considerable sum. Don't you think I'm entitled to an explanation?'

'I can't explain.'

His eyes fixed on her and she knew he was telling her that there was an easier way – stay in Ottawa, get to know me, we're both lonely. But she gave him no comforting answer in her gaze.

'I'll think it over,' he said, and stood up, buttoning his jacket, the state functionary once more faced with a recalcitrant subordinate.

The next morning there was an envelope on her desk with five twenty-dollar bills inside. She felt a strange rush of emotion: gratitude, relief, shame, comfort, humbleness. Never trust anyone, never trust a soul on this earth – except, she thought, the Witoldskis and the Comeaus of this world.

She moved hotel, again, twice before 18 January, collected her ticket and documentation from the travel bureau in the ministry – ticket and documents made out in the name of 'Mary Atterdine' – and she allowed herself to think of the future for the first time, really, of what she would do when she made landfall, where she would go, what she would do, who she would become. England – London – was hardly her home, but where else could she go? 'Lily Fitzroy' awaited her in Battersea. She could hardly travel to France to try and find her father and stepmother, whatever had become of them. The war would have to end first and it showed no sign of doing that. No, London and Lily Fitzroy were her only options, for the short term at least.

12

SAVAK

HUGUES ASKED ME IF I wanted another drink – I knew I shouldn't accept (I had drunk too much already) but, of course, I said yes and went eagerly with him to the puddled, ashy bar of the Captain Bligh.

'Can I have a packet of peanuts, as well, please?' I cheerily asked the surly barman. I had arrived late and had missed the food provided in the upstairs room – the sliced baguettes and cheese, sausage-rolls, Scotch eggs and mini pork pies – all good drink-soaking carbohydrate. There were no peanuts, it transpired, though they had crisps; but only salt 'n' vinegar. Salt 'n' vinegar it would have to be, I told him, and in fact I found myself craving that saline bitterness, all of a sudden. This was my fifth vodka and tonic and I knew I would not be driving home.

Hugues handed me my drink and then my bag of crisps, held daintily between thumb and forefinger. *'Santé,'* he said.

'Cheers.'

Bérangère sidled up beside him and slipped her arm through his, proprietorially, I thought. She smiled hello at me. I had a mouthful of crisps so couldn't speak: she looked too exotic for the Captain Bligh and the Cowley Road, did Bérangère, and I could sense her keen urge to leave.

'On s'en va?' she said plaintively to Hugues. Hugues turned and they talked in low voices for a moment. I finished my crisps

– it had taken me about three seconds to consume the packet, it seemed, and moved off. Hamid had been right, they clearly were an item, Hugues and Bérangère – P'TIT PRIX meets Fourrures de Monte Carle – and right under my roof.

I leant on the bar, sipped my drink, and looked around the smoky pub. I felt good; I was at that level of inebriation – that hinge, that crux, that ridge – where you can decide to proceed or step back. Red warning lights were flashing on the control panel but the aeroplane was not yet in a screaming death-dive. I checked out the crowd in the pub: virtually everyone had moved down here from the function room above once the food and the free drink (bottled beer and screw-top wine) had run out. All of Hamid's four tutors were here and the students he shared them with – and also the small band of Dusendorf engineers – mainly Iranian and Egyptian this season, as it turned out. There was a raucous, teasing mood in the air – a lot of banter was going on around Hamid about his impending departure to Indonesia that he was taking in good grace, smiling resignedly, almost shyly.

'Hi, can I buy you a drink?'

I turned to find a man, a thin tall guy, in faded denim jeans and a tie-dyed T-shirt, with long dark hair and a moustache. He had pale blue eyes and – as far as I could tell in the state I was currently occupying, poised on my ridge, wondering which way to go – he looked pretty damned nice. I held up my vodka and tonic to show him.

'I'm fine, thanks.'

'Have another. They close in ten minutes.'

'I'm with a friend, over there,' I said, pointing with the glass at Hamid.

'Shame,' he said, and wandered off.

My hair was down and I was wearing new straight-legged jeans and a puff-sleeved ultramarine V-neck T-shirt that showed three inches of cleavage. I had my high boots on and I felt tall and sexy. I would have fancied me, myself . . . I let the illusion warm me for a while before adding the pointed reminder that my five-year-old son was staying with his grandmother and I didn't want to be hungover when I went to pick him up. This would be my last drink, definitely.

Hamid came over to the bar and joined me. He was wearing his new leather jacket and a cornflower-blue shirt. I put my arm round his shoulders.

'Hamid!' I exclaimed in feigned dismay. 'I can't *believe* you're leaving. What're we going to do without you?'

'I can't believe it neither.'

'Either.'

'Either. I'm very sad, you know. I was hoping that –'

'What were they teasing you about?'

'Oh – Indonesian girls, you know. Very predictable.'

'Very predictable. Very predictable men.'

'Would you like another drink, Ruth?'

'I'll have another vod and ton, thanks.'

We sat on bar stools and waited for our drinks to be served. Hamid had ordered a bitter lemon – and it struck me suddenly that he didn't drink alcohol, of course, being a Muslim.

'I'll miss you, Ruth,' he said. 'Our lessons – I can't believe I'm not coming to your flat on Monday. It's over three months, you know: two hours a day, five days a week. I counted: it's over 300 hours we've spent together.'

'Bloody hell,' I said with some sincerity. Then I thought, and said, 'But you've had three other tutors as well, remember. You spent as much time with Oliver . . .' I pointed, 'and Pauline, and Whatsisname, over by the juke-box.'

'Sure, yeah,' Hamid said, looking a little hurt. 'But it wasn't the same with them, Ruth. I think it was different with you.' He took my hand. 'Ruth –'

'I have to go to the loo. Back in a tick.'

The last vodka had tipped me off my ridge and I was sliding, tumbling down the other side of the mountain in a skidding flurry of schist and scree. I was still lucid, still functioning, but my world was one where angles were awry, where the verticals and horizontals were no longer so fixed and true. And, curiously, my feet seemed to be moving faster than they needed. I barged brusquely through the door into the passageway that led to the toilets. There was a public phone here and a cigarette machine. I suddenly remembered I was almost out of cigarettes and paused by the machine but, fumbling, rummaging for change, I realised that my bladder was making more importunate demands on my body than my craving for nicotine.

I went into the loo and had a long, powerfully relieving pee. I washed my hands and stood in front of the mirror. I looked at myself square in the eye for a few seconds and pushed my hair around a bit.

'You're pissed, you silly bitch,' I said out loud, though softly, through my teeth. 'Go home.'

I walked back into the passageway and Hamid was there, pretending to be making a phone call. From the pub the music surged louder – 'I heard it on the grapevine' – almost a Pavlovian sexual trigger for me and somehow, in some manner, in some brief gap in the space/time continuum, I found myself in Hamid's arms and was kissing him.

His beard was soft against my face – not raspy and jaggy – and I stuck my tongue deep in his mouth. I suddenly wanted sex – it had been so long – and Hamid seemed the perfect man. My arms were around him, holding him tight to me, and his body felt absurdly strong and solid, as if I was embracing a man made from concrete. And I thought: yes, Ruth, this is the man for you, you fool, you idiot – good, decent, kind, a friend to Jochen – I want this engineer with his soft brown eyes, this solid, strong man.

We broke apart and, as it inevitably does, the dream, the wish, seemed immediately less potent and desirable, and my world steadied slightly.

'Ruth –' he began.

'No. Say nothing.'

'Ruth, I love you. I want to be your husband. I want you for my wife. I'll come back in six months from my first tour. I have a very good job, a very good salary.'

'Don't say anything more, Hamid. Let's finish our drinks.'

We went back into the bar together – last orders were being called but now I didn't want any more vodka. I searched in my handbag for my last cigarette, found it and managed to light it reasonably competently. Hamid was distracted by some of his Iranian friends and they had a quick exchange in Farsi. I looked at them – these handsome, dark men with their beards and moustaches – and watched them shake hands in a strange way – high, gripping thumbs, then smoothly altering the grip again, as if they were exchanging some covert signal, acknowledging some membership of a special club, a secret society. And it was this thought that must have made me recall Frobisher's invitation and, for some stupid, over-confident, drunken reason, it suddenly seemed worth pursuing.

'Hamid,' I said, as he sat down beside me again, 'do you think there might be SAVAK agents in Oxford?'

'What? What are you saying?'

'I mean: do you think some of these engineers have been planted here, pretending to be students but all the while working for SAVAK?'

His face changed; it became very solemn.

'Ruth, please, we must not talk of such things.'

'But if you suspected someone, you could tell me. It would be a secret.'

I misread the expression on his face – that can be the only explanation for what I said next. I thought I had stirred something in him.

'Because you *can* tell me, Hamid,' I said, softly, leaning closer.

'I'm going to be working with the police, you see, they want me to help them. You can tell me.'

'Tell you what?'

'Are you with SAVAK?'

He closed his eyes and, keeping them closed, said: 'My brother was killed by SAVAK.'

I tried to vomit by the wheelie bins at the back of the pub, but failed, managing only to hawk and spit. You always think you'll feel better if you vomit but actually you feel much worse – and yet still you try to empty your stomach. I walked with due care to my car and methodically checked it was locked and that I hadn't left anything temptingly thievable on any seat and then set off on the long walk home back to Summertown. Friday night in Oxford – I'd never find a taxi. I should just walk home and, perhaps, it might sober me up. And tomorrow Hamid was flying off to Indonesia.

The Story of Eva Delectorskaya

London. 1942

EVA DELECTORSKAYA WATCHED ALFIE Blytheswood leave the side entrance of Electra House and duck into a small pub off the Victoria Embankment called the Cooper's Arms. She gave him five minutes and then went in herself. Blytheswood stood with a couple of friends at the bar of the snug, drinking a pint of beer. Eva was wearing spectacles and a beret and she approached the bar herself and ordered a dry sherry. If Blytheswood glanced up from his conversation he would easily spot her, though she was confident he wouldn't recognise her, the new length and colour of her hair seeming to alter her appearance significantly. However, she had put on the spectacles at the last moment, suddenly a little unsure. But she had to test her disguise, her new persona. She took her sherry to a table by the door, where she read her newspaper. When Blytheswood left, walking past her table, he didn't even glance at her. She followed him to his bus stop and waited with the others in the queue for his bus to arrive. Blytheswood had a long journey ahead of him, north to Barnet, where he lived with his wife and three children. Eva knew all this because she had been shadowing him for three days. At Hampstead a seat behind him was vacated and Eva slipped quietly into it.

Blytheswood was dozing, his head repeatedly nodding forward then abruptly jerking up as he regained consciousness. Eva leant forward and placed her hand on his shoulder.

'Don't turn round, Alfie,' she said, softly in his ear. 'You know who it is.'

Blytheswood was completely rigid and completely awake.

'Eve,' he said. 'Bloody hell. I can't believe it.' He moved to turn his head reflexively but she stopped him with her palm on his cheek.

'If you don't turn round, then you can honestly say you haven't seen me.'

He nodded. 'Right, yes, yes, that would be best.'

'What do you know about me?'

'They said you'd flown. Morris killed himself and you flew away.'

'That's right. Did they tell you why?'

'They said you and Morris were ghosts.'

'It's all lies, Alfie. If I was a ghost do you think I'd be sitting on this bus, talking to you?'

'No . . . No, I suppose not.'

'Morris was killed because he'd found something out. I was meant to be killed too. I'd be dead now if I hadn't flown.'

She could see him struggling with his desire to turn and look at her. She was fully aware of the risks involved in this contact but there were certain things she had to find out and Blytheswood was the only person she could ask.

'Have you heard from Angus or Sylvia?' she asked.

Blytheswood tried to swivel his head again but she stopped him with her fingertips.

'You don't know?'

'Know what?'

'That they're dead.'

She jolted visibly at this news, as if the bus had braked suddenly. She felt suddenly sick, saliva flowing into her mouth as if she were about to gag or vomit.

'My God,' she said, trying to take this in. 'How? What happened?'

'They were in a flying boat, a Sunderland, shot down between Lisbon and Poole Harbour. They were flying back from the States. Everyone on the plane was killed. Sixteen, eighteen people, I think.'

'When did this happen?'

'Early January. Some general was on board. Didn't you read about it?'

She remembered something, vaguely – but of course Angus Woolf and Sylvia Rhys-Meyer wouldn't have been mentioned among the casualties.

'Jerries were waiting for them. Bay of Biscay, somewhere.'

She was thinking: Morris, Angus, Sylvia. And there should have been me too. AAS Ltd was being rolled up. She had flown and disappeared; that left only Blytheswood.

'You should be all right, Alfie,' she said. 'You left early.'

'What do you mean?'

'We're being rolled up, aren't we? It's only because I flew that I'm still here. There's only you and me left.'

'There's still Mr Romer. No, no, I can't believe that, Eve. Us being rolled up? Just bad luck, surely.'

He was wishful-thinking. She knew he could read the signs as well as she could.

'Have you heard from Mr Romer?' she said.

'No, actually, as a matter of fact I haven't.'

'Be very careful, Alfie, if you hear that Mr Romer wants to meet you.' She said this without thinking and she immediately regretted it as she could see Blytheswood's head instantly shaking slightly as he ran through the implications of her remark. For all that he had been part of AAS Ltd for several years, Blytheswood was essentially an immensely skilled radio operator, an electrical engineer of some genius; these kinds of complexities – dark nuances, sudden contradictions in the established order of things – disturbed him, made no sense, Eva could tell.

'I've got a lot of time for Mr Romer,' he said finally, with a bit of petulance in his voice, as if he were a loyal estate worker being asked to pass judgement on the lord of the manor.

Eva realised she couldn't leave it like this. 'Just . . .' she paused, thinking fast, 'just don't ever tell him we've had this conversation or you'll be as dead as the others,' she said, her voice harsh.

He took this in, his head slightly bowed now, his shoulders slumped, not wanting this information at all, and Eva saw her opportunity and was out of her seat and down the stairs before he had time to turn round to see her go. The bus was slowing for some traffic lights and she jumped off and ran into a newsagent's. Blytheswood, had he looked, would have seen the back of a woman in a beret, nothing more. She watched the bus pull away from the lights but he didn't get off. Let's hope he took me seriously, she thought, wondering all the same if she'd made a bad mistake. The worst, the very worst, that could happen was that Romer would know for sure that she was now back in England, but that was all, and in any event he was probably working with that possibility in mind – nothing had really changed – except that she knew now about Angus and Sylvia. And she thought about them both, and the times they had shared, and she remembered, with bitterness, the vow she had made to herself in Canada and how it hardened her resolve. She bought an evening paper to discover the latest news of the air raids and the casualty figures.

The convoy had left St John, New Brunswick, on 18 January 1942, as planned. It was a stormy crossing but, apart from the bad weather, uneventful. There were twenty passengers on their ex-Belgian cargo ship – the SS *Brazzaville* – carrying aero-engines and steel girders: five government secretaries from Ottawa transferring to the London embassy, half a dozen officers from the Royal Regiment of Canada and an assortment of diplomatic staff. The heaving ocean kept most of the passengers to their cabins. Eva shared hers with an inordinately tall girl from the Department of Mines, called Cecily Fontaine, who needed to vomit every half-hour, as it turned out. By day Eva spent her time in the cramped 'staterooms' trying to read, and for three nights managed to claim one of the two empty beds in the *Brazzaville*'s sick bay before a stoker with a grumbling appendix drove her back to Cecily. From time to time Eva would venture on deck to gaze at the grey sky, the grey turbulent water and the grey ships with their belching smokestacks butting and smashing onward through the waves and jagged swells – disappearing in explosions of wintry spume from time to time – gamely making for the British Isles.

The first day out of St John they did their life-jacket evacuation drill and Eva hoped she'd never have to trust her person to those two canvas-covered cork-filled pillows she slipped over her head. The few seasickness survivors gathered in the mess under naked light bulbs to eat horrible tinned food three times a day. Eva marvelled at her redoubtability: four days into the voyage, only three of them were mustering for meals. One night a particularly large wave wrenched one of the *Brazzaville*'s lifeboats from its davits and it proved impossible to winch it back into its original position. The *Brazzaville* slipped back through the convoy because of the lifeboat's drag until – after furious signalling between the accompanying destroyers – it was cut free and allowed to drift away into the Atlantic. The thought struck Eva that if this unmanned lifeboat was found drifting wouldn't it be assumed that its mother ship had gone down? Perhaps this could be the little bit of luck she was looking for. She did not rest her hopes upon it, however.

They arrived at Gourock eight days later just before sunset and, as the sulphurous peachy light illuminated their surroundings, they found themselves docking in a harbour-graveyard of scuttled, listing and damaged ships, masts askew, funnels missing, bleak testimony to the U-boat gauntlet that they had managed to run unscathed. Eva disembarked with her pale and shaky colleagues and they were taken by bus into Glasgow's Central Station. She was tempted to leave them there and then but decided that a discreet departure overnight *en route* to London would be more efficacious. So she stepped off the sleeper at Peterborough, leaving her sleeping colleagues unaware, and carefully positioning a note for Cecily, saying that she was going to visit an aunt in Hull and would rejoin them in London. She doubted she would be missed for a day or two and so caught the next train for London and headed directly for Battersea and Mrs Dangerfield.

She burned her Margery Atterdine passport, leaf by leaf, and dropped the ashes here and there all over Battersea. She was now Lily Fitzroy, at least for a short while, and she had almost £34, all told, to her name once she had converted her remaining Canadian dollars and added them to the money she had hidden beneath the floorboards.

She lived quietly in Battersea for a week or two. Elsewhere in the world the Japanese seemed to be moving effortlessly through South-East Asia and there were new reverses for the British forces in North Africa. She thought of Romer every day and wondered what he was doing, confident that he'd be thinking of her too. The air raids were still coming in but without the regularity and remorseless ferocity of the Blitz. She spent a few nights in Mrs Dangerfield's Anderson shelter at the bottom of her narrow garden, where she regaled her with tales of her fictitious life in the USA, making Mrs Dangerfield's mouth open and eyes widen at the news of the wealth and profligacy of America, its superabundance and democratic generosity. 'I would never have come back myself, dear,' Mrs Dangerfield said with sincere feeling, reaching for her hands. 'A few days ago you were having cocktails in the Asporia-Waldorf, or whatever it's called – now you're sitting under a useless piece of tin in Battersea, being bombed by the Germans. I would've stayed put if I'd been you. Better off there, my darling, than in sad old London, blown to blazes.'

She knew this curious limbo couldn't last and indeed it began to chafe on her. She had to take action and get information, however meagre. She had escaped, she was free, she had her new name, passport, ration book and coupons but she was aware she was only drawing breath, pausing for a while: there was still some distance to run before she could truly feel at ease.

So she went to Electra House on the Embankment and spent two days watching the employees arrive and depart before she spotted Alfie Blytheswood emerging one evening. She followed him home to his house in Barnet and the next morning followed him from home to work.

She sat in her room in Battersea, thinking over the news Blytheswood had given her. Morris, Angus and Sylvia dead – but she had been destined to be the first. She wondered if her overturning of the Las Cruces operation had in a way made the others' deaths inevitable. Romer couldn't risk anything more, now Morris had exposed him as a ghost, and there was also the fact that Eva knew, also. What if Morris had hinted to Sylvia or, more likely, Angus? Angus's mood had been odd those last days – perhaps Morris had hinted at something . . . Romer couldn't risk it, in any event, and so he began rolling up AAS Ltd – carefully, guilefully – leaving no trace of his hand in the matter. Morris's suicide, then a leak of information about a Sunderland flight from Lisbon to Poole – date and time – and a high-ranking soldier on board as cover . . . It spoke of real power, she realised, a huge and powerful network with many intermediate contacts. But Eva Delectorskaya was still unaccounted for and she began to wonder if the chain of identities she had acquired for herself could be extended *ad infinitum*. If Romer could engineer the shooting-down of a flying boat in the Bay of Biscay it wouldn't take him long to find Lily Fitzroy – a name he already knew. Only a little time would elapse before, one way or another, via the cumbersome but dogged bureaucracy of wartime Britain, the name of Lily Fitzroy surfaced. And then what? Eva knew all too well how these things turned out: a motor accident, a fall from a high building, a black-out robbery turned to murder . . . She had to break the chain, she realised. She heard Mrs Dangerfield climbing the stairs.

'Fancy a cup of tea, Lily dear?'

'Lovely, yes please,' she called.

Lily Fitzroy, she realised, had to go.

It took her a day or two to calculate how it might just be done. In bombed-out London, she logically supposed, people must constantly be losing everything they owned. What did you do if your block of flats collapsed and burned while you were cowering in your basement shelter in your underclothes? You stumble out, dressed in pyjamas and dressing gown, into the dawn after the 'all clear', to find that everything you possessed had been incinerated. People had to start again, almost as if they were being reborn: all your documentation, clothing, housing, proofs of identification had to be re-acquired. The Blitz and now these night raids had been going on since September 1940, over a year, now, with thousands and thousands of dead and missing. She knew black-marketeers exploited the dead, kept them 'alive' for a while to claim their rations and petrol coupons. Perhaps there was an opening for her, here. So she began to scan the newspapers looking for accounts of the worst attacks with the biggest number of casualties – forty, fifty, sixty people killed or missing. A day or two later names would be printed in the papers and sometimes photographs. She began to look for missing young women about her age.

Two days after the encounter with Blytheswood there was a

big raid over the East End docks. She and Mrs Dangerfield went down the garden to the shelter and sat it out. On clear nights the planes often followed the meandering line of the Thames upriver looking for the power stations at Battersea and at Lots Road in Chelsea, unloading their bombs somewhere in the general vicinity. The residential areas of Battersea and Chelsea, consequently, received more bombing than they might ever have expected.

The next morning on the wireless she heard the news of the raids on Rotherhithe and Deptford – whole streets flattened, an entire housing estate evacuated, blocks of flats burned out and destroyed. In the evening paper more details were supplied, a small map printed of the most grievously damaged areas, the first lists of the dead and missing. She was looking – ghoulishly, she knew – for whole families, groups of four or five people with the same surname. She read of a charitable-trust estate in Deptford – three blocks almost totally destroyed, a direct hit on one, Carlisle House – eighty-seven people feared dead. The West family, three names, the Findlays – four names, two of them young children, and worst of all the Fairchilds with their five children: Sally (24), Elizabeth (18), Cedric (12), Lucy (10) and Agnes (6). All missing, all believed dead, buried under the devastation, hope for survivors remote.

Eva caught a bus to Deptford the next day and went in search of Carlisle House. She found the usual fuming moonscape of dereliction: hills of brick rubble, teetering cliffs of walls and exposed rooms, gas mains still burning through the tumbled masonry with a pale wobbly light. Wooden barriers had been erected around the site and were manned by police and ARP volunteers. Behind the barriers small crowds gathered and looked forlornly on, talking about the senselessness, the mindlessness, the agony and the tragedy. In a nearby doorway Eva took out her passport and then she walked along the line of barriers as far from the crowds as possible and as close as she could get to a flaring gas main. The winter evening was drawing in quickly and the pale flames were becoming more lurid and orange. Darkness meant another raid, possibly, and the muttering groups of neighbours, survivors and spectators began to drift away. When she was sure no one was looking she gently threw her passport into the heart of the flames. For an instant she saw it flare and shrivel and then it disappeared. She turned and walked quickly away.

She went back home to Battersea and told Mrs Dangerfield, with a gallant sigh, that she had a new posting – 'Scotland again' – and had to leave that very evening. She paid her two months rent in advance and left blithely, happily. At least you'll be away from these raids, Mrs Dangerfield observed enviously, and pecked her goodbye on the cheek. I'll telephone when I'm coming back, Eva said, probably March.

She booked into a hotel near Victoria Station and the next morning banged her head hard against the rough brick embrasure of her window until the skin broke and the blood began to flow. She cleaned her wound and covered it with cotton wool and sticking plaster and took a taxi to a police station in Rotherhithe.

'What can we do for you, Miss?' the constable on duty asked.

Eva looked around, acting disorientated, as if she were still concussed, still in shock. 'The hospital said I should come here,' she said. 'I was in the Carlisle House raid. My name's Sally Fairchild.'

She had provisional identity papers by the end of the day and a ration book with a week's supply of coupons. She said some neighbours had taken her in and gave an address of a street near the bomb-site. She was told to report to a Home Office department in Whitehall within a week in order to have everything regularised. The policemen were very sympathetic, Eva wept a little, and they offered to have a car drive her to her temporary home. Eva said she was going to meet her friends, thanks all the same, and visit some of the wounded in hospital.

So Eva Delectorskaya became Sally Fairchild and this, she thought, was at last a name that Romer didn't know. The chain was broken but she wasn't sure how long she could keep her new identity going. She thought he would take some perverse pleasure in her skill at evasion – I taught her well – but he would always be thinking: how to find Eva Delectorskaya now?

She never forgot this and she knew that more had to be done before she could feel even half secure, and so, in the early evenings, she took to drinking – while her money lasted – in a better class of public house and restaurant bar. She knew that for these next few days while she lived in her hotel and while she did nothing she was safest; as soon as she took up any form of work again, the system would remorselessly claim her and document her. So she went to the Café Royale and the Chelsea Arts Club, the bar of the Savoy and the Dorchester, the White Tower. Many eligible men bought her drinks and asked her out, and a few tried unsuccessfully to kiss and caress her. She met a Polish fighter pilot at the Leicester Square Bierkeller whom she saw twice more, before deciding against him. She was looking for a particular someone – she had no idea who – but she was confident she would recognise him the minute they met.

It was about ten days after she had become Sally Fairchild that she went to the Heart of Oak in Mount Street, Mayfair. It was a pub but its saloon bar was carpeted and hung with sporting prints and there was always a real fire burning in the grate. She ordered a gin and orange, found a seat, lit a cigarette and pretended to do the *Times* crossword. As usual, there were quite a few military types in – all officers – and one of them offered to buy her a drink. She didn't want a British officer so she said she was waiting for a gentleman friend and he went away. After an hour or so – she was thinking of leaving – the table next to her was taken by three young men in dark suits. They were in merry mood and after listening in for a minute or two she realised their accents were Irish. She went to buy another drink and dropped her paper. One of the men, dark, with a plump face and a thin pencil moustache, returned it to her. His eyes met hers.

'Can I buy you that drink?' he said. 'Please: it would be both a pleasure and an honour.'

'That's very kind of you,' Eva said. 'But I'm just going.'

She allowed herself to be persuaded to join their table. She was meeting a gentleman friend, she said, but he was already forty minutes late.

'Oh that's no gentleman friend,' the man with the moustache said, making a solemn face. 'That's what you call an English cad.'

They all laughed at this and Eva noticed one of the men across the table – fair-haired with a freckly complexion and a big, easy, slouching presence – who smiled at the joke, but smiled inwardly, as if there were something else funny about the statement that amused him and not the obvious slur.

She discovered that all three of them were lawyers attached to the Irish Embassy, working in the consulate office in Clarges Street. When it was the fair-haired man's turn to buy the next round, she let him go to the bar and then excused herself to the others, saying she had to go and powder her nose. She joined the man at the bar and said she'd changed her mind and would rather have a half pint of shandy than another gin and orange.

'Sure,' he said. 'A half pint of shandy it shall be.'

'What did you say your name was?' she asked.

'I'm Sean. The other two are David and Eamonn. Eamonn's the comedian – we're his audience.'

'Sean what?'

'Sean Gilmartin.' He turned and looked at her. 'So what would be your name again, Sally?'

'Sally Fairchild,' she said. And she felt the past fall from her like loosened shackles. She stepped closer to Sean Gilmartin as he presented her with her half pint of shandy, as close as she could without touching him, and she lifted her face to his quietly knowing, quietly smiling eyes. Something told her that the story of Eva Delectorskaya had come to its natural end.

13

Face to Face

'SO THAT WAS HOW you met my dad?' I said. 'You picked him up in a pub.'

'I suppose so.' My mother sighed, her face momentarily blank – thinking back, I assumed. 'I was looking for the right man – I'd been looking for days – and then I saw him. That way he laughed to himself. I knew at once.'

'Nothing cynical about it, then.'

She looked at me in that hard way she had – when I stepped out of line, when I was being too smart-aleck.

'I loved your father,' she said, simply, 'he saved me.'

'Sorry,' I said, a bit feebly, feeling somewhat ashamed and blaming my sourness on my hangover: I was still paying the price for Hamid's farewell party. I felt sluggish and stupid: my mouth was dry, my body craving water, and my earlier 'mild' headache had moved into the 'persistent/throbbing' category in the headache leagues.

She had quickly told me the rest of the story. After the encounter in the Heart of Oak there had been a few more dates – meals, an embassy dance, a film – and they realised that slowly but surely they were growing closer. Sean Gilmartin, with his diplomatic-corps connections and influence, had smoothed the processes involved in Sally Fairchild acquiring a new passport and other documentation. In March 1942 they had travelled to

Ireland – to Dublin – where she had met his parents. They were married two months later in St Saviour's, on Duncannon Street. Eva Delectorskaya became Sally Fairchild became Sally Gilmartin and she knew now that she was safe. After the war Sean Gilmartin and his young wife moved back to England, where he joined a firm of solicitors in Banbury, Oxfordshire, as a junior partner. The firm prospered, Sean Gilmartin became a senior partner, and in 1949 they had a child, a girl, who they named Ruth.

'And you never heard anything more?' I asked.

'Nothing, not a whisper. I'd lost them completely – until now.'

'What happened to Alfie Blytheswood?'

'He died in 1957, I believe, a stroke.'

'Genuine?'

'I think so. The gap was too big.'

'Any lingering problems with the Sally Fairchild identity?'

'I was a married woman living in Dublin – Mrs Sean Gilmartin – everything had changed, everything was different; nobody knew what had happened to Sally Fairchild.' She paused and smiled, as though recognising her past identities, these selves she had occupied.

'Whatever happened to your father?' I asked.

'He died in Bordeaux, in 1944,' she said. 'I got Sean to track him through the London embassy, after the war – I said he was an old friend of the family . . .' She pursed her lips. 'Just as well, I suppose – how could I have gone to him. I never saw Irène, either. It would have been too risky.' She looked up. 'What's the boy up to now?'

'Jochen! Leave it alone!' I shouted, crossly. He had found a hedgehog under the laurel bush. 'They're full of fleas.'

'What're fleas?' he called back, stepping away all the same from the dun, prickly ball.

'Horrible insects that bite you all over.'

'And I want him to stay in my garden,' my mother shouted as well. 'He eats slugs.'

In the face of these joint remonstrations Jochen backed off some more and crouched down on his haunches to watch the hedgehog cautiously unroll. It was Saturday evening and the sun was lowering into the usual dusty haze that did duty for dusk in this endless summer. In the thick golden light the meadow in front of Witch Wood looked bleached-out, a tired old blonde.

'Have you got any beer?' I asked. I suddenly wanted beer, some hair of the dog, desperately, I realised.

'You'll have to go to the shop,' she said and glanced at her watch, 'which will be shut.' She looked shrewdly at me. 'You do look a bit the worse for wear, I must say. Did you get drunk?'

'The party went on a bit longer than expected.'

'I think I've got an old bottle of whisky somewhere.'

'Yes,' I said, brightening. 'Maybe a little whisky and water. Lots of water,' I added, as if that made my need less urgent, less blameworthy.

So my mother brought me a large tumbler of pale golden whisky and water and as I sipped it I began, almost immediately, to feel better – my headache was there but I felt less jangled and tetchy – and I reminded myself to be extra specially nice to Jochen for the rest of the day. And as I drank I thought how perplexing life could be: that it could arrange things so that I should be sitting here in this Oxfordshire cottage garden, on a hot summer evening, with my son pestering a hedgehog, and my mother bringing me whisky – this woman, my mother, whom I had clearly never really known, born in Russia, a British spy, who had killed a man in New Mexico in 1941, become a fugitive and who, a generation later, had finally told me her story. It showed you that . . . My brain was too addled to take in the bigger picture that the story of Eva Delectorskaya belonged to, all I could enumerate were its component parts. I felt at once exhilarated – it proved we knew nothing about other people, that anything about them was possible, conceivable – and at the same time vaguely cast down as I realised the lies under which I had lived my life. It was as if I had to start to get to know her all over again, reshape everything that had passed between us, consider how her life now cast mine in a different and possibly unsettling new light. I decided, there and then, to leave it for a couple of days, let it brew for a while before I attempted fresh analysis. The events of my own life were sufficiently complicated enough: I should worry about myself, first, I said to myself. My mother was made of stronger stuff, clearly. I should think it over when I was more alert, more intellectually articulate – ask Dr Timothy Thoms a few leading questions.

I looked over at her. She was idly turning the pages of her magazine but her eyes were fixed elsewhere – she was looking fixedly, anxiously across the meadow at the trees of Witch Wood.

'Is everything all right, Sal?' I asked.

'You know there was an old woman – an elderly woman – killed in Chipping Norton the day before yesterday.'

'No. Killed how?'

'She was in a wheelchair, doing her shopping. Sixty-three years old. Hit by a car that mounted the pavement.'

'How awful . . . Drunk driver? Joy-rider?'

'We don't know.' She tossed the magazine on the grass. 'The driver of the car ran away. They haven't found him yet.'

'Can't they identify him from the car?'

'The car was stolen.'

'I see . . . But what's it got to do with you.'

She turned to me. 'Doesn't it make you think? I've been in a wheelchair recently. I often shop in Chipping Norton.'

I had to laugh. 'Oh, come *on*,' I said.

She looked at me: her gaze steady, unfriendly. 'You still don't understand, do you?' she said. 'Even after everything I've told you. You don't understand how they operate.'

I finished my whisky – I wasn't going down this tortuously twisting road, that was for sure.

'We'd better go,' I said, diplomatically. 'Thanks for looking after the boy. Did he behave well?'

'Impeccably. Excellent company.'

I called Jochen away from his hedgehog studies and we spent ten minutes gathering up his widely dispersed belongings. When I went into the kitchen I noticed there was a small assembly of packaged foodstuffs on the table: a thermos flask, a Tupperware container with sandwiches inside, two apples and a packet of biscuits. Odd, I thought, as I picked up toy cars from the floor, anyone would think she was about to go off on a picnic. Then Jochen called me, saying he couldn't find his gun.

Eventually we loaded the car and said goodbye. Jochen kissed his granny and when I kissed my mother she stood stiff – everything was too strange today, making no sense. I had to leave first, then I would tackle the anomalies.

'Are you coming into town next week?' I asked, nicely, in a friendly way, thinking I would have lunch with her.

'No.'

'Fine.' I opened the car door. 'Bye, Sal. I'll call.'

Then she reached for me and hugged me, hard. 'Goodbye, darling,' she said and I felt her dry lips on my cheek. This was even odder; she hugged me about once every three years.

Jochen and I drove away from the village in silence.

'Did you have a nice time with Granny?' I asked.

'Yes. Sort of.'

'Be precise.'

'Well, she was very busy, doing things all the time. Cutting things in the garage.'

'Cutting? What things?'

'I don't know. She wouldn't let me go in. But I could hear her sawing.'

'Sawing? . . . Did she seem different in any way? Was she behaving differently?'

'Be precise.'

'*Touché*. Did she seem nervous, jumpy, bad-tempered, strange?'

'She's always strange. You know that.'

We drove back to Oxford through the fading light. I saw black flights of rooks taking to the air from stubbly fields as the smoky light of evening blurred and hazed the hedgerows and the darkening copses and woods seemed as dense and impenetrable as if they had been cast from metal. I felt my headache easing and, taking this as a sign of general improvement, I remembered that I had a bottle of Mateus Rosé in the fridge. Saturday night in, telly on, twenty cigarettes and a bottle of Mateus Rosé: how could life get any better?

We ate supper (there was no sign of Ludger and Ilse) and watched a variety show on television – bad singers, clumsy dancers, I thought – and I put Jochen to bed. Now I could drink my wine and smoke a couple of cigarettes. But, instead, twenty minutes after I had washed up the dishes, I was still sitting in the kitchen, a mug of black coffee in front of me, thinking about my mother and her life.

On Sunday morning I felt about a hundred per cent better but my thoughts still kept returning to the cottage and my mother's behaviour the day before: the edginess, the paranoia, the packed picnic, the untypical touchy-feeliness . . . What was going on? Where could she be going with her sandwiches and thermos – and made up the night before, which would seem to indicate an early start. If she was planning a trip, why not tell me about it? And if she didn't want me to know, why leave the picnic out in such prominent display?

And then I realised.

Jochen accepted the new arrangements to his Sunday with good grace. In the car we sang songs to pass the time: 'One Man

Went to Mow', 'Ten Green Bottles', 'The Quartermaster's Store', 'The Happy Wanderer', 'Tipperary' – these were songs my father had sung to me as a child, his deep vibrating bass filling the car. Like me, Jochen had a terrible voice – completely out of tune – but we sang along, lustily, carelessly, united in our dissonance.

'Why are we going back?' he asked between verses. 'We never go back the next day.'

'Because I forgot something, forgot to ask Granny something.'

'You could speak to her on the phone.'

'No. I have to speak to her, face to face.'

'I suppose you're going to have a row,' he said, wearily.

'No, no – don't worry. It's just something I have to ask her.'

And, as I had feared, the car was gone and the house was locked. I retrieved the key from under the flower pot and we went in. As before, everything was neat and orderly – no hint of a rapid departure, no sign of panic or fearful haste. I walked through the rooms slowly, looking around, looking for the clue, the anomaly that she would have left me, and, eventually, I found it.

On these baking sultry nights, who in their right mind would light a fire in their sitting-room? My mother had, clearly, as a cluster of charred logs lay in the grate, the ashes still warm. I crouched down in front of it and used the poker to disturb the pile, looking for the remains of burned papers – perhaps she was destroying some other secret – but there was no sign: instead my eye was caught by one of the logs. I picked it out with the fire tongs and ran it under the tap in the kitchen – it hissed as the cold water rinsed the ashes away – and the glossy cherrywood grain of the wood became immediately evident. I dried it off with some paper towels: there was no mistaking it, even half charred: it was obviously the main part of the butt of a shotgun, sawn off just behind the hand-grip. I went out to the garage where she had a small work-bench and kept her gardening implements (always oiled and neatly racked away). On the bench was a hacksaw and vice and scattered around it the small silver corkscrew frills of worked metal. The shotgun barrels were in a burlap potato sack under the table. She had taken no real care to hide them; indeed, even the shotgun butt had been more scorched than burned away. I felt a weakness in my gut: half of me seemed to want to laugh – half of me felt a powerful urge to shit. I understood, now, that I was beginning to think like her: she had *wanted* me to come back this Sunday morning to find her gone; she had wanted me to search her house and find these things and now she expected me to draw the obvious conclusion.

I was in London by six o'clock that evening. Jochen was safe with Veronica and Avril and all I had to do was find my mother before she killed Lucas Romer. I took the train to Paddington and, from Paddington, a taxi delivered me to Knightsbridge. I could remember the street that my mother had said Romer lived on, but not the number of the house: Walton Crescent was where I told the taxi driver to take me and drop me close to one end. I could see from my street map of London that there was a Walton Street – that seemed to lead to the very portals of Harrods – and a Walton Crescent that was tucked away behind and to one side. I paid the driver, a hundred yards off, and made my way to the Crescent on foot, trying all the while to think as my mother would think, to second-guess her *modus operandi.* First things first, I said to myself: check out the neighbourhood.

Walton Crescent breathed money, class, privilege, confidence – but it did so quietly, with subtlety and no ostentation. All the houses looked very much the same until you paid closer attention. There was a crescent-shaped public garden facing the gentle arc of four-storey, creamy stuccoed Georgian terraced houses, each with small front gardens and each with – on the first floor – three huge tall windows giving on to a wrought-iron filigreed balcony. The small gardens were well tended and defiantly green despite the hosepipe ban – I took in box hedges, roses, varieties of clematis and a certain amount of mossy statuary – as I began to walk along its curving length. Almost every house had a burglar alarm and many of the windows were shuttered or secured with sliding grilles behind the glass. I was almost alone on the street apart from a nanny wheeling a pram and a grey-haired gentleman who was cutting a low yew hedge with pedantic, loving care. I saw my mother's white Allegro parked across the street from number 29.

I bent down and rapped sharply on the window. She looked round but seemed very unsurprised to see me. She smiled and reached over to open the door to let me in beside her.

'You took your time,' she said. 'I thought you'd be here ages ago – still, well done.' She was wearing her pearl-grey trouser suit and her hair was combed and shiny as if she'd just left the hairdresser's. She was wearing lipstick and her eyelashes were dark with mascara.

I allowed a shudder of anger to pass through me before I clambered into the passenger seat. She offered me a sandwich before I could begin to reproach her.

'What is it?' I said.

'Salmon and cucumber. Not salmon out of a tin.'

'Mayonnaise?'

'Just a little – and some dill.'

I took the sandwich and wolfed down a couple of mouthfuls: I was suddenly hungry and the sandwich was very tasty.

'There's a pub in the next street,' I said. 'Let's go and have a drink and talk this over properly. I'm very worried, I have to say.'

'No, I might miss him,' she said. 'Sunday evening, coming back from the country somewhere – his house or a friend's – he should be here before nine.'

'I will not let you kill him. I warn you, I –'

'Don't be absurd!' She laughed. 'I just want to have a brief chat.' She put her hand on my knee. 'Well done, Ruth, darling, tracking me here. I'm impressed – and pleased. I thought it was best this way – to let you figure it out for yourself, you know? I didn't want to ask you to come, put pressure on you. I thought you would figure it out because you're so clever – but now I know you're clever in a different way.'

'I suppose I should take that as a compliment.'

'Look: if I'd asked you outright you'd have thought of a hundred ways of stopping me.' She smiled, almost gleefully. 'But, anyway, here we are, both of us.' She touched my cheek with her fingers – where was all this affection coming from? 'I'm glad you're here,' she said. 'I know I could see him on my own but it'll be so much better with you beside me.'

I was suspicious. 'Why?'

'You know: moral support and all that.'

'Where's the gun?'

'I'm afraid I rather buggered it up. The barrels didn't come off cleanly. I wouldn't dare use it – anyway, now you're here I feel safe.'

We sat on talking and eating our sandwiches as the evening light seemed to thicken dustily, peachily, in Walton Crescent, turning the cream stucco the palest apricot for a few moments. As the sky slowly darkened – it was a cloudy day but warm – I began to notice a small squirm of fear entering me: sometimes it seemed in my guts, sometimes my chest, sometimes in my limbs, making them achy and heavy – and I began to wish that Romer wouldn't come home, that he'd gone away for a holiday to Portofino or Saint Tropez or Inverness, or wherever types like him vacationed, and that this vigil of ours would prove fruitless and we could go home and try to forget about the whole thing. But at the same time I knew my mother and I knew it wouldn't simply end with Romer's non-appearance: she had to see him just once more, one last time. And I realised, as I thought further, that everything that had happened this summer had been designed – manipulated – to bring about this confrontation: the wheelchair nonsense, the paranoia, the memoir –

My mother grabbed my arm.

At the far end of the crescent the big Bentley nosed round the corner. I thought I might faint, the blood seemed to be rushing audibly from my head. I took a huge gulp of air as I felt my stomach acids seethe and climb my oesophagus.

'When he gets out of the car,' my mother said evenly, 'you go out and call his name. He'll turn to you – he won't see me at first. Keep him talking for a second or two. I want to surprise him.'

'What do I say?'

'How about: "Good evening, Mr Romer, can I have a word?" I only need a couple of seconds.'

She seemed very calm, very strong – whereas I thought I might burst into tears at any moment, might bawl and blub, I felt suddenly so insecure and inadequate – not like me at all, I realised.

The Bentley stopped, double-parking with the engine running, and the chauffeur opened the door and stepped out, walking round the car to the rear. He held the back door open on the pavement side and Romer climbed out with some difficulty, stooped a little, perhaps stiff from the journey. He had a few words with his driver, who then got back into the car and pulled away. Romer went to his front gate; he was wearing a tweed jacket and grey flannels with suede shoes. A light came on in the transom of number 29 and simultaneously the garden lights were illuminated, shining on the flagged path to the front door, a cherry tree, a stone obelisk in the hedge corner.

My mother gave me a shove and I opened the door.

'Lord Mansfield?' I called and stepped out on to the road. 'May I have a word?'

Romer turned very slowly to face me.

'Who are you?'

'I'm Ruth Gilmartin – we met the other day.' I crossed the road towards him. 'At your club – I wanted to interview you.'

He peered at me. 'I've nothing to say to you,' he said. His raspy voice even, unthreatening. 'I told you that.'

'Oh, but I think you have,' I said, wondering where my mother was – I had no sense of her presence, couldn't hear her, had no idea which way she'd gone.

He laughed and opened the gate to his front garden.

'Good-night, Miss Gilmartin. Stop bothering me. Go away.'

I couldn't think what to say next – I had been dismissed.

He turned to close his gate and I saw behind him someone open the door a few inches, left ajar for easy access, no bother with keys or anything as vulgar as that. He saw I had remained standing there and his eyes flicked automatically up and down the street. And then he became very still.

'Hello, Lucas,' my mother said from the darkness.

She seemed to materialise from around the box hedge, not moving – just suddenly standing there.

Romer seemed paralysed for a moment, then he drew himself erect, stiffly, like a soldier on parade, as if he might fall over otherwise.

'Who're you?'

Now she stepped forward and the dusky late evening light showed her face, caught her eyes. I thought: she looks very beautiful, as if some sort of miraculous rejuvenation were taking place and the intervening thirty-five years of ageing were being erased.

I looked at Romer – he knew who she was – and he kept himself very still, one hand gripping the gatepost. I wondered what this moment must have been like for him – the shock beyond all shocks. But he gave nothing away, just managing to produce a small erratic smile.

'Eva Delectorskaya,' he said, softly, 'who would have thought?'

We stood in Romer's large drawing-room on the first floor – he had not asked us to sit down. At the garden gate, once he had recovered from the shock of seeing my mother, he had composed himself and his old bored urbanity re-established itself. 'I suppose you'd better come in,' he'd said, 'no doubt you have something you want to tell me.' We had followed him up the gravel path to the front door and into the house, where a dark-haired man in a white jacket stood waiting cautiously in the hall. Down a corridor I could hear the sound of dishes clattering in a kitchen somewhere.

'Ah, Petr,' Romer said. 'I'll be down in a minute. Tell Maria to leave everything in the oven – then she can go.'

Then we followed him up the curving staircase into the drawing-room. The style was English country house, 1930s: a few good dark pieces of furniture – a bureau, a glass-fronted cabinet with faience inside – rugs on the floor and comfortable, old sofas with throws and cushions, but the paintings on the wall were contemporary. I saw a Francis Bacon, a Burra and an exquisite still life – an empty pewter bowl in front of a silver lusterware vase containing two wilting poppies. The painting looked lit but there were no picture lights – the thickly painted gleam on the bowl and the vase did that work, astonishingly. I was looking at the paintings as a way of distracting myself – I was in a strange giddy panic: a combination of excitement and fear, a mood I hadn't truly experienced since childhood when, on those occasions when you wilfully do something wrong and proscribed, you find yourself imagining your own discovery, guilt and punishment – which is part of the heady appeal of the illicit, I suppose. I glanced over at my mother: she was looking fiercely but coolly at Romer. He would not meet her gaze, but stood proprietorially by the fireplace, looking thoughtfully at the rug at his feet – the fire laid, unlit – his elbow resting on the chimney-piece, the back of his head visible in the tarnished freckled mirror that hung above it. Now he turned to stare at Eva too but his face showed no expression. I knew why I felt this panic: the air seemed thick and curdled with their crowded, turbulent, shared history – a history I had no part of, yet was now compelled to bear witness to its climax: I felt like a voyeur – I shouldn't be here, yet here I was.

'Could we open a window?' I said, hesitantly.

'No,' Romer said, still looking at my mother. 'You'll find some water on that table.'

I went over to a side-table that had a tray of cut-crystal glasses and decanters of whisky and brandy on it as well as a half-empty carafe of visibly dusty water. I poured myself a glass and drank the warm fluid down. The noise of my swallowing seemed terribly audible and I saw Romer glance over at me.

'What relation do you have to this woman?' he said.

'She's my mother,' I replied instantly and felt, absurdly, a small stiffening of pride, thinking of everything she'd done, everything she'd been through to bring her here, now in this room. I went and stood closer to her.

'Jesus Christ,' Romer said. 'I don't believe it.' He seemed profoundly disgusted in some way. I looked at my mother and tried to imagine what could possibly be going on in her head, seeing this man again after so many decades, a man she had genuinely loved – or so I believed – and who had also taken diligent pains to organise her death. But she seemed very calm, her face set and strong. Romer turned back to her.

'What do you want, Eva?'

My mother gestured to me. 'I just want to tell you that she knows everything. I wrote everything down, you see, Lucas, and gave it to her – she has all the pages. There's a don in Oxford who is writing a book about it. I just wanted to tell you that your secret years are over. Everyone is going to know, very soon, what you did.' She paused. 'It's finished.'

He seemed to chew his lip for a moment – I felt that this was the last thing he had expected to hear. He spread his hands.

'Fine. I'll sue him, I'll sue you and you'll go to prison. You can't prove a thing.'

My mother smiled at this, spontaneously, and I knew why – this was already a kind of confession, I thought.

'I wanted you to know that and I wanted to see you for one last time.' She took a little step forward. 'And I wanted you to see me. To let you know that I was still very much alive.'

'We lost you in Canada,' Romer said. 'Once we realised that was where you must have gone. You were very clever.' He paused. 'You should know that your file was never closed. We can still arrest you, charge you, try you. I just need to pick up this telephone – you'd be arrested before the night was over, wherever you happen to be.'

Now my mother's slight smile proclaimed her moment of power – the balance had shifted, finally.

'Why don't you do it, then, Lucas?' she said easily, persuasively. 'Have me arrested. Go on. But you won't do that, will you?'

He looked at her, his face giving nothing away, the control absolute. All the same, I savoured my mother's triumph over him – I felt like cheering, whooping with delight.

'As far as the British government is concerned you're a traitor,' he said, his voice flat, without the trace of any threat or bluster.

'Oh yes, yes, of course,' she said, with massive irony. 'We're all traitors: me and Morris and Angus and Sylvia. A little nest of British traitors in AAS Ltd. Only one man straight and true: Lucas Romer.' She looked at him, with a kind of pure scorn, not pity. 'It's all finally gone wrong for you, Lucas. Face it.'

'It all went wrong at Pearl Harbor,' he said, with a pursed ironic grin, as if he finally realised he was impotent, all control having passed from his hands. 'Thanks to the Japanese – Pearl Harbor rather fucked everything up.'

'You should have left me alone,' my mother said. 'You shouldn't have kept looking for me – I wouldn't have bothered with all this.'

He looked at her, baffled. This was the first genuine emotion I had seen his face register. 'What on earth are you talking about?' he said.

But she wasn't listening. She opened her bag and took out the sawn-off shotgun. It was very small, it couldn't have been more than ten inches long – it looked like an antique pistol, some highwayman's firepiece. She pointed it at Romer's face.

'Sally,' I said. 'Please . . .'

'I know you won't do anything stupid,' Romer said, quite calmly. 'You're not stupid, Eva, so why don't you put it away?'

She took a step towards him and straightened her arm, the two blunt stubby barrels were aimed full at his face, two feet away. He did flinch a little, now, I saw.

'I just wanted to know what it would be like to have you at my mercy,' my mother said, still perfectly under control. 'I could happily kill you now, so easily, and I just wanted to know what that moment would feel like. You can have no idea how imagining this moment has sustained me, for years and years. I've waited a long time.' She lowered the gun. 'And I can tell you it was worth every second.' She put the gun away in her bag and snapped it loudly shut, the click making Romer jump a little.

He reached for a bell on the wall, pressed it and the awkward, nervy Petr was in the room in a second, it seemed.

'These people are leaving,' Romer said.

We walked to the door.

'Goodbye, Lucas,' my mother said, striding out, not even looking round at him. 'Remember this evening. You'll never see me again.'

I, of course, did look round as we left the room to see that Romer had turned away slightly and his hands were in the pockets of his jacket, pushing down hard, I could tell, from the creases that had formed, and how the lapels of his jacket were deformed; his head was bowed and he was staring at the rug in front of the fireplace again, as if it held some sort of clue as to what he should do next.

We climbed into the car and I looked up at the three tall windows. It was growing dark now and the panes glowed orange-yellow, the curtains still unpulled.

'The gun freaked me out, Sal,' I said.

'It wasn't loaded.'

'Oh, right.'

'I don't want to talk at the moment, if you don't mind. Not yet.'

So we drove out of London, via Shepherd's Bush on to the A40 heading for Oxford. We sat in silence all the way until we reached Stokenchurch and saw, through the great gap that they had carved through the Chilterns for the motorway, the lazy summer night of Oxfordshire laid out before us – the lights of Lewknor, Sydenham and Great Haseley beginning to sparkle as the land darkened and the residual warm agate glow of the sun set somewhere in the west beyond distant Gloucestershire.

I was thinking back over everything that had happened this summer and I began to realise that, in fact, it had started many years ago. I saw how my mother had so cleverly manipulated and used me over the last few weeks and I began to wonder if this had been my destiny as far as she was concerned. She would have lived all her life with the thought of that final meeting with Lucas Romer and when her child was born – maybe she was hoping for a boy? – she would have thought; now I have my crucial ally, now I have someone who can help me, one day I will bring Romer down.

I began to see how my return to Oxford from Germany had been the catalyst, how the process had begun – now that I was back in her life and the entanglement could slowly begin. The writing of the memoir, the sense of danger, the paranoia, the wheelchair, the initial 'innocent' requests, all designed to make me part of the process of finding and unearthing her quarry. But, I realised something else had triggered her into acting now, after all these years. Some sense of perceived danger had made her resolve to settle this matter. Perhaps it was paranoia – imagined watchers in the woods, the unfamiliar cars driving though the village at night – perhaps it was sheer fatigue. Maybe my mother had grown tired of being eternally watchful, eternally guarded, eternally prepared for that knock on the door. I remembered her warnings to me when I was a child: 'One day someone will come and take me away,' and I realised that in reality she had been living like that since she had fled to Canada from New York at the end of 1941. It was a long, long time – too long. She was tired of watching and waiting and she wanted to stop. And so, resourceful, clever Eva Delectorskaya had engineered a little drama that had drawn her daughter – her necessary ally – into the plot against Lucas Romer. I couldn't blame her and I tried to imagine what the toll had been over the decades. I looked across at her, at her fine profile, as we drove through the night towards home. What are you thinking, Eva Delectorskaya? What duplicities are still fizzing in your brain? Will you ever have a quiet life, will you ever truly be at rest? Will you now, finally, be at peace? She had used me almost in the same way Romer had tried to use her. I realised that, all this summer, my mother had been carefully running me, like a spy, like a –

'I made a mistake,' she said, suddenly, making me start.

'What?'

'He knows you're my daughter. He knows your name.'

'So what?' I said. 'He also knows you've got him cold.

Everything's going to come out. He can't lay a finger on you. You told him – you challenged him to pick up the phone.'

She thought about this.

'Maybe you're right . . . Maybe that's enough. Maybe he won't make any calls. But he might leave something written.'

'What do you mean: "leave something written"? Leave something written where?' I couldn't follow her.

'It would be safer to leave something written, you see, because . . .' She stopped, thinking hard as she drove, hunching forward almost as if, in that posture, she could drive the car home more swiftly.

'Because what?'

'Because he'll be dead by tomorrow morning.'

'*Dead?* How can he be dead tomorrow morning?'

She glanced at me, an impatient glance that said: You still don't get it, do you? Your brain doesn't work like ours. She spoke patiently: 'Romer will kill himself tonight. He'll inject himself, take a pill. He'll have had the method ready for years. It'll look exactly like a heart attack, or a fatal stroke – something that looks natural, anyway.' She flexed her fingers on the steering wheel. 'Romer's dead. I didn't need to shoot him with that gun. The second he saw me he knew that he was dead. He knew his life was over.'

14

A True-Blue English Gentleman

MY MOTHER, JOCHEN AND I stood close together under my new russet umbrella on the pavement outside the entrance to St James's Church, Piccadilly. It was a cool, drizzly September morning – packed seal-grey clouds moved steadily above us – as we watched the dignitaries, guests, friends and family arrive for Lord Mansfield of Hampton Cleeve's memorial service.

'Isn't that the Foreign Secretary?' I said, as a dark-haired man in a blue suit hurried out of a chauffeur-driven car.

'He seems to be getting a good turn-out,' my mother said, almost eagerly, as if it were a marriage rather than a funeral, as a small queue began to bulk shapelessly at the entrance to the church, behind the iron palings of the small sunken forecourt. A queue of people not at all used to queuing, I thought.

'Why are we here?' Jochen asked. 'It's a bit boring, just standing out here on the pavement.'

'It's a church service for a man who died a few weeks ago. Someone Granny used to know – in the war.'

'Are we going to go in?'

'No,' my mother said. 'I just wanted to be here. To see who was coming.'

'Was he a nice man?' Jochen said.

'Why do you ask?' my mother said, now taking full notice of the boy.

'Because you don't seem very sad.'

My mother considered this for a while. 'I thought he was nice at the beginning, when I first knew him. Very nice. Then I realised I had made a mistake.'

Jochen said nothing further.

As my mother had predicted, Lucas Romer did not live to see the next morning after we had left him. He died that night from a 'massive heart attack', according to the newspaper obituaries. They had been prominent but rather sketchy and David Bomberg's portrait had been frequently reproduced, in the absence of any decent photographs, I supposed. Lucas Romer's war-work had been summarised as 'for the intelligence services, later rising to a senior position within GCHQ'. Many more words had been expended on his publishing career. It was as if they were commemorating the passing of a great literary figure rather than a spy. My mother and I looked at the guests as the queue to enter the church lengthened: I thought I spotted a newspaper editor, frequently on TV, I saw an ex-cabinet minister or two from distant governments, a famously right-wing novelist and many grey-haired elderly men in immaculately tailored suits, their ties discreetly signalling aspects of their past – regiments, clubs, universities, learned societies – that they were happy to acknowledge. My mother pointed out an actress: 'Isn't that Vivien Leigh?'

'She's long dead, Sal.'

Jochen tugged discreetly at my sleeve. 'Mummy: I'm getting just a little bit hungry.' Then he added considerately, 'Aren't you?'

My mother crouched down and gave him a kiss on the cheek. 'We're going to have a very nice lunch,' she said. 'The three of us: at a lovely hotel up the road called the Ritz.'

We sat at a table in the corner of the beautiful dining-room with a fine view of Green Park, where the leaves of the plane trees were turning yellow, giving up the fight prematurely after the broiling summer – autumn would be early this year. My mother was paying for everything, so she announced at the beginning of the meal, and we were to have nothing but the best on this memorable day. She ordered a bottle of vintage champagne and when it had been poured into our flutes we toasted each other. Then she let Jochen have a sip.

'It's rather nice,' he said. The boy was behaving very well, I thought, polite and rather subdued, as if he sensed there was a complicated and secret sub-text to this unusual trip to London that he would never fathom.

I raised my fizzing glass to my mother.

'Well, you did it, Eva Delectorskaya,' I said.

'Did what?'

'You won.' I felt absurdly emotional, suddenly, as if I might cry. 'In the end.'

She frowned, as if she'd never considered this before.

'Yes,' she said. 'In the end. I suppose I did.'

Three weeks later we sat in the garden of her cottage on a Saturday afternoon. It was a sunny day, but bearable: the unending heat of the summer was a memory now – something to reminisce about – now we welcomed a bit of early-autumn sunshine, with its fleeting warmth. There were swift, scudding clouds and a freshening wind thrashed the branches of the trees across the meadow. I could see the ancient oaks and beeches of Witch Wood heave and stir restlessly as the rattle of their yellowing leaves carried across the uncut blond grass towards us – hushing, shushing – as the unseen currents of air hit the trees' dense massiness and set their weighted heavy branches moving urgently, making the great trees seem alive somehow, shifting, tossing, provoked into a kind of life by the effortless power of the wind.

I was watching my mother reading a document with stern concentration. I had brought it with me, having just come from a meeting with Timothy 'Rodrigo' Thoms at All Souls, where he had given me a typewritten analysis of my detailed summary of *The Story of Eva Delectorskaya* – and this is what she now had in her hands. Thoms had tried, but failed, to seem unexcited as he spoke but I could sense the scholar's plea underneath his calm explanations of what he thought had gone on in America between Lucas Romer – 'Mr A' as far as Thoms was concerned – and Eva Delectorskaya. Give me all this, his eyes said, and let me run with it. I made him no promises.

Much of what he told me was over my head or else I wasn't fully concentrating – clustering acronyms and names of *rezidents* and recruiters, members of the Russian politburo and NKVD, possible identifications of the men who had been in the room when Eva was interrogated about the Prenslo Incident, and so on. The most interesting verdict, it seemed to me, was that he identified Romer unequivocally as a Russian agent – he seemed absolutely convinced about this – arguing that he had probably been recruited while he was studying at the Sorbonne in the 1920s.

This fact helped him explain the background to what had gone on in Las Cruces. He felt that the timing was the vital clue and all to do with what was happening in Russia in late 1941 when, coincidentally, another Russian spy – Richard Sorge – had told Stalin and the Politburo that Japan had no plans to attack Russia through Manchuria, that Japanese interests were concentrated and directed towards the west and the Pacific. The immediate consequence of this for the Russians was that it freed large numbers of divisions to fight against the German army, still marching towards Moscow. But the German invasion of Russia was faltering: the tenacity of Russian resistance, the over-extended lines of supply, fatigue and the encroaching winter meant that it was stopped and held finally just a few miles from Moscow.

Thoms had reached for a book and opened it at a marked page at this juncture.

'I'm quoting from Harry Hopkins here,' he said. Harry Hopkins – all I could think of was Mason Harding.

Thoms read, ' "As the new Russian armies from the Manchurian front began to mass and gather around Moscow, waiting to launch the inevitable counter-attack there began to grow in the Russian high command – and notably within the NKVD and the other secret services – the realisation that the tide had finally turned: the prospect of Russia defeating the Germans was finally realisable. Certain elements within the Soviet government began to think ahead, about political settlements in the post-war world." '

'What's this got to do with agent Sage stuck in a car in the deserts of New Mexico?' I asked.

'That's what's so fascinating,' he said. 'You see, some people, particularly in the intelligence services, began to think that, for the Russians, it might actually be for the best, in the long term, if the USA did *not* enter the war in Europe. If Russia was going to win, then the last thing they wanted was a strong US presence in Europe. Russia could do it on her own, given time. Not everyone agreed, of course.'

'I still don't follow.'

He explained: towards the end of 1941, NKVD interest began to focus on the strenuous efforts that the British were making to persuade the USA to ally themselves with Britain and Russia against the Nazis. These efforts seemed to be working: to the Russians it appeared as if Roosevelt was looking for any excuse to join the war in the Allied cause. The discovery of the Brazilian map was a key factor in this propaganda war – it seemed to have genuinely tilted the balance. A great coup by BSC, so it was judged. US public opinion could understand much better a threat that lay at their own borders, rather than one that was a distant 3,000 miles away.

So, Thoms argued, it was probably at this juncture that whoever was running Mr A issued him with instructions to try to do something to undermine this increasingly successful BSC propaganda, and expose it as such. To his mind the events at Las Cruces looked very typical of this sort of destabilising exercise. If indeed agent Sage had been found dead with a forged German map of Mexico, he said, then the whole BSC South American case would have been exposed as the sham it was and the isolationist, non-interventionist cause in America would have been hugely strengthened.

'So Sage was meant to be the smoking gun,' I said. 'BSC exposed – perfidious Albion, yet again.'

'Yes, but Mr A's hands were totally clean. It was a brilliant, very, very clever operation. Mr A issued no instructions to Sage beyond the initial courier delivery – everything Sage did on the way to New Mexico and in Las Cruces was impromptu, completely unplanned and the result of decisions made on the spot. It was as if agent Sage could be relied upon to engineer his own destruction. Remorselessly, unthinkingly.'

Engineer *her* own destruction, I thought – but she was too smart for them all.

'Anyway, it didn't matter in the end,' Thoms said, with a wry smile. 'The Japanese came to the rescue with the attack on Pearl Harbor – and so did Hitler with his subsequent unilateral declaration of war on the USA a few days later: everyone tends to forget about that . . . Everything changed, for ever. All this made sure that, even if Sage had been compromised, it would have made no difference at all. The US was finally in the war. Mission accomplished.'

Thoms had made a few other points. He felt that the assassination of Nekich seemed very significant. Information from the FBI debriefing of Nekich appeared to have reached Morris Devereux in November 1941, hinting about serious Soviet penetration of the British security and intelligence services ('We know now just how extensive it was,' Thoms added, 'Burgess, Maclean, Philby and whoever else in the gang is still lurking out there'). Devereux would never have suspected Mr A as a 'ghost' had not agent Sage's experiences in Las Cruces caused grave doubts to be raised and the finger of culpability to be pointed. Devereux was clearly very close to unmasking Mr A before he was killed. His death – his 'suicide' – bore all the signs of an NKVD assassination squad, which again supported the case for Mr A being a Russian agent, rather than German.

'I think Mr X is probably Alastair Denniston, director of the Government Code and Cypher School,' Thoms said as he walked me to my car. 'He would have sufficient power to be able to run his own "irregulars". And, think about this, Ruth, if, as seems highly likely, Mr A was an NKVD "ghost" in GCHQ then he probably did more for the Russian cause during the war than all the Cambridge spies put together. Amazing.'

'In what way?'

'Well, this is the real dividend of the stuff you gave me. It would be shocking if it was made public. Huge scandal.'

I said nothing more. He asked me if I wanted to go out for a meal some time and I said I would call – life was a bit frantic at the moment. I thanked him very much and drove out to Middle Ashton, picking up Jochen on the way.

My mother seemed to have reached the final page. She read out loud: ' "However, this is not to denigrate the story of agent Sage. The material you gave me provides a fascinating account into both the huge extent and the minutiae of BSC operations in the USA. This is all compelling stuff to someone like me, needless to say – the lid has been kept very firmly pressed down on what the BSC was up to over the years. Until now, no one on the outside has really had *any* idea of the extent of British intelligence operations in the USA before Pearl Harbor. You can imagine how this information might be received by our friends on the other side of the Atlantic. Forging a 'special relationship' clearly wasn't enough – we needed British Security Coordination to go the extra mile." '

She tossed the pages down on to the grass; she seemed upset and stood up, ran her hands through her hair and went into the house. I didn't go to her – I thought she probably needed some time to let all this analysis filter through to her, to see if it fitted, made sense.

I reached over and picked up the typed pages, tapping them into shape on my knee, deliberately thinking about other things, such as the intriguing news the morning's post had brought – an invitation to the marriage of Hugues Corbillard and Bérangère Wu in Neuilly, Paris, and another letter from Hamid, sent from a town called Makassar on the island of Celebes, Indonesia, announcing that his salary had risen to $65,000 and that he hoped to take a month's leave before the end of the year, during which he intended to come to Oxford to see me and Jochen. Hamid wrote to me regularly once a week: he had forgiven me my crassness in the Captain Bligh without my having to ask for it or before I could apologise. I was a very bad correspondent – I think I'd replied briefly to him, twice – but I sensed Hamid's dogged wooing would continue, none the less, for a long time to come.

My mother came back out of the house, a packet of cigarettes in her hand. She seemed more composed as she sat down, offered me one (which I refused, I was trying to give up, as a result of Jochen's persistent nagging).

I looked at her and watched her light her cigarette.

'Make any sense, Sal?' I asked, tentatively.

She shrugged. 'How did he express it? "The minutiae of BSC operations in the USA . . ." I suppose he's right. Suppose de Baca had killed me – it wouldn't have made any difference. Pearl Harbor was right around the corner – not that anybody ever guessed it would happen.' She managed a chuckle, but I could tell she didn't find it funny. 'Morris used to say that we were like miners chipping away at the coal-face miles underground – but we hadn't a clue how the mining industry was run on the surface. Chip-chip-chip – here's a piece of coal.'

I thought for a while and then said, 'Roosevelt never made that speech, did he? When he was going to use your Mexican map as evidence. That would have been amazing – might have changed everything.'

'You're very kind, darling,' my mother said. I could tell she was not going to be bucked up today whatever I tried: there was a kind of resigned weariness about her – too many unhappy memories swirling around. 'Roosevelt was due to make the speech on 10 December,' she said. 'But then Pearl Harbor happened – and he didn't need a Mexican map anymore.'

'So Thoms is saying that Romer was a Russian agent. Like Philby, Burgess, Maclean – I suppose that's why Romer killed himself. Too old to run like they did.'

'It makes more sense,' she said. 'I could never understand why Morris thought he was an Abwehr ghost.' She smiled an empty smile. 'Still,' she added with heavy irony, 'it's good to know how insignificant and petty it all was in the "big picture", I must say.'

'It wasn't insignificant and petty to you,' I said, putting my hand on her arm. 'These things all depend on your point of view. You were the one in the desert with de Baca – no one else.'

She looked suddenly weary, said nothing and stubbed out her cigarette, half smoked.

'You all right, Sal?' I said.

'I'm not sleeping well,' she said. 'Nobody's been in touch with you? Nothing suspicious?'

'I'll get in the car and drive home if you bring that up again. Don't be ridiculous. It's over.'

She paid no attention. 'You see, that was the mistake, my mistake. It's bothering me: you should have gone to meet him under a false name.'

'That wouldn't have worked. He'd have checked up on me. I had to tell him honestly who I was. We've had this conversation a hundred times. Please.'

We sat in silence for a while.

'Where's Jochen?' I said.

'Inside – drawing.'

'We should head off.' I stood up. 'I'll get his bits and pieces.' I folded away Rodrigo's letter and as I did so I thought about something.

'What I still don't understand,' I said, 'is why Romer would have become a Russian agent in the first place.'

'Why did any of them?' she said. 'Look at them: they were all middle-class, well-educated, privileged, establishment figures.'

'But look at the life Romer was leading – everything about him, the way he lived. Money, position, power, influence, lovely houses. "Baron Mansfield of Hampton Cleeve" – he even had a title. The boy locked in the English establishment sweetshop, wouldn't you say?'

My mother had risen to her feet also and was now wandering about the back lawn, picking up Jochen's scattered toys. She stood up, a plastic sword in her hand.

'Romer used to say to me that there are only three reasons why someone will betray their country: money, blackmail and revenge.'

She handed me the sword and picked up a water pistol and a bow and two arrows.

'It wasn't money,' I said. 'It wasn't blackmail. So what revenge was he after?'

We walked back to the cottage together.

'In the end it comes down to a very English thing, I believe,' she said, seriously, thoughtfully. 'Remember, I didn't come here until I was twenty-eight. Sometimes, if you don't know a place, you can see things the locals miss. Remember, also, Romer was the first Englishman I really got to know . . . Got to know well,' she added, and I sensed the pain of her past still living, stirring beneath the recollection. She looked at me, with her clear-eyed look, as if daring me to refute what she was about to say next.

'And knowing Lucas Romer, as I did, and talking to him, being with him, watching him, it struck me that sometimes it's just as easy – and maybe sometimes more natural – to hate this country as to love it.' She smiled, knowingly, ruefully. 'When I saw him that night: Lucas Romer, Lord Mansfield with his Bentley, his butler, his Knightsbridge house, his club, his connections, his reputation . . .' She looked at me. 'I thought to myself: that was his revenge. He'd got it all: everything that seems most desirable – money, reputation, esteem, style, class – the title. He was a "Lord", for God's sake. He was laughing all the time. All the time, laughing at them all. Every minute of the day, as his chauffeur drove him to his club, as he went to the House of Lords, as he sat in his Knightsbridge drawing-room – he was laughing.'

She made a resigned face. 'That's why I knew – absolutely, without question – that he'd kill himself that night. Better to die acclaimed, fondly remembered, admired, respected. If there was a heaven he'd still be laughing, looking down at his memorial service with all those politicians and dignitaries celebrating him. Dear old Lucas, fine fellow, salt of the earth, a true-blue English gentleman. You say I won – Romer won, too.'

'Until Rodrigo publishes his book. It's going to blow everything wide open.'

'We must have a talk about that one day soon,' she said, severely. 'I'm not all that happy about it, to tell you the truth.'

We found Jochen; he gave her his drawing – of a hotel, he said, nicer than the Ritz – and we packed everything away in the car.

'Oh, yes,' I said, 'one thing that's been on my mind, I keep thinking about. It seems silly, but – what was he like, my uncle Kolia?'

She straightened up. 'Uncle Kolia,' she repeated, as if testing the phrase, savouring its unfamiliarity. Then I saw her eyes narrow, keeping the tears back. 'He was rather wonderful,' she said with false briskness, 'you would have liked him.'

I wondered if I had made a mistake, recalling him to her like that, at this particular moment, but I had been genuinely curious. I fussed Jochen into the car and settled myself inside.

I wound down the window, wanting to reassure her, one last time.

'Everything's fine, Sal. It's over, finished. You've no need to worry anymore.'

She blew us a kiss and wandered back inside.

We had just driven out of the gate when Jochen said, 'I think I left my jersey in the kitchen.' I stopped the car and climbed out. I went back in through the front door, pushing it open and calling cheerily, 'It's just me,' and walked through to the kitchen. Jochen's sweater was on the floor under a chair. I stooped and picked it up and realised my mother must have gone back out to the garden.

I peered through the window, looking for her, and saw her, eventually, half hidden by the big laburnum by the gate in the hedge that gave on to the meadow. She was looking through her binoculars, trained on the wood, traversing slowly this way and that. Across the meadow the big oaks still heaved and thrashed in the wind and my mother searched amongst their trunks, amongst the darkness of the undergrowth, for signs of someone watching for her, waiting to find her unguarded, at ease, uncaring. It was then that I realised this was exactly how she never would be. My mother would always be looking towards Witch Wood, as she was now, waiting and expecting that someone was going to come and take her away. I stood there in the kitchen, watching her staring across the meadow still searching for her nemesis and I thought, suddenly, that this is all our lives – this is the one fact that applies to us all, that makes us what we are, our common mortality, our common humanity. One day someone is going to come and take us away: you don't need to have been a spy, I thought, to feel like this. My mother watched on, staring across the meadow at the trees.

And the trees in the dark wood moved and shifted in the wind, and the sun patches skidded across the meadow, cloud shadows rushing by. I saw the blond uncut grass bend and flow almost like a living thing, like the pelt or fleece of some great animal: wind-combed, wind-stirred, ever-moving – and my mother watching, waiting.